A Gambling Man

David Baldacci is one of the world's bestselling and favourite thriller writers. With over 150 million worldwide sales, his books are published in over 80 territories and 45 languages, and have been adapted for both feature film and television. David is also the co-founder, along with his wife, of the Wish You Well Foundation®, a non-profit organization dedicated to supporting literacy efforts across the US. Still a resident of his native Virginia, he invites you to visit him at DavidBaldacci.com and his foundation at WishYouWellFoundation.org.

Trust him to take you to the action.

BY DAVID BALDACCI

Aloysius Archer series
One Good Deed • *A Gambling Man*

Amos Decker series
Memory Man • *The Last Mile* • *The Fix* • *The Fallen*
Redemption • *Walk the Wire*

Atlee Pine series
Long Road to Mercy • *A Minute to Midnight* • *Daylight*

Will Robie series
The Innocent • *The Hit* • *The Target* • *The Guilty* • *End Game*

John Puller series
Zero Day • *The Forgotten* • *The Escape* • *No Man's Land*

King and Maxwell series
Split Second • *Hour Game* • *Simple Genius* • *First Family*
The Sixth Man • *King and Maxwell*

The Camel Club series
The Camel Club • *The Collectors* • *Stone Cold* • *Divine Justice*
Hell's Corner

Shaw series
The Whole Truth • *Deliver Us From Evil*

Vega Jane series
The Finisher • *The Keeper* • *The Width of the World*
The Stars Below

Other novels
True Blue • *Absolute Power* • *Total Control* • *The Winner*
The Simple Truth • *Saving Faith* • *Wish You Well*
Last Man Standing • *The Christmas Train* • *One Summer*

Short stories
Waiting for Santa • *No Time Left* • *Bullseye*

DAVID BALDACCI

A Gambling Man

MACMILLAN

First published 2021 by Grand Central Publishing, USA

First published in the UK 2021 by Macmillan
an imprint of Pan Macmillan
The Smithson, 6 Briset Street, London EC1M 5NR
EU representative: Macmillan Publishers Ireland Limited,
Mallard Lodge, Lansdowne Village, Dublin 4
Associated companies throughout the world
www.panmacmillan.com

ISBN 978-1-5290-6178-9

1 3 5 7 9 8 6 4 2

A CIP catalogue record for this book is available from the British Library.

Printed and bound by CPI Group (UK) Ltd, Croydon, CR0 4YY

Visit **www.panmacmillan.com** to read more about all our books
and to buy them. You will also find features, author interviews and
news of any author events, and you can sign up for e-newsletters
so that you're always first to hear about our new releases.

To Trisha Jackson:
a superb publisher and editor, a wonderful person,
and one of my dear friends

A Gambling Man

CHAPTER

I

WITH A NEW DECADE LOOMING, Aloysius Archer was on a creaky bus headed west to California to seek as much of a life as someone like him could reasonably expect. A roof over his head, three squares a day, a pint of decent liquor every now and then, and a steady supply of his Lucky Strikes to keep his mouth supple and amused. And a job. Actually, more of a profession. He needed that right now. It was like seeking water while in a desert, you just required it and didn't care how you got it. Otherwise, he'd be a chump, and there was no future in that.

He took off his hat and swiped at his short, dark hair before resettling the fedora into place.

Hell, maybe I am shooting for the moon after all. But why not?

Archer wasn't yet thirty. After fighting in the Second World War, he'd spent time in prison for a crime of which he was essentially innocent, though the law hadn't recognized such nuance and stuck him behind bars anyway. However, he *would* have gladly pled guilty to a charge of gross stupidity. It had involved a woman, and Archer just seemed to lose all of his common sense when they were around.

He was a little over six-one, and his frame had been hardened first by the Army and then by prison, where the strong didn't necessarily survive, but such an attribute certainly improved your chances. He had a serviceable brain, quick-enough wits, and a work ethic deep enough to carve a good life somewhere given the chance. Archer was hoping to find that opportunity in a town on the water in California where he was eager to start his new phase in life under the tutelage of a veteran private eye named Willie Dash.

But first, he had to get there. And these days, nothing was easy, particularly long-distance travel across a country that was so big it never seemed to end.

He looked out of the bus's grimy window and eyed the street-spanning metal sign they were passing under:

RENO THE BIGGEST LITTLE CITY IN THE WORLD

He had no idea what that meant, but it sounded intriguing. They pulled into the bus terminal and he grabbed from the overhead rack his large, brand-new leather satchel. He had on a two-piece tan wool pinstripe suit, with a patterned green single-Windsor-knotted tie, fronting a starched white shirt and topped by his crown-dented fedora with a brown band. Everything else he owned in the world was in the satchel. It wasn't much, but it was a lot more than he'd had when the prison doors had opened not that long ago.

He got a recommendation on a place to stay the night from a gal behind the bus counter with blonde hair that wrapped around her neck like a naughty mink stole and mischievous blue eyes to match. She had a curvaceous figure that reminded him of the photo of a swimsuit-clad Ava Gardner he had kept in his helmet during the war. After telling her he was headed to California, she handed him a map, along with a recommendation for where to grab his dinner.

"My name's Ginger," she said with a broad smile. "Maybe I'll see you around town later."

He doffed his hat to her, returned the smile, and trudged on, his grin fading to a grimace. He didn't care if she was Ginger Rogers, he was keeping his distance, naughty hair and eyes be damned.

"You look lost, soldier," said the voice.

Archer was outside the depot now, fully immersed in the delicious heat that seeped up from the pavement and gave him a hug. The speaker was a man in his late sixties, straight as a rake, thin as a lathe, with tumbleweed-white hair and a fluffy mustache that dipped nearly to his chin. He had on a dark suit that needed a good sponging and a creased black hat with a soiled burgundy band. A silver watch chain spanned his dappled white vest, which covered a sunken chest and belly.

Archer put his satchel down on the pavement, pulled a half-full pack of Lucky Strikes from his pocket, struck a match on the bottom of his shoe, and lit the end of the cigarette. He waved the spent match like a sparkler and tossed it down. The man looked so lustfully at his smoke that Archer slid one out and offered it to him. He accepted with gratitude on his features and used a dented chrome lighter to do the honors. They puffed for a bit, each squinting at the other through the spawned, mingled fog of twin Luckys.

"Just in town," replied Archer with a bit of a shiver as the sun began its descent after a hard day's labor, and the heat shriveled down into the pavement like a receding flame.

The man eyed both the satchel and the bus depot behind and nodded. "Can see that."

"And I'm not lost. Just going to my hotel."

"Didn't mean geographically. More metaphorically."

"You sound educated, or are you just fortunate with how words spill out of your mouth?"

"Time fills your head up, if you allow it. Some don't. They just put a lid on and end their life as they began it, ignorant as babies." He put out a shaky, thinly veined hand with dark spots here and there. "I'm Robert Howells, but my friends and some of my enemies call me Bobby H. And you are?"

Archer shook his hand but said, "Why do you want to know?"

"Just making small talk, son, don't get jumpy on me."

"I go by Archer."

"Your first time in Reno?" asked Howells.

Archer puffed on his smoke and nodded slowly. "Just passing through."

"On to California? San Fran? Los Angeles? That's where Hollywood is. Most beautiful women in the world. Streets paved with gold, and the water tastes like wine."

"And none of that is true."

"Not a bit. Well, maybe the gals. But they ain't free, son. And there goes all my standard conversation right out the window."

"Fact is, I *am* heading to California, but it's a place north of Los Angeles. According to the Rand McNally."

"You have a certain look the camera might find interesting. Maybe I'm staring at the next Gary Cooper?"

"I have no interest in being the next Gary Cooper or looking into cameras. I'm not saying I can't act, because I pretty much do every time I open my mouth."

"What *is* your ambition then?"

Archer finished his smoke and patted it dead on the pavement with the heel of his right wingtip. "No offense, Bobby H, but I don't know you. And trouble with strangers is not something I'm casting about for."

Howells frowned. "You seem closer to my age, at least in your lack of adventurous nature."

"I'll take that as a compliment."

"Do you know why they call Reno the biggest little city in the world?"

Archer shook his head.

"It's because you can get whatever New York or Philadelphia or Boston or even Los Angeles can provide."

"And what do you think I want?"

"What do most young men want after a war? You fought, I take it?"

"That's nearly five years gone by now."

"But it was a big war with long legs. We won't be forgetting it anytime soon."

"So what *do* I want?" Archer asked again.

"A good time with no duties appurtenant thereto."

"*Appurtenant*? Now you sound like a lawyer. They run second to dead last in popularity with me to undertakers. And it's a long way up from there."

"Do you wish a good time with no consequences?"

Archer wondered if the old man was drunk or doped or both. "I never assumed there was such a thing."

"In Reno there is."

"Well, good for Reno. And what do you get out of telling me that?"

"You don't believe in generosity for generosity's sake?"

"And I don't believe in Santa or pennies from Heaven either. Ever since age seven."

"For a young man you seem old and gray in spirit."

"And getting older every minute I'm standing here gabbing with you."

"The passion of youth has been smote clean from you, and that's a damn shame, son."

Archer lit another Lucky and eyed the man, awaiting his next move. It was at least passing the time in the biggest little city on earth.

"Okay, I can understand your cynicism. But let me make another observation. One that has personal advantages to me."

Archer flashed a grin. "Now we're getting somewhere. I knew you had it in you."

Howells fingered his chin. "You look like a man able to take care of himself."

"That doesn't tell me anything I don't already know."

"Here it is then: Can you protect others?" asked Howells.

"Who are we talking about here?"

"We are talking about me."

"And why do you need protection?" asked Archer.

"I have enemies, as I said."

"And why do you have enemies?"

"Some folks have them, unfortunately, and I'm one of those folks. So what do you say?"

"I have no interest in making your enemies my enemies. So you have a good day."

Archer tipped his hat, turned, and walked off with his satchel. Howells called after him. "You would desert an old man in need, soldier?"

Over his shoulder Archer said, "Just wait for a fellow to fall off a truck and *he's* your man, *Bobby H.*"

2

In his hotel room, which looked like a shower stall with half-hearted ambition, Archer ditched his hat on the bed, tucked his satchel in the narrow closet with two feeble hangers dangling from the wooden rod, and sat in the one chair by the one window. He parted the faded and frayed curtains and stared out at Reno. It just looked average, maybe a little below that, in fact. Yet maybe it punched above its weight, like he always tried to do.

He smoked another Lucky and took a drink from the flask he carried in his jacket pocket. Archer didn't need beautiful women, watery wine, or golden boulevards. He just desired a steady paycheck, something interesting to do with his time, and the small slice of self-respect that came with both.

The rye whiskey went down slow and burned deliciously along the way. Thus fortified, he took out the letter typed on sandpaper stationery with the name "Willie Dash, Very Private Investigations" imprinted at the top and giving an address and a five-digit phone number in Bay Town, California. Included with the letter was the man's business card, stiff and serious looking with the same address and telephone information as the letter. A tiny magnifying glass rode right under the business name. Archer liked the effect. He hoped he liked the man behind it. More to the point, he hoped Willie Dash liked him.

The missive was in response to one Archer had written to Dash at the advice of Irving Shaw, a state police detective Archer had met while in a place called Poca City, where Archer had served his parole. Shaw and Dash were old friends, and Shaw believed Archer had the makings of a gumshoe; he'd thought Dash might be a good mentor for him. Archer had mentioned Shaw in the letter because he hoped it would move Dash to at least write back.

Not only had Dash written back but he'd suggested that Archer come to Bay Town and see what might be possible. He had promised Archer no job, just the opportunity to seek one, depending on how Dash viewed things. Archer didn't need false promises or mealymouthed platitudes. He just needed a fair shot.

He put the letter and business card back in his jacket pocket, gazed out the window again, and noted that it was nearing the dinner hour. He had passed clusters of eateries along the way here, and one had stood out to him because it had also been the establishment naughty Ginger had told him about.

He grabbed his hat, pocketed his hefty room key, which could double as a blunt instrument if need be, and set out to fill his time and his belly.

It was a short walk to the Dancing Birds Café. The place was tucked away down a side street off Reno's main drag. The broad windows were canopied by red-and-green-striped awnings, the door was solid oak with a brass knocker barnacled to the wood, and a flickering gas lantern hung on the wall to the right of the door. Archer took a moment to light up a Lucky off the open flame. Breathing in the methane reminded him of the war, where if you weren't sucking foul odors like cordite into your lungs, you'd think you were either dead or someone had upped and taken the war elsewhere.

He opened the door and surveyed the place. Seven in the evening on the dot, and it was packed as tight as a passenger ship's steerage class, only these people were better dressed and drinking niftier booze. Waiters in black bow ties and short white jackets seemed to hop, skip, and jump in frenetic furtherance of their duties. Archer looked for the "dancing birds" but saw no evidence of winged creatures performing the jitterbug. Either the place was misnamed, or he was in for a real surprise at some point.

At the far end of the room was a raised stage with a curtain, like one would see at a theater. As Archer stood there, hat in hand, the curtains parted and out stepped four long-limbed platinum blondes dressed so skimpily they looked ready to hop into bed for something other than sleep. Each of them held a very large and very fake bird feather in front of them.

A short, tubby man in a penguin suit waddled onstage and over to a microphone the size of two meaty fists resting on a stand. With deliberate dramatics he announced that the four ladies were the eponymous Dancing Birds and would be performing for the entertainment of the patrons now either eating or, in the case of half the tables that Archer could see, *drinking* their dinners.

About the time the ladies started to sing and hoof it across the wooden stage while twirling their feathers and twitching their hips, a bow-tied gent came up and told Archer there was room for him if he didn't mind sharing a table.

"Works for me," Archer said amiably.

He was led to a table that was nestled right next to the stage, where a man in his fifties sat. He was short and well-fed, and his calm, regal expression and sharply focused eyes told Archer that he was a man used to giving orders and seeing them obeyed, which was a decent gig if you could get it and then hold on to it. The tux handed Archer a stiff menu with the food items written in free-flowing calligraphy, took his order for three fingers of whiskey and one of water, and departed. Archer hung his fedora on the seat back and nodded to the other man.

"Thanks for the accommodation, mister," he said.

He nodded back but didn't look at Archer; he kept his gaze on the Birds.

When Archer's drink came the man turned and eyed the whiskey. "Good choice. It's one of the best they serve."

"You have knowledge of the bar here?"

"In a way. I own the place. Max Shyner." He raised a flute of champagne and clinked it against the whiskey glass.

"Nice to meet you, Mr. Shyner. My name's Archer. And thanks a second time for the table spot, then. Wondered why you had such a good seat for the show."

"You like the Dancing Birds?" he said, returning his gaze to the stage.

Archer gave a long look at the Bird on the end, who responded with a hike of her eyebrows, the lift of a long fishnet-stockinged leg in a dance kick, and a come-hither smile before she tap-tapped to the other end of the stage with the rest of the feathered flock.

"Let me just say how could a breathing man not?"

"You just in town?" Shyner asked.

"Why, do I look it?"

"I know most of the regulars."

"Passing through. Bus out tomorrow."

"Where to?"

"West of here," he said vaguely, not wanting to offer anything more.

"California, then?" Shyner said.

"Maybe."

"Well, son, any farther west and you'd be drinking the Pacific."

"Suppose so," replied Archer as he took a sip of the whiskey. He picked up the menu. "Recommend anything?"

"The steak, and the asparagus. They both come from near here. Get the Béarnaise sauce. You know what that is?"

"We'll find out." Archer gave that order to the waiter when he next came by and got a finger of whiskey added to what he had left. "So how long have you owned this place?"

"Long enough. I was born in Reno. Most are from someplace else, at least now. Great transition after the war, you see."

"I guess I'm one of them," replied Archer.

"Where in California? I got contacts, in case you're looking for work."

"Thanks, but I think I got something lined up."

"The Golden State is growing, all right, why people like you are rushing to get there. Me, I'm more than content with this piece of the pie."

"Who's she?" asked Archer, indicating the Bird who had given him the eye.

"Liberty Callahan, one of my best. Sweet gal." He pointed a finger at Archer. "No ideas, son. She wants to get into acting. Don't think she'll be here long, much to my regret."

"I'm just passing through, like I said. I've got no ideas about her or any other lady."

Shyner leaned forward, his look intense and probing. "You like to gamble?"

"My whole life's been a gamble."

"I mean, in a casino?"

Archer shook his head.

Shyner drew a fist of cash from his pocket and peeled off fifty dollars in sawbucks.

"You take this, with my compliments, and go try your luck at the Wheelhouse. It's my place."

"You give out folding money to all the folks passing by?" said Archer. "If you do, you might want to stop before you run out."

Shyner leaned in more so Archer could smell the champagne on the man's breath and Old Spice cologne on the ruddy cheeks. "Little something you need to know about casinos, young fella. No matter what the game, the casinos have the edge. With blackjack and roulette it's a little less, with craps and slots a little more. But there's no game where the House *doesn't* have the advantage. My job is to get folks into my place. Even if I have to front them a bit. In the long run it pays off for me."

"Well, with that warning, aren't you defeating your purpose of recruitment?"

Shyner laughed. "You forget the element of human nature. I give you a little seed money and you'll pay that back and more on top in no time."

"Never got the point of gambling. Life's uncertain enough as it is."

"Gambling will be here long after I'm dead and buried, and you too. People are born with weaknesses and they pass them on. Sort of like Darwinism, only the stupid survive."

"I might try your place, but I'll do it with my own coin, thanks."

"You sure?"

"Sure as I'm sitting here with a man who owns a casino."

Shyner put the cash away and lit up a short, thin cigar and blew wobbly rings to the high plastered ceiling. "You surprise me, Archer. I've done that fifty-dollar bit more times than I can remember and you're the first to turn it down."

"So what about all those casinos in Las Vegas? Don't they give you competition?"

Shyner waved this concern away. "In twenty years it'll be a ghost town and no one will even remember the name Las Vegas, you mark my words."

His steak and asparagus came, and Archer ate and washed it down with another two fingers.

"Can I at least comp your meal, Archer?"

"What do I have to do in return?"

"Just go to my casino. Two blocks over to the west. You can't miss it."

Archer laid down a dollar for his meal and drinks.

"So you're not going to the Wheelhouse then?" said Shyner in a disappointed tone.

"No, I am. Just on my terms instead of yours."

"Action doesn't start up till around ten. You'll want the full picture."

As he left, Archer gave Liberty Callahan a tip of his hat as she was singing a solo while reclining on a baby grand piano that had been wheeled onstage. She hit him with a dazzling smile and then kept right on singing without missing a beat. Her voice sounded awfully good to Archer. She waved bye-bye with her fake feather as he left the nest.

Archer had to admit, he liked the lady's style.

3

The Wheelhouse was located in a building about as big as an aircraft carrier, but with nicer furniture, no portholes, and enough booze to launch her. Inside an army of gamblers was looking to win big, although almost all would lose what they had brought plus what they hadn't brought. Archer didn't need Shyner to tell him the odds favored the House. Somebody had to pay for the liquor, the neon, and the ladies, and the chubby old man who owned it all and liked his champagne and fifty-dollar suckers.

Pretty much every game of chance invented was being played in the main room as cocktail waitresses in black stockings and low-cut blouses made their rounds with drinks, smokes, and the occasional teasing look that hinted at additional services available after hours for those few with any cash left. The bar set against one wall was packed because the liquor was half price, or so said the sign overhead. Drunk people no doubt increased the casino's odds even more, figured Archer.

As ten struck on his timepiece, he checked his hat and strode across the main floor to the cashier booths. He had never gambled in a casino, but Archer *had* gambled. First in prison, and then in private games where the odds were a little better than at this place, the booze came out of flasks or thimbles masquerading as shot glasses and the only ladies present were housewives coming to drag their no-account hubbies home while they still had twin nickels to their names.

He paid for ten bucks' worth of chips, then ambled over to a craps table and from a distance studied the bets on the board until the table opened up for new action like the jaws of a prowling gator. He continued to watch three guys crap out after two tosses each. Then two more rollers in the wings fell out, one passing out drunk, the other blowing his whole stake on the last throw of the dice.

A man at the rail turned and saw Archer. He beckoned for Archer to join him.

After Archer did, the man said, "Listen up, son, this here fella about to throw has been hot three nights in a row."

Archer looked down at the gent speaking. He was small and around sixty with fine white hair and a pair of rimless specs worn low on his squat, red-veined nose. He was encased in a seersucker suit with a snazzy blue bow tie and two-tone lace-up shoes. His nose and flushed face stamped him as a man who liked his drink more than he liked just about anything else.

"Is that right?" said Archer.

"Yes sir. That boy can roll." He held out a flabby hand. "Roy Dixon."

"Archer."

They shook hands as the stickman standing behind the casino's table bank called for fresh bets. The new shooter stepped up to one end of the table shaking out his arms and undoing kinks in his neck, like he was about to enter a boxing ring and not the green felt of a craps table that might be the most complicated betting game ever devised. Archer thought he could even see the guy's eyes roll back in his head for a second before he shook it all clear and got ready to either do the House damage or get grizzly-mauled by a pair of dice weighing an ounce. The two base dealers handled all the chip traffic, while the seated boxman, a burly man wearing a green visor and a sour expression, watched all of this like his life and all those he knew and loved depended on his not missing *anything*.

"Okay, son, let's make some money," said Dixon, who made his bet on the Pass line.

"How?" said Archer.

"Hey, you."

Archer looked up to see one of the base dealers drilling him with a stare. "The button's off, pal. Got a new shooter coming up, no point made. You stand by the rail, you got to bet. That's prime real estate, buddy. Didn't your mama ever teach you that?"

Everyone laughed and more than a few gave Archer patronizing looks. He placed some chips next to Dixon's on the Pass line.

"Thank you, sonny boy, now don't you feel all better inside?" said the dealer.

Dixon leaned over and whispered to Archer, "He's gonna roll seven on his come out roll."

"How do you know that?"

"Shit, 'cause he always does."

The stickman presented the shooter, a tall, thin man with curly brown hair and wearing a two-piece beige suit with a wrinkled white shirt and no belt, with five dice. He picked his deuce and handed the trio back to the stickman, who dumped them in his shake-out bowl.

"Dice out, no more bets allowed," announced the stickman.

The shooter blew on the dice and rattled them once in his right hand.

"Throw with one hand only, and both dice have to hit the back wall," instructed the stickman.

The shooter looked at him incredulously. "Hell, you think I don't know that? How long I been throwing here, Benny?"

"Just saying," was Benny's only reply.

The shooter let fly, and the dice bounced off the far U-wall of the table.

The stickman announced, "We got a Big Red, natural seven. Pass line wins, no-pass goes down."

Dixon said, "What did I tell you? We just doubled our money."

Their chips doubled, and Archer looked intrigued as the dealers worked the payoffs and oversaw new bets.

"Now what?" asked Archer.

"He's going to make his point on this next roll."

Dixon set his chips down on certain betting squares and Archer followed suit.

A few moments later: "Shooter rolls a ten," announced Benny. "Point is made, folks."

The bets were posted again and the shooter was handed the dice. They banged off the far end of the table and came to rest.

"Little Joe on the front row," bellowed Benny. "Hard four."

Archer looked at the twin twos staring up from the faces of the dice. Then he looked at his pile of chips growing. He and Dixon bet again.

"Boxcars," called out Benny as double sixes stood up after careening off the wall. "Twelve craps, come away triple."

"What does that mean?" asked Archer.

"The Wheelhouse pays triple the field on boxcars," Dixon said, looking down with relish at his now-towers of chips.

"Hey, pal, shouldn't we quit while we're ahead?" said Archer.

"What the hell's the point of that?" countered Dixon.

Archer took some of his chips off, while Dixon did not.

The next roll was another winner and Dixon grinned at Archer. "You're too timid, son. First rule of craps, you ride a hot shooter all the way to the very end."

Archer glanced at the shooter. A cigarette dangled from his lips, a line of sweat rode on his brow, and his eyes spoke of too much booze, drugs, and maybe overconfidence. If ever a man looked done in and done out, this was the hombre, Archer thought. He lifted all his chips off the edge of the fabric and slid out his reserve chips from the slots in the table and took a step back as the boxman eyed him with contempt.

"Running out on a hot shooter, bub?" Archer just stared at him. The boxman added with a sneer, "Then go find your mommy. It's time for your bottle of milk, *junior*."

Dixon moved every single one of his chips forward onto new bets on the Pass line and come field a second before Benny handed the dice to the shooter.

As Archer walked away, a huge groan went up from the table as Benny gleefully called out, "Seven out." The next sound was his stick coming down and raking away all the chips that had bet on the shooter continuing to roll. The House had come roaring back and the lives of the bettors gathered round came careening down to earth like a doomed plane.

Archer looked back to see Dixon staring at the spot where all his chips used to be. The king had lost his kingdom, as they all eventually did.

"I better go find that bottle of milk," Archer said to himself.

4

"Hᴇʏ. Hᴇʏ, ʏᴏᴜ!"

Archer looked over and saw the woman waving enthusiastically at him.

It was Liberty Callahan, of the Dancing Birds troupe, sitting at the roulette table. She had changed out of her stage outfit and lost her condor-sized feather. While her sparkly dress was tight, her welcoming smile, promising skittish fun with few rules, was even more appealing to Archer. And yet when he more soberly took in her toothy smile and frisky appearance, Archer saw in it prison guards itching to bust his head, chain gangs to nowhere, and food that was not food at all. That was what had happened to him the last time a gal had called out to him like that. A sob story, a poorly planned escape from her tyrannical father, the arrival of the police, a change in heart by the gal after her old man put the screws to her, with the result that Archer had donated a few years of his life to busting up rocks and seeing the world through the narrow width of prison cell bars. Still, he ordered a highball from the bar and took a seat next to her. He just couldn't seem to help himself. He was an internal optimist. Or just stupid.

"I'm Liberty Callahan."

"I'm Archer."

She shot him a curious look. "That's a funny name."

"It's my surname."

"What's your given name?"

"Not one I 'give' out."

Her features went slack and put out, but Archer didn't feel unduly bothered by this. Any first meeting was a nifty place to lay out the ground rules. And his new universal ground rules were to take no one into his confidence and to listen more and talk less.

"Suit yourself, *Archer*." She turned to play with her little stack of chips.

He said, "Mr. Shyner pointed you out to me back at the café. Told me your name too."

She eyed him cautiously. "That's right, you were at his table."

Archer eyed the wheel and the dealer standing in the notch cut out of the elongated table, while the gamblers sipped on drinks and conspired on their future bets. He heard all sorts of talk coming in one ear about this method and that superstition coupled with that infallible telltale sign of where a spinning ball would come to rest in a bowl full of colored numbers in slots that were spinning the other way. People had colorful chips in hand that looked very different from the ones Archer had been using at the craps table.

The table had a sign that said minimum and maximum bets differentiated between inside and outside bets. Archer had no idea what any of that meant.

"He told me you want to get into acting?" said Archer.

Her smile emerged once more, showing every tooth in her arsenal, including a jacketed porcelain crown in the back that was so white it looked nearly pewter in the shadowy cave of her mouth.

She nodded, her smile deepening. "People calling out your name and wanting your autograph. Your picture in the newspapers. Somebody else driving you around and you travel with your own maid. It all sure sounds swell. So, yeah, I want to try my hand at it. Stupid, maybe. Long shot, sure, but why not me, right?"

"So what are you going to do about it?" asked Archer evenly.

"Hey, hey!" called out the dealer. He was beady-eyed and thick at the waist but with a steady hand in which the little ball already rested. "You got a seat, you got to bet."

"Sorry," said Callahan. She quickly put a chip on ten black.

Archer pulled out some of his crap chips.

The dealer shook his head. "No, no, you need to use *roulette* chips here, sonny. Let me see what you got there."

Archer pulled out all of his chips and showed them to the dealer. The man eyed him with interest as he totaled them up, scooped them away, and placed a stack of colorful chips in front of Archer.

"Okay, what do you want each to be worth?"

"Excuse me?" said Archer.

The dealer told him what his crap chips had been worth. "But you get to pick how much each of *these* chips are worth, while not going over the total value of the chips you just turned in."

"Why so complicated?"

"It's not complicated. It's roulette. Everybody at the table has a different color chip. They tell me what they're worth and I keep that in my head. What's complicated?"

Archer glanced over the chips and gave the man a number.

"Thanks, genius," the dealer said as he placed a like-colored chip atop the rail by the wheel and then placed a number marker on it that coincided with the chip value Archer had given him.

The dealer grinned at Archer. "Memories are iffy, marker chips make it easy."

"Yeah, I can see that, *genius*." He put a chip on ten black next to Callahan's.

The ball was dropped and the wheel spun by the dealer. People kept betting until the ball was about to drop and then the dealer called out, "No more bets." Seconds later Archer and Callahan lost their chips because the ball decided twenty-one red all the way on the other side was a much more comfortable resting place than ten black.

Callahan took a sip of her cocktail and said, "I'm going to Hollywood. That's what you do if you want to be in the movie business, Archer. Ain't you heard of that place?"

"I don't go to many movies. Never saw the point. They're not real."

"Well, that *is* the point."

"If you say so."

"Life is crap, Archer. You go to the movies to get away from that for a little bit. Get some pixie dust thrown on you for a precious two hours."

"And when the two hours are up and the pixie dust falls off, your life is still crap."

"Boy, it must be fun walking in your shoes," she observed.

"But then you go back to the movies for more pixie dust, right?"

"Yeah, so?"

Archer said, "So you're an addict. Might as well be smoking reefer. Movies are about making money. And putting butts in seats. No butts in the seat, no autographs, no maids, and no newspaper pics."

She frowned. "Thanks for popping the one dream I have."

Archer sipped his highball and tapped a finger against the tabletop. "We all have dreams. Point is, what are you going to do about it? Just *going* to the place doesn't seem like enough. I'll bet it's chock-full of people wanting to do the same thing as you."

"I *know* that. I need to take some classes and work on how I walk and how I talk."

"You can already walk and talk. And dance, too, and sing. I'm witness to that. You do it pretty swell, in fact."

Surprisingly, her frown deepened at this compliment. "But there's a lot more to acting than that. You have to have what they call the 'it' factor. The camera has to love you. It has to capture something in you that maybe even you don't see. That's how a star is made."

"Heard that a bunch of actors fought in the war. Hank Fonda, Clark Gable. Lots."

"Oh, poor Clark Gable. Wasn't it awful what happened to his wife, Carole Lombard?" said Callahan. "That plane crash after she was out promoting war bonds. Her mom was with her but didn't like to fly. She wanted to take the train back. Lombard wanted to take a plane to get back to Gable faster. They said she and her mom flipped a coin. Her mom lost and they took the plane. And it flew right into a mountain."

"Yeah, I heard about that while I was overseas. Damn shame."

"So you fought?"

Archer shrugged. "Sure, like most everybody else."

"I worked in a factory making bombs."

"Dangerous work."

Callahan took a moment to pull a Camel from a pack she slid from her purse. She held out the smoke for Archer to light, which he did, using a box of matches he took from a stack next to a green glass ashtray overflowing with smoked butts. The air was thick with so much smoke Archer thought a fog had materialized inside.

She cupped his hand with hers as he lit the Camel. She glanced up at him as their skin touched, but he wasn't looking at her, with good reason. He waved the match dead and plunked it with the other wreckage into the ashtray. Then he sat back and watched her smoke. She did it well.

She said, "One girl I knew at the factory got killed in an accident. And I lost a brother and a cousin in the war. One in Germany and one in France. They're buried over there. I want to make enough money to go see their graves and put flowers on them," she added, her expression growing even more somber, but her eyes lifted to his. "You lose anyone in the war?"

"Just almost myself."

"Right," she said, apparently disappointed by this.

"So Hollywood then?" prompted Archer. "Your dream?"

"Yes. And don't give me a hard time about it," she added in a pouty voice that Archer didn't much care for. Women, he'd found, did that to move men one way or another.

The dealer suddenly barked, "Hey, lovebirds, you gonna bet or you gonna give up your seats, 'cause that's the choice you got to make. And do it before I die of old age, will ya?"

Callahan looked at the man with an expression that gave Archer pause. It was akin to a snake sizing up its next meal. He didn't like it, but he could understand it. With a slow, methodical, full-of-meaning motion, she pushed her remaining chips onto twenty-two black.

"You sure about that, honey? Just that one bet," said the dealer, giving her an eye back as though to evaluate her mental acuity.

Turning to Archer she said, "It's the year I was born, 1922. And I like black better than red, always have."

Archer slid all of his roulette chips next to hers.

She jerked so violently her Camel came close to hitting her in the eye.

"Archer, that's too many chips for a single ride on the wheel. Soften the blow with other bets on white, black, even, odd. Don't be a dummy, spread the risk."

"Lady's talking smart," said the dealer.

Archer finished his highball and sensed the others at the table watching him, wondering whether he was mad, rich, just stupid, or all three. "Thing is, I didn't earn it. I just followed a guy over at the craps table and got out before I lost it all. For me, it's free money."

"Ain't no such thing, buddy," barked the dealer.

Archer eyed him. "You in the business of *not* taking bets, *buddy*?"

The man chuckled and spittle ran down his chin. He didn't bother to wipe it away. "Your funeral, pal. So just to be clear, you're doing a straight up bet on twenty-two black with no outside odd or even, red or black column bets? How about some inside splits, corners, street, double street? Last chance, amigo."

"If I knew what any of that meant, I'd answer you," said Archer. "But all I know is if that little ball drops on twenty-two black, we win."

"You know the odds?" asked the dealer nervously.

Archer glanced around the bowl. "You got thirty-six numbers." Then he noted the zero and double zero slots that were in green felt rather than red or black.

"What are those numbers?" he asked.

The dealer grinned. "That's where the House gets its advantage, pal, didn't you know?"

"You mean, it doesn't count for the odds?"

The grin deepened. "Nope, just two more numbers to add to the thrill. See, that's what *advantage* means."

"So thirty-six minus one means the odds are longer than the road from heaven to hell and the payoff is thirty-five to one, although the wheel has *thirty-seven* opportunities to lose."

"You're picking it up real fast, pardner," said the dealer, eyeing the big stack of chips on twenty-two black. His eyebrow twitched and a sweat bubble sprouted over this twitch like a mushroom after a hard rain. "Like taking candy from a baby," he said, but there was no spirit behind it.

"So you gonna spin the wheel and drop the ball, or do I have time for a smoke break?" asked Archer.

Callahan gripped Archer's hand under the table and gave him a pointed smile that showed all teeth and the jacketed crown that now looked more white than pewter.

The dealer looked around the table and then glanced to the ceiling and muttered something Archer couldn't hear.

The wheel was spun, the dealer sent the ivory ball spinning in the opposite direction, and Archer and Callahan waited for

what seemed an eternity for the game to do what it was designed
to do.

The bona fide absurdity of the endeavor was not lost on Archer.
He watched a dozen reasonable-looking adults eyeing a little ball
like it was the most important thing they would ever witness in
their entire lives.

It's a damn miracle we won the war and aren't speaking German.

"No more bets," barked the dealer.

A moment later, Callahan shrieked, "Omigod," as the ball
dropped into the slot for twenty-two black.

She threw her arms around Archer and kissed him on the lips,
almost knocking him out of his seat.

"Damn," said the dealer, shaking his head.

"How much did we win?" asked Archer quietly. "I mean in
money, not wafers."

The dealer eyed the bets and then the markers and said mournfully, "Little over four grand for you. Two hundred and eighty
bucks for the lady."

"Holy Jesus," exclaimed Callahan.

"We'll cash out now," said Archer, giving the dealer a dead stare.

The man slowly counted out a number of regular casino chips.
He slid a small pile to Callahan and a far larger stack to Archer.

Archer took his stacks of chips, split them evenly, and handed
one stack to Callahan.

"What are you doing?" she said, bug-eyed. "You won those,
not me."

"I just followed your bet, Liberty. I would've won nothing except
for you. So a fifty-fifty split seems fair." He lit a Lucky Strike and
eyed the dealer through the mist. "After all, it was free money."

"Do you...? I mean, are you...? Oh, Archer." She kissed him
again, this time on the cheek and not with as much fury, so he held
firm in his seat.

The dealer said, "Hey, look, the night's young. You folks sure you won't let me try to win some of that back? My boss ain't gonna be happy with me."

Archer flipped him a fifty-dollar chip. "He might still be unhappy. But you won't be, amigo."

The man caught the chip and looked surprised. "Didn't figure you for a class act. My mistake, buddy."

"I think you figured me just right, but four grand can bring class to any bum."

After Archer and Callahan reclaimed their hats from the hat check girl, they turned chips into dollars at the cashier's desk, and Archer carefully folded the money over and put it through a slit in his hat's lining. Callahan's stash disappeared into her purse.

"How about a drink?" she said. "To celebrate? On me? Not here. They water everything down. I know a place."

He studied her for so long she finally said, "What!"

"Works for me."

"What took you so long?"

"The guy usually does the asking, not the girl."

"Well, I'm the other way around, Archer. You hang around me long enough, you'll figure that out."

"Maybe I will. Or maybe I won't. But let's go get that drink," he added with a measure of calm bordering on ambivalence.

"You're a strange bird. Most folks after winning all that would be sort of giddy."

"I don't think I have any giddy left."

CHAPTER

5

I̲ᴛ's ʀɪɢʜᴛ ᴅᴏᴡɴ ᴛʜɪs sᴛʀᴇᴇᴛ," said Callahan as they turned off the strip. "A friend told me it used to be a speakeasy back when they had Prohibition." Callahan slipped her arm inside his. "Isn't life just grand sometimes, Archer? I mean, five minutes ago we had nothing, really. And now look at us."

Archer wasn't sure what to make of her move on him, but he let the lady stay right where she was, even as her soft hip bumped his. He could figure that out later, if need be.

"It took guts what you did back there, betting all those chips."

"Doesn't seem anything like that."

"I suppose you'd feel that way, I mean, after fighting in a war."

"I guess so," he said.

"You want to talk about it?"

"No."

"You sure?" she asked, glancing at him.

"Yes."

"How come? It might make you feel better."

"I don't need to feel better. And the guys who didn't come back can't talk about it, so what gives me the right? The lucky stiffs shouldn't write the histories or tell the stories."

"Okay, okay, Archer. Don't bite my head off for caring."

They took a few more steps when Archer said, "What was that?"

"Sounds like a fight or something," said Callahan, looking startled. "But they have lots of those around here. No business of ours." She tightened the grip on his arm.

Next they heard a man calling out in fear: "Please, don't!"

Archer said, "That sounds like..."

"What?"

"Let me just see something." He pulled free from her and hustled down the street.

"Archer!"

She hurried after him, holding on to her hat as she did so. "Dammit, I don't like to run with heels on!"

Archer reached an alley and turned down it. He ran toward the noise and eventually saw three burly men surrounding another man, far frailer and older, like hyenas circling prey.

Robert Howells was just picking himself up off the ground; his lip was split and his cheek was bruised, and his crumpled hat was lying off to the side. His concave chest was heaving as he held up his hands futilely in a defensive measure as the younger and larger men bore down on him. The blood leached down his face and made a spot on his shirt like a crimson teardrop.

"You boys having fun at an old man's expense?" said Archer as his hand slipped into his pocket and wrapped around something he was probably going to need.

The three men turned around. They were all bigger and beefier than Archer, and not one of them carried a friendly expression.

Archer advanced on them and pointed at Howells. "You feel good about that? Something to write home to Mom about, if you got one."

The biggest and meanest looking of the trio took a few steps toward Archer. "This ain't your business, buddy, so shut your trap, just turn around, and keep moving, if you know what's good for you. You get one warning and that's it."

"Bobby H, come on over here," said Archer.

The other two men put out their thick arms to bar the old man from moving.

"Look here, I don't want to do this the hard way," said the big man. He held up a fist as large as a bowling ball. "You beat it now or this is the last thing you'll see until you wake up."

"All you have to do is let him go," said Archer. "Then you don't get hurt."

The men just gazed stupidly back at him, as though wondering whether Archer was simple-minded or thought way too much of himself.

"Do you got a death wish, bub?" For added emphasis and to let Archer see things as clear as possible, the man took out a blackjack and slapped it against an open palm. One of the other thugs drew out a switchblade and made a slashing motion with it. He grinned and made another slash. Archer didn't bother to watch the performance. His immediate focus was on the blackjack.

"I was about to ask you the same thing," said Archer, still marching toward the big man.

"So just turn around and get out of here. Last warn—"

Archer pushed off the balls of his feet, which separated him from the pavement. With his wingtips rising about six inches off the surface, he moved in a graceful arc. As he leaped he rotated his arm back, his elbow making a V pointing in the opposite direction from which he was heading. As Archer made his descent, his hand, now a mean fist, came forward. Archer leaned his weight into it, thereby accelerating the blow about to be delivered. His fist struck the man so hard on the chin on a downward slope that the man's upper jaw jammed into his lower; two of his teeth were ejected by this collision and landed on the ground along with a stream of blood. A split second later, their owner joined them, facedown and lights out.

Archer came to rest on the ground, his knuckles cracked and bleeding and the stinger flowing all the way to his rotator. You couldn't hurt another man in that way without hurting yourself, he knew. But he would take the pain he was feeling over the one the big man would endure when he awoke.

The knife man lunged at Archer, making attacking motions with his blade. Archer waited for a few seconds as he sized him up until the man drew close enough. Then he lashed out, gripped the man's wrist holding the knife, and used his foot to hook his opponent's ankle while at the same time he pushed his foe backward. The man fell, but he did so without the blade, since Archer had twisted it free with a violent downward tug on the man's wrist.

Archer closed the blade and threw it behind him. He didn't like knife fights for the most part and would rather finish this skirmish with his fists. The man regained his balance and flew at Archer, only to collapse backward from a shot directly to his nose that had painfully moved it about an inch closer to his face. He had less room to breathe now, but air was the least of his concerns at present. Like his friend, he collapsed on the pavement for an involuntary nap after Archer's haymaker.

The third man, taking no chances, had drawn a snub-nosed Colt .32 with oak grips from his jacket pocket. He pointed the barrel at Archer and took no pains to conceal his delight at what he was about to do. It took something to kill a man at close distance and with your own hands. It took only an index finger and not a shred of nerve to do the same with a gun.

The shot made Archer flinch, because the sound of gunfire just did that to a man. But it hadn't come from the snub-nosed.

He looked back to see Callahan standing there holding a nickel-plated Smith & Wesson .38 Special. She had fired the shot into the air, but now had her gun pointed at the other man's chest. "Drop the piece, or I drop you," she said, her features set like a slab of pretty granite. "And I don't miss, mister."

The man eyed her up and down, a slick smile creeping onto his lips. "I ain't worried about no girl pulling no trigger on me."

Her response was to place a shot through the top inch of his porkpie hat, neatly blowing it off his head. He cried out, dropped his gun, and knelt down, blubbering like a baby.

"Then stop worrying," said Callahan calmly, holding the gun as expertly as the best-trained soldiers Archer had seen. "Unless you want the next slug drilling your balls. Which one do you love the least?"

Still whimpering, the man instinctively covered his crotch.

"Come over here, Bobby H," said Archer again as he grabbed the .32, slipping it into his waistband. He also picked up the knife and put it in his jacket pocket.

Howells snatched up his hat, spat on the big man lying at his feet, and tottered over to Archer. They all three hustled out of the alley and back to the main street.

"What was that about?" said Archer. "Why were they giving you the business?"

Howells turned to the side and spit blood and possibly part of his inner lip out of his mouth. "I told you I got enemies, Archer. It's why I wanted you to help me, son."

"You know this piece of work?" said Callahan, who had put her revolver back in her purse as casually as though it were merely her lipstick and powder.

He shook his head. "We don't even qualify as acquaintances. And how come you have a gun?"

She gave him an illustrative eye roll. "I'm a good-looking, young dancer and I live in Reno. What else do you need to know, choirboy?"

"Let's get you cleaned up," said Archer to Howells. The old man was trying to wipe the blood off his face, but he just made a mess of it.

"The bar we're going to has a washroom," said Callahan. "If he can make it that far."

"I'll make it," said Howells. "But only because I sure as hell need a drink."

"Okay, but you can buy," said Callahan.

"Why's that?" said a startled Howells.

"We just saved your bacon is why, you old geezer. Don't be simple."

"Well, okay," said Howells doubtfully. "But my funds are limited at the moment."

"Great," she said spitefully.

Howells turned to Archer, "And who is your *charming* friend, Archer?"

"Hey, bub, I'm right here," she said. "Archer doesn't have to speak for me. And the name's Liberty Callahan."

"I'm sure it is," said a bug-eyed Howells.

She turned to Archer. "Hey, how'd you knock those two guys out with one punch anyways?"

Archer held up the set of aluminum knuckles he had earlier pulled from his pocket. "I always keep these around for emergencies."

"Is that legal?" she asked. "You could get in trouble."

"I figure if you can carry a gun, I can carry these."

She cracked a smile. "I'm starting to like you, Archer."

"Hell, what took you so long?"

6

ARCHER HELPED HOWELLS CLEAN UP in the men's washroom and then they joined Callahan at the bar, after he dumped both the snub-nosed and the knife in the waste can. They didn't want to be near any windows, in case the three guys came looking for them. Although Archer was of the opinion that at least two of them would need a doctor when they came to, and the third a change of undershorts after Callahan's antics with her .38.

Archer ordered a bourbon straight up, Callahan a Tom Collins, and Howells a sidecar.

"Go heavy on the brandy and triple sec, hon," the old man told the waitress, a tired-looking woman in her forties with a Dutch boy haircut and a way of looking at you that made you feel like a heel even if you weren't one. "I got serious troubles," he added by way of explanation.

"Tell it to somebody who cares, *hon*," she said before walking off.

"So give it to us straight, Bobby H," said Archer. "Why were those guys giving you the heavy lifting?"

"I...I, uh, got a little gambling debt issue."

"Then maybe you should stop gambling," said Callahan. "That ever occur to you, genius?"

Howells looked down at the shiny surface of the bar. "I tried but it didn't go too well."

"How much do you owe?" said Archer.

"Eighteen hundred and fifty dollars."

"Eighteen hundred and fifty dollars!" exclaimed Callahan. "Are you that bad a gambler or what?"

"Every bettor loses if he plays long enough, missy."

"*Can* you find that kind of dough?" asked Archer.

"I have no, what you would call, *liquid* assets. But I have a car. A mighty fine one. I'm loath to part with it, but I'm more loath to part with my life."

"What kind of car?" asked Callahan.

"A Delahaye."

"What's that?" said Callahan. "Like a Ford?"

"It is *nothing* like a Ford," said Howells indignantly as he tapped his fingers against the mahogany bar. "It is a work of art. It's French made, truly one of the most beautiful cars ever conceived. Indeed, only five of this model were ever built."

"How come? Was it no good?" asked Callahan.

"No, a little thing called World War II intervened," retorted Howells in a bristling tone. "It is in every respect a spectacular example of automotive genius."

"How'd you get your mitts on something like that?" asked Archer suspiciously. "Your story isn't adding up to me. You're going to have to fill in the holes."

"I didn't get *my* mitts on it. My son did. He left it to me when he passed away last year."

"Sorry to hear that. He must've been a young guy."

"He was. You're not supposed to bury your children," Howells added somberly, staring at his hands.

Callahan and Archer exchanged a sympathetic glance.

"How'd your son get the car?" Archer asked quietly, after a few moments of silence. "There has to be a story in there worth telling," he added encouragingly.

"He, like you, fought in the war. And did so bravely."

"Okay, but I didn't get a car in the bargain," said Archer. "What did he do?"

"Why should I tell you anything?" replied Howells sharply.

Archer took out the aluminum knuckles and placed them between himself and Howells. "Because a few minutes ago I made your enemies my enemies. That's at least worth a little information, friend."

Howells eyed the knuckles and nodded, his expression now contrite.

"Near the end of the conflict my boy saved the life of a French soldier who was the son of one of the Delahaye company owners. As a gesture of thanks they shipped the car here. It's a 1939 model, but it's never really been driven and looks brand-new. It was actually built for a wealthy Englishman and was supposed to be delivered in early 1940. For obvious reasons, it was never shipped out to him."

"How'd your son die?" asked Archer.

"He, too, had gambling debts."

"You mean, they killed him over that?" said Archer.

"That *can* happen," Callahan said knowingly, drawing a meaningful glance from Archer.

He rubbed at one of his swollen fingers and stretched out his stiff arm. "Go on, Bobby H, don't stop now," he said. "It's just getting good."

"He left the car to me. It was really all he had."

"How come the folks he owed money to didn't try to get it?"

"They didn't know he had it. They don't know *I* have it."

"You mean, he never drove it?" said Callahan.

"Never. It's an unforgettable-looking automobile. If they had seen him in it…well, he wouldn't have had it long. Same goes for me. Plus, I don't even know how to drive a car."

"Where is it?" asked Archer.

"Outside of town in a safe place. Why?"

"Well, looks like you're going to have to sell it. Like you said, you're more loath to part with your life than with the car."

Their drinks came, and they each lighted up cigarettes and drank their spirits with enthusiasm.

Through a sheen of smoke Archer eyed Howells. "And you'll need to make a decision fast. We saved you tonight, but I at least won't be here tomorrow to do the same."

"And saving you is not *my* job," added Callahan. "We all have problems."

"There's no one I know with enough money to buy it."

"How much you asking?" said Archer.

"Don't be crazy," said Callahan sharply. "Why do you need a car like that?"

"I'm just asking," replied Archer, whittling down his Lucky and his bourbon. "No harm in that."

"What *would* you do with a car like that?" asked Howells cautiously.

Archer didn't answer right away as he blew lazy smoke rings to the filthy ceiling. "Maybe drive it to California."

"California?" Callahan snapped. "Is that where you're headed? Why didn't you tell me that before?"

He tilted his gaze at her. "Before *what*? We just met."

"But I told you that's where I'm going."

"Well, hell, you two can go out west *together*," said Howells, smiling happily as if Archer and Callahan had just exchanged marriage vows.

"Don't tell me what to do," said Callahan. "And I barely know Archer. I can't drive all the way to California with someone I barely know."

"Well, the same goes for me," replied Archer. "Particularly a gal with a gun."

"What are you going out to California for?" Howells asked her.

"To get into pictures, what else?"

"Well, once you see the Delahaye, you may change your mind about not wanting to drive out there with Archer in it."

"Why?"

"Because you'll arrive in style. You'll be in all the newspapers."

"But I'm not going to Hollywood," said Archer.

"Oh, hell, son, California is California. Do you want to see it or not?"

"What do you say?" Archer asked Callahan.

She mulled over this. "It can't hurt to look."

"But how about one more round of drinks first?" suggested Howells.

"Only if you're buying," said Archer. "I busted a knuckle for you. That's enough without you attacking my wallet, too."

"Well, I will, on the condition that you buy the car."

Archer sat back on his stool. "How do we get out to this place?"

"Got a buddy who can give us a lift in the back of his truck." Howells checked his watch. "He gets off work in about ten minutes."

"The back of his truck?" exclaimed Callahan.

"Well, you can sit in the front. Me and Archer can ride in the back."

Callahan threw down money for the booze. "But let's just keep it to the *one* round then, in case Archer doesn't buy the damn car."

7

The friend's pickup truck was a rambling, ancient mess of a Plymouth held together by wire, tape, and probably prayer by the gent driving it. That "gent" was a burly fellow dressed in blue overalls, dusty brogans, and a dirty, tan snap-brim hat with a fat cigar stuck in the red band. Howells didn't provide a name for the man, and the man didn't volunteer one.

Howells's friend ogled Callahan as he held open the rusted passenger door for her. She tucked herself primly inside the cab and wouldn't look at him. The lady didn't need a magnifying glass to discern the man's primal desire. Archer noted that Callahan kept a firm hand on her clutch purse, in which the .38 lay like a coiled rattler.

Archer hefted Howells into the back, where he sat next to a passel of tools. Archer rode higher up on the truck bed's side panel. He buttoned up his jacket and turned up his collar because the air had gone cool. As they headed west, the sky was clear and the stars were stitched to the dark fabric in random patterns of elegance.

They were moving at too brisk a pace for Archer to light up a cigarette, so he just watched the dirt pass by. The land was flat, the vegetation uninteresting, and the occasional animal unremarkable.

"Not much out this way," Archer commented after a few miles.

"Men came here for gold a long time ago. Now it's just a

stop on the way to somewhere else, unless you're enamored of desert land."

"I like the water."

"You grew up on the ocean?"

"No. But I took a long boat ride home and it was the sweetest ride I've ever had."

"Smooth, was it?"

"No, we actually went through a hurricane. Thought we were going to sink for about three straight days, guys puking and praying all over the place. I'd settled on the fact that I was gonna drown right then and there in the old Atlantic."

"So why the hell do you like the water then?"

"I survived the war and that boat was taking me home. It affects a man."

"I can see that," said Howells thoughtfully. "I fought in the First World War."

"I'm hoping there won't be a third."

"So California, eh?"

Archer shrugged. "Good a place as any, I reckon."

"I wish I'd done more moving about when I was young."

"You from here, then?"

"Not exactly. But I call it home now, for better or worse."

"If you pay those boys off, who's to say you won't get back into debt? And you won't have another car to sell."

"You make a fair point, Archer, but right now I don't see another option."

Archer shrugged. "It's your funeral, and any man who can't see that deserves what he gets."

"That's a hard line, friend," Howells replied, frowning.

"No, that's life. And you've seen more of it than me, so you should know better."

The truck rolled on until they reached an unwieldy conglomeration of buildings. A gas station, an automobile repair garage, and a small bungalow that looked like someone had let the air out. Out front was parked a big sparkling-blue Buick and a smaller dented Ford two-door, Mutt and Jeff in mechanical splendor.

"What is this setup?" asked Archer as he helped Howells down.

"My buddy's place, like I told you. He has the garage and a filling station. And he lives in that little house there."

"Your buddy have a name?" asked Callahan, who had gotten out of the cab before the man had stopped the truck fully, probably so he couldn't hurry around and try to see up her skirt like he had when she'd gotten in.

Howells pointed to the sign above the garage. It read: LESTER'S AUTO REPAIR. "Lester's had this place a long time."

The truck shot back onto the road and disappeared quickly from view.

"Why's your friend in such a hurry?" asked Archer.

"Lester doesn't like Calvin. And if Lester doesn't like you, you know it."

Archer eyed the fleeing Plymouth and then glanced at Howells. "So how do we get back to town then, Bobby H?"

Howells considered this dilemma and said, "Well, that's a pickle for sure."

The door to the bungalow opened at Howells's knocking. In the doorway stood the largest human being Archer had ever seen. About six feet eight, his body was so thick it needed every inch the doorway provided. Archer figured him for 350 or more pounds, if he weighed an ounce. He looked like a statue whose sculptor had gotten carried away.

"Holy Lord," whispered Callahan. "Is that one man or two?"

"Dunno," said Archer. "But either way, don't make him or *them* mad."

Howells threw up a hand and said, "Howdy there, Lester."

Lester did not seem pleased to see him or any of them, thought

Archer. He looked like he would prefer to snap their necks like chickens and then pluck and cook them for dinner.

Lester had curly dark hair and a crooked nose that seemed to go on and on. His lips were thick, and his teeth were relative to the size of his wide mouth. He wore a stained, sleeveless undershirt that showed off thick, broad shoulders, arm muscles that seemed too weighty for the bones they were attached to, and matted black chest hair where the fabric dipped low. His stiff dungarees, while enormous, strained to contain his legs. His feet were surprisingly small for his huge frame. His nails were thick with grease, and the smell of gasoline shrouded the man like wrapping paper around a present, a big one. A cigarette was stuck behind one ear like a pale, severed finger lingering.

He looked them over one by one and said nothing.

Callahan took a subtle sniff and wrinkled her nose, taking a step back to allow the man some space and her lungs some reprieve.

Lester once more ran his gaze up and down Archer and Callahan before turning to Howells. "It's late for a visit, Pops. What are you here for?"

His voice was low, like rumbling thunder. It didn't quite match his girth, but it still made Archer notice his words with particular care.

"Came to see the car." He looked at Archer. "Got a prospective buyer in Archer here."

Lester turned once more to Archer. His gaze went from the hat to the feet and then came back up like an elevator car and stopped at the floor containing Archer's eyes.

"He doesn't look like he can afford it."

"Well, looks can be deceiving," said Archer.

Lester did not appear to take too kindly to this mild rebuke. He took a few steps toward Archer before Howells said, "So is it in the garage then?"

Lester snapped a glare at him that in the dim light seemed

ferocious somehow. "Where else, Pops? Under the cover, like always."

"Well, let's get to it," said Howells hastily. "Don't want to waste what's left of your night, Lester."

To Archer, the old man seemed uneasy at having to deal with the giant, and that uneasiness transferred to Archer like a virus.

Lester took them to the garage, pulled a key from his pocket, unlocked a massive padlock, and slid open the doors with outward thrusts of his two-by-four arms. Inside they saw automobiles and pickup trucks in various stages of disassembly. Large rolling toolboxes stood next to some of these vehicles. Single bulb work lights were strung from the exposed rafters. The smell of grease was predominant but barely winning out over the odor of burned nicotine. Archer saw a Maxwell House coffee can full of cigarette butts. He next eyed a fifty-gallon drum marked GASOLINE with a hose and nozzle attached, and he wondered how the man had not managed to blow or burn himself up.

"Business looks good," noted Archer in a friendly tone. He really did not want to have to try his luck with the aluminum knuckles against a man the size of this one. He doubted he could reach Lester's chin to see if, despite his size, it was made of glass.

"Looks can be deceiving." Lester was the only one to smile at his little joke, and it was a weak, grim effort.

In a separate room behind another set of locked slider doors was a vehicle draped with a brown canvas tarp. Lester flicked on a light and glanced at Howells, who nodded.

Archer stood next to Callahan, who had reached out and clutched his arm, as though what was about to be revealed was a wild animal instead of something you drove on the road.

Lester grabbed one end of the tarp and with one tug pulled it free of what was underneath.

"Damn," Archer and Callahan said collectively.

Howells stepped forward and rubbed the silver trim on the side of the bloodred car, which also had a red convertible top that was now set in the down position.

"Folks, feast your eyes on a 1939 Delahaye Model One Sixty-Five, Figoni and Falaschi convertible cabriolet."

Callahan gushed, "It…it looks like it's floating on air."

Archer eyed the long hood, which ended in a shiny grille that ran from top to bottom on the front of the vehicle like a knight's metal vestments. Its front and rear fenders looked like waves crashing on a beach and enormous teardrop-shaped pearls, respectively. There were slashes of chrome trim on the sides and running along the bottom of the chassis. It rode so low that he could see only the bare bottoms of the whitewall tires.

"It looks…more like a dream than a car," said Archer quietly.

Lester said, "It ain't no dream, buddy. This baby weighs three thousand pounds, has a twelve-cylinder all-aluminum, four-point-five-liter engine, triple overhead cam, three downdraft Solex carburetors, and a four-speed transmission, with a top speed of around a hundred and fifteen miles an hour."

"Holy hell," said Callahan. "Just the car you want if you're robbing a bank."

This comment made Howells and Archer exchange a startled look.

"Figoni and Falaschi?" said Archer.

Lester replied, "Figoni and Falaschi were the designers of the car. Delahaye was an engineer and he didn't have an in-house body shop. He built the mechanics of the car and left the body design to coachbuilders, like Figoni and Falaschi. They make really pretty cars. They're I-talians."

Howells said, "So what say you, Archer?"

Archer pointed at the front seat. "Well, for starters, the steering wheel's on the wrong side."

"No, the steering wheel is on the *right* side for the simple fact that it was built for an Englishman, and that is where a steering wheel is located over there," said Howells.

"I'm not English," said Archer. "And I'm over here, not *there*."

"So do you want it or not?" said Howells.

"I can't decide on buying a car I haven't driven."

"Fair enough. Lester, the key?"

Lester slipped a key off a hook on the wall and held it out to Archer. "You ever driven anything like this?"

"Hell, I've never *seen* anything like this, pal. What a sheltered life I've led."

"You want me to drive it out of the garage for you, so you won't bang nothing up?"

Archer reached out and took the key from him. "I got it."

Lester held his hand up without the key for longer than was necessary. For a moment, Archer thought the hand would change to a fist and be swung at him. With his free hand he felt for the aluminum knuckles in his pocket. He would have preferred a howitzer.

But Lester shrugged, lowered his arm, and said, "You break it you bought it, mister."

"Let's go, Liberty," said Archer.

"What, me?"

"I don't see anybody else named Liberty hanging around."

They climbed into the car, and Lester pushed the other door open, providing a wide space for the Delahaye to roll through.

Archer put the key in the ignition and turned it. Then he hit the starter button, and the car purred to life with suppressed power.

"Sounds like a lion yawning," said Callahan.

Howells grinned. "This beast hasn't been out of its cage. It needs to run free."

Archer worked the clutch and put the car in gear using the tiny gearshift that was mounted on the steering column. The steering wheel was the same color as the car. It was like he was holding a circle of fire in his hands. He was relieved that there was no grinding sound as he geared up, and they pulled through the opening. They passed the other humbled cars, which seemed to bow to the Delahaye like a pride to its king. As they rolled through the double doors, Archer turned on the headlights; they overcame the darkness with stunning visibility.

Howells and Lester followed them out.

"Which way should we go?" Archer asked.

"Well, first things first. Move over, gal," said Howells to Callahan.

"What?" said Callahan, staring up wide-eyed at the old man.

"You think I'm going to let you ride off into the night all by your lonesome in the most beautiful car ever built before giving me a dime for it?"

"I'm no car thief," said Archer.

"Glad you think so. I'm not convinced myself."

"I can ride with them," said Lester.

"Hell, Lester," said Howells. "I don't think you would fit in there if it was just you."

Callahan slid over tight to Archer, and Howells climbed into the car, crowding the other two. "Now go west, young man," he said pointing to the left. "That way."

Archer pulled onto the road and pressed down the gas.

Howells pursed his lips. "Come on, Archer. Let it rip."

Archer mashed the pedal down.

The acceleration was immediate, popping their heads back and exhilaratingly so.

"My goodness," exclaimed Callahan. "If this car was a man, I think *I'd* propose."

CHAPTER

8

"So how much are you asking for it?" Archer said as they spun around a tight curve in the road before reaching a long straightaway.

Howells scratched his cheek and then smoothed down both ends of his white mustache. "Like I said, there's only five known One Sixty-Fives around. And a fellow in Beverly Hills, California, just bought one for $12,000."

"Christ Almighty," yelled Callahan.

In her agitation she hit Archer's arm, and he nearly drove the car off the road and into some cacti. Archer quickly righted the vehicle and slowed. He looked down at his hands holding the wheel of a $12,000 car. That amount of money was unimaginable to someone like him. It was far more than a *house* cost. To his mind, it was far more than anything *should* cost.

"I don't have $12,000, Bobby H. And I don't know anyone who does besides Rockefeller, and I don't *know* him."

"Well, I didn't say that's what I was asking for it. I was just conveying some information to lend you some perspective."

"Well, you'd have to *lend* me the twelve grand too."

"You said your gambling debts were $1,850," Callahan reminded him.

"Well, yes, but I can't let it go for just that. I'm many things, but an idiot is not one of them."

"Then I'm not your man."

"Now hold on, Archer, I'm in a bit of a dilemma, obviously, so let's just have a discussion on what might be possible."

"Well, $12,000 will never be possible."

Callahan said, "Let's hear the man out."

"Okay, but that's going to have to wait," said Archer as he glanced in the mirror.

"Why?" asked Callahan.

"Because we have company and they're coming fast."

Both Howells and Callahan shot looks behind them to see a pair of headlights coming with alarming velocity toward them.

"Hold on to whatever you need to," said Archer calmly. Then he asked for everything the Delahaye had to give by pushing the pedal all the way to the floor. And the loveliest car in the world responded with the heart of a champion.

They shot far ahead of the chase vehicle, which Archer had seen in the moonlight was a big-butted, two-tone Buick with a long hood and whitewall tires. It wasn't the Buick that had been parked in front of Lester's place, so Archer doubted it was the giant back there. The car receded so fast into the darkness that for a moment Archer imagined he might be on a plane about to take off.

Yet no car or plane could outrun a bullet.

Archer cut the wheel to the right and then the left as shots flew past them.

Callahan shrieked and fell sideways onto Archer's lap as Howells dove to the floorboard.

Archer draped one hand over the doorframe and used that as a fulcrum to keep himself rigidly in place as he continued to steer the car in evasive maneuvers. The Delahaye executed every one of these movements with surprising agility for such a heavy car.

"Aren't you scared?" said Callahan, lifting her head and looking up at him as he nimbly whipped the car through a hail of bullets.

"Sure I am. But I got used to people shooting at me in the war,

Liberty," he said. "And if you get so scared you can't do something about it, then you probably deserve to die."

A bullet glanced off the metal post supporting the windscreen, dinging it.

"Son of a bitch!" screamed Howells, rising up and looking back at the Buick. "They put a mark on this car. That's…that's like wiping varnish over the *Mona Lisa*. It's…it's blasphemy is what it is."

"If you say so," replied Archer. "And while it rides nice, it's a little heavy in the turns, Bobby H. You might want to check the front alignment."

"That's crap, Archer," roared Howells. "You're a Philistine who doesn't know how to dance with a queen."

Archer cut the wheel to the right, slid into a turn, and said when they came back out on the straightaway, "So, really, how much do you want for this thing?"

"You want to negotiate now!" screamed Callahan as the Buick appeared behind them and commenced firing again.

"Well, unless Bobby H has enemies other than the ones he owes the gambling debts to, then I'm thinking that's them back there. That means they know he has the car now. So how much?"

Howells said sharply, "I can see you're looking to exploit my current situation with your newfound leverage."

"Wouldn't you?"

"What'd you say you could afford again?"

"I didn't. But if you were to ask I'd say the amount of your debt, eighteen fifty."

"I told you I couldn't take anything close to that."

"But that would pay off the boys back there," pointed out Callahan, who had now risen and sat with her head below the seat top, her long legs bent, her shoes off, and her feet pressed against the dashboard. This position had allowed her dress to float all the way up to the very tops of her stockinged thighs. And under any other conditions Archer would have been mesmerized by the view. But not now.

"I need to do better than that," said Howells, shaking his head. "As I intimated earlier, I'm probably going to be back in debt soon. I need a cushion to allow for that. You can see that, surely."

"And you also said you wanted to have a discussion on what might be possible," noted Archer. "Only I haven't seen that discussion yet and I'm thinking time is running short, unless the Delahaye has wings."

Before Howells could respond, Archer downshifted, slammed into a tight turn, and came out high on the curve, then upshifted and laid the pedal to the floor. The Delahaye wound up like a rocket. The landscape was going by so fast that everything was a blur. If another car was up ahead, they were all dead.

"Lester was wrong," said Archer.

"How so?" asked Howells.

In answer Archer pointed to the speed gauge on the red metal dashboard. "We're doing a hundred and twenty-one."

Callahan closed her eyes and made the sign of the cross.

"So about those discussions?" prompted Archer.

Howells took a look behind him, swallowed nervously, clutched the edge of the windscreen tightly, and said, "I can take the eighteen fifty as a *start*, but there's got to be more down the road."

"How exactly does that work?" asked Archer.

"When you get to where you're going, and get yourself all set up, you send me a hundred dollars a month."

Archer shook his head. "That's steep. I might not even make that much."

"Well, I'm a betting man, Archer, as you know, and I'm betting on you to do just fine out there in California."

"But for how long do I make the monthly payments?"

"Oh, let's say six years, and I like you so I'm not even going to charge you interest over that time."

"Well, I'm starting to like you, too, so let's say one year and I'll allow you to continue *not* charging me interest."

Howells said, "Three years, Archer. It's still quite a steal for you. You'll be driving this car as an old man."

"Two years for a total of $4,250, and if I can pay it all off early, I will. You have my word."

"Jesus H. Roosevelt Christ," screamed Callahan as more bullets whizzed by them.

"Okay, that's a deal," said Howells.

Archer eyed the mirror. "Great. Liberty, take your gun out of your purse."

"Why?"

"Because I want to make it useful out here." There was a sense of urgency in his voice that compelled Callahan to do just as he asked.

She held out the Smith & Wesson. "Now what? Do you want me to start shooting?"

"No. I need you to take the wheel."

"What! How?"

"Put your hands on the wheel. I'll slide under you and you go over me. I'll keep my foot on the gas as long as I can. Soon as you're in place, you mash it to the floor."

"Archer, I don't think I can do this."

"I wouldn't be asking unless I knew you could. And Bobby H can't drive."

"Oh, Lord help me."

"The Lord helps those who help themselves," interjected Howells in a knowing manner.

"Oh shut up, you old fool. *You* got us into this. And I doubt very seriously you of all people know anything about the *Lord*."

Archer said, "Go up. Now."

Callahan put her hands on the wheel, took a deep breath, then arched her back and slid to the right while Archer sunk low and edged to the left. A moment later Archer dropped into the middle of the seat and she into the driver's. "Floor it," he called out as he gripped the .38, turned around in the seat so he was facing backward, and lined up his shot through the revolver's iron sights.

Archer turned to Callahan. "On the count of three start to ease off the gas until you get it down to around sixty."

"But you said—"

"Just do it, Liberty!"

She gave him a sulky look and waited.

"One...two...three."

The Delahaye slowed to a hundred and then eighty, and then stuck at sixty as Callahan eyed the speed gauge.

"We're there," she said.

The Buick was now catching up fast.

Archer aimed but didn't fire.

Wait for it, wait for it...

He placed two quick shots into the grill and followed those with one each in the front tires. When he pulled the trigger again, the hammer banged empty. He was out of bullets. But he didn't need any more.

Steam immediately started pouring out of the Buick's radiator, covering the windshield in a thick fog. The blown-out front tires wobbled madly, and finally rubber separated from the metal rims, and the treads went spinning off into the darkness.

The Buick ended up crashed in a ditch while the Delahaye roared triumphantly on.

"Nice shooting there, Archer," complimented Howells.

Archer sat forward in his seat and looked at Callahan. "You okay to drive?"

"Yes. But I'm sure as hell not going as fast as you did."

"Okay, the three of us are staying together until the government building opens and we can get the title to the car transferred all official."

"I got a room," said Bobby H.

"And I'm sure those boys back there know it, too," replied Archer. "So that's out."

"We can stay at my place," said Callahan, drawing surprised looks from both men. "Well, it's got *two* rooms. One of you can sleep on the couch, the other the floor. *I'll* be in the bedroom."

Howells looked at Archer with a pained expression. "I got me a real bad back, son. Real bad."

"Of course you do," said Archer as the Delahaye roared on.

9

THEY HAD TO GO UP THE FIRE ESCAPE to Callahan's place because the landlady was, in Callahan's words, "an old battle-ax determined not to let young women have any fun." And that obviously included no men staying the night.

They had parked the car in a lean-to attached to a garage behind Callahan's building. Archer had found a cover in the trunk and thrown that over the Delahaye.

As she led them into her room via the fire escape and then a window she said, looking at Howells, "Now, she probably wouldn't mind you. But Archer is definitely a no-no."

Howells seemed to swell up with indignity. "I may not be as young as I once was, and who among us is, but I'm still a man who can appreciate female beauty when it is so obviously presented to me."

"Well, thanks for the compliment, I guess," responded Callahan, giving Archer a funny look.

Howells took the couch, which was lumpy but serviceable. He took off his hat and coat and shoes, revealing toeless socks, and then promptly fell asleep, his soft snores settling over Archer and Callahan as they watched him.

"Exciting times must have exhausted him," noted Archer, holding his hat and peering down at the man.

Callahan shook her head. "I'm not ready for bed. I'm a night owl."

"What *are* you ready for?" asked Archer.

"A drink."

"Afraid my flask is almost empty."

"I've got a bottle and two glasses hidden away under my bed. Old Fitz Kentucky bourbon work for you? It's wheat, not rye."

"I like pretty much any grain that's been liquefied."

They sat on the fire escape as they sipped their drinks.

"So California, huh?" said Callahan.

"Yep."

"What's out there for you?"

"A private eye named Willie Dash. I'm hoping he'll take me under his wing and teach me the business."

"So you wanna be, what, a gumshoe like Humphrey Bogart?"

"Bogie just pretends to be a gumshoe. I want to be one for real."

"Taking pictures of married men and women cheating? Running down lousy deadbeats for money? Poking into people's secrets? That's your idea of a job?"

"Must be," said Archer bluntly. "Because I haven't thought of another one."

She cocked her head and appraised him carefully. "You could be in the pictures, Archer. Sure, you're rough around the edges and you're definitely not Cary Grant, but you're all right. And you're tall and you have broad shoulders and you got a nice voice."

"Funny, those are exactly the requirements for a private eye."

"Stop teasing and pour me another drink."

He did so, then helped himself to another finger of Old Fitz and settled back against the hard metal of the fire escape. After the wild ride in the Delahaye, it felt good not to be moving or shot at.

"So you got any family hereabouts?" he asked.

"No, because I'm not from here."

"Where then?"

"None of your business."

He gave her a bemused look. "I thought we were getting along okay."

"I don't like talking about myself all that much. And I told you where I worked during the war and about my brother and cousin. Hell, that's pretty much my life story. What about you? Where are you coming from?"

"Little town called Poca City, nearly fifteen hundred miles due east of here."

"That's one long trip."

"And my butt and back felt every mile."

"Never heard of Poca City."

"I wouldn't recommend you going there and finding out for yourself."

"You had a bad time there?"

"You could say that," Archer replied evenly.

"And what were you doing there?"

"Just passing through." He paused, took a drink, and said, "So the car. What would you say to driving west with me?"

"I don't know. How far is this place from Hollywood?"

"They're both in southern California. Bet there's a bus to Hollywood from where I'm headed."

She eyed him nervously. "You looked real good with that gun back there."

"Everybody looks good with a gun, until they get shot by somebody else with a bigger gun or better aim."

"I don't necessarily mean that as a compliment. You're no criminal, are you? I mean, you haven't been to prison, right?"

"Do I look like I've been in prison?"

"I don't know. I've never met any ex-cons before."

"You telling me in a place like Reno there are no ex-cons?"

"I'm sure there are. I've just never met any."

"That you know of, you mean. They wouldn't exactly come out and tell you."

"Does that include you, Archer?"

Archer almost winced at how neatly she had played him on that one.

He finished one more finger of the Old Fitz before answering her. "Truth is, I served three years. Got out early for good behavior. Spent my parole time in Poca City. Only reason I was there. Now I'm done with my parole. I'm as free as any other man."

"What were you in for? If you only spent three years in the slammer, it couldn't have been too bad," she added hopefully.

"I didn't hurt anybody and I didn't steal a dime. And I was innocent, by the way. But I guess they all say that."

"I guess they do."

"It…it was actually about a gal and another car. Her father's. She wanted to get away from him, start life fresh somewhere."

"Well, my father's long since dead, but sounds like my situation."

"It didn't turn out the way I thought it would. For either one of us."

"Did you love her?"

"No," he said sharply. "It was nothing like that."

"Okay, Archer, don't get sore."

"Maybe I was just trying to be a hero. You know, save the gal."

"I was just asking because with a guy and a gal it usually is about love, or lust, or a combo of the two."

He eyed her curiously. "You sound like you know all about it."

"You think you're the only one life's dumped on? I got my bruises, too, maybe they don't show as well as yours, is all. And I never got to play the hero."

"So were you the damsel in distress?"

She finished her drink. "I don't recall getting saved one time. Quite the opposite."

He put his empty glass down. "So I suppose you riding with me to California is out then."

"What makes you say that?"

He looked up at her in some surprise. "I'm an ex-con, whether I deserve it or not."

"But you gave me half your winnings at roulette when you

didn't have to. And I saw how you were with the old guy. You defended him from those thugs when you didn't have to. They could've killed you, and you didn't even really know him. And you saved our lives tonight with a nifty piece of driving and shooting. And you're going to buy a car you don't really need to help that old man from getting killed. And..."

"And what?"

"And we're sitting out here all alone and you haven't made one move on me. Now, I can tell you that has never happened to me before, least since my breasts came in."

Archer actually blushed at this last remark.

She added, "And you get embarrassed when a girl says 'breasts.' That makes you all right in my book, Archer."

"Funny the things you learn along the way. So California?"

"I can be ready to go after you get the car squared away."

"What about the Dancing Birds? What about Mr. Shyner?"

"Oh, they've got lots of gals waiting to take my place. And Mr. Shyner knows I want to go to Hollywood. I'll write him a note in the morning and get it to him. It'll be okay."

Archer nodded. "Well, I guess we better get some sleep then. Long day tomorrow."

"I guess so." She leaned over and kissed him on the cheek.

"What was that for?"

"Just for being a nice guy. There aren't that many out there, least from where I'm sitting." She eyed the window. "I've got carpet in my bedroom if you want to sleep on the floor. Might be easier on you."

He eyed her long legs, the curve of her hips and bosom, the hair bouncing off her graceful shoulders, and, best of all, the woman's warm, tender smile.

"For a lot of reasons, and I'm not saying they're all good ones, I'll sleep next to the snoring old man."

"You sure?"

"No. But it might actually be harder, not easier, on me if I took you up on your offer."

Her smile deepened. "Just confirmed everything I've been saying about you, Archer."

"Yeah, well, good night."

"Good night."

She climbed in one window and he the adjacent one.

And neither one got much sleep at all.

10

The next morning, with all the paperwork done, Howells shook Archer's hand on the steps of the government building.

"Well, good luck to you," said Howells as he folded the cash and put it away in his billfold.

"And good luck to you, too, Bobby H. But if I were you I'd get out of town while you still can. Reno isn't a good place for you. You can do better, and live longer, somewhere else."

"You might be right about that, Archer. In fact, I'm certain of it."

Archer read the man's face like a telegram form. "But you're staying?"

"Yes I am. It's principle, sort of. Convoluted and perhaps nonsensical to some if not most, but principle all the same." He twirled the ends of his mustache, as though putting an exclamation point at the end of his words.

"Like I said before, it's your funeral, Bobby H, and I don't mean that *metaphorically*. I mean six feet under just like for everybody else."

Howells's face crinkled at this remark. "You're a good man, Archer. Take care out there in California. What I've heard of the Golden State there might be danger there as well."

"There's danger everywhere, if you take the time to look for it. And sometimes even if you don't. By the way, where do I send the payments?"

Howells took a card from his pocket and passed it across. "This address will find me."

Archer studied the card. It had a street address and read: "Robert Howells c/o Reno City Jail. To be held until picked up."

"So do you live at the jail? Is that where the room you mentioned is?"

"A truly remarkable notion, Archer."

"Which isn't exactly a no." Archer slid the card into his jacket. "You're a strange one, you are, Bobby H."

"So will the beautiful and vivacious Liberty Callahan be making the journey with you?"

"A long trip is better with some companionship."

"And companionship of a beautiful young woman trumps all other companions of my acquaintance."

"If you say so."

Howells patted his breast pocket and said, "Nice doing business with you, Archer."

On that, Howells walked off with his head held cockily high and his pocket chock-full of money that Archer was sure the man would not use to pay off the debt, but rather lose at gambling. He might be dead before the sun rose the next morning.

Archer had already gotten his bag from the hotel and placed it in the trunk of the Delahaye. He hoofed it back to Callahan's building to find her carrying two suitcases down the front steps. She was in her traveling outfit, complete with a hat that had a bird clinging to the side like a barnacle to a hull. He helped her with the bags and closed up the trunk. Then he pulled out the car key and slipped into the right-hand drive seat of the Delahaye while Callahan took up a perch on the left.

"This is going to take some practice," noted Archer as he put the key in the ignition, turned it, and then thumbed the starter button. The Delahaye roared to breathless life.

"What's that?" she asked.

"Driving on the wrong side of a *car*."

They headed out of town.

People on the streets turned to stare at the ride.

"It does draw attention," observed Callahan.

"Yeah, I'm actually not too thrilled about that right now."

"Too late for that thinking, Archer. Hey, do you even know which way to go?"

"Looked at my nickel map this morning. We basically keep driving west and then we turn south for a bit and then we turn west again and we stop right before we plunge into the Pacific."

"This is so exciting, Archer, don't you think?"

"Sure. I can barely keep my teeth from chattering."

"New lives for us both. You a shamus and me a movie star."

"I think you have the harder road."

"Do people shoot at shamuses?"

"If they do, I got some practice with that last night."

She took the .38 Special from her purse. "Don't worry, I reloaded last night."

He shot her a curious glance.

"You never carry an empty gun around, Archer. What would be the point?"

"As a former soldier, I can't argue with that logic."

"How long will it take us to get there?"

"We'll never make it to where we're going in one day, not even in this rocket ship. We'll have to stop for the night."

Archer glanced at the woman in time to see her let slip an anticipatory smile at his remark. He tossed this one around in his brain for a few moments and came away with several possibilities. One of which intrigued him, and the others of which bothered him, with at least one of *those* putting the fear of God in him.

He glanced at the dinged metal post, the only blemish on an otherwise pristinely beautiful piece of art, at least according to

Howells. Next, he focused on the road, but in his head other things commanded his attention.

This was the start of a new life for him. Or at the very least, the *potential* of a new life. What if he screwed it up? What if California and his dream of becoming a PI came to nothing? Then what would he do? He'd be out there without a dime to his name, in a car he couldn't afford to make the payments on, without the prospects of anything getting better.

"You look nervous," said Callahan.

Archer glanced over to see her staring at him with an earnest look, but then she smiled, which he liked better than earnest.

She patted his hand. "If it makes you feel any better, Archer, I'm scared, too."

"Who says I'm scared?"

"You didn't have to say it. I can see it. But we're young. So what if we got a bum ride so far in life? We're looking for something better. So why not take our shot?"

"Easy to say."

"Hell, Archer, if it were easy, everybody would be fat and happy."

11

THEY DROVE DUE SOUTH TOWARD CARSON CITY and soon passed an enormous body of water.

"Now that's a sight for sore eyes," said Callahan. "Considering we're in the middle of a desert."

"Lake Tahoe," said Archer as the Delahaye whizzed past it on State Route 27.

"How do you know that?"

"Read a travel brochure."

She eyed the dashboard. "Does this thing have a radio?"

"Afraid not," said Archer. "Nineteen thirty-nine apparently was a long time ago."

"I like George Burns and Gracie Allen. They make me laugh. And they seem to really love each other even though they're married."

"Well, that's sort of the point, isn't it?"

"What you don't know could fill a library, Archer."

"What I don't get is how come on the show Gracie always outsmarts George."

"Well, they just like to keep it realistic."

They crossed into California and then doglegged southwest before entering the Sierra Nevada Mountains. As the ground rose swiftly around them, Callahan clutched the edge of her seat.

"You okay?" asked Archer.

"I didn't know we had to go through mountains to get there."

"You ever been to California before?"

"Never. You?"

"When I was in the Army. Trained at Fort Ord and then at Camp San Luis Obispo."

As they passed close to the edge of a long drop, she closed her eyes and said, "Well, I prefer flat land."

"Well, with the right-hand drive and the direction we're going, I'm the one close to the edge, not you."

"I'm close enough, thank you very much."

They drove past slopes full of chaparral, flatter lands of grass savannas, stands of big-leaf maples and white alders, thick, rugged live black and blue oaks, and armies of Coulter pines.

"What the hell kind of tree is that?" asked Callahan.

They were passing what looked to be a whole forest of them. They seemed to reach to the stars, and an Army column, complete with armor, could have ridden through an opening in one broad trunk.

"Giant sequoias, biggest trees there are. We came up here to train a few times. Ended up just staring at those suckers for about an hour."

They started upward again with jarring swiftness and Callahan clamped her eyes shut.

"How'd you end up in Reno?" asked Archer, trying to draw her mind away from the ascending elevation.

She slowly opened her eyes. "After the war, I wasn't sure what to do. My brother was dead, and my parents both died before the war started. The factory I worked in closed down, and with all the boys coming back from fighting there weren't any jobs left for the women. Those who were married went back to their homes and husbands, those who came back anyway. I worked at a diner in Tennessee for a bit, then decided to just pull up stakes and totally change the direction of my life."

"So you headed west?"

"Yes, like a lot of people." She eyed him with a heavy-lidded look. "Like you."

"And the stint at the Dancing Birds Café?"

"I got to Reno and was wandering around town, checking things out when I literally bumped into Mr. Shyner. I guess he liked the looks of me. I started out working as the hostess, prancing around in my tight little gown, getting my butt pinched and my boobs felt up and taking dollar tips from gents for the privilege. Then I became a waitress. The tips were better, and the ass pinchers had a tougher angle to work with, but I couldn't see a future in it. I was practicing my dancing and singing the whole time though, you see. Out in Hollywood, the girls have to be able to do lots of things. I read about that in magazines. If I can sing and dance, I can get parts. Bit parts, sure, but then people get to know you. And your roles get bigger. That's how it works. And if you're lucky enough and work hard enough, you get to be a star."

"Sounds like you gave this a lot of thought," replied Archer.

"You *have* to give it thought when you're changing your whole life."

Archer considered this. "I'm not sure I gave my course change a lot of thinking. It was sort of a spur-of-the-moment thing."

"I couldn't afford to do that, Archer. This is my last chance at something big."

"Why? You're still young."

"In the movie business, I'm getting close to middle age. I need to get going before the only parts left to me are playing the heroine's spinster aunt."

"Um-hmm." Archer checked the mirror.

She noticed this and said, "You don't think we're being followed?"

"Never can be too careful."

They passed over the San Joaquin River and watched the rushing water below. It was the fourth such river they had crossed. It seemed to Archer that California was a very well-hydrated state. It grew dark as they continued heading south through the San Joaquin Valley, which was flat and filled with plants of every description, and all lush and green.

"So are we done with the mountains?" asked Callahan, looking relieved. "This place is pretty level."

"Valleys usually are, but no, we're not. We have to go through the Diablo Range next," noted Archer.

"Then is that it for the mountains?"

"No. There's a whole mess of coastal ranges, north to south. After Diablo, we cross the Santa Lucia Range to get to Bay Town, which is where I'm going."

"Lots of Spanish names in California," she said suspiciously.

"Well, they *did* discover it first."

"Where are we stopping for the night?" she asked as she lit up a cigarette and nervously blew smoke to her side of the car.

"There's a place called Coalinga in Fresno County. Route 198 will take us there."

"Never heard of Coalinga."

"Neither have I. But it's a place to stop."

"Do we go through the Diablo mountains to get there?"

"No, it's still pretty much in the valley. It's farmland, mostly level."

"How much farther after Coalinga to Bay Town?"

"On these sorts of roads, I'm not sure. We cross the Diablos, head for the coast and then go south for a way, cross the Santa Lucias, and then go straight for the Pacific. It'd be good if we could make it in one trip, but I'm getting pretty tired and it's another three hours just to Coalinga."

"Then why don't you pull over and rest your eyes, at least? I don't want us running off a cliff because you're beat."

He found a rest area on the side of the road that had a small picnic table and an old, rusted charcoal grill. They sat at the table with their coats wrapped around them, since the sinking sun had brought drastically cooler temps, and the winds, funneled down the valley, had picked up. Callahan had brought a paper sack of sandwiches, and they ate one each and split a fat pickle. As they smoked their cigarettes and Callahan took a pull on Archer's flask, he said, "We'll need to gas up again. We can do that in Coalinga. And maybe we can get a cup of coffee."

"Or a slug of gin."

"Right. Then we're good until we get to Bay Town."

"And you can be a private eye," said Callahan. "Or die trying."

Archer glanced over at her. "And you can go to Hollywood and be a movie star. And ditto."

She looked over at the Delahaye admiringly. "Nice ride so far."

"Except for the mountains, you mean."

"I'm getting used to them, actually. I can learn to accept pretty much anything."

"That's real good, lady, 'cause you're gonna have to."

They looked up to see three men standing there.

12

ARCHER STARED OVER AT THE TRIO of intruders. One guy was small, but he stood in front of the other two. He was clearly the leader. Archer sized up the pair as the necessary muscle on a mission of this kind. They were built like pickup trucks, and their expressions betrayed as much intellect as an exhaust pipe.

The little fellow was dapperly dressed in a blue serge suit with two-tone shoes, black and gray, toe to heel, and a white felt hat with a black band and ribbon. The hair Archer could see around the temples was slick, just like the facial features. The eyes were dulled ball bearings. His waistcoat was dark gray and matched the shoe color. His tie was dark red and knotted in the double-Windsor style. He had a straight line of mustache above a thin, chapped top lip. It looked waxed. *He* looked waxed.

The pair of strongarms was outfitted in 46 long pinstripes that still looked squeezed by their bulk. Tweedle-dee held a .45 loosely at the side of his hammy thigh. His partner in crime cradled a far more menacing Remington side-by-side sawed-off shotgun in his hands like a newborn. They both had matching fedoras, light blue with black bands, and no ribbons thereon.

The boss took a step forward and the big boys did likewise; the menace in their features was palpable.

Archer rose from the picnic table while Callahan remained in her seat staring at the men.

"Hello, fellas, are you lost?" said Archer by way of greeting. He pointed to his right. "The Pacific's that way, at least I think."

The little man snickered and then apparently thought better of it and his features turned nasty. "We know exactly where we are. If anybody's lost, it's you two." He aimed a finger at Archer and then Callahan for emphasis that wasn't needed; the shotgun and .45 did that just fine.

"We know where we are and where we're going," said Archer.

Tweedle-dee's twin brought the sawed-off up and leveled it at Archer's belly.

Archer wasn't prepared to fight a Remington with his bare hands; he couldn't outrun buckshot, and assuming the fetal position seemed like a lousy idea, too.

"The fact is, mac, you ain't going anywhere," said the little man.

Archer glanced at Callahan to see her gaze still holding on the three men. She seemed concerned but not desperate. Archer didn't quite know how to read that.

"Is there something you want?" asked Archer, his gaze now swiveling between the little man and the Remington. The night air was suddenly thick with the choking smells of the eucalyptus trees, and the chaparral seemed to close upon them like a band of hungry wolves. If Archer dared close his eyes he could be back in the European theater, on the outskirts of another village, the names of which he could never pronounce. He would be creeping along, he and two buddies, M-1s in hand, cig packs in their pockets, dog tags dangling from quivering necks, equal parts hope and dread in their hearts, just wanting to finish the mission of the moment and get back to safety, if there was any to be had in the middle of a world war.

The dapper fellow pointed to the Delahaye.

Archer followed the finger. "You want the car?"

"What a smart guy you are." There was no joviality behind the remark, only stark insult.

Archer eyed the muscle. There was nothing behind their eyes. They were here to dispose of a problem. *Two* problems.

"You been following us, right?"

"Ever since you left Reno. Wasn't that hard. Roads like this, you can only go one way, probably why you never eyed us."

"Reno? Really?"

"Yeah, really."

"You happen to know somebody named Robert Howells?"

The man grinned. "He was the one who told us you were heading to California. This was after we roughed him up a little. Made it easy to follow you. It was one of my guys who put the ding in that car last night. And you ruined my Buick, pal. You owe me for that. I'm here to collect."

"Okay, but why do you want the car? Howells was going to pay you off with the money he got for it."

"Yeah, thing is, he owed me a lot more than he got from you."

"How do you know how much he got from me?"

The man pulled out a wad of cash. "'Cause soon as he left you I took it from him and counted it. He owes another six grand. I figure the car will make up the difference."

"He didn't mention owing you that much. If he did I'm surprised he let the car go for what I gave him."

"Well, thing is, old Bobby H must've forgot to add in the interest. At a hundred percent a day, it adds up quick."

"Yeah, I bet. And where is Howells now?" asked Archer, his face starting to tingle.

The man gave him a forced grin. "You ain't *that* stupid, are you?"

"You didn't have to kill him, you know."

"I don't remember asking for your opinion."

Callahan broke the silence. "If you take the car, how the hell do we get out of here?"

Archer couldn't believe the woman was serious with her question, and when he looked over at her he could tell by her expression that she wasn't. Maybe she was stalling for time, allowing Archer to come up with a plan. What a disappointment he would be for her.

"That won't be a problem, for *you*," said the little man.

"Well, I don't find that acceptable," said Callahan.

Archer almost laughed at this comment but when he looked at her the thought of humor faded.

The little man seemed to want to say something, but the words stalled in his throat. He just shrugged, lit a half-smoked cigarillo, and contemplated the dirt for a few moments.

"Take the car," said Archer. "And we can walk to where we're going."

The muzzle of the cigarillo came up and pointed in Archer's direction; like the Remington, it seemed a direct threat to his personal well-being.

Archer added, "We don't know you from Adam. You'll be long gone before we reach a telephone box or a cop. Why make two bodies if you don't have to? Stealing a car is one thing. The other is something else. The gas chamber at San Quentin is a shitty way to kick it."

Smoke curled off the end of the cigarillo and lifted to the sky like a fragment of a memory gone to Heaven. Archer looked up at the sky, and when his gaze came back down, the little man was staring dead at him.

"No can do, pal. I never did like loose ends."

Archer felt his adrenaline actually ease for some reason. This unusual physiological reaction in the face of danger came from his fighting in the war. If you wanted to live, you had to remain calm. He moved to his left, drawing the attention and angle of attack of the thugs.

"Don't try to run," said the little man. "It won't matter and you'll just embarrass yourself, mac."

"I don't remember asking you for *your* opinion," said Archer.

"And just so you know, the outer killing range on a sawed-off is about six feet. I'm double that." He eyed the .45. "And in the dark, that revolver is bumping up against the wall of accuracy at ten feet."

He took a long stride backward. "And now I'm at fifteen feet."

"Son, don't end your time looking like a fool," said the little man somberly. "Have some self-respect and let's get this over with nice and clean."

Archer moved in a slow curve, and they curved with him.

Sawed-off, perhaps sensing a loss of control of the situation, took a few quick strides forward.

"Still not enough," said Archer. "The buckshot will sting but it won't kill." He didn't really believe this, but then *he* didn't have to.

Now .45 moved forward, joining his twin along the line of attack. The little man, sensing the end coming, took a step back, burned off the remnants of his smoke, and dropped it to the dirt. The orange embers winked dead in the darkness like a miniature sun burrowing into the horizon.

"Now just hold still," said .45, his voice surprisingly high-pitched for such a big larynx. He took aim with the revolver, but Archer could see his dominant arm shaking like a twig in a breeze; .45 clearly wanted to be big and tough but maybe he was just big.

Archer kept moving for two more strides, turning the men's attention even more fully to him.

What they hadn't foreseen was that his movements had put their backs to Callahan. They seemed to have forgotten all about the woman. That was about to change, but not exactly in the way Archer intended.

Callahan fired and her .38's round hit Sawed-off in the right shoulder blade. He grunted once as the slug penetrated first skin, then tendon, then severed bone and plowed right through an intersection of blood vessels.

He groped around, pawing with his free hand at the entry wound, and screaming in pain. His hat came off and landed in the pool of blood now avalanching from him, for the shot had split a fat artery right in two. Snot blew out of his nose in his rage and fear and pain. He threw up whatever he'd last eaten and drunk, fouling the air. A urine stain emerged around his zipper as the shock of the round's hitting him overcame his ability to hold this bodily function in check.

His fingers lost their strength, and the Remington hit the hard dirt. The impact with the ground must have sprung its filed-down hair triggers, because the twin barrels of the sawed-off boomed sideways and caught .45 at both ankles with hundreds of pebbles of angry buckshot at a distance of about seven inches, severing that part of his body as neat as a bone saw and miraculously leaving him upright. At that range, the sawed-off wasn't a gun, it was a bomb.

The big man looked down and saw that his black wingtips, and the feet in them, were resting next to him, instead of under him. He was suddenly three inches shorter and standing on twin shattered bone tips, and his mind didn't seem able to cope with this because he made no sound. He toppled sideways but fired his gun, maybe as a knee-jerk reaction.

He killed a eucalyptus tree next to Archer.

.45 commenced dying as he lay on the ground probably not knowing who or what had killed him. Archer watched as the man turned to him, his hemorrhaging eye an inch above the forest floor. The man blinked once, then shock took over. He convulsed once, then again, and the eye closed and the man died quick and silent.

Archer knew that pulling the trigger and killing a man was easy. What was hard was everything leading up to that point. And everything coming after it.

Archer turned to Sawed-off. He, too, had left this life in a dark, burgundy spread of blood that the dirt did not seem to want, because it lay on top of the ground like water in a pool.

"Don't," the voice barked out.

Archer turned to see Callahan now pointing her Smith & Wesson at the little man, who, dazed by the sudden elimination of his comrades, had pulled a .22 Derringer from his waistcoat and was pointing it around, though Archer could tell the fellow had no firm idea of an actual target.

"Don't do it," Callahan said. Her voice was assured, in command, with an ice-in-the-veins sort of rhythm. It was like a dagger needling your ribs before it went in for the kill.

Archer looked at her. Unlike .45, there wasn't a twitch in her gun hand. The Smith & Wesson was held as sure and steady as a foot-round oak branch in still air. Callahan's features looked like the mountain peaks they had passed, chiseled, foreboding, impenetrable. The last one got to Archer the most, confounding him.

The little man dropped the Derringer and backed away from it, his hands palm up in front of him, as though that would matter against the .38.

"Okay, okay," he said, a line of sweat glistening around the whiskers above his lip. "Don't do nothing crazy, lady."

"You mean, kill you? Like you were going to kill us? So, who's crazy?"

"Please, lady," he moaned.

"Don't *please* me," she retorted. "It's a little late for that."

Archer said, "It's over, Liberty. Just let him go."

She spoke without looking at him. "And let him do what? Keep following us? Tell somebody else what happened? I killed a man, Archer."

"In self-defense."

"I shot him in the back."

"I'm your witness to what happened."

The little man said, "He's talking sense. And all the fight's gone right out of me. Wish I'd never come up here. I'll take my money and go. You got my word, honest to God."

"Too late to be talking about God," snapped Callahan.

"Just wait a minute," said Archer.

"You can't trust guys like this, Archer. They say one thing and do another." She took closer aim with her revolver. "And he confessed to killing Bobby H."

Archer stepped forward, blocking her sight line. "Killing a man in self-defense is one thing. Shooting him in cold blood is something else. And I'm no saint, but I can't be a party to that, so you might as well shoot me first."

"I like you, Archer, but I'm not sure I like you that much."

"Well, keep this in mind. We have more mountains to go over. You want to drive it alone? Go ahead."

This did what apparently her conscience could not. She lowered her gun. "Pick up his piece and the shotgun and the revolver."

Archer did as she asked, holding the trio of weapons so their barrels pointed to the dirt.

"Where's your car?" Callahan asked the little man.

"Around the bend back there."

"Show us."

He led them around a curve in the road. It was a wonder they hadn't heard the engine, but the wind up here was loud, funneled between the peaks.

It was a Chrysler sedan painted an ugly green with the biggest chrome bumper Archer had ever seen. It was large enough for him to take a nap on.

"You got a spare tire?" asked Callahan.

"Of course," replied the man.

She shot out the Chrysler's right front tire and the air hissed out as the rubber fell flat.

She lowered her gun, studied what she'd done, and said, "I still want to shoot him."

"I know," said Archer, drawing a sharp look from her. "But I say we get back in the car and keep going."

"I'll go along with that plan, for now." She eyed the man, who looked like a fellow who thought he was still on death row. "You follow us, Archer won't save you next time. You go back to where you came from and stay there. And you keep your mouth shut." She lifted her .38 and took aim at a spot between his ball-bearing eyes.

The man backed away. "Yes ma'am."

"One more thing," said Archer. He walked over to the man and drilled him so hard in the face with his fist that the fellow was lifted off his feet and slammed against the side of the car before crumpling to the dirt.

"That was for Bobby H. And if I ever see you again, I'll be the last thing you ever see."

The man sat on the ground holding his broken nose and sobbing in pain.

Callahan turned and walked back to the Delahaye. "Let's go, Archer."

Archer stood there for a bit until she was almost out of sight. Then he did just as she said.

CHAPTER

13

THE DELAHAYE PROWLED THROUGH THE VALLEY like a muscular river drilling through rock. Archer had placed the weapons they'd taken in the trunk. Both he and Callahan were visibly shaken by what had happened. Archer's mind was going a million miles an hour, and Callahan looked pale and distraught.

"I guess you think I'm a bad person," Callahan said quietly, finally breaking the silence after about twenty-five minutes of nothing but the French car's purr.

"I don't think anything one way or another."

"Girls have to know how to take care of themselves, Archer, at least *this* girl does. You think that just applies to guys?"

"No. But maybe I assume, just like all other guys."

"Assume what?"

"That gunplay is for the men. Clearly, I'm wrong about that."

"Fact is, my daddy taught me to shoot starting when I was eight years old. I could barely hold the deer rifle."

"He taught you well. That was not an easy shot tonight with the bad light and distance."

"He was as big as a barn. If I'd missed that lug I'd need glasses. And the other guy died from an accident. So that had nothing to do with me."

Archer downshifted as the road began to curve sharply. They'd put up the car's top because the temperature had dropped and the wind was pushing the cold into them like a railroad spike between the ribs.

"How about the little man then? You were going to shoot him in cold blood."

"Maybe I was bluffing."

"Don't think so."

She lit up a Camel and blew a puff of angry smoke at him. "How the hell do you know? How the hell do you know anything about me?"

"I've seen you gamble. You don't have a poker face."

She gave him a sideways glance that Archer—who was doing the same to her—felt to his toes. He wasn't sure how to properly read this situation, mainly because he'd never met a woman like Callahan before.

So is that my fault or hers?

With an exhale of Camel smoke followed by a brush at her hair with a shaky index finger, she said, "Do we have to tell anybody about it?"

"I think there might be trouble if we don't."

She cranked her window down and flicked her Camel away. It caught a shaft of wind and glanced off an oak before sinking into the asphalt. She cranked the glass back up.

Archer continued, "But we have to think this through. They're going to find the bodies. It was at a picnic area. Folks are going to stop there, just like we did. They're going to unwrap their sandwiches, take out the potato salad, pour coffee out of the thermos, and then look around and start puking."

"Maybe the other guy will get rid of the bodies," she said.

"Why would he do that?"

"He's got exposure, too, Archer. *He's* a criminal, not us. We were just protecting ourselves."

Archer shook his head. "I told Howells to get the hell out of Reno. And now he's dead."

She shot him a look. "So I say we forget it happened and if anybody asks we don't know anything. Two murderers are dead; so what? They got what they deserved."

He glanced at her purse. "Well, no matter what, you might want to do something with the Smith & Wesson, then."

"Why?"

"Because your slug's in the man's back, that's why. They can match bullets. And speaking of, we need to get rid of the guns in the trunk."

She started to bite at a nail painted bright green until it bled, as she thought about this. "We still stopping at Coalinga?"

"Right now I feel like I'm never going to close my eyes again, but we need gas, and I need some coffee. And staying someplace feels like the right thing to do. We both can sort of calm down."

"Can I have a pull on your flask?"

He worked it free from his pocket and passed it across.

She took a healthy swallow, sucked her lips inward in satisfaction, and recapped the flask. "That's better. You want a shot?" she asked, holding it out.

"I've had enough shots for today, thanks." He pointed to the river rushing parallel to the road. "That's a good spot to dump them."

"Okay, Archer, go ahead. But not my gun. We might need it in case that guy comes after us again."

He got out, grabbed the shotgun, Derringer, and .45 from the trunk, walked down to the riverbank, and tossed them all in. He watched them float for a few moments in the strong current, and then they were gone, like fog in the heat of a rising sun.

He walked to the car, got back on the road, and sped up.

"You feel better?" she asked.

"Yeah. How about you?"

In a tone he had not heard her use before she said, "I...I killed a man back there, Archer. I...I'm not sure I'll ever feel right again."

He saw her hands suddenly start to shake and the muscles around her throat tense. Sweat bubbles rose up on her forehead.

He quickly pulled off the road, leaned over, and opened her door. "Go ahead. Do it out there. Quick!"

She jumped out and ran behind a tree, and he could hear her being violently sick. She came back a couple minutes later rubbing at her mouth. Then she got into the car and shut the door.

"You okay?"

She nodded but still looked unwell.

"Sometimes there's a delayed reaction. Like your mind can't wrap itself around something right away."

"Yeah."

"They were going to kill us, Liberty, like you said."

She pressed her face against the cool glass, closed her eyes, and exhaled a long breath. "Yeah. Now just shut up and drive."

14

Coalinga wasn't a thriving metropolis, nor was it the one-horse town Archer thought it was going to be.

Liberty eyed the welcome sign. "Where'd they get the name Coalinga? Is it Spanish?"

He pointed to his right. "There's a railroad spur over there and those are loaded coal cars, so maybe there's your answer."

It was nearly ten o'clock, and the town seemed to be sound asleep, with no one out and most of the buildings closed up.

"I don't know if we can get gas or coffee now, and we might end up sleeping in the car till morning," said Archer. "Because the filling station over there is shut down for the night, and this doesn't look like a two-gas-pump kind of town."

"There's a light on in that building over there."

They stopped in front and climbed out. The air was cool and dry, and the wind had died down some. Archer slipped on his hat and locked up the Delahaye. The sign out front of the building read: CLANCY'S SALOON. OPEN AT NOON, CLOSE WHENEVER.

"I like Coalinga better already," said Callahan as she saw this, too.

Archer held the door for her and they walked in.

The four hundred square feet inside consisted of a mahogany bar with ten backless stools, a jukebox with neon tubes blinking wearily, four tables with a pair of low-backed chairs designed in the form of a ship's wooden wheel around each, a small dance floor made of scratched herringbone parquet on which not a soul was dancing, and a pay phone on the wall. A pencil dangled from a string tacked to that wall, and lines of phone numbers had been scribbled across the paint like math equations. A small window behind the bar was where the food came through for the patrons seated there. A single swing door to the left of that was where the meals came through for the dining area.

Two men sat at the bar. One young and lean, one old and spreading. They both held mugs of beer, and both looked to be listing to the right in alcoholic zeal. Behind the wooden counter was a beefy man with curly red hair, a stained white apron, and shirtsleeves rolled up to reveal twin anchor tattoos, one on each forearm. A cigar was clamped on one side of his wide, toothy mouth. He was staring down at the cloth in his hand like he was wondering how it had gotten there.

Of the four tables, only one was occupied. On one side was a woman in her fifties with white hair and a long, horsey face. Her cherry-red purse sat on the table next to her plate of raw oysters on the half shell and a bourbon, neat, percolating in a short glass. Across from her was a gentleman, also in his fifties, suited in a three-piece worsted wool with a loosened dark tie. He was chubby and sweaty, and his napkin was pinned across his white shirt front like a bull's-eye. A plate of spaghetti and clams lay in front of him, and he methodically worked his fork and spoon in tandem as he ate. He had a glass of red wine as his meal's liquid companion.

At first no one looked up when they walked in. Then Chubby with the clams saw Callahan and made such a fuss that White Hair turned to see. Her long face became pinched and sour. She turned back to her tablemate and said something low, snappy, and apparently pointed as a spear because the clams once more became Chubby's sole focus. The bartender looked up, saw Callahan, grabbed a glass, and started polishing it to a fine sheen, a sloppy grin spreading across his face, as though he'd just won a prize that would take him away from here. The young drunk turned, eyed Callahan, and almost fell off his stool. The old drunk would probably have done likewise, but he had already fallen face-first into the mahogany and was now snoring.

The swinging door did its thing and a woman in her twenties with sandy brown hair and short, muscular legs and attired in a light brown waitress uniform with faded red piping came out carrying a platter of clean glasses. She saw them and pointed with her free hand to a table.

"Have a seat, be with you folks in a sec."

Archer and Callahan sat, and after the waitress deposited the glasses in a double-door wooden cabinet, she came over with menus and cloth napkins folded around cutlery. She handed it all out and said, "Can I get you something to drink? If you want food, the kitchen closes in twenty minutes."

"Then we must be getting close to 'whenever,'" noted Archer.

"Yeah, you're the first person to come up with that line," she said in a bored tone.

"I'll have coffee, black," said Archer. "You folks know how to make a gimlet?"

"Yes. We've done those before."

"Great, then a gimlet chaser for the coffee, and go easy on the Rose's and let the gin make its mark for me. Or do I tell that to friendly behind the bar?"

"I'll give him the order," she said as she turned to Callahan. "And you, ma'am?"

"You got cranberry juice?" asked Callahan.

"Yes. Is that all you want?"

"Yeah, so long as it goes with the vodka."

The woman grinned and gave Archer a condescending look. "Now, *that's* wit, buckaroo. I'll get your drinks."

Archer took his hat off and set it on the table. He looked around the room. He'd been in bars better than this and lousier than this.

The same alcohol was served here that was dished out in the best bars in the world, LA, New York, Paris, London, and Berlin, what was left of it. So in that respect a bar in Coalinga, California, was as good as any of those. But Archer was still in Coalinga and not Paris.

Callahan slipped out a Camel and tapped the lighting end on the hard surface to make the tobacco as good as it could be. "You think that little goon headed back to Reno?" she said.

Archer shrugged. "Maybe. He's out of guns and bigger goons. I don't see him following us alone."

"He might still come after us with some other muscle."

"Good luck finding us. California is a pretty big place."

"That's true," she replied, her spirits seeming to lift.

They sat there in silence until his coffee and gimlet came along with her cocktail. The waitress pulled out her pad and pen.

"You folks had a chance to look over the menu? No more oysters and no more clams, by the way."

"What would you recommend?" asked Archer.

"The steak. We got two pieces left. And baked potato. We got two of those left, too."

"Steak and potatoes, why didn't I think of that?" said Callahan. "Sold."

"Make it a deuce," added Archer.

The waitress went off. Archer drank down the rest of his coffee and turned his attention to the gimlet.

Callahan shot him a nervous glance. "You're looking pensive again, Archer."

"You still want to go on to Hollywood?"

She gave him a pointed look that seemed to peek right into his soul. She finished a long drag on her smoke before saying, "That was the original plan. You see any reason why I should change it?"

"Yeah, two of them, same as the number of bodies we left up in the mountains."

"Do we have to go over that again?"

"Hear me out."

"Okay."

She sat back and crossed one long leg over the other, which rode her skirt way up, and commenced to jiggling her foot, letting her high heel dangle precariously off her toes. Chubby glanced over and saw this, and seemed to whimper before his companion kicked him under the table.

"It might be better if we stuck together, at least for a while."

"You mean, if he comes after us with more goons?"

"Yeah."

"But you said he wouldn't be able to find us, Archer."

"I know I did, but I've been thinking about that. I'm not sure I didn't let it slip when I was in Reno about where I was headed. And the Delahaye sort of sticks out. And if you go to Hollywood and start making a name for yourself? He sure as hell knows what your name is. He would've gotten it from Howells. Mine too."

"But then should we go to Bay Town, if he knows that's where you'll be?"

"I have to, Liberty. I want a shot at this job. And I told the guy I'd be coming." Archer now looked uncertain. "But maybe you shouldn't go to Bay Town. Maybe you should go to Hollywood, but change your name. All those folks do, right?"

"But if I get in pictures, he'll recognize me, even if I change my name. Hell, he might even try to blackmail me."

Archer nodded slowly. "That's true. So what do you want to do?"

"I think we should stay together," she said. "And go to Bay Town. I can hang around long enough to see if the guy shows up."

"But you don't have to do that. You can go lie low somewhere else."

"And leave you all by your lonesome? What kind of a fink do you think I am?"

They sat in silence until their meals came. Archer was lost in thought and Callahan was lost in more Camels.

They ate and put down money for their bill. When the waitress came over to collect it, Archer asked if there was a place to stay the night.

"Yes, it's right down the street, called the Coalinga House. They do overnights and they have vacancies right now. Knock hard, they might have gone to bed. Mildred Hawks is the owner's name. She's nice. Tell her Katy sent you."

* * *

They walked out, got into the Delahaye, and drove the short distance to the Coalinga House. It was a broad plank-and-brick building with a porch down the front and a row of rocking chairs lined up like toy soldiers alongside little pots with fresh flowers. There was a concrete statue of a kitten playing cute on the first step up to the porch.

"Well, at least it doesn't look like a place where we can get into too much trouble, Archer."

The door was painted red and Archer had to pound on it for a full minute before they heard footsteps pecking on the floor toward them.

The door opened and there stood, presumably, Mildred. She was in her sixties with long, braided gray hair flipped over one granny-robed shoulder. She looked sleepy and annoyed at the same time.

"Yes?"

"We need a place to stay," said Archer. "Just got in town. Katy at Clancy's recommended you. I'm assuming you're Mildred?"

Mildred nodded warily and then eyed Callahan with a severe eye. "I've only got one room available."

Callahan said, "One is all we need."

"Then you're married?"

She said, "We're driving in from Reno. Who goes to Reno except to get hitched?"

Mildred's gaze swept down to their hands. "And where are your rings then?"

Callahan's expression turned to one of despair. "Can you believe it, we were robbed on the way? We've reported it, but the police don't hold out much hope."

"If you were just married, you must have your certificate."

"That was with the things that were stolen," said Callahan mournfully. "Along with something borrowed and something blue. Crappy way to start a honeymoon, huh? I've had to work hard not to cry my eyes out."

This stream of lies so confidently told seemed to soften Mildred up. She opened the door wider. "I have a place at the top of the stairs. Bathroom down the hall."

"That sounds perfect," replied Callahan. She turned to Archer. "Well, honey?"

"Well what?" said Archer.

"Aren't you going to carry me over the threshold?" She looked at Mildred. "Men, right? They're like little boys who have to be constantly told to blow their noses and to lift the seat on the toilet."

Mildred gave her a knowing look and stepped back out of the way. "Okay, young man, go ahead. Do your duty."

He picked Callahan up effortlessly, swung her through, and set her down.

"There you go, honey," he said. "Hope you're happy."

Mildred said, "Well, aren't you going to kiss, too? That's all part of it."

Callahan and Archer exchanged nervous glances. "Sure," said Callahan. She leaned over and planted a kiss on Archer. She was about to pull away, but then didn't. They wrapped their arms around each other and lingered. When they pulled apart, each looked as surprised as the other.

A breathless and flushed Callahan smoothed down her dress while Archer adjusted his tie.

Mildred said, "Well, you two are definitely married. I know love when I see it."

On that comment, neither Callahan nor Archer would look at the other.

"There's a pot of coffee on that table over there in the morning," said Mildred. "Let's get you signed in."

Later, after they were in their room, they took turns changing in the bathroom down the hall. Archer put on dark pajamas and Callahan a long white sleeping gown with a slit of interesting elevation, a few fluffy feathers, and nothing on underneath.

They lay in the one narrow bed and Callahan said, "You really thought I'd just up and leave you to those killers?"

He turned to the side to look at her. She did likewise, perching her cheek on her palm as she studied him.

"It's not like you owe me anything, Liberty."

"We're friends, aren't we?"

"We just met."

"So is there a rule that you have to know somebody a certain amount of time before they can be friends?"

"No."

"And it seems to me that we've already shared a bunch of stuff that people who are friends their whole lives haven't."

"Well, being almost killed on three separate occasions over the span of twenty-four hours is unusual, I'll give you that."

"Do you consider yourself my friend?"

"Yes, I do," he said.

"Okay, then it's all settled."

She lay back down. But Archer didn't move. He just watched her. She seemed to sense this because she said, "Under normal circumstances, Archer, I'd be having certain feelings for you lying here like we are. Especially after that kiss…" She shot him a glance full of curiosity. "Just so you know."

"Nothing remotely normal about our circumstances. But I feel the same way, just so you know."

This made her smile. She reached out a hand and he took it.

Archer lay back down. And they both fell asleep hand in hand.

15

Archer was up early, and he brought a sleepy Callahan a cup of coffee from the pot Mildred had mentioned. After that he took the Delahaye for a gas fill-up. When he got back Callahan was dressed and ready to go.

"That's some traveling outfit," noted Archer as he observed the hip-hugging white dress that fell to above her knee and showed enough cleavage to make a man temporarily forget his name. Her heels were high and the color of lavender, and the slim leather belt around her waist was black. Her hair fell to her shoulders, and her head was topped by a turban the color of which matched her shoes.

"If I'm going to be a star, I have to look the part," she replied. "So you think I look okay?"

"That would not be the adjective I would use."

"What *would* be the adjective?" she asked, her eyes lifting to meet his gaze.

"I think I'll keep that to myself."

"And I have to compete with that damn car. I feel like such a second billing."

"Don't worry. Guys like cars, but they like beautiful women better."

"That's the nicest thing you've said to me all morning, Archer. Now, let's blow this joint."

He was loading the bags into the trunk of the Delahaye as a

prowler drifted by. The two cops inside gave the Delahaye, and then Archer, long looks, before floating on to the next street.

By the time they were about to drive off, the prowler had drifted back downstream and docked next to them. The passenger's-side window was cranked down, revealing the meaty face of a guy in his forties with a clean-shaven slab of skin that was sunburned and windburned around the neck and forehead. His brown hair was cut close to the scalp. Archer thought he might be ex-military. His shoulders were wide enough to swallow the window on the prowler. His partner was tall and reedy, and seemed not nearly as interested in them as Meaty was.

"Nice car," said the cop.

"Yeah, isn't it," replied Archer with a friendly grin. He wanted this to go only one way, when it could so easily go the other.

"Where'd you get something like that?" Meaty had apparently read the name located on the chrome front of the car, because he said, "A Dela-haye? What the hell is that?"

"French made. But it was built for an Englishman, which is why the steering wheel's on this side."

"Where'd you get it, pal?"

Archer had been expecting this and said, "From a collector over in Reno. He had some money setbacks and needed to sell."

"You look pretty young to have the dough to lay down for this piece of chrome."

"Yeah, it was a sweetheart deal, but I have to keep paying on it for a while."

The cop pushed back his cap and thought about this, his eyes going back and forth and then reaching to Archer's eyes and holding like the searchlight bolted to the side of the prowler.

Archer didn't like that look. It was probing and distrustful and seemed to be angling for any reason to bust his head open and put the cuffs on. Pretty much every cop he'd ever run into had, at some point, given him that very same look.

"You got papers that prove that?"

"If you really need me to get them, yeah."

The cop's features turned to stone at this slight pushback, and the glare he shot Archer was all official and aggressive and the look of a dog who'd just found a dinosaur bone to crack open and then devour.

"Let me tell you something, buddy—" he began sharply.

Callahan stuck her head around Archer's. "Are you from Coalinga, Officer?" She smacked him with an ear-to-ear smile.

He eyed her features and grinned. "Born and bred, ma'am."

"I'm from back east, but I wouldn't have minded growing up here."

"Yes ma'am." Then the cop's grin faded as he looked at the Delahaye's damaged windscreen post where the bullet had struck. Next his gaze dropped to the door panel and held there; his expression grew even more serious. *Felony* serious, thought Archer, who was noting every changing nuance of this little confrontation.

"What the hell is that?" the cop asked, pointing.

Archer dropped his gaze and saw it. His first instinct was to hit the gas. His second was to look up to see the cop watching him closely.

"Looks like blood to me," said the cop. "What's it look like to you, mister?"

Archer knew that blood was exactly what it was. The car had been parked in the picnic area near the shoot-out. The blast from the shotgun had obviously driven some of the dead man's blood spatter onto the Delahaye's metal. Archer hadn't noticed it in the dark and, for some reason, hadn't noticed it in the light of morning, either. It was, unfortunately, clearly revealed to him now.

"We hit something on the road last night. A deer, a coyote, some animal. Banged the windscreen and then I guess it brushed the side of the car."

"But no dent," said the cop, getting out to look closer. His buddy joined him, coming around the side of the prowler, his hand on the butt of his leather-holstered Colt .45. He looked like he wanted something to shoot.

"You'd expect a dent, right, Jimmy?" Meaty said, looking at his partner, who had an Adam's apple so pronounced it looked like a tumor. "Ain't no dent that I can see. You hit a deer or a big cat, you're gonna have a dent or at least some paint scratches, yes sir. Something weird going on here. I got me some questions, mister."

He bent down to look closer, while Jimmy kept his distance, probably in case he had to draw and shoot Archer on the fly. Meaty looked up and said, "Step out of the car, buddy."

It was right then that *Callahan* got out of the car and came around to them.

Both cops took a whiff of her nectary perfume and came to rigid attention, like a bailiff had just called the court to order. Archer was gratified that their full focus was on the lady and her tight dress rather than the blood and absence of dents.

"I was driving at the time when we hit something. Scared the bejesus out of me," she said. "Didn't it?" she added, looking at Archer.

"The bejesus," repeated Archer.

"'Bejesus,' that's an Irish term," said Meaty. "Hey, are you Irish, Miss?"

She put out a gloved hand for him to shake. "Name's Callahan, Liberty Callahan, so that would be a yes. I am most definitely Irish, officer."

His grin threatened to run off both sides of his face. He pointed to the name sewn onto his uniform. "I'm Sean, Sean *Regan*. My parents came from the county of Offaly."

"My grandparents were from Cork."

"Talk about a small world." He turned and looked at his partner. "Hell, Jimmy, this gal's family is from Cork."

Jimmy couldn't take his gaze off Callahan's prominent bosom. "Cork," was all he managed to say.

Archer noted that Callahan stood so that she was entirely blocking the door panel.

"I'm heading to Hollywood. I want to be in the pictures." She put a hand on her hip and bumped it out and placed the other hand behind her long neck, turned into a profile shot, curved that long neck back like a swan's, and hit them with a dazzling smile. "Think I have a shot? Tell me the truth now, fellas."

Regan said, "Hell, you're lots prettier than Rita Hayworth." He glanced down at her stockinged legs. "Ain't that right, Jimmy?"

Jimmy looked like he had downed two bottles of Old Forester as a warmup to really hitting the juice. "Cork," he said throatily.

Jimmy was down for the count, Archer concluded. He'd probably forgotten about his Colt .45, or the fact that he was even a cop. And Regan wasn't far behind.

"You are so sweet." She gave Regan a hug and Archer watched the cop's hand slide down to her buttocks. He made his landing and dug into her soft flesh. She made no attempt to move his fingers back to a respectable spot. Archer had to appreciate the lady's self-control.

When Callahan stepped back, she said, "I was so nervous, but you've cheered me up no end. So thank you and now I'll let you go on your way. I know how important police work is. My uncle's a cop in Boston."

Regan beamed. "Now there's a big city, all right. They say on Saint Paddy's Day every bar in Boston gives free drinks to every Irishman. Is that true?"

"Every Irishman and Irish*woman*," she added, giving him another broadside of a smile fired right from the biggest quarterdeck cannon she had.

He chuckled and tipped his cap at her. "Best of luck to you, Ms. Callahan."

She did a little curtsy. "Thank you kindly, Officer Regan."

They climbed into the prowler, Regan gave one more enthusiastic wave, and they were gone, just like that. It was hard for Archer to believe everything that had just happened was not a by-product of his imagination or a drunken binge.

Callahan watched them until they were out of sight and then got back in, tugging her dress sharply so the hem wouldn't get caught in the door as she closed it.

"Okay, now I'm convinced," said Archer.

She looked at him curiously. "Of what?"

"That you actually might make a go of it as an actress."

"That wasn't acting, Archer, that was just lying."

"Isn't it the same thing?"

"I don't know. I've done a lot of one, but not necessarily the other."

"It was lucky about the Irish thing."

"What lucky? I saw Regan's name sewn into his uniform. And I *am* Irish. I thought I would give it a shot. What could we lose, right?"

"*Is* your family from Cork?"

"Hell, who knows? Now, let's get out of here before that dumb mick forgets the pleasure of grabbing my ass and remembers the blood and no dent. So *hit* it."

And so Archer hit it.

16

Hours later Callahan awoke with a start and looked over at Archer. Only he wasn't there. The car was empty except for her. The Delahaye was pulled off to the side of the road, next to a river. She looked out the window and saw Archer skimming rocks across the water.

She slipped her heels back on and got out, walking carefully over to him across the uneven terrain.

"What are you doing?" she asked.

"Just taking a break. You were asleep, seemed like a good time to stop."

He reached down and picked up an opened bottle of Coke. "Got this back in Coalinga at the filling station. Just cooled it in the river for a few minutes."

She took the bottle from him and took a couple of swallows before handing it back.

"So where are we?"

"Salinas Valley." He pointed at the water. "That's the Salinas River. Its mouth is way up at Monterey Bay."

"It's beautiful around here."

"It's farmland and very fertile. Nearly a hundred miles of it in the valley. Mountains on both sides. They raise a lot of crops here."

"Were you a farmer?"

"Never plowed a field a day in my life. But I can read. You ever heard of *The Grapes of Wrath*?"

"I saw the movie. Henry Fonda, right?"

"Right. But first it was a novel by a fellow named John Steinbeck. The title comes from a line in the song, 'The Battle Hymn of the Republic.' Read it when I was in college." He took a drink of the Coke. "It's about the Joad family. The Depression and the Dust Bowl wiped out their farming prospects in Oklahoma, so they gathered all the possessions they had left, converted their sedan into a rattling truck, and set off for California for a better life."

Now Callahan looked interested. "Well, hell, that's what we're doing." She took the Coke from him and took another swallow before handing it back and settling her gaze on the rushing water and the picturesque land beyond.

He continued, "The trip didn't turn out too well. Some died on the way. And when they got to where they were going the good-paying jobs turned out not to exist, at least for them. The Joads fell on hard times. It got pretty bad."

"Well, then, I'm surprised you want to go anywhere near California."

"There's a line in the book I'm partial to."

"What is it?"

" 'How can you frighten a man whose hunger is not only in his own cramped stomach but in the wretched bellies of his children? You can't scare him—he has known a fear beyond every other.' "

"So what 'fear beyond every other' have you known, Archer?"

Archer handed her the Coke and spun a beauty of a six-skipper over the face of the Salinas as the sun blazed down on them.

He tipped his hat back. "Life, really, Liberty. Just life. How about you?"

She gave him a look that was between a sob and a smirk. "Hell, Archer, I'm a woman. So yeah, I can say the same, only double."

Archer was about to skip another rock, but then let it drop. He put his hands in his pockets and stared out over the water.

"Don't leave me in suspense, Archer. How'd it really end for the

Joads? Were they all dead? Or did it turn into a fairy tale and they woke up rich?"

"Some of them fought back. Tried to do the right thing. Organized labor, that sort of thing. Fight the rich men. Sort of like trying to beat a Sherman tank with a pistol for all the good it'll do you. But if a man doesn't even try...?"

"Or a *woman*, Archer," she said firmly.

"Or a woman," he conceded.

"So was the trip worth it for them?"

"I guess any trip is worth taking if standing still isn't an option."

"So why aren't we moving then?"

They were walking back to the car when Callahan noticed it. "The blood on the door is gone."

"Why do you think I stopped by the river? A rag and water equals no blood."

"Smart thinking, Archer."

They got back on the road, and very soon they entered the Santa Lucia Mountains. As the land rose around them, Archer looked over at Callahan as she closed her eyes and gripped the seat again.

"You know, for a tough lady like you who knows her way around a gun, I'm surprised anything scares you. We could have used you in the Eighth Army. You're a better shot than a bunch of the guys I served with."

"Flattery will only get you so far with me." But she opened her eyes and smiled at him. "And where I grew up the land was pretty flat. I don't really care for this."

"How'd you get to Reno?"

"Trains, and buses, and hitching rides when my money ran out, which it did pretty regularly."

"That can be dangerous for a gal on her own."

"Yes it can, Archer," she said but did not elaborate.

"Well, glad you made it."

She gazed out the windscreen. "I didn't really run into any mountains on the way." She looked at him. "But I guess there's always something in the way of where you want to go."

"Well, once we clear *these* mountains, we'll be able to see the Pacific Coast and the ocean."

This perked Callahan up. "Really?"

"The mountains affect the weather coming west from the Pacific. Lot wetter on the coast side. Learned that while I was out here training. You'll see the plants and trees and things are a lot different on the western-facing slopes. The mountains bump the weather systems. They drop their rain and then head over the peaks. They call it the rain shadow effect. It's drier in the Salinas Valley because of that. They have to irrigate a lot from local water sources, although they do get some rain."

They cleared the top of a peak on the winding road and started down. They passed coastal redwoods, ponderosa pine, fir trees, Pacific madrones, and cypress.

Later, at a lower level, they rounded a curve and Archer said, "And there's the Pacific."

Callahan actually sat on her haunches on the seat, one hand clutched on her turban, as she surveyed the breath of the largest body of water in the world.

"That whole thing is the Pacific?" she exclaimed.

"Well, you can only see a little bit of it from here. Keep going straight west and you'll hit Japan. Same ocean, though."

Her expression was one of unbridled wonder. "Jesus, that's something, Archer. I thought that Lake Tahoe was big."

"A drop in the bucket."

"Gosh, it's just...swell. I mean, really swell."

He eyed her sitting on her haunches looking like a little girl who'd just been shown the most beautiful doll in the world and then been told it was all hers. He next eyed the glove box, where the .38 Special that had killed a man sat. He wondered about the complexities of human beings in general, and this woman in particular.

"How much farther to Bay Town?" she asked, finally resettling in her seat.

"We head out of the mountains, and I think the rest of the drive is out along the coast." He slowed the car and then stopped on the shoulder. He popped open the glove box and took out a map and unfolded it. He studied the route while she watched him.

"Yep, along the coast. It looks to be a few hours. If we could rev the Delahaye up we'd be there in no time, but from the looks of the route, we won't be going that fast."

"And it'll be pretty flat?"

"Pretty flat."

She said, "Well, hallelujah for small miracles."

"Are there any other kind?" he said.

17

Coming down the steep Santa Ynez Mountains they entered the vibrant-looking town that was perched like a gargoyle right on the coast.

Welcome to Bay Town, said the sign. Where a good life begins.

"Place seems to think a lot of itself," Callahan remarked.

They reached a wide boulevard named Sawyer Avenue and admired the row of fine homes there.

"Nice places. But they don't look cheap," she said. "Do you have somewhere lined up to stay?"

"Rooming house on Porter Street."

"Think they got 'room' for one more?"

"We can always ask."

"Or do you want to play the husband and wife routine again? You could carry me over the threshold. Of course we'd have to do the kissing thing," she added, giving him a sharp, hopeful glance.

"That might be a little awkward now that I'm making this place my home."

"You take all the fun out of everything," Callahan replied, but she smiled to show she wasn't serious.

Archer stopped and asked a woman walking her dog where Porter Street might be. She told him and then said, "What kinda car is that? Steering wheel's on the wrong side."

"French," said Archer.

The woman looked at him funny. "French? How'd it get to America?"

"We drove it over," said Callahan. "It turns into a boat when you press that button," she added, pointing to a knob on the dash.

"Well, isn't that something," said the woman.

"*You* sure are," said Callahan as Archer pulled off with a grin. He hung a left and headed up a steeply ascending road.

"When do you meet with that private eye who's going to teach you all the dirty tricks you'll need to be a full-fledged shamus?" asked Callahan.

"I was going to call him when I got in and arrange to meet him."

"What was the name again?"

"Willie Dash."

"*That* Willie Dash?"

She was pointing at a large faded sign pasted on the side of a brick building.

On it was the image of a short, broad-shouldered man in his late forties with a pugnacious expression dressed in an old-fashioned pinstripe suit, and sporting a fedora worn at a sharp angle on his wide head. He was pointing a sausage finger apparently at the world in general. The words written below him read:

GOT A PROBLEM NEEDS SOLVING? PRIVATE EYE WILLIE DASH IS YOUR MAN.

After that was a five-digit phone number but no address. It was the same phone number as on Archer's letter from the man.

Archer stopped the car and looked up at the sign, gaping. "Yeah, *that* Willie Dash. I thought he'd be older. But he came highly recommended."

"Yeah? And who recommended the guy who recommended *him*?"

Archer drove on without answering her.

They pulled to a stop in front of the rooming house, a broad building with a narrow front porch, wood siding painted gray, red shutters, and a peaked metal roof the color of olive green. It looked old and seemed to be slightly leaning to one side. A sign out front said there were vacancies.

"My lucky day," remarked Callahan as she noted this. "But we might have to spend half our time holding the sucker up."

They took out their bags and walked up to the front porch. The screen door opened, revealing a woman standing there. She was seventy if she was a day. Her rimless specks made her small eyes enormous. One pupil hugged the inner wall of its socket. She had on a threadbare sweater over a homemade dress that dipped below her knee. She eyed, with a certain disdain, the turbaned Callahan in her tailor-made outfit.

"Can I help you?" she said sharply.

"Name's Archer. I have a room reserved."

"Yes. I already have you on the books." She eyed Callahan. "And who might this be?"

"This might be Liberty Callahan. I need a room, too."

"For how long?"

"I'll have to let you know. My plans are what you call *fluid*."

The woman glanced past them to the Delahaye and her already giant eyes became the size of a full moon.

"Is that your car?"

"Yes ma'am," said Archer.

"It's a Delahaye."

Surprised, Archer said, "Yes it is. How'd you know?"

"I'm French. I came over long before the war. I don't really sound French anymore, do I?"

"No ma'am, you don't."

She looked upset by this. "Well, that's my problem, isn't it? *J'ai perdu la beauté de ma culture. Je suis américaine maintentant.*"

"If you say so," replied Archer.

"And you are?" asked Callahan.

"You may call me Madame Genevieve."

"You're married, then?" said Archer.

"Not anymore," she said.

"I'm sorry."

"I'm not. Come in and sign the register and I'll show you to your rooms. I take a week's rent in advance. No exceptions."

"Seems like a nice town. You like it here?" asked Archer.

"I like it fine. If I didn't, I wouldn't stay."

She turned and walked off down the hall. Archer and Callahan exchanged a glance and then followed.

18

Archer took a moment to look around the small room that he would be calling home at least for a while. Everything in it was old, but the place was spotless and smelled of soap and furniture polish. He pocketed the large metal key, put his suitcase down, dropped his hat on the small bed, and went over to the rear window. His immediate view was the back of another building. But rising behind that and the rest of Bay Town were the Santa Ynez Mountains. The high rock dwarfed the town like Goliath had David.

But then look who won that fight.

He crossed the room and looked out the front window. They weren't on the ocean side of town, but the elevated position of the boardinghouse allowed an unobstructed view of the Pacific. To the right of that was a long wharf where ships were docked, and Archer could see large cranes either taking off or loading on cargo. Men swarmed around this operation like ants on a hunt. Archer knew that directly up the coast was the Army's Camp Cooke. Farther down he saw a couple of oil derricks bowing and straightening like ostriches pecking for food as they lifted black gold from the earth. He knew off the coast and farther to the south were the Channel Islands.

Archer unknotted his tie, pulled his flask, and took a sip of his rye. It quenched his thirst just enough to persuade him to take another belt. From his suitcase he hung up the clothes that needed hanging and put away the others in the chest of drawers stacked against one wall. They held the scent of Murphy's Oil soap, a product he'd often used in prison to clean his own cell. He would have to find a board and an iron to press everything.

He went back downstairs and out to the Delahaye after finding out from Madame Genevieve where he could park the car. He drove it into a two-bay garage behind the boardinghouse. After that he went back up to his room, took off his jacket and shirt and undershirt, but kept his pants and shoes on.

He had just lighted a Lucky when someone rapped on his door.

Callahan had taken off her turban but was otherwise dressed the same. She came in without invitation and looked at his space. "Seems every room is the same."

"Nice views."

She eyed his bare torso. "Yeah, they are nice. Hey, where'd you get all those big muscles, Archer?"

"Sears and Roebuck. They were having a sale. Got 'em cheap."

She slid a hand along his right shoulder and down his arm. Archer breathed in her perfume but remained unbowed by conjuring the image of her shooting a man dead.

She said, "Remind me to place an order with them sometime. The *quality* is really good." She slowly slid her fingers free but scraped his bare skin with her nails as she did so.

"What's up?" he asked.

"I put my things away and now I'm bored."

"We just *got* here, Liberty."

"I've got a low tolerance for having nothing to do. I need to find a place to work."

"I can ask around."

"I already did that."

"When?" he asked in a surprised voice.

"Madame Genevieve. She said there's a place outside of town.

Like a burlesque theater. It's called Midnight Moods. She said it sounded right up my alley."

"How would she know what was up your alley?"

"She's already got her opinion of me, Archer, after one look and two minutes of conversation. Women tend to do that a lot faster than men. She sees me, I'm sure, as what she would call a 'loose' lady. And maybe I am. And I don't really care what she thinks. But I do care about supporting myself. Maybe you can drive me over there at some point and I can see if they need a new girl."

"Sounds like a plan."

"Hey, you want to take me to lunch?"

"No, but I'll take you to dinner."

"Okay. See you around, Archer."

She went back to her room. Archer put on his undershirt and grabbed the letter from Willie Dash. Then he walked down to the main floor and slipped into the phone box in the small foyer just outside the rectangular-shaped dining area. He closed the booth door, dropped in his coin, and dialed the number.

A moment later: "Willie Dash, Very Private Investigations," said a female voice.

"Hello, this is Archer. I'm in town. I'd like to set up a time to meet with Mr. Dash today."

"Yes, Mr. Archer. This is Connie Morrison. I'm Mr. Dash's secretary."

"Nice talking to you, Miss Morrison. So when can I see him?"

He heard paper being shuffled. "He has an opening now if you want to come by."

Archer checked his timepiece. "I'm staying over at a boarding-house on Porter Street, down by the wharf. How long do you reckon it would take me to get there?"

"Depends. Do you have a car?"

"I do."

"Then ten minutes should do it. Do you have our address?"

"Yeah, it's on the letter. 1533 Encino Street."

She gave him directions and added, "It's a four-story brick office building with a green awning out front. We're on the top floor. Suite 401."

"Thanks. Um, I saw one of his billboards in town."

"I'm sure you did. But they're pretty old."

"I'll see you shortly."

He rushed back to his room and put on a fresh shirt, wound a tie around his neck, lined his pocket square just so, and angled his hat the same. He was bouncing down the stairs when she called out.

"Good luck, shamus-to-be."

He looked back up to see Callahan standing at the top of the stairs. She had taken her dress off and was wearing a pale blue robe that hung only to midthigh and was clingy enough to get Archer's undivided attention. In her right hand she held a lit cigarette, its burning muzzle pointed straight down.

He made a show of checking his watch. "You look like you're going to bed," he said.

She played with the belt on the front of the robe. "Then I'd have to take off all my clothes."

"That surely won't take you long."

Her fingers undid the knot on the belt. The panels of the robe parted ever so slightly.

Archer let that sink in and said, "You trying to seduce me?"

"Not *trying*, no."

"You told me good luck. How do you know where I'm going?"

She said, "I don't need to be the world's greatest gumshoe to figure that one out. You have the look of a guy just itching to get going."

"Okay. Maybe *you* should go see Willie Dash about the job instead of me."

"Dressed as I am, you probably think I'm just a floozy with

a bottle of hooch behind my back and pegging you as a sucker I *briefly* need for a good time."

"I don't think you're anything like a floozy unless you're *pretending* to be one, and *I* don't need to be the world's greatest gumshoe to deduce that the only thing behind your back is *you.*"

"Well, aren't you a true gentleman to notice."

"You know, you should charge for all this."

"Oh, I do, handsome. You just haven't gotten the bill yet."

She blew Archer a kiss, turned, and sauntered away.

After her door closed, Archer slapped his face hard to stun himself out of everything he was feeling, and it was a lot. All he wanted to do was run upstairs to her.

But instead he walked off to take care of business.

Maybe you're finally growing up, Archer. It's about time.

19

ARCHER CLIMBED INTO THE DELAHAYE, turned the key, thumbed the starter button, and put the car in gear. Heads turned to stare at the car as he followed the precise directions Morrison had given him, and he made it to Encino Street in short order. The buildings down this way seemed a lot older than others he had passed, and they became dingier still the longer he was on it. The very last building was Dash's, and it was the dingiest of all. It looked like something erected at the end of the last century merely as an afterthought.

Mortar splotches had permanently stained its brick surface. The green awning that covered its entrance was torn, with a sleeve of it flapping in the stiffening ocean breeze. The sidewalk in front was missing a few chunks, like teeth punched out of a mouth.

He parked the car in front of the entrance and opened the single glass door, finding himself in a tiny lobby that smelled of stale tobacco, spilled gin, and a few odd odors that he couldn't readily place but made his nose crinkle in displeasure. The space was badly lighted, and he had to blink a few times to transition his pupils from daylight to enforced dusk.

There was an occupant register on the wall. Though he knew the suite number, Archer wanted to check out who his potential neighbors might be. It didn't take him long. There were only twelve suites in the building, three on each floor, and only four were currently occupied; the other eight had VACANT next to them.

There was a doctor on the first floor by the name of Myron O'Donnell. On the second floor was a chap named Bradley Wannamaker, attorney-at-law. Dash was on the top floor along with a business called Gemology Incorporated. There was no girl at the tiny reception desk in the lobby. A dusty telephone switchboard sat in one corner. There were no cobwebs covering it, but there easily could have been.

Archer saw the sign for the elevator and headed that way. He figured the stairs would be in the same direction. Ever since being in prison he did not like small, enclosed spaces where he could not open the door when he wanted to.

He came to the single elevator, where a black man who looked to be about a hundred, wearing an ill-fitting gray bellhop's uniform with white piping down the legs and arms, sat on a small, ragged, pillow-topped, wooden dropdown seat just inside the car, reading a nickel copy of the *Bay Town Gazette*. He was short and too thin, with hands that bent upward, apparently against their owner's will because he held the paper in an awkward grip. The unlit, short, cheap stogie in his mouth was rolling from one side to the other with delicate flicks of his tongue.

With an effort he put the paper aside, sat on it, and said, "What floor, young man?"

"It's okay, I'll take the stairs."

He scratched his nose and looked interested. "Give me something to do if you let me take you. My first customer all day."

"Aren't Willie Dash and his secretary here?"

The man grinned. "Hell, they don't count. They work here. I need me some fresh, smiling faces like yours. Keeps me going. You going to see Willie?"

Archer nodded.

"Fourth floor. Suite 401. Let's get to it, young man."

Archer hesitated for a moment, glancing at the wooden door with a wired pane of glass leading to the stairs for a few moments until the man said, "Time waits for no man, mister, and don't I know it. I'll be worm food before long."

Archer stepped on.

The man closed the cage door and then hit the button for the fourth floor, which automatically closed the car's outer solid metal door.

Archer sucked in a breath and felt his body stiffen and his pulse race. He shut his eyes and pretended he was outside with all sorts of possibilities for escape.

The man had swiveled around in his seat and stared at him as the car began its glacial ascent of thirty or so feet.

"When'd you get out, friend?" asked the man with a knowing look.

Archer opened his eyes. The old fellow smiled, showing off perfectly white teeth, and all of them real, as far as Archer could tell.

"Get out of where?"

The fellow snorted. "Come on, don't BS me. The *joint*, man."

"How do you figure that?"

"How do I *not* figure it, you mean. Been inside myself, lots of times, all together longer than you been alive. And carried lots of men up to see Willie who got the elevator disease, same as you. Stair doors you can open all by yourself." He tapped the cage. "Not like these. Remind you of bars, don't they?"

"Does it go away?"

"Look at me. I *live* in a goddamn elevator, son."

"How long did it take you?"

"I won't say 'cause I don't want to discourage you."

"I got on, didn't I?" retorted Archer.

"Sure you did. Now stop sweating and looking like you gonna puke and we getting somewhere."

Archer put a hand against the wall. "What can you tell me about Willie Dash?"

The man picked up his paper but his brown eyes stayed on Archer. "What you want to know?"

"What kind of a man is he?"

"You looking to hire him?"

"No, work for him."

This surprised the man. He took a moment to light up his stogie, sticking the burned match in a metal cup that stuck out from the wall of the car. "Work for him? What, you a baby shamus or something?"

"Something like that."

"Well, Willie is getting up there, all right. Can't be doing this forever."

"But he's good at what he does?"

The man puffed on the cigar to get it going as the car slowly moved past the second floor and began its assault on the third. "You know he was a G-man with Hoover's boys before he left to be a copper in Frisco."

"No, I didn't know that."

"He was one of the best. Worked with that there Eliot Ness."

"Why'd he leave?"

The man shrugged. "Who knows? Why'd he leave Frisco to come here and be a private dick?"

"So he's really good, then."

The man smiled slyly. "Hell, he caught me. It was his second day on the job as a detective in Frisco and he nailed my ass."

"For doing what?"

"Held up a liquor store. Done my time at San Quentin. I don't recommend it, son. Death row there. Used to hang 'em. Now they gas 'em."

"Either way you're dead," said Archer.

"Now, Willie put in a real good word for me, so I didn't get nearly as long a sentence as I might have and then I got time off for good behavior, and I was getting up there age-wise and they needed more room for younger bad guys needing prison beds. It was Willie got me a job here after I left prison."

"So he kept in touch after you went into the joint?"

"Visited me at the prison a few times. Said I did what I did because I was down and out and the wrong color; all stuff I knew. Hell, I'm a Mississippi boy. Only thing the police do down south is march in parades on July Fourth and shoot folks look like me. Why I got outta the south. But I ain't find it all that different no matter where I go. Figgered robbing a place might get me three squares and a roof over my head, so I hit that liquor store. But Willie said I could make an honest living, if I wanted to."

"So you came down here and climbed into this car?"

"Naw. Willie got me a job at the docks, loading shit on and taking shit off the boats. Did that for years." He held up his gnarled hands. "Where I got these. Then Willie got me this sitting job when I couldn't lift the shit no more. I can still poke a button and close a gate, see?"

"Did that surprise you? I mean, what he did for you?"

"Nothing surprises me, young man. Not no more. You live to be my age *and* you colored to boot, life ain't got no more surprises, 'cept why no white man ain't shot me dead at some point along the way for no reason 'cept he wanted to, see?"

A minute later the slow-moving car passed the third floor and settled into the home stretch.

"What about his gal, Connie Morrison?"

The old man cackled. "Connie? They used to be hitched."

Archer shook out a Lucky. The old man struck a match and lit it for him before depositing the spent match in the chromium cup.

"So, they *were* married? But not anymore?"

"That's right. Think Willie was married way back to some gal when he was a G-man, but guess that didn't work out. Pretty sure he's done walking down the aisle now. Not sure 'bout Connie. She's forty-two, which is long in the tooth for getting hitched. But maybe some man'll snatch her up."

"What's your name, by the way?"

"Earl. You?"

"Archer. So if I go to work for him, what's your advice?"

"Go in with both eyes and ears open and pray that's enough."

"Think he can teach me stuff?"

"He's forgot more about gumshoeing than you'll ever know, young man, no offense."

With a jolt and a hiss, they reached the fourth floor, and Earl slid open the cage door. When the outer door disappeared into the wall, Archer quickly stepped through and gratefully sucked in even the stale air at his sudden freedom.

Earl poked his head out. "Down the hall and to the left, Archer. Good luck to you."

"At this point in my life you'd think I wouldn't need so much damn luck," muttered Archer as he headed on to meet ex–G-man and former copper Willie Dash.

20

THE DOOR WAS PEBBLED GLASS with painted letters on its surface that spelled out: WILLIE DASH: VERY PRIVATE INVESTIGATIONS.

The image of a lawman's five-point star was etched below this as though to lend gravitas to the entry point, a certain officialness. Or maybe it had been thrown in for the price of the name above, mused Archer.

The doorknob was brass and looked worn down, probably by the thousands of nervous, sweaty hands that had touched it looking for some help of a "very private" nature.

The door was locked. He noted the buzzer next to the door and pressed it.

"Yes," said the voice, from the little intercom screen.

"It's Archer."

Archer heard a lock click free. He turned the knob and swung the door open.

Six feet directly across from him was, presumably, Connie Morrison. He could have laid flat on the floor, his hat against one wall, and the bottom of his shoes would have touched her desk. Morrison was a honey blonde with shoulder-length hair parted in the middle with the sides winging their way down. The lady was sitting behind a carved oak desk that looked like it had come over on the *Mayflower* and gotten wet along the way.

Archer took in the small reception area. Four walls, one window, five dented metal file cabinets with alphabet letters on their fronts, and a square of faded carpet that was so worn it looked like the plank floor had reclaimed it. There was a fuzzy light overhead, and a table lamp with a patterned shade on the desk.

A Royal typewriter about the size of a Sherman tank sat on the desk in front of her with a black blotter underneath that. A jar of finely sharpened pencils was near her elbow, along with a stapler and a roll of tape in its holder. A Boston sharpener bolted to the wall just behind her, and standing ready to take care of all those yellow number twos, completed this dream of an office setup.

On the walls were diplomas and certificates from places Archer had never heard of, and framed photos of people he didn't know, except for President Harry S. "The buck stops here" Truman dressed in a cream suit and a dotted bow tie, who smiled all alone from one wall.

A rubber tree that looked fake and still somehow dead leaned out of a blue-and-white ceramic planter with an elephant on it that sat next to the desk.

When Morrison rose and came around to the front of the desk, Archer could see that she wore a blue tailor-made suit dress and that she was medium height, and thin. She had fine lines all over her chiseled face, like the depth markings on a shipping channel map.

Morrison slipped on a pair of rimless cheaters that she was holding in her hand. They accentuated the woman's eyes, which Archer decided were closer to periwinkle blue than any other blue he knew of. They were slightly washed out, as were the woman's features. Her heels were black and matched the color of her hosiery and added about two inches of height to her frame. A slender platinum watch graced her left wrist.

A dark hat with a blue ribbon was on a wall hook. A tan raincoat hung next to it, though there wasn't a cloud in the sky. Next to that hung a dented crown fedora with a bloodred ribbon. He assumed that belonged to Willie Dash.

He tipped his hat in greeting as she reached him.

"Mr. Archer, nice to meet you."

Her long fingers managed a grip that was firm and reassuring, her expression less so. The periwinkles took him in as thoroughly as his gaze had done her. She seemed to come away impressed, although that could have simply been Archer's wishful thinking.

"Nice to meet you, Miss Morrison. I'm really hoping I can go to work for Mr. Dash."

The periwinkles dulled a bit, and the firm jaw clenched even tighter, and the lines around her eyes and mouth deepened into ditches. "Um, yes. Give me a minute. We've had a, uh, *development* since you called."

She turned and left him there, opening and then quickly closing the door to the interior office, where, Archer was certain, Willie Dash bided his professional time.

A development since I called ten minutes ago?

He took off his hat, twirled it between his fingers, and took a long, slow loop around the room, arriving at the Royal typewriter and the paper wound into its maw that had clickety-clack marks all over it. He bent over to read the typing better.

It was addressed to the First National Bank of Bay Town.

Dear Mr. Weaver, Due to my recent illness coupled with a sudden downturn in business, I will be unable to meet my payment obligations on the loan to your institution in the near term. I would like to discuss a different payment plan that might

The words ended here. Archer slid back around the desk as the inner office door opened, and Morrison appeared once more. She wouldn't meet his eye but said, "Mr. Dash will see you now, Mr. Archer."

"Great. Everything okay?"

She lifted her elegant chin and dead-eyed him with the periwinkles that had instantly hardened to glowing bits of molten iron. "Why shouldn't it be okay?" She glanced sharply at her typewriter.

Archer said, "You mentioned developments. I took that as maybe there was a problem. My mistake, sorry."

The fire in the eyes dimmed and the periwinkles sparkled back at him. "No apology necessary." She held the door open for him.

He passed by her and went in. He heard the door close firmly behind him and listened to the efficient heels of Connie Morrison marching the short distance back to her desk to finish her boss's letter of developments.

Next, Archer heard a belch and swiveled his attention to a battleship-sized dark walnut desk that turned out to not have a single sailor on board. This office was three times the size of the outer room but seemed far smaller because it was crammed with so much stuff Archer wasn't sure whether he was in a private eye's office or a fence's warehouse.

Against one wall was a Murphy bed that was in the down position. It was neatly made up with two pillows plumped on its surface like white geese on a rectangular pond.

"Keep your eyes looking, Archer, you'll get there, son."

Archer did as the voice suggested and came to rest on the man lying shoeless on a pale blue davenport. His cuffed pants were held up by white plastic suspenders rather than a belt or leather braces. His collar was undone, and his blue dotted bow tie hung off limply to one side of his neck like a broken arm dangling.

His broad face was flushed, and his scalp was as bald as a cue ball and close to the same color, which provided an odd and unsettling juxtaposition. His white shirt was wrinkled beyond perhaps the remediation of an iron, and one of his dark socks needed darning where his little toe poked out like a hatching chick.

His eyes were cloudy gray, like the color of a naval ship. They seemed to peer right through Archer.

On the coffee table in front of the davenport was a bottle of Jim

Beam Kentucky Bourbon and two glasses, one of which had been used. A newspaper lay next to them.

"Willie Dash, sir. Come on and take a seat and let me have a closer look at you."

Archer crossed the room and noted the plank floor was worn smooth, perhaps from a man pacing in his socks for a number of years.

He sat down, placed his hat next to the Beam, and leaned forward, his elbows resting on his knees, waiting.

Dash had a line of sweat on his broad forehead, each drop perfectly lined up with its neighbor—blackbirds on a phone line. When he opened his mouth wide, Archer saw twin porcelain crowns, one on either side and occupying the lower back forty.

A grinder who has worn down his grinders.

"You live here?" said Archer, eyeing the bed.

"I *sleep* here sometimes. Depends on the job. This ain't no nine-to-fiver, son. You want that life, go apply at the bank to count other people's money and be bored to death for the next forty years."

"So how are *developments*?" asked Archer. "Things looking up or still down? To put it as squarely as I can, will you be able to hire me if I pass muster?"

With an effort Dash sat up and swung his short, thick legs down to the floor. The toes touched, but not the heels. He was no more than five-seven, but his burly build looked strong. He wasn't much under two hundred pounds. His age was difficult to say. Archer thought over sixty rather than under.

"I like your directness, Archer. It's good, up until it's not so good. And you eyeballed the letter in Connie's typewriter because she sure wouldn't have told you. That shows initiative and a certain disregard for the rules. Both okay in my book and maybe essential to the task."

He pulled a handkerchief from his pants pocket, hocked into it, and set it down next to him.

"The developments can come later, and maybe not the ones you're thinking of. Now, Irving Shaw wrote very highly of you."

"He's a good man. Learned a lot from him."

"And you no doubt want to continue your education under me."

"I hoped my letter to you made that clear."

"You're coming in from this Poca City place? Irv told me that in his letter."

"Yes. I stopped over in Reno for a little bit and then headed west."

Dash hocked once more into the cloth and sat back, lifting his feet fully off the floor. "You got a ticket?"

"Come again?"

"A PI's license."

"Nope. Do I need one?"

"State of California says you do. Law enacted back in 1915."

"What do I have to do to get it?"

"You have to apply to the State Board of Prison Directors."

Archer felt like someone had just shivved him in the carotid. "Prison Directors!"

"Yes. You have to provide background on yourself, where you were last employed, and where in the state you intend to work as a PI. And you have to provide facts that you're of good moral character. You have to sign that application, and then you have to find five reputable people in Bay Town who will approve of the application and also sign it before an officer duly authorized to take acknowledgment of deeds."

"I don't even know five people in town."

"And the State Board will review the application and may do its own investigation to confirm that you are indeed a person of good moral character and integrity. If they do, they will issue a license good for five years, and the fee is ten dollars a year."

Archer stared at him. "And if they find out I've been in prison, will that knock out any chance of me getting my license?"

"It might. But there's another way."

"What's that?"

"There's a provision in the law that allows you to act under the auspices of the license I have for this firm."

"So I don't even have to apply?"

"But you might want to anyway, sometime down the road, Archer. I won't be around forever, and the license I have is not transferable to you. And I have to tell you that there's talk of changing the law, making it even more restrictive next year. It might well require several years of apprenticing as a PI, and also require that the applicant not have been convicted of any serious crime."

Archer nodded. "Okay."

"So you might want to find five people and get yourself grandfathered in, if you can. Me and Connie can be two of them, so you're nearly halfway home on that score. In the meantime, I can provide a ticket for you that allows you to operate under the license of this firm. I'll have Connie get going on that."

"Didn't know it was so involved."

"It's a profession, Archer. And it's getting all the riffraff out and making way for us professionals. I went to the CAPI conference last year and it was quite informative."

"The what?"

"California Association of Private Investigators. Had a woman named Mildred Gilmore speak. She's a licensed PI *and* an attorney, and good at both jobs. She argued for adopting a code of ethics for PIs. She also said that women make better operators because they're more ethical and no one would suspect them of being PIs."

"What do you think?"

"I've got my own ethics, and I don't want other folks telling me what they should be."

"Yeah, okay."

"What's your first name again?"

"Aloysius."

"Then I'll just call you Archer."

"I, uh, I saw the billboards around town. Miss Morrison told me they were from a while ago."

Dash cocked his head and the mouth flatlined. "Don't play me for a fool, son. You put up billboards to get business, least I did when I first got here. The fact is I soon had more than enough business, so no need for more billboards. Plus, I sort of like driving around and seeing what I used to look like."

"But you need business now, sounds like."

"Things have slowed, I won't debate that point with you."

"So you were with the FBI?"

Dash poured out small measures of Beam in both glasses and nudged one toward Archer.

"How is Earl? In fine form? Man loves to talk."

"He thinks the world of you."

"I did him one act of kindness and he did the rest."

"Nice of you after sending him to San Quentin."

Dash said sharply, "He sent himself to San Quentin. That liquor store didn't rob itself."

"Right. I guess not."

"And it was the Bureau of Investigation when I was there. Didn't become the FBI until 1935."

"He said you worked with Eliot Ness. Is that true?"

"It is. But Ness worked with a lot of guys. I was just one of them."

"Didn't he take down Ma Barker, Dillinger and Machine Gun Kelly, and folks like that? Were you in on that, too?"

"Ancient history, Archer."

"Why'd you leave?"

"I had my reasons."

"So then you went to Frisco to be a cop?"

"A detective," corrected Dash. "I grew up on the West Coast and wanted to get back here."

"So why the shamus route?"

"I don't like following orders, particularly if they're lousy ones. And I like being my own boss. But enough about me, Archer, how'd you find the joint?"

"It wasn't so different from being in the Army, actually. And I was innocent, if that makes a difference to you."

Dash sipped his Beam, and slowly shook his head. "Were you tried and convicted?"

"No, I did a deal. Otherwise, they were going to throw the book at me."

"Then you were guilty?"

"You think all men who do a deal are guilty?"

"Of course I don't. Just as I know that all men who are tried and convicted aren't guilty. But it's the only system we have. Fact is, I'm not concerned with the past, Archer, yours or mine. I look toward the future."

"So where does that leave us?"

"With a possibility, nothing more and nothing less." He bent over and worried at the hole in his sock, tucking the little toe out of sight before straightening. "What do you know about the detective business?"

"What Lieutenant Shaw taught me."

"Which was?"

"Listen, ask questions, don't believe anything is true unless you can corroborate it, and don't trust anyone."

He nodded approvingly. "That's a good start. Irv knows his way around an investigation, that's for sure. He said in his letter that you saved his life."

"He did the same for me."

"And you have a good war record."

"I did my bit."

"Care to talk about it?"

"No."

He nodded approvingly again. "I fought in the First World War, the one that was supposed to end any future ones, right? Basically living in holes and only climbing out of them when the Army felt it had to show it was doing something, giving folks their money's worth, so to speak." He slapped his right leg. "Got some metal here they never took out. But I was one of the lucky ones. Left a lot of good buddies back there."

"I can understand that," said Archer, sipping his drink and letting it go down as slow as possible.

"What else?" asked Dash.

"That fingerprints can do a man in and the police check for that. That honest people lie all the time when they're in a jam. And that sometimes it's the last person you suspect who did the deed."

Dash put his glass down, sat forward so his toes were touching the planks once more, and said, "Now, this possibility I'm talking about."

Archer hunched forward and settled in to listen.

The buzzer on the desk phone sounded off like a warning shot across the bow.

Dash moved across the space with surprising speed and snatched up the phone. He listened for a moment and said, "Give me one minute, hon."

He put the phone down, stepped into his brown wingtips, which were set next to his desk, and rapidly put his collar and bow tie in place before slipping on his jacket and pinching his cheeks. Next he opened a desk drawer, slipped out something hairy, squirted on its underside something wet from a bottle on his desk, and then plopped a black toupee on the top of his bald head. He fussed over it in the slanted shaving mirror on his desk until he came away satisfied with the look. To Archer the thing looked like a baby skunk without a stripe.

"Put the Beam away in that cabinet over there, Archer, and hoist up the bed."

Archer quickly did so and said, "What's up, Mr. Dash?"

"The possibility, Archer, the possibility has just walked in the door."

CHAPTER

21

THE DOOR OPENED AND THERE appeared Morrison looking breathless from her three-foot walk from desk to door. She stepped to the side and said, "Mr. Douglas Kemper and Mr. Wilson Sheen."

Two men walked past her and into the room. She hastily closed the door, but Archer did not hear her trademark heel clatter going away. He glanced at Dash, who was staring at the door and apparently thinking the very same thing.

Dash moved slowly across the room to greet the men. Where he had been frenetic seconds before, Archer could see the man was now all cool, calm, and as collected as a preacher about to dispense an easy dose of religion and then follow that up with an ask for money.

"Gentlemen," he said, shaking their hands. He motioned to the sitting area across from his desk. "Please, sit. Would you like something to drink? Coffee, tea?"

Both men shook their heads, dutifully marched across the room, reached Archer, and stood there, each sizing him up.

Dash said, "This is my associate, Mr. Archer. Just in town from working with the police in another state on a very important investigation. His former boss there is a good friend of mine and a fine police investigator. Archer will be truly helpful to me in this matter. And his discretion is legendary."

Archer returned his attention to Kemper and Sheen, looking

them over as he shook their hands. Kemper was in his late thirties, an inch shorter than Archer, trim, good-looking, and well groomed. *Elegant* was the descriptive term that came to Archer. His shoulders were narrow and his hips narrower still. His grip was a dishrag clench—whether that was for Archer's benefit or the man did that with everyone, Archer didn't know. He had a dark pencil mustache that matched his hair, which was slicked and parted and rode on his head like a flat crown. His eyes were green and his manner seemed bored, as though what he was here for held no particular interest.

He was dressed immaculately in a dark blue double-breasted worsted wool suit framing a starched gray shirt so sparkling it looked like liquid chrome. His muted red-and-blue-striped tie was double knotted and held against his throat by a gold collar pin. He looked soft but maybe wasn't, was Archer's conclusion.

Wilson Sheen was a different sort altogether. He was around five-eight and overweight with a bulging gut that preceded him everywhere. He had broad shoulders and hips to match. His suit was light brown, single-breasted, with a dim blue shirt and a dark brown tie that rode uncomfortably against his meaty neck like a tree leaning into a hurricane. His pants were cuffed and pleated, and his shoes were scuffed fore and aft. His manner was as intense as Kemper's was indifferent. His ice-blue eyes raked across Archer. He drew in his nostrils like a scent dog. Archer took an instant dislike to the man and then reprimanded himself. What would Irving Shaw say? Let it play out. Don't judge on emotion. Let the facts rule.

Both men dropped their fedoras on the table and sat down.

Dash and Archer joined them.

Dash said, "Everyone in Bay Town knows who you are, Mr. Kemper. But for the sake of my new associate understanding things, perhaps you could start from the very beginning."

Kemper did not appear to like this suggestion, but he glanced at Sheen, who nodded in agreement. Kemper took out a gold cigarette case and pulled a gold-tipped cigarette from it. Sheen instantly lighted it with a gold-plated beauty of an ignitor that was stamped with a name that to Archer looked French.

Golden boy all around, maybe.

Kemper primed his smoke, sucked in a long one, and let it gush out both nostrils like steam from a train coming right at Archer. In a smooth, bored voice he said, "It's like this, Archer. I'm running for mayor of Bay Town. Wilson is my right-hand man in my business and is also my campaign manager. I was chairman of the town council for two years and was content with that, but a number of very smart, important people asked me to consider running for mayor, and I decided to do just that. We're growing fast, and a steady hand is needed to manage that growth. Otherwise it can get out of whack."

"And we don't need a dentist in charge," chimed in Sheen.

While Kemper's voice was silk, Sheen's was like a bulldozer. It banged off all four walls of the office and fell on them like mustard gas.

"Yes, well," said Kemper, tapping ash into a blue ashtray set on the table. "As far as personal history, I married into a very prominent family, the Armstrongs. My wife is Beth Armstrong Kemper."

When Archer made no reply to this, Dash said, "For generations the Armstrong family dominated the cattle business around here, which made money hand over fist. They were astute enough to get out of it before the whole industry went down to nothing, and they used those funds to basically invest in and expand Bay Town, a large part of which they still own. Sawyer Armstrong is Beth's father and the richest man in town."

"I drove down Sawyer Avenue coming into town," noted Archer.

Kemper blew smoke to the ceiling as he crossed his legs, showing off canary yellow socks, and swished his tasseled loafer like a leather metronome. "Sawyer loves to make his presence felt wherever he can. Naming the best and most beautiful boulevard in the town after himself was one way to do that. Hell, I'm surprised we're not called Sawyerville or Armstrongburg. If I win the election he might just insist I do it."

Archer continued to watch as Sheen touched Kemper's sleeve and shot his boss a look of caution.

Kemper said, in a more controlled tone that would work well on the political stump, "He's really made this place what it is, I have to give him that. We're not always on the same page about what direction the town should go in now, but that's to be expected. But I value his opinion."

"And the matter that has brought you here?" said Dash.

Kemper glanced at Sheen before lighting another cigarette, this time with his own lighter. He took so long doing it that Archer could have rolled two of his own and smoked them both down. Kemper was apparently a man used to taking his time and used to people allowing him to do it, thought Archer.

"Yes, well, this must remain confidential, of course."

"Once the retainer is signed and money exchanged, privilege attaches," said Dash. "I've already communicated my rates to you."

Kemper gave him a once-over sneer. "Look, Willie, you'll get your damn money, all right? Don't put the squeeze on me from the get-go. It affronts my sensibilities, to the extent that I have any left. It's a damn nuisance that I have to do this at all. It's ridiculous, in fact, but I have been persuaded that it's in my interests to do so."

"By the very important, smart people," noted Archer.

Kemper turned his gaze to him and smiled. "It's difficult to say no to such influence."

Dash said, "I'm sure I'll get the money, Mr. Kemper. As privilege attaches *at that time*. But that doesn't get us to the heart of the problem. You came here to ask us to help you get answers, solve your dilemma. The money obviously is secondary to that. Or am I being off base?"

Archer eyed Kemper and saw the hostility fade in the latter's eyes.

Kemper said, "No, you're doing okay." He impatiently stubbed out his newly lit smoke. "Well, let me get to the point then, gentlemen. I received this in the mail." He took an envelope from his jacket pocket and handed it to Dash. Archer slid closer so he could read it as well.

"There was no return address and no signature, of course," added Kemper.

It wasn't a long letter, and after both men read it, Dash looked up and said, "Okay, we're talking blackmail. If you don't drop out of the race for mayor, details of an affair between you and a Miss Ruby Fraser who works at Midnight Moods will be made public." He glanced at Archer. "That's the burlesque place on the edge of town."

"Yeah, I heard of it. I have a friend who might try to get a job there."

Dash gave him a puzzled look. "You make friends fast, Archer."

"She actually drove out here with me."

"Right," said Dash before turning to Kemper. "Do you know this Miss Fraser?"

"I know her."

"How well?"

"Not nearly as well as they claim in the letter."

"So no affair?" said Dash.

"No."

"If there's no truth to it, why worry?" said Archer.

Kemper snapped, "Because the damage will be done. I'll get creamed in the election. Women *can* vote, Archer. And they won't vote for an alleged philanderer."

Dash interjected, "So our means of attacking this sucker are limited but they're still there."

Kemper sat back. "And pray tell, what might those be?"

Sheen interjected, "You're not going to suggest paying off the blackmailer?"

"There's no such thing as paying *off* a blackmailer," replied Dash. "They just keep coming back. You might as well open a bank account for them to access."

"So, what then?" asked Kemper.

"Any idea who's behind this?" asked Dash.

"I might have some ideas."

"Then let us have them."

"What would you do with that information?" asked Sheen quickly.

"Both sides can play the game," said Dash.

"Meaning?" said Kemper sharply, his indifferent manner vanishing.

Archer piped in, "Meaning you fight fire with fire. If what they say about you isn't true but is still potentially damaging, then the same holds for them."

"And if their reputation means nothing to them?" inquired Kemper.

"Easy to say, another to endure," replied Dash.

Kemper tap-tapped his ash. "Okay. We can provide you with a list later this afternoon. Once we put it together I'll have Wilson send it over. It will be a short one probably, and there's no guarantee that the real culprit is on there."

"It's still a good place to start," said Dash. "But you have to be prepared for them making this public if you don't pay, or if blackmail is not their intent."

"You mean, they might just want to smear Douglas and make him lose the election?" suggested Sheen.

"Maybe," said Dash, keeping his gaze on Kemper.

The man sat forward, his brow furrowed. "Look, Willie, the last thing I want is for my wife to find out about this garbage in some cheap paper. She's just recovering from an illness. She doesn't need this on top of it."

"What illness? I hadn't heard."

"Appendicitis. She had an operation. In fact, the doc in this building performed it. He handles the whole family."

"Right. O'Donnell. He's very good. It's always surprised me he's stayed here. He makes enough money to rent on the other side of Sawyer Ave. I hope she's going to be okay."

"She will. Beth's strong. But this won't help."

"We'll do all we can to keep it under wraps."

A moment later there was a knock at the door, and Morrison entered with a sheaf of pages.

"Mr. Kemper," said Dash, eyeing Morrison. "You can sign off on the retainer, get your duplicate copy, and then leave the check with Miss Morrison. And we can get to work."

"The election is in four weeks," Sheen told him.

Dash offered up a smile. "Then, by God, we haven't a moment to waste."

Kemper rose and joined Morrison over at the desk where he signed the papers, as did Dash. Archer came over to stand next to the desk. Kemper took his duplicate copy and passed it over to Sheen, who had risen and joined him. It was Sheen who took out a checkbook and made out the retainer check in the amount of one thousand dollars, signing it with a flourish. He handed it to Dash.

Archer saw that it was drawn on an account in the name of "Kemper for Mayor."

Dash said, "Expenses are of course separate, and will be itemized and sent to you regularly."

Kemper glanced at Dash and then at Archer. "Oh, joy. I wish you both luck in this endeavor."

He and Sheen picked up their hats and left.

Dash turned to Morrison, passed her the check, and said

urgently, "Okay, hon, carry that down to the bank and get it deposited ASAP. Then go over the list of outstanding bills, prioritize and whittle, stiff who you can, and negotiate the must-pays down as best you can. In the future I'll need credit, and this is where I build it back up."

Morrison nodded, glanced anxiously at Archer, and hurriedly left. A few moments later Archer heard the office door open and close.

Dash plucked a briarwood pipe from a stand on his desk, stuffed it with tobacco pulled from a pouch in his desk drawer, and took a moment to light it, puffing thoughtfully. He settled back on the davenport and glanced at Archer.

"Well?" asked Dash.

Archer said, "A dentist in charge? What did Sheen mean by that?"

"Kemper's running against a fellow named Alfred Drake, who's a dentist. But he's no dummy. And Drake's been on the town council for years. He knows the difference between floating a water bond and filling up a pool with water."

"Nice of Kemper to provide a list of possible suspects."

Dash lit his pipe again and sucked on the end to prime it. "The list, *if* we get it, will be worthless. He'll put on there anyone he has a grudge against, hoping we can find dirt on *them*, whether it has anything to do with the election or not."

"But if the truth won't set Kemper free, what will?"

"I'll tell you what, Archer, for a thousand bucks plus expenses, *we* will." Dash stood and said, "Now, follow me."

22

Dash led Archer out the door, past Morrison's empty desk, and over to another door on the other side of the reception area that Archer had missed seeing before.

Dash opened the door and turned on the light. A long naked tube hissed and popped overhead before gaining purchase and staying on, feebly illuminating the small space so it looked like a partially exposed photograph. Archer looked around and took in the room that held a desk, a chair, another chair, a three-drawer metal file cabinet, and one window about as wide as his head.

Dash swept a hand across the space. "Your new office, Archer."

"So I have the job then?"

"Not if you continue to be that slow on the uptake. Now, it's a little dusty, but I can get Connie to spruce it up a bit. Maybe get a fresh flower for that vase over there."

"No, that's okay. I can clean it up."

"You sure?"

Archer surveyed his office. "Pretty sure, yeah."

"PIs don't spend a lot of time on their duff in their office, Archer," Dash said warningly.

"Give me a sec to breathe it all in, Mr. Dash. Then I'll be raring to go."

Dash smiled. "Well, first thing, not even my old man was Mr. Dash. I'm Willie, capiche?"

"Got it, Willie. So, do we wait on the list from Kemper?"

"I don't like depending on clients for answers. If they can do it themselves, I might as well put myself in a coffin and pay the digging fee up front."

"But if we find the blackmailer, what can we really do?"

"Dirt, Archer. It sticks both ways, like you said. And I've never met anyone who didn't have something they'd prefer other people didn't know."

"So is Kemper the favorite in the race?"

"By a wide margin yes. He's young, handsome, wealthy, smart, smooth as silk. Pure class, as I'm sure you saw for yourself. For a minute there I thought I was talking to Errol Flynn. Alfred Drake looks like a day-old cadaver by comparison."

"And so Kemper married into a wealthy family. Talk about good fortune raining down."

"Well, Kemper looks like he was always rich. In fact, his father came from money. Then he blew it all and Kemper went from being a rich kid to a poor adult. But he worked hard. Yeah, he married well, but the guy isn't afraid of work, I'll give him that."

"And Sawyer Armstrong?"

"Armstrong is a son of a bitch. But he's a cunning son of a bitch."

"And his daughter?"

"She's cut from the same wood. But she's more nuanced than her old man, and Armstrong can be subtle when the need arises."

"Do you believe Kemper about there being nothing between him and Fraser?"

"Yeah, and I believe that Dewey beat Truman. Assume the worst of your clients, Archer, and you'll never be disappointed. They don't come to us because they're good little boys. They come because they screwed up and they want us to clean the mess." He pointed to the desk. "In one of them drawers is a little notepad and a pen. Take 'em with you and write stuff down. Memory makes mistakes; what you write down is a lot better."

Archer got the pad and pen, and he and Dash went back to the reception area. Dash plucked his fedora off the hook and said, "Hey, you got a car?"

"It's outside."

"Good, mine's in the shop."

"What's wrong with it?"

"Nothing that paying the money owed won't fix."

"What model is it?"

"A 1942 Lincoln Continental Cabriolet, the prettiest blue with a canvas top and fat whitewalls. Did you know 1942 was the last year Detroit made cars before the war intervened?"

"Nope."

"After that the big boys turned to the war effort, building trucks, tanks, planes. My ride was one of the last off the assembly line before Detroit turned to being the engine of the 'arsenal of democracy,' as Roosevelt termed it."

"Car's nearly eight years old then. You looking for a new ride?"

Dash frowned. "You don't let a filly go when she's just starting to hit her stride."

"Miss Morrison seems efficient."

Dash gave him a nuanced look. "And I'm sure Earl told you we were married and are now divorced."

"He did mention that. Surprised you two can still work together."

"We always worked together just fine. It was *marriage* together that didn't work."

"Okay."

"You got a heater?" Dash said abruptly.

"Not on me, no."

Archer followed Dash back to his office. Out of a desk drawer Dash drew a Colt .38 in a leather belt holster. "Irv said you were in the Army and know your way around a piece."

"I'm sure you do, too."

"I do. But at this point in my life, I'd rather think than shoot. So clip it on and don't pull it unless you're going to use it."

"By the way, what's my salary and how often do I get paid?"

"Don't go too fast, Archer. Let's take it nice and slow. I need to see you in action first."

They rode the elevator down. Earl gazed up at Dash, the grin stretching to both cheeks and maybe beyond.

"You going to work, Mr. Dash? Going to get yourself some cri-mi-nal?"

"That's the plan, Earl."

"Saw Miss Morrison run outta here with a check in hand. She going to the bank, I 'spect?"

"You'd make a good shamus."

"Can't lose you, Mr. Dash. You the only one takes the elevator, 'cept this young man here. I be out of a job."

"Uh-huh. Well, we don't want that to happen."

Outside, Archer said, "Is he always like that with you?"

"Like what?"

"I don't know, gushing."

"Hell, Archer, the man hates my guts."

"How do you know that?"

"No man ever went to prison who comes out liking the man who put him behind bars."

"So did you get him the job here because you keep your enemies close?"

"I felt for the guy. But he'd stick a knife in my back in a New York minute."

When Dash saw the Delahaye he stopped and stared suspiciously at Archer. "This your car?"

"Yep."

He read off the name. "Delahaye?"

"It's French."

"The hell you say." As he started to get in, he stopped. "Steering wheel's on the wrong side."

"Don't worry, I'm getting the hang of it. By the way, where are we going, Willie?"

"Straight to the source, Archer. To talk to Ruby Fraser."

"You think she'll cop to blackmailing Kemper?"

"She's not blackmailing anybody. She's what you call a pawn. I don't expect her to be honest, don't get me wrong. Midnight Moods doesn't care about honest people. They just want gals with long legs and big tits. Miss Ruby isn't quarterbacking this one."

"So, Kemper's enemies?"

"Or his friends."

"Friends who are enemies, then?"

"Do you know of any other kind, son? Because I sure as hell don't."

23

As THEY WERE HEADING OUT OF TOWN, Dash pointed to a large billboard. "There's our man."

Douglas Kemper's face was about ten feet tall. He was looking off into the distance, his expression intelligent, visionary even. Next to this profile was the slogan: KEMPER FOR MAYOR. A MAN FOR OUR TIMES.

"Catchy," said Archer drily as they passed by and drove north.

A half hour later they arrived at their destination. Midnight Moods looked to Archer like every shallow fantasy a man could reasonably expect to have in his life. Constructed like a faux castle, complete with turrets and towers, bastions and battlements, the high walls covered with enormous posters of the most beautiful women wearing the most alluring outfits that Archer had ever seen.

The place had a vibrant view of the nearby salty ocean. Its large asphalt parking lot held about thirty cars, from junkers to lean rides, to police prowlers, to a couple of Bentleys, though it was still the afternoon.

As they pulled to a stop Archer ran his gaze over the front of the place once more and said, "Who the hell built this thing?"

"Who do you think? Sawyer Armstrong. He's the only man around with the sawbucks to put up a joint like this."

"When *did* he do it?"

"During the war. Sawyer has X-ray vision when it comes to seeing opportunities and making money off poor saps who don't have a lot of it but don't mind spending what they do have. It's *volume* that matters."

"And where did that volume come from? This isn't exactly New York City."

"Trains full of soldiers came through here, Archer. Sawyer put this place up in six months and made a fortune and then some for about three years just off the GIs."

"And now? How's business?"

"Popular as all get out. Lots of young guys, and older gents, coming through looking for something new." He paused. "But in the long run, who knows."

"Meaning?"

"Bay Town is turning into something that tends to shun places like this."

"What's that?"

"Bay Town is doing its best to turn *respectable*. But there will always be an audience for this sort of thing. Even if wives and girlfriends show up here from time to time to make their feelings known. Sometimes with an iron skillet in hand and not caring who they hit with it."

"You ever been here?" asked Archer.

"A few times. Some laughs, some drinks, nothing more."

"How many times did Connie Morrison crack you in the head with her skillet?"

"I'm starting to like you, Archer. But don't make it personal."

They climbed out and crossed over a short wooden bridge that spanned a fake moat that was filled with not water but gravel. There were chains on either side of the bridge that ran to some wheels affixed to the outside wall of the place.

"They ever raise the drawbridge?" asked Archer.

"Yeah, every night after the last penniless drunk falls out the door."

Inside it was dark, quiet, and, at least to Archer, palpably ominous. Until a woman in her late forties came to greet them. She was dressed in a long, dark gown and wearing red high heels that drove her height to a head above Dash's. Her hair was platinum with darker roots, her skin white as cream. Her lipsticked mouth housed a smile as wide as her face, but it never once reached her baby blues. She smelled of talcum powder and ginger.

"Can I help you, gentlemen? We're not open quite yet. The sun's still up."

"The front door was wide open," pointed out Dash.

"They lowered the bridge to let the beer, wine, and liquor deliveries through."

"And all those cars in the parking lot are…?"

"Just visitors," she replied, keeping her tone and expression professional. "The performers live here."

"You mean, the *female* performers?"

"Do I? And what business is that of yours, Mister…?"

Dash pulled out his ID card and flashed it for her. "Willie Dash, PI. My associate Archer here. We'd like to talk to Ruby Fraser."

The woman eyed the card. "Gumshoes at Midnight Moods. My my."

"And you are…?" asked Archer.

"*I* would be Mabel Dawson, sonny boy. I manage this place. At least the girl part of it."

Dash said, "Speaking of girls, is Ruby here?"

"Why do you want to see Ruby?"

"It's confidential. She should be expecting us," Dash lied.

"Is that a fact? She never mentioned it to me."

"That's because it's confidential," said Archer. "While you're getting her, mind if we look around?"

"Yes, I would mind. And who said I was getting Ruby, handsome?"

"Any reason why you won't?" asked Dash.

"I can think of about ten. And I can call the cops if this turns into harassment."

"Why bother the cops with something so trivial? We'll talk to Ruby and then we'll leave, nice and simple, no trouble to anyone," said Dash.

"I don't have to do nothing except ask you to leave." She tacked on a smile as though she were enjoying all this. "So scram."

"But I *do* know things about this place," added Dash, looking around. "Like why have the bridge down at this hour?"

"I told you, buster, for deliveries. You want to see the booze for yourself?"

"I happen to know that your deliveries come in the morning. And through the tradesman entrance on the side."

"Like I said, we have the bridge down for the visitors to our performers. They're entitled to have visitors, aren't they?"

"Sure. But they're not entitled to get paid for it, if you know what I mean?"

"I really have no idea what you're getting at."

"Would Ruby be engaged in the thing you have no idea what I'm getting at?"

She pursed her lips and said indignantly, "Prostitution is illegal, Mr. Dash!"

"Lots of things are illegal, and that just makes some people want to do them even more. And there are prowlers out there, so I guess I'll include the cops in that."

Dawson bristled slightly. "Ruby's a good girl." A chrome cigarette case appeared from down her bosom and Archer lit up her smoke when she beckoned him with a generous glance to do so. She drew in the smoke deeply. "You really just want to talk to her?"

"We do."

She slid a hand along Dash's face. "You wouldn't lie to me, would you, mister? I don't like men who lie to me, and most of them do, so that's why I don't like most men."

"Not on your life would I lie to you, Miss Dawson."

She lightly slapped his pudgy face. "Right." She glanced upward. "Is that rug on tight enough for you? It can get sort of rough sailing inside here."

Dash tapped his toupee and said, "I never get seasick."

"Hey, you boys packing?"

"And if we were?"

"Just asking."

"Good for you. Nice to be curious, ain't it, Archer?"

"Follow me then, gents. Watch your footing. They haven't brought the firehoses through yet to clean up from last night's rummies. Would it surprise you that I don't touch the stuff myself?" She eyed Archer when she said these words, running her gaze from top to bottom in a way that made Archer feel like she had peeled off all his clothes.

"Apparently nothing could surprise me about you, Miss Dawson," replied Archer.

"Brawn *and* brains. And here I'd just about given up all hope."

CHAPTER

24

THEY HEADED DOWN A LONG HALL and then walked up three flights of thickly carpeted stairs.

They passed a sand bucket under a spooled firehose. Archer noted it was filled with discarded cigarette butts. If the place caught fire, the sand probably would too.

"Is that reefer or has my sense of smell gone to hell?" said Dash.

"Marijuana is illegal, Mr. Dash," said Dawson.

"Yeah, just like prostitution. And make it Willie. We're friends now."

They reached the end of the hall and walked up one last set of stairs that carried them to the very top of Midnight Moods.

"Only the best room in the house for the kid, I see," said Dash. "Nosebleed seats. Can't see home plate from here, no sir."

"In this setup, you work your way *down*, not up, *Willie*," retorted Dawson.

She led them to a scarred door painted black. On a stiff card inserted in a brass holder was written: RUBY FRASER.

Dawson knocked and called out, "Ruby, you decent? Two gumshoes here to talk to you. One's old and chubby with a rug on top, and one's tall and could give Clark Gable a run for it. I'll leave it to you to decide which one to concentrate your efforts on."

They heard footsteps approach, hesitant, maybe fearful, thought Archer.

The door opened and there she was, looking like a Conover model, all tall and long limbed, and supple and fresh-faced and innocent and violet-eyed. She had on silk pajamas, a top and a bottom that was a good two inches too short for her and revealed long, pale feet with nails painted a dull red. She was maybe all of twenty, and maybe not even that, yet.

She looked from Dawson, to Dash, to Archer, holding on him, and her lips curled ever so slightly upward as she did so.

"Yes?" she said.

Her voice was surprisingly deep, thought Archer.

"These gents want to talk to you, Ruby. They're private eyes."

Archer thought their appearance might knock this lady for a loop; however, her smile deepened. But when he looked at her eyes more closely, he saw an unnatural languidness there, a bullet jacket with no bullet in it.

She opened the door further and stepped back, motioning them in.

Dawson looked at them. "I'll leave you to it then." She walked off.

"I'm Ruby Fraser," she said, holding out her hand for them to shake.

"We know, that's why we're here," said Dash, shaking her hand. He looked at Archer. "Pull out the notepad and pen, Archer. I'm sure Ruby has lots to tell us."

Archer did as Dash had asked. He looked around and noted that the room was small, with a pale blue davenport on one side and a dormant electric heater on the other. Against another wall was a built-in breakfast nook. A small black Emerson radio sat on a side table. It hummed low, like she might have just turned down the volume. Next to it was an ashtray stand with a burning stub resting in it. A small fan sat on the floor lazily pushing the air from one side to the other, like a cat leisurely flicking its tail.

"What do you do for food in this joint?" asked Dash, taking a seat in a chintz chair, the only one in the room.

"Got another room over there with a little icebox and a hot plate, and a table and two chairs. Room next to it has a Murphy bed and a closet. But mostly I go downstairs for meals. Food's not bad. In fact, it's pretty good."

"Toilet?"

"Down the hall. We take turns with the shower. Me and three other girls."

"Good to know," said Dash. "Take a seat on the davenport and let's have a little chat."

She did so, and Archer leaned against the wall with his notepad and pen. The woman was calm, patient, and unmoved. All things she shouldn't have been with them. The room had a scent to it other than the cigarettes. He eyed her clothes. The pajamas were polka-dotted and looked like a man's outfit, wide in the shoulders, narrow in the hips. He wondered where she had gotten them. Not from Kemper, they were too short for him.

"What is it that you do here, Ruby?" asked Dash.

"I sing and dance and do skits. And I work with Ralph Jeffries. He's good, showing me the ropes. He was in vaudeville before the war. You know him?"

Dash shook his head. "Where you from?"

"Illinois."

"Chicago?"

"Never been to Chicago. I usually tell people I'm from Peoria because that was the closest big city to where I'm from. But I've never been there neither."

"What are you doing out here?"

"Looking for something besides Peoria."

Archer noted that she put her hand to her mouth while speaking. When she removed it, he noted the line of yellowed uneven teeth, with scraggly points at either end.

Archer said, "You sticking around here long, Miss Fraser?"

"Just call me Ruby. Long enough to learn my craft, that's what they call it. Then I'm off to Hollywood. I want to be in pictures. Soon as I get my teeth fixed. I'm saving up." She now opened her mouth wide to show them.

"Hollywood, huh?" said Archer. "That seems to be going around like the flu."

"Douglas Kemper?" said Dash.

"What about him?"

"So you know him?"

"He comes here pretty regular. They have a card club here. He's a member."

"Card club?" said Archer.

Dash said, "California doesn't allow casino gambling like they do in Nevada, Archer. They used to have gambling ships just past the three-mile mark, but before the war a state attorney general by the name of Earl Warren, and who is now our esteemed governor, got them outlawed. Now the card clubs are the only game in town, unless you're into horse racing, which is allowed as well."

"But isn't card playing still gambling?"

"There's no House to play against. The players are pitted against one another."

"How does the House make money, then?"

"Various fees. Players pay for their seats, they pay by the hand, things like that. The House provides the space, the dealer, the cashier. They make good money. The clubs are real popular. The one here does very well. The more players, the more money you make."

Fraser said, "Mr. Kemper is married to some important lady, so's I hear. He's very nice."

"How nice, meaning to you?" said Dash.

She picked up the lit stub and took a long drag on it, shooting both men probing looks. "Who wants to know?"

"For starters, I do. And maybe *Mrs.* Kemper, the very important lady."

She looked relieved. "She's got nothing to worry about. He's a perfect gentleman."

"Then you have no idea who might be claiming that Kemper and you are far more than friends?"

She presented him with a knife-sharp glare. "What are you trying to pull here, mister? Who says that?"

"Mr. Kemper has received a blackmail demand and you figure prominently in it."

"Well, I don't know nothing about that. Sweet Jesus."

"Then if someone asked, you'd say that there was nothing there?"

"That's what I'm telling you. That's what I'd tell anybody who asked."

"I need you to tell *me* that you're speaking the truth."

"I am. I never slept with Mr. Kemper. Swear to God."

"Okay, Archer, you got that?"

Archer nodded. "Got it. Swear to God."

"Okay, the next time we come back it'll be with an affidavit for you to sign. Do you know what an affidavit is?"

She shook her head.

"Well, it's a document where you tell the truth and then sign it, to make it official. Then, if you change your story, it can be used against you."

"Well, why would anyone want to sign that?" she asked.

"It can also help you, but only if you're telling the truth. And since you are, there's no problem, right?" said Archer.

She didn't respond. She just looked at Archer like he was the last thing standing between her and death row.

Dash rose. "One more thing. How much do you make here?"

"Hundred dollars a week, room and board included. Most dough I ever made. Why?"

"Just setting a baseline, Ruby. That's all."

"I don't get it."

"I suppose not. You're not thinking of leaving town anytime soon?"

She eyed him like a chicken did a fox. "I don't know. Should I?"

"Not till you hear from me, no. But if I do tell you to go, Ruby, you need to go like nobody's business."

"You're scaring me."

"Good. Then I'm getting my point across." He added, "Maybe we'll be back to take in your show. What time does it start?"

"Ten o'clock sharp."

"I'll have to take a nap. You be a good girl, Ruby, and *we'll* get through this."

Downstairs, Dash made a call from the front office of Midnight Moods to Connie Morrison and then waited for a few minutes for her to ring him back with an answer. After that, as they were leaving, Archer said, "Do you believe her?"

"I'm not sure. What I am sure about is that she's a drug user."

Archer looked startled. "How do you know?"

"The eyes don't lie. From the looks of her I'd say opium. Don't think she's taken heroin yet. Hope she never does. That's the difference between getting shot with a .22 and a bazooka."

"Where are we off to now?"

"The next piece of the puzzle, Archer."

"Mrs. Kemper?"

Dash gave him an admiring look. "You might just make a decent gumshoe after all."

25

ARCHER DROVE BACK TOWARD TOWN and then up a road that zigzagged as they passed canyons with clefts that crept through the rock like capillaries inside the body. As they reached a plateau in the rise and the ground flattened out like a skillet, he was then directed by Dash to pass through a pair of impressive wrought iron gates embossed with the letter *A* in scrollwork that appeared when the gates were closed and the two halves came together. The gates were mounted on two enormous stone columns. With the ocean on the left and the foothills of the Santa Ynez Mountains on the right, the Delahaye roared along on a curved, pale cobblestone road.

The trees up here were lush and covered the ground like a vast, decamped army. Fifty-foot-tall live oaks with their jumble of branches lined their way. Spanish moss hung off them like veils on blushing brides.

This botanical spectacle held forth until they rounded a bend where the columns of trees retreated. There the greenest, widest patch of grassy lawn Archer had ever seen commenced; it led up to a peninsula of land on which sat a long two-story structure that was built of limestone block, round gray and brown stone, and other elements thrown in for interesting architectural measure. A sea of French doors ran along the front and were anchored by a pair of massive wrought iron doors with impressive scrollwork that served as the main entrance. On either side of them were lit gas lanterns about the size of Archer's torso, and still they seemed small next to the doors.

Thick, plush, variegated ivy covered much of the home's lower front façade. Throughout the landscape were well-tended flower beds creating patterns of color, green hedges, and lush topiary bushes set in either pots or the ground. It was an idyllic setting powered by money, and presumably a lot of it. Along with a ton of sweat labor.

As they turned and came up the long drive running along the face of the house, Archer got a glimpse of the rear grounds, which faced the ocean and held a stunning vista of the Pacific. There was a tennis court with a tented seating area on one side and an oval-shaped pool with deep, dark blue water on the other. A long stone wall ran along the rear perimeter of the property, which presumably ended in a cliff. The Pacific stretched out nearly a thousand feet below like a private body of water.

Next, he looked at a large metal-roofed barn from which two men in denim work clothes were coming out, while another man pushed a wheelbarrow full of brush; a fourth man hosed down a dark blue Triumph Roadster with its canvas top up. A green John Deere tractor sat idle near the barn; a man had the engine cover open and was tinkering with the motor.

Archer pulled to a stop in the paved motor court next to a red-and-black Bentley with a topless front compartment for the chauffeur. Next to that was a silver-and-black Rolls-Royce Phantom.

As Dash got out he said, "Hey, now your ride's in good company."

"I'd say so," replied Archer. "Nice place the Kempers have."

"Didn't you note the letter *A* on the gates? Sawyer Armstrong built this place for his daughter as a wedding present but couldn't resist putting his 'name' on it."

Dash breathed in the sea air that rose up from below like it had taken an express elevator car to get there. "Smell that, Archer?"

"Yeah. Fish."

"Bet you never seen a house this big before?"

"I have."

"Get outta here, you're having one on me."

"The one I saw back in Poca City was bigger than this place, but not by much. But it was also phony and so were the people in it. The jury's still out on this one."

"It won't be much longer. But I wouldn't call Beth Kemper a phony."

"How do you know she'll see us?"

"I phoned Connie from Midnight Moods and had her set up an appointment. She called back to confirm it. That's what I was waiting on."

They walked up to the massive double front doors. They, too, were embossed with an *A*, but here each door held its own letter.

Archer said, "Boy, the guy likes to remind people of the origins of this place."

Dash said, "For me, it's a sign of insecurity, but I could be wrong."

He poked at a buzzer. From somewhere distant they heard the peal of a bell, its sound dulled by distance.

About twenty seconds later footsteps approached.

The opening door revealed a Chinese man who wore a waist-long white tuxedo jacket, black pants with lighter black stripes down the sides of the trousers, and a bow tie the color of the pants. His skin was tanned, and he had three moles that marched across his forehead like a line of ants. His dark hair was trimmed with silver at the temples, like the best character actors in the movies, and was slicked back. He had a long, tapered mustache that dovetailed around his mouth and ended in a stringy goatee. He had the sort of face that made it hard to guess the correct age. Archer put the range at forty to sixty.

"Willie Dash and Archer to see Mrs. Kemper. We're expected."

"May I see identification, please?"

"Oh, so you're one of those butlers? Okay, pal, feast your eyes."

Dash held out his ID card and the man examined it long enough to have copied out all the information it contained three times over. He handed it back and motioned them in. He closed the door, and they followed him down a marble hall that had a cushiony Oriental rug running right down the middle of it for what seemed like miles. The walls were festooned with enough paintings that Archer could have been forgiven for believing he had mistakenly stepped into a museum. They passed large rooms that were all furnished with just the right amount of furniture and not a smidgen more. White, gray, and pale blue were the dominant colors. Archer could see how that scheme would play well off the California sun that was streaming in through all the windows and French doors that also lined the rear of the home.

The interior was as quiet as a tomb and nearly as joyful, Archer thought as he walked next to Dash. Even with all the beautiful things, he couldn't imagine living here.

The man stopped at double curved doors made of walnut, which shone with elbow-greased polish, and knocked on one of them.

"All right," said the voice within. To Archer it sounded dulled and joyless, like a knife blade left outside to rust.

He steeled himself to meet Beth Armstrong Kemper.

26

THE MAN OPENED THE DOOR and stepped to the side for them to pass through. They did so and he closed the door, and Archer heard his soft footsteps moving away.

Archer glanced around the room. He didn't have to be a world-class shamus to deduce that this was the library. Three walls of floor-to-ceiling shelves bursting with books would have been his first and only necessary clue. The carpet was white with subtle dashes of orange and muted teal done up in a breaking-wave pattern. It felt deep and springy, like he was standing on a trampoline. The furniture was large and tasteful and well laid out over the room's expanse. A fireplace at one end was mounted in stone and topped by a mantel consisting of one enormous worm-eaten piece of blackened and distressed timber that someone could have built a boat out of with wood left over. Despite the warmth outside, it was deliciously cool in here, and a small fire flickered in the hearth. There were two camel-haired wingback chairs set in front of the fireplace. One of them was occupied.

When Beth Kemper rose and turned to them, Archer had to catch his breath and almost dropped the notepad and pen he'd taken from his pocket. She was not the most beautiful woman or the one with the finest figure he had ever seen. Yet he wasn't sure he had ever been in the presence of a *lovelier* woman, and right now he couldn't explain the distinction. It was just a feeling, an overpowering one.

She was tall and slim, with blonde hair that had not come out of the bottle. It skimmed her shoulders like a shade tree does its underlings. Her skin wasn't pale in keeping with her hair. It had a healthy glow that radiated right up to her eyes, which were cornflower blue but seemed enhanced by something inside the woman that transformed soft cornflower into electrically charged sapphires.

Her features were classical in the sense that there wasn't a flaw to be detected or criticized. The cheek bumps, the jawline, the slender, plum, line-straight nose, the shallow sockets the eyes rested in, the high forehead without trace of wrinkle or brow furrow, all seemed molded by the sure hand of a sculptor intent on perfection, or at least most people's view thereof.

She was dressed simply in a lavender day dress that dropped straight down her tall frame, with a strip of white around the neck and also at the ends of the elbow-length sleeves. The hemline just touched her knees. She wore a strand of small pearls, a platinum, engraved wrist cuff, and white unadorned heels of simple, elegant design. Her engagement and wedding rings were the stuff of royalty, thought Archer.

He also observed that Beth Kemper had the weary expression of a woman who wished to tolerate others only on her terms but had never yet been afforded that singular opportunity.

He figured she couldn't be much older than he was, maybe thirty at the most.

"Gentlemen," she said, her voice bubbling like a brook, but he thought that might be just for a certain effect.

"Mrs. Kemper. I'm Willie Dash. You might remember me. Our paths have crossed at certain functions from time to time. This is my associate, Archer."

Kemper barely looked at Dash. "Is Archer your surname or given one?" she asked.

For a moment Archer couldn't remember the answer. He twirled his hat in his hands, a trait of his when nervous, and said, "Archer's my last name."

"And your Christian name?"

"Aloysius."

She nodded, satisfied, and motioned to the two chairs while she stood with her back to the fire. "Yes, Mr. Dash, I do remember you. You and my father go way back."

After they sat, Dash said, "We've known each other a long time, yes."

"To the extent that anyone really knows my father."

"Yes ma'am. I understand what you mean. He and I have butted heads a few times, and I can't say I understand him any better now than I did then."

"Then you and I have something in common."

"Yes ma'am."

"Would you like something to drink? A bit early in the day but I'm having one if that influences your decision."

It was then that Archer saw the bar set up a few paces from the fireplace and on the same wall.

"Bourbon straight is fine by me," said Dash, running his eye along the rows of bottles.

She nodded and looked at Archer with hiked eyebrows that were as rigid as a pencil, even in the uplifted position, and far darker than her hair. The combination of the two colors for some reason had a deeply unsettling effect on him. As though he were looking at two women instead of merely one.

"And you, Mr. Archer?"

"Whatever you're having. And you can just call me Archer."

She nodded, turned to the bar table, and fixed their drinks. Her motions were practiced and efficient, Archer thought as she jiggered, measured, and mixed. That bar must see a lot of work, he figured.

He glanced at another table that was bedecked with framed

photographs. He rose and started looking over them. They were all signed either to Beth or Douglas, but none together. There was one of the vice president, and another signed, "Best wishes, Earl Warren." Then he glanced at another one. "You know Jimmy Stewart?"

She turned to him from the bar table. "My husband did. They flew together in the war."

"Your husband's a pilot?"

"Yes, at least he was." She presented Dash with his bourbon and nothing else in a cut crystal glass. Then she handed Archer his drink. "Dry Manhattan, Archer."

"You don't care for the sweet vermouth, then?"

She looked impressed. "I like a man who knows his cocktails. For me, it's an essential skill. And no, I care for nothing sweet at all."

Unsure of how to take this, Archer retook his seat and said nothing. She eyed the notepad and pen he had placed on the table. "This must be serious if you're to chronicle all I have to say."

"Just standard procedure," interjected Dash.

She took up residence in front of the flames once more and looked down at the two men, her drink held loosely at her side. She was apparently waiting for them to sample their libations.

Dash took a sip of his and smiled. "Good bourbon."

"From Kentucky. That's where they first distilled whiskey into what we call bourbon. In a county of the same name."

"Didn't know that," said Dash, giving the woman the once-over in a single glance.

Archer drank from his Manhattan. "Nice," he said. "Thank you."

Dash eyed her closely. "Heard you were ill recently. Appendicitis. You're looking fine now."

"How did you know?"

Dash glanced at Archer before saying, "Myron O'Donnell is in my building. He happened to mention that he performed the operation."

"He was my mother's doctor, too. And many years ago he saved my father's life after a car accident. That's how I came to use him. He's a fine surgeon."

As soon as she finished speaking, her look hardened like wet cement solidifying. "Now, to business."

"You know why we're here?" said Dash.

"In a general sense, yes."

She sipped her drink and then placed it on a doily set on the timber mantel. "But please feel free to enlighten me as to particulars." She picked up a cigarette case from a side table, clicked it open, and extracted a cigarette. Then she placed it into an ivory holder, which she also took from the case, and ignited the end with a platinum lighter that had sat next to the case. She replaced both exactly where they were before.

A careful, measured woman, Archer observed. Who likes things just so. At least the things she can control. He wrote this impression down.

She blew smoke out and picked up her drink, taking another sip.

Dash said, "Some of this may be troubling to hear."

"Much of what I have to deal with is troubling, Mr. Dash. And people like you and your associate do not get called in when things are *not* troubling, do you?"

"I appreciate that you understand the situation."

She took another puff of cigarette and a sip of her drink. "I'll understand it even better when you tell me the *particulars*."

Archer took another swallow of his drink and eyed the room once more, this time with a nuanced approach.

Everything in this place is for show. He eyed Kemper. *Maybe including the woman.*

He didn't write this down; he didn't have to.

Dash laid it all out for her, piece by piece, regurgitating everything that her husband had earlier told them, including his denials of a relationship with Ruby Fraser.

Kemper took it all in and drained the rest of her drink, then turned and started toward the table as though to make another but seemed to think better of it. It was the only moment of indecision Archer had seen in the woman. And from that glimpse he considered the possibility that she actually might be human, with real blood flowing through her thin veins.

She returned to face them in front of the fire, which now seemed to Archer somewhat metaphorical. She perched on the leather-topped fender surrounding the fireplace opening.

"Have you talked to your husband about this...matter?" asked Dash.

She took a moment to finish her cigarette and tossed it, minus the holder, into the fire. She dexterously rolled the ivory holder around and around between her thumb and index finger. "Not really, no. Douglas is running for mayor, I'm sure you know."

"Which makes the matter even more delicate, and the timing suspicious."

The cornflower eyes focused on him with an astonishing degree of severity. "Mr. Dash, you are not a fool, I take it?"

"My worst enemies would accuse me of a lot, and they would be right, but being a fool is not one of them. I've seen too much of life and suffered through quite a bit of it. It strikes foolishness clean from you, least it did for me."

"Then do not intimate that the timing of the election makes this accusation scurrilous."

"Now that's a fifty-dollar word," replied Dash.

"And the only one that comes to my mind to fit the situation."

"Then you believe that your husband *did* have an affair with Ruby Fraser?"

Her angry look quickly faded. "I...I don't know about that. I would hope not. But..."

"Did you ask him?"

"No, I didn't." She paused and studied her shoes. "Maybe I didn't want to know his answer," she added quietly.

"His political opponents would love to make hay out of this."

"Alfred Drake most assuredly knows of it, or at least his associates do, which in politics is a difference without meaning."

"I forgot your father was mayor here and once took a run at the governor's mansion in Sacramento."

Her lips pursed for a moment. Archer wasn't sure if she was holding back a smile or not.

She said, "He won the mayor's race by a landslide and lost the governor's contest by the same margin."

"Is there a lesson in that?" asked Archer.

She turned to him, her look now one of amusement. "Fame and influence are both often fickle and *localized*."

"I'm sure it was a hard loss for your father," said Dash.

"It was, if only because it was the only time he *did* lose at anything."

"But Drake may be behind this blackmail attempt."

"He may, or he may not. I have no idea, really. I actually always thought Alfred Drake was a decent man. But I think that of many people and I've been proven wrong before."

"If he is the blackmailer, we could use that against him," noted Dash.

"No one expects Drake to win, even with this allegation bubbling up."

Archer spoke up. "Then why would your husband hire us to investigate the matter if it will have no impact on the outcome of the election?"

She graced him with a look that hit Archer somewhere between his gut and his heart. Her slender tongue slid over the pale, glossy, and full lips.

"An excellent question to which I have no viable answer. Did you ask him that?"

Dash said, "I don't usually discourage clients from hiring me, and in our defense, we didn't know the lay of the land yet. But what you said does give me something to chew on."

Archer said, "So you know Alfred Drake, then?"

"I used to go to him for my teeth." She smiled. "He's actually an orthodontist and an excellent one. I think he did a rather marvelous job, taking out some teeth and putting braces on which straightened the ones that were left. I was hopeless as a child. My father was ready to give up on my having any sort of a social life simply because of the atrocious state of my teeth. But it was my mother who finally put her foot down and took me to Drake."

"I hardly think anyone would have agreed with your father's assessment," noted Archer.

This did not earn him a second graceful smile. The eyes grew cold.

"In many ways, his observation was spot-on because people are invariably shallow, at least here. But you can know nothing of that, so don't bother rendering an opinion."

Archer held up a hand in a motion of acquiescence and also apology.

This also did him no favors with the woman. "You surrender quite easily, Mr. Archer. I hope you're not as squeamish in your work. If so, my husband will certainly be overcharged."

She turned her attention to Dash, as though now totally discounting the value of Archer's presence. "Anything else, or can you both leave me in relative peace now?"

"Not unless you can think of anything that might help our investigation."

"If I did, I probably wouldn't tell you."

"So, you don't want to help out your husband here?"

"If Douglas got himself into this, he can get himself out of it."

"I apologize in advance for this question, but is he the sort of man who has the wandering eye?"

"What man doesn't?" was her reply.

"Well, I think that's it for now, ma'am. Thank you for your time."

She leaned over and pushed a button on the wall. Five seconds later the same man appeared to lead them out.

As they were leaving, Archer put his notepad and pen away and glanced back at Kemper.

She caught him looking and said imperiously, "Something on your mind, Archer?"

"Nothing wrong with having that second drink now. It might taste better at this point."

"And why is that?" she asked in a disinterested tone.

"You got your piece off your chest and didn't stumble once over your lines. I'd clap in appreciation except I'm holding my hat."

27

As Archer and Dash approached the Delahaye, the man who had been washing the Triumph out back came up to them rubbing his hands on a white towel. He was around thirty-five with a muscular build, good looks, a trim black mustache, and brooding eyes. A short-barreled stogie perched from one corner of his slash for a mouth. He was wearing a white T-shirt and dark brown jodhpurs tucked into leather lace-up boots and a chauffeur's black cap.

General George Patton would have been proud of the man's wardrobe choices, thought Archer. Now all he needed were the twin pearl-handled Colt pistols.

"Nice ride," said the man, looking the Delahaye over.

"Right back at you," said Archer, pointing to the Phantom and the Bentley. "And I saw you washing the Triumph. Rode in one of those over in England."

The man pinched his stogie and nodded. "I was over there too. Hundred and First Airborne. Name's Adam Stover."

"Meaning you jumped out of perfectly good airplanes," noted Dash with a grin.

"I was Eighth Army," said Archer. "Name's Archer. That's Willie Dash."

Stover eyed Archer. "Eighth Army? Then you got your share of killing and nearly being killed."

"I think we all did."

"You two here visiting Mrs. Kemper?"

Dash said, "Yes, on some private business."

Archer said, "Nice place."

Stover laughed. "One way to see it. They got more money than God."

"How'd you end up here?"

"I'm from Bay Town. Came back after the war. Know my way around cars. So there you go." He eyed the house and then Dash. "Seen your billboards around town, Mr. Dash. You're a private dick."

"That I am. So is Archer here."

"Got trouble here, then?"

"Again, we're *private* dicks, so that's as far as it can go, Mr. Stover."

Stover touched the bill of his cap and walked off.

As Archer climbed into the car, he glanced at one of the French doors to see Beth Kemper watching him. With his gaze still locked on her, Kemper turned and walked away.

As they drove away from the mansion and out through the gates, a marine fog was coming in off the ocean and accumulating like fire smoke in the clefts and fingers of the foothills after already invading the lower canyons. The wind had picked up, and it looked like rain was coming as the temperature dropped.

"I guess it can get pretty tricky driving up or down here when the mist rolls in," said Archer.

"It's tricky driving up or down here at any time, and I'm not necessarily referring to the weather."

"Where to now, Willie?"

"Back to the office. I need to think some."

Archer checked his timepiece. "It's still early for me. How about I do some sleuthing on my own?"

"And how exactly would you go about doing that, I'd like to know."

"I wouldn't mind having another go at Ruby Fraser. She's got more to say than she did. I can go back to see her show, and talk to her after. I can bring my friend along with me. She's looking for work."

"Ruby might not talk to you again, Archer."

"She might with another woman there. Let me work it, Willie. You have to trust me at some point."

"Right, only I don't know if I've gotten to that point yet, Archer. We did just meet."

"I won't louse it up. I'll just be listening."

Dash rubbed his stomach and grimaced in some pain.

"You got something going on down there?" asked Archer.

"I got something going on lots of places. It doesn't concern you."

"If his wife maybe believes he's having an affair, what are we supposed to do about the blackmail angle? And Kemper might very well win the election, affair or not, like his wife said."

"The election isn't the thing, Archer. Somebody is committing a crime. And they need to be punished for it."

"Now you're sounding like Mr. Shaw."

Dash looked down. "I was a cop for a long time. Sticks to your bones and your brain. But since you're an ex-con maybe I'm speaking to a wall."

"I've got morals, Willie, maybe more than you think."

"And I've got to always keep in mind that I work for the client, not the blindfolded lady holding the scales of justice."

"I can see how that might be hard."

"If it ever stops being hard, I need to see about another line of work."

"So drop you off at the office then?"

"Yeah, and keep your eyes on the road, or the only place we'll be going is off this mountain, the hard way."

After leaving Dash at the office, Archer turned the Delahaye around and drove back to the boardinghouse. He passed Madame

Genevieve in the hall. She spoke to him with only her eyebrows, which rose toward the ceiling.

"Is there a problem?" he asked.

"Your lady friend is very demanding."

"Tell me something I don't know."

He raced up the steps and knocked on Callahan's door.

"Who is it?"

"Archer."

"Come on in."

"You decent?"

"Well, if I were, I wouldn't have told you to come on in."

Even Archer had to grin at that one.

He opened the door and closed it behind him. Twirling his hat, he moved over to the bed where Callahan was lying and wearing the same pale clingy robe she'd had on before.

"Had a busy day?" he began, eyeing her closely.

She stretched like a cat, yawned, and wiggled a bit, lifting the robe to a fascinating height. "Yeah, I'm worn out just being little old me."

Archer looked at the floor and said, "Madame Genevieve says you're a tough customer."

"If asking for hot water and a towel is a tough customer, then I plead guilty."

She sat up against the pillow, pulled out a cigarette from her case, and lit it. Archer did the same and perched on her bed.

"I did run out for smokes. Do you know what they're charging for a pack of Camels? A quarter. It's eighteen cents back in Reno. What's so special about this place?"

"Maybe it's the ocean premium."

"Yeah, right. Oh, did you get the job?"

Archer nodded. "Already working a case."

"Why are you here then?"

"You still thinking about trying for a job at Midnight Moods?"

"Yeah, I am. Seems to be the only game in town."

"How do you know that?"

"I haven't been lying here all day waiting for you, Archer."

She swung her legs over the side of the bed so they were sitting shoulder to shoulder. He breathed in her perfume and watched as she crossed one bare leg over the other. He closed his eyes and thought of every sad thing that had ever happened to him. It was almost enough. It gave him a fighting chance.

"I was there earlier today because the case I'm working has to do with one of the gals who performs out there. I'm planning to go back there tonight. So I came back here to ask if you want to come along with me tonight and see about getting a job out there. Like you said, it's the only game in town. And then maybe you could be there while I talk to the lady again. She might feel more comfortable with another woman there."

She rubbed her toes against his pants leg. "You promised you'd take me to dinner."

"Her show doesn't start until ten. So we can go there *after* dinner. And my treat. I'm gainfully employed, and now I have some leads to follow up on. So how about it? Will you come?"

"Sure, Archer, I'll come."

"Great." He rose.

"Hey, do you have to rush off?" She eyed her bed. "I'm…kind of lonely."

"No can do, Liberty. I'm a workingman now."

She looked resignedly up at him. "You're sure taking this shamus thing to heart, Archer."

"Only way to do it." He tipped his hat and walked out the door wondering how he'd found the fortitude to do that.

28

ARCHER WENT BACK TO THE DASH AGENCY.

Morrison told him that Dash had left almost immediately after Archer had dropped him off.

"Where does he live?" asked Archer. "Nearby?"

"If he hasn't told you, I don't think it right that I should."

"Okay, did a message arrive from Kemper? It was supposed to be a list of people for us to check out."

"No, nothing like that."

"Do you have Kemper's address, then? I could run over and get the list."

Morrison looked at him.

"Willie knows I'm going to do some investigating on my own."

"I know. He told me. He said he was coming to trust you." She paused, wrote something down on a piece of paper, and handed it to him. "Kemper's address."

"Is he going to be okay?" Archer asked, taking the paper. "He seems to be in pain."

"Ulcers. He just needs to rest from time to time and watch his diet." Morrison opened her desk drawer and took out a black leather card case. "Here."

"What is it?"

"Your ticket. It just came in twenty minutes ago."

Archer looked surprised. "But didn't I have to sign something?"

"I did all the paperwork for you."

Archer opened the case and saw the printed card with his name and other information on it. "Aloysius Archer, Licensed Private Investigator in the city of Bay Town under the auspices of Willie Dash, Very Private Investigations, Incorporated. Licensed under California Law, Bonded and Insured."

"The cost of getting it will be deducted from your earnings."

"How much *are* my earnings?"

"Willie didn't discuss that with you?"

"No, and I asked him."

"Well, I'll have to leave that to him."

"He said I should apply for my own ticket because the law might change and this might not be enough."

"If he said so, I would believe it."

"He said I need five people to vouch for me. He said you would be one of them."

"Sure, Archer, whatever you need."

"Just like that?"

"If Willie said it was okay for me to sign, then that's good enough for me."

Archer left her and looked at the address as he walked down the hall. Kemper's office was on Idaho Avenue. He rode back down in the elevator with Earl, who was not nearly as talkative as before, but just sat on his little chair and read his newspaper.

Archer drove to a Rexall drugstore and bought a map of Bay Town and the surrounding area. As he sat at the counter drinking a cup of coffee and studying it, the pink-frocked soda jerk girl with a matching cap said, "You looking for someplace in particular, mister?"

"Idaho Avenue?"

"On the rich side of town," said the girl.

"Is that right?"

She had curly red hair, a skinny frame, and a freckled face with a button nose barely large enough to support both nostrils. She placed her long index finger on a spot on the open map. "We're here, okay?"

"Right."

"And Sawyer Ave cuts right through the middle of town. Anything to the mountain side is the working-class side, at least for the most part. Anything to the ocean side is the rich side, except for obviously where Sawyer's Wharf is. And Idaho Ave is right here," she added, stabbing the paper with her finger once more.

"So I guess folks want the water view?"

"I guess rich folks *get* whatever it is they want," she replied gamely.

"How about up in the foothills? That's not ocean side."

"Now that's where the *really* rich live. See, you don't just get the ocean views up there, you get to look down on the rest of us." She laughed at her own little joke.

"You mean, like the Kempers?"

Her freckles seemed to bulge at the mention of the name. "You know them?"

"I met them today. Husband and wife."

She gave him an appraising look and adjusted her pink cap. "Old man Armstrong and his family really built up this town."

"His son-in-law, Douglas Kemper, is running for mayor."

She shrugged. "Don't know nothing about that. I'm more into flicks than politics."

Archer noted the movie pulp magazine stashed under the counter behind her. "Do you know anything about Kemper?"

"He's got a bunch of businesses. My mom and dad work for him, and my two brothers work for him, too."

This got Archer's attention. "What sort of businesses?"

"He builds houses and apartment buildings, for one. My dad's a carpenter with that company. Lots of people moving to this area and they need some place to live. And he has a vineyard, too, a little north of here. My older brother works there building the casks and working in the grape fields. And Kemper owns a members-only country club, the Winward. It's a mile north of here and right on the water. They have a marina and folks keep their boats there. My middle brother works there as a valet. He says it's really nice. And Kemper owns the Mayport Hotel. That's near Idaho Ave. My mom's a maid there. It's probably the nicest hotel in town."

"Sounds like the Kempers only deal in the nicest of everything." He handed her a buck tip.

Her fingers closed around it and she flashed him a smile. "Thanks, mister."

Archer left, fired up the Delahaye, and started off in the direction of Idaho Avenue. He glanced at the passenger seat where he'd placed the map.

The traffic was light, and he figured he could make it in under twenty minutes. Bay Town was bustling, Archer could see that easily enough. Folks were driving and walking and biking and riding the trolleys that were gold in color and promoted Bay Town as the "place of paradise." Folks seemed to have taken this to heart and were dressed up and shopping and working and hauling stuff and generally moving both commerce and contentment from here to there with smiles on their faces.

Archer passed several dance halls, two buildings advertising card clubs, and a filling station where helpful uniformed attendants pumped gas, cleaned windshields, and gave out shiny toy metal cars to little boys jumping up and down in the rear seats. There was an open-air food market on a patch of green town square, where farmers in bib overalls were offering their wares from the beds of ancient pickup trucks to discerning shoppers. There was a new-looking movie theater playing *The Fountainhead* with Gary Cooper and Patricia Neal.

The fog had burned off down here and the sun was warm, but the air was still damp and thus chilly. He looked toward the foothills where the Kempers resided and saw higher-level winds swirling up the west-facing slopes and ruffling the canopies of the sea of trees. And up there silver strands of marine fog still crept into the clefts of the rock like a thief's hand slipping into a pocket. To his left the ocean shimmered broad and fine, with seagulls dipping for their meals and boats puttering along as they made to port or away from it. About a hundred boats of all sizes were moored in the bay, bobbing up and down to the beat of the Pacific. An airplane, a Western Airlines DC-4, glided along about a thousand feet above the water, its four propellers whirling in precise synchronization.

Archer had flown on the military version of the DC-4 during the war. That brought back memories of a harrowing flight in dense fog that resulted in a crash landing in which not everyone had survived. But since it was World War II, the grunts who did survive got off and took up the fight once more as though nothing remotely unnerving had happened. He had never really cared for riding in planes after that.

He crossed Sawyer Avenue going toward the ocean, and he could see what the soda jerk girl had meant. Even the dogs looked healthier over here, as did the flowers, trees, and bushes. And the sidewalks held not a scrap of paper or other trash. People were clothed in nicer duds. The price tags of the cars cruising along became elevated, pickup trucks and old, dented Fords were replaced with Coupe de Villes, Eldorados, and chromed Buick Roadmasters that looked big enough to live in. The shop fronts were classier and catered to a clientele that obviously had money. Archer had passed one beauty parlor on the other side of Sawyer. It was dingy with two cracked vinyl chairs, a dirty window, and two old women in their housecoats getting their hair dyed a color he didn't recognize offhand. He had already passed four beauty parlors on the ritzier side of Sawyer, and each one was nicer than the one before, where each well-heeled patron was greeted at the door with a smile, a handshake, and a symbolic kiss on the behind.

Archer slowed down for traffic and then stopped in front of a shop selling furs. He peered through the front glass and saw a hostess in a long pale green gown and silver shoes catering to an old woman and what looked to be her twenty-something granddaughter, while a tall young woman modeled an ankle-length mink coat. Both granny and granddaughter looked enthralled at the prospect of draping the remnants of dead things over themselves.

He next passed the Mayport Hotel, which Kemper owned. It was six stories high and had twin columns out front, along with a top-hatted doorman in full faux military regalia. A long, pristine burgundy awning was stenciled with the hotel's name in fancy swirls and loops of calligraphy. A cabstand out front was doing a brisk business. Tall windows were on the street side, and an oak revolving door near the end of the left side of the hotel invited folks into the Mayport Bar and Lounge for libations, live music, and good times, or so the sign said. Through one window Archer could see women in stylish hats and dress gloves having what looked to be a refined tea in the main dining area.

He kept driving and turned left and then right before reaching Idaho Avenue. It was a trim street, shadowed and cooled by a canopy of overhanging trees. The road here transformed from asphalt to cobblestones, and the Delahaye bumped uncomfortably over them. A policeman was on the corner telling traffic where and when to go, and Archer waited his turn until the uniformed gent sent him on his way with a sharp wave of a white-gloved hand.

He'd seen six prowl cars on the other side of Sawyer Avenue and not one on this side. As though the rich didn't commit crimes, thought Archer. Yet, he also knew that those with lots of money didn't do it in the open with a gun or knife or a fist like a workingman might employ. They did it in the shadows four layers removed from the actual dirty deed, and nobody came after them because they could afford the best lawyers, knew all the judges, gave to charity, and had good teeth.

He parked in front of a ten-story limestone building that was as neat and refined as the street.

THE KEMPER BUILDING, the gold wall plaque outside read. Archer thought Kemper might operate all his myriad businesses out of this place and then he probably rented the rest of it to other tenants. The receptionist took his name and request and got on her sleek telephone switchboard to call up to Douglas Kemper's office. With that done, she sent him on his way with the suite number on the very top floor.

He eyed the marquee in the lobby, and it showed that the place was fully leased, to businesses with impressive-sounding names. Overcoming his fear of enclosed spaces, Archer rode an automatic elevator car up to the top floor. It had been a bit easier to beat his phobia this time, because the elevator was mostly all glass wrapped in chrome. He thought Earl from Dash's building might go crazy riding up and down all day in the thing. And he assumed at night that one might get some unsettling reflections. He, for one, didn't want delusions occurring at a hundred feet in the air.

But then again, they probably exist at street level, too.

29

A PAIR OF REFLECTIVE GLASS DOORS with platinum wrappers greeted Archer at the entrance to Kemper Enterprises. Two large rubber plants in thousand-pound cast stone pots with lions in raised relief on their sides guarded this portal. Since there was no sunlight in the hall Archer wondered how these beauties could manage, but when he touched them and then smelled them, he realized they were fake.

He opened one of the doors and stepped through. It was then that he realized the revealed anteroom was just a tease. There was no one and nothing here. Just four walls painted black and a hat and coat rack, stuck in one corner, that was bereft of both hats and coats.

The door set directly across from him was thick oak and he found out it was locked. He saw the buzzer and the voice box, so he buzzed and prepared to use his voice.

A woman answered, "Yes?"

"Aloysius Archer here to see either Mr. Kemper or Mr. Wilson Sheen."

"Do you have an appointment?"

"No, but they should be expecting me. We met this morning at Willie Dash's office."

"Oh," said the voice, and Archer heard what he expected to hear—the door being buzzed open.

He gripped the knob, pulled, and stepped into la-la land, at least at first blush. His opinion didn't change much on the second blush.

The room was cavernous, awash in light, indeed so much light that stepping from a dark hall into a darker anteroom and then into this burst of illumination made Archer's eyes squint, his pupils contract, and his head momentarily pound. The windows were floor-to-ceilings and let in as much of the descending California sun as was humanly possible. There was not a drape to be had in the whole space, apparently.

There were six uniform desks, each lined up with the other. And on a raised dais behind them was one desk, twice as large as the others. Six women sat in the lower section. They all looked to be in their twenties, well scrubbed, professionally dressed, efficient, earnest, smart, ambitious, and platinum blonde right down to the part in the middle of the scalp. They could be sextuplets, down to their bone marrow. Carriage typewriters clicked and clacked, phones rang, and a stock market tape rattled along on one walnut-carved credenza spelling doom or fortune, depending on one's Wall Street position. There was a frenetic energy here that was hard for Archer to wrap his head around. These ladies seemed to be living life at a different speed from the rest of humanity.

Since the hat rack outside was empty, he figured they must keep theirs in their desk drawers.

The walls were upholstered in what looked to be brown leather two-by-two tiles. On these walls hung paintings of seascapes and landscapes and mountainscapes, as well as other scapes Archer had never contemplated before. A marble statue of a naked woman and baby stood in one corner. Real plants whiled away their time in cast stone pots that dwarfed the ones in the hall. The overhead light fixtures were grand chandeliers with about a thousand pieces of cut crystal each, and they looked like a bitch to clean and even more of a bitch to raise to the ceiling. And that ceiling. It was flat metal copper plates acid-washed with blue, black, brown, and teal slashes. It looked like something you'd see in Europe before the war took its pound of flesh and everything else.

The rug underneath his feet sank in two inches under his weight, and Archer didn't think he'd hit rock bottom yet. To Archer's mind there was too much woodwork everywhere, like an over-abundance of makeup on an aging film star; in trying to hide every perceived flaw, it succeeded in wiping out all that was authentic.

Yet the whole outfit made Willie Dash's operation look like a plot in a desperate Depression-era Hooverville with cardboard homes and not an ounce of hope in sight. Despite that, Archer found himself preferring Dash's humble space over this over-the-top setup.

The large desk on the raised dais was occupied by a very different sort. She was in her thirties, tall and well shaped, and so brunette that in the sea of platinum she looked like the puppy that had gone lost. Her face held starkly intelligent features, and her eyebrows, as dark as the hair, acted like antennae, sniffing out everything before it became an issue. She was dressed all in black except for a high white collar and slips of white around the ends of her long dress sleeves. Her hair was thick and wavy and graced her head like a tiara. She had stacks of files on both sides of her desk, a phone in the middle next to an open ledger book, and no typewriter in sight, which told Archer that in addition to her heightened position behind the half-dozen ladies, she was the boss of this little dynasty. And unlike the frenetic activity going on around her, this lady exhibited an aura of languid calm, like the eye of a hurricane.

She suddenly harrumphed, and one of the platinums obediently rose like a pet on voice command and came over to greet Archer. She was dressed in a tailored brown pants suit with dark heels, a white blouse, a yellow carnation in her buttonhole, and a splash of yellow in her breast pocket. An earthy-colored cravat was around her throat. She looked like she was just about to step onto a maga-zine cover for smartly dressed professional women who wanted to take over the world by 1950.

"Mr. Archer?" she said.

"The one and only."

The efficient face sparked for a moment and the lips looked like they might uplift to a smile, but then the moment was gone and the mask went back on. "Miss Darling will see you now."

"But I didn't ask to see Miss Darling."

"Yes, please step this way."

Archer stepped that way and was led up onto the dais and deposited next to the brunette aka Miss Darling, as the platinum returned to her glorified niche and commenced to attack her typewriter once more.

Darling looked him up and down, perhaps gaining insights into him that Archer lacked himself. He twirled his hat and said, "I'm here to see either Kemper or Sheen."

"Yes, I heard. Take a seat, it might be a while for either Mr. Kemper or Mr. Sheen."

"I only need to see them for a minute."

"That's what they all say. You see that chair over there? Take it and we'll see what happens."

"And if you just buzz them?"

"You're currently twelfth on the 'buzz' list."

"And where are the other eleven?" asked Archer.

"They gave up. Let's see how much stamina you have."

"Can you put in a good word for me?"

"Do you have a reason why I should?" she said.

"I'll go smoke a cigarette like a good boy and think of one."

This line seemed to please her even as she deftly waved him off.

He sat in the prescribed chair, a leather monster of a baseball mitt that looked like it might reach around and hug him to death, but ended up minding its own business. He slid a chrome ashtray stand over, lit up a Lucky, and tapped ash into it as he gave the place the once-over, once more. He came away even more impressed with its organization and blazing efficiency. The platinums worked away like ants on a hill, occasionally venturing to Darling for some reason or another, showing a piece of paper, whispering something, or in one instance writing something down for her while casting worried glances at Archer. Darling took everything in, her eyebrows flicking and clicking like knitting needles. She made firm decisions and sent the girls on their productive way.

He finally stood and wandered over to a large map of the area that sat on a wooden stand and had red stick pins inserted all over. By reading the accompanying information section he was able to discern that these were ongoing Kemper projects, and there were an enviable number. He caught the platinums eyeing him from time to time, and Darling once. Each time he smiled, which sent them scurrying back, goggle-eyed, to their work, all except for Darling. She nodded and leisurely returned to what she was doing.

Finally, the door opened and there was Wilson Sheen, dressed just as frumpily as before, with the front part of his shirt coming dangerously close to pulling free of the pants. Compared to the sea of efficient femininity spread out before him, he looked as out of place as a eunuch in a brothel. He eyed Darling, who nodded in Archer's direction. By Archer's timepiece, two hours had passed, and it was getting close to dinnertime, but none of the ladies had reached for their purses or hats. They continued to work like obedient bees before the queen.

"This way, Archer," said Sheen brusquely.

Archer got up, stubbed out his smoke, and headed up to the dais, where Darling said, "So you couldn't find a good enough reason, I take it."

"You're just very intimidating, Miss Darling. It set me off my mark."

This line seemed to please her more than the first one. She

actually smiled so he could see even white teeth that he thought were as real as the rubber plants outside.

The next room Archer stepped into was not much of a letdown from the previous. It was large and comfortably furnished, and its enormous windows had drapes, which were now all the way open to let in the dwindling light.

"How'd your guardian grizzly bear signal that I was here?" asked Archer. "She never left her desk or lifted the phone."

"She and I can read minds."

"If that's so, I might be in real trouble with her."

"Something makes me think you're always in trouble, Archer."

"Quite the operation you have out there," noted Archer. "Those ladies seem to move at the speed of light."

"That's what we pay them to do," said Sheen, glancing at a file on his desk, a Victorian-era piece that would have looked at home in Buckingham Palace.

"You might want to issue them sunglasses. It's pretty tough on the eyes out there."

"Well, at least they won't be catching a nap. And enhanced sunlight is good for productivity."

"Unless you go blind in the process. And I don't think you need the sun, so long as you have Miss Darling."

Sheen sat down and said abruptly, "And what can I do for you?"

Archer eyed one door set against the wall, on the other side of which was the outside hall. Sheen obviously used this to come and go without going through the working stiffs. The door set in the far wall no doubt led to Mr. Kemper's inner sanctum. He doubted he would get in there. He had run his share of the gauntlet and it appeared to be ending one room shy of the finish line. He imagined Kemper, as the boss, had at least two escape hatches to get out of here without engaging the minions, platinum or not.

Archer said, "The list? The one with the people's names who

might be behind the blackmail? It was supposed to be dropped off at our office, but it wasn't."

"Right, the list." He opened a drawer and rummaged through it while his gaze lifted to Archer's.

"Hard to see what you're looking for that way," noted Archer.

"What I'd like to know is what you've done so far. And where is Dash?"

"Thinking."

"And you're out what, running his errands?"

"Yeah, my next stop is for the sardines, crackers, and a bottle of Old Forester. You might want to come and join the party."

Sheen slammed shut the drawer without taking anything from it.

"We're paying your bill, Archer, so don't play it cute with me. I have neither the time nor the interest."

"Well, I'd like to have back the last two hours of my life, but that's apparently wishful thinking."

"We *are* busy here."

"Yeah, I saw the map out there. So, the list?"

"What have you done since we met earlier? Give me a report."

"Shouldn't I be talking to your boss?"

This comment made one of Sheen's eyes commence to twitch. "I am Mr. Kemper's authorized representative for all things."

"All things? That's pretty heady stuff. If I were you, I'm not sure I'd want all that responsibility. But to answer your question, we went to see Ruby Fraser."

Sheen sat up straight and gripped the front of his desk. "You did what?"

"She denies any affair happened, and also denies blackmailing Mr. Kemper. She could be lying, of course, and probably is."

"But if she denies it, that's good for us."

"Sure, why not."

"You don't sound convinced."

"Neither did she, if you get my drift."

"What else?" asked Sheen as he drummed his fingers on the desktop.

"We took a ride up into the foothills and saw Mrs. Kemper. Do you think she's intense, or was it just me?"

"Are you insane? Douglas will be furious."

"For the record, I'm not certain Mrs. Kemper shares Ruby Fraser's opinion that Ruby Fraser is not being diddled by her hubby."

"You are a crude man," he snapped.

"But?"

"But nothing, you are a crude and vulgar man. What else did Beth say?"

"She knows nothing about nothing and really wasn't interested."

Sheen nodded. "Well, that's good then."

"So that list?"

Sheen reached into his pocket, pulled out a piece of folded paper, and handed it across to Archer.

He unfolded it and looked at the list of names. "And there it was all the time in your pocket."

"Is there anything else?" Sheen said gruffly.

"Yeah, when do the girls out there knock off for the day? It's getting late."

"Why in the world do you care about that?"

"I don't, but it looks like they don't know, either. And they keep up that pace, they'll be dead by morning."

Sheen pointed to the other door. "You can leave this way."

"No thanks. I opt for public entrances and exits at all times. I find it safer."

Archer put the paper in his pocket and left.

He passed by Darling, who looked at him. "Good meeting?"

"The best. I might make it a habit. When do you all call it a day here?"

"When I say we do."

"Right. Okay, look me up some time. I'm over on Porter Street. We'll have a drink. Name's Archer, in case you forgot."

"Porter Street?" she said with a hiked brow.

"Yeah, it's on the *other* side of Sawyer Avenue. Do a border crossing some time. We don't bite, at least I don't."

"I doubt we will ever have a drink together, but I will have no trouble remembering your name."

"Oh yeah, why's that?"

She smirked. "You look to be a pretty decent shot."

"Then maybe we *will* have that drink together."

"What's your first name?"

"Aloysius. What's yours?"

"Well, Aloysius, mine is Wilma."

"Wilma Darling, has a ring to it."

"Archer, quit while your head's still above water."

He graced the woman with a smile and a tip of his fedora, before winking at the row of platinums. He got smiles back from half. He considered that his best odds since Reno.

30

THIS LOOKS LIKE A NICE PLACE. Are you sure you can afford it?"

Callahan glanced around the interior of the restaurant called Burbanks. It was all brick with a drive-through portico, white-jacketed and -gloved valets, gas lanterns providing flickering light, and a parking lot full of high-dollar cars. It was after seven and the place was packed with the well-heeled of Bay Town in all their glory.

"Not to worry. Remember, I'm a workingman now." He took out his PI license and held it out to her.

"Wow, Archer, this looks official and everything."

"Hey, if I needed you to vouch for me, sign a document saying I was okay in your book, would you do that?"

She handed the license back to him. "Why do you need me to do that?"

"Apparently, it's part of being an honest-to-God PI in California."

"But I thought you were already licensed. Isn't that what the card said?"

He slipped it back into his jacket. "It's sort of complicated, Liberty."

"Everything with you is sort of complicated."

"Look who's talking."

"Yeah, sure, I'll do it. Then maybe you can put in a good word for me with Warner Brothers," she quipped. "Now, let's go eat. I'm starving."

They walked arm in arm into the dining area, where they were met by the hostess, who was draped in a silky white number that fell off one shoulder and was barely clinging to the other. Her cleavage was so prominently revealed that even Callahan looked taken aback. The shimmery hostess glided through the sea of tables like a siren to a floundering ship as she led them to a private corner alcove with a built-in banquette seat. She positioned them side by side and looking out at their fellow diners.

She bent down and placed the menus in front of them, giving Archer another peek at her bosom. She whispered in a working-class British accent, "You look to me like a gent that doesn't like having his back exposed. Am I right, guv?"

Archer thanked her with a nod and she sashayed off for her next victims.

Archer eyed the drinks section of the menu and glanced at Callahan. She was dressed in a pale blue polyester skirt and jacket with black trimmings with a white blouse underneath and dress gloves. A hat with a short veil tacked up to the rim and black four-inch heels over sheer stockings completed her outfit. Every man in the room had given her the eye, even those there with other women seated across from them.

"What's your poison?" asked Archer.

"Champagne cocktail, for starters."

"Remember, we have to work tonight."

"You think a champagne cocktail is going to put me under the table, Archer? Where have you been since we met?"

The waitress came over, and Archer ordered the champagne cocktail for Callahan and a martini for himself.

"Bring the onions and hold the olives," he tacked on.

They pulled out their cigarettes and lit up, dropping ash into the bowl provided on their table.

"How'd you find this place?" she asked.

"Just looked west of Sawyer Avenue and there it was. Like shooting fish in a barrel."

"You talking code or something?"

"Or something."

Their drinks came and they toasted Archer's new job.

"So how did this afternoon go?" she asked. "Have you solved the case yet?"

"Not exactly. When I do you'll be the second to know, right after Willie Dash, unless he gets there first."

"So how's it going with him? You think you're going to learn a lot?"

"The guy's good, knows the town and the people in it. For the most part."

"What does that mean?"

"It means for the most part." He picked up the menu. "What looks good?"

"You order for me, Archer."

He shot a glance. "Really? Why's that?"

"I'm not used to nice places like this. In Reno, we just had crap, really."

"And you think *I'm* used to them?"

"No, I mean, I don't know. But you can tell the people in here are somebody. They have class. The men probably all went to college for an education, and the women probably all went to college to find a husband."

Archer eyed the woman closely because this was the first real hint of insecurity he had seen in her.

He tapped her hand. "You're as good as all of these people, Liberty, and don't think you're not."

"Sure, sure, Archer, and I'm the queen of England, too."

"Where is this coming from?" he asked. "Until we walked in here I never would have thought you had an ounce of self-doubt or gave a damn what anybody thought about you."

"Shows how good an observer you are."

"I guess," he said.

They both ended up with the trout, which was moist and tender. And rice pilaf and a green vegetable that was not readily identifiable to either of them. But it was good if oversalted. Their cocktails were followed by a bottle of wine, recommended by a short man wearing a bow tie and holding a cork opener on a chain. It cost three dollars, which almost gave Callahan a fit and amused Archer.

Archer examined the bottle's label. It had the silhouette of a woman on it that looked familiar to Archer. The wine was called the BK. On the back he read off the name of the vineyard that had produced it. "Kemper Enterprises. BK must stand for Beth Kemper."

Archer explained who she was and what they were investigating. "Her hubby has a vineyard and he named the wine after her."

"Well, wasn't that sweet? I guess the louse figures he owes her after cheating on her."

"Could be, yeah. Although I probably shouldn't have told you that, so keep it to yourself."

She gave him the eye. "Gee, what's it worth to you, Archer?"

"See, you keep charging and I keep retreating. Thing is, I don't want you to be disappointed. You have such a high opinion of me and everything."

"You're actually getting funnier, and I mean that."

They finished their meal, retrieved the Delahaye, and drove out of town toward Midnight Moods.

It was well dark now and cool enough to ride with the top up.

"No mountains, right?" said Callahan.

"Scout's honor."

"You were no Boy Scout."

"What do you have in that thing?"

She had earlier placed a small, hard-sided piece of luggage on the seat between them.

"*Things* for the job interview, Archer."

"Okay."

They reached Midnight Moods forty minutes later. It was very different from earlier in the day. The parking lot was packed, the façade of the building was ablaze in neon and spotlights, and the sounds inside reached all the way to the parking lot as they pulled in.

"Gee, this place is dead," said Callahan sarcastically.

He found a space in the back of the parking lot and Callahan grabbed her bag. They walked in and looked around. Mabel Dawson, now bedecked in a black sequined number with shoes that matched, greeted them at the door.

"Oh, the puppy dog came back," she said to Archer before giving Callahan the long eye. "And who is your friend?"

"Liberty Callahan," said Callahan, putting out her gloved hand. "Archer said you might be looking for some new girls."

"Is that right, Archer?"

"New blood," said Archer. "Can't hurt to take a look."

She turned to Callahan and gave her an even longer scrutiny. "So what's your shtick?"

"Singing, dancing, acting, skits. You name it, I can slot it. And that includes the fast hands and lousy stage timing from the guys."

Dawson pursed her lips and inched up her nose like a smell had come along she didn't care for. "You strike me as being *overly* confident."

Callahan put a hand on her hip and stuck it out wide like a door opening. "And you strike me as the sort that if I can't cut it here, you'll gladly throw me out on my very cute derriere."

Dawson lit a cigarette and blew a lungful of smoke at Archer. She eyed Callahan through the mist. "Sure, I'll see what you got. But if you get the gig, there's no drinking or drugging on company time. You're here, you serve the house. You get paid a salary. Tips are your business. Whatever else you can earn on your own time, that's your business, too."

"I've heard the song before."

Dawson eyed the bag. "Your working clothes in there? We got some of our own."

"But these show me off the way I like."

Dawson again blew a lungful of smoke at Archer. "You can really find them, Archer. And where's your gumshoe twin?"

"Thinking."

"Right." She looked at Callahan. "Okay, let's go back to the dressing room, and I can put you through your paces. Sound good?"

"You sure you can spare the time now? You look busy."

"I can teach a monkey to greet people at the door. And I'm not just saying that. I have. Shirley!" she called out.

A little minx with bushy red hair flew out of some hidey-hole like a mouse stirred by a cat's charge and stood cringing in front of her boss.

"Yes, Miss Dawson?"

"Take Archer here, get him a drink on the house, and find him a seat at the next show. I'll wait here until you get back, and then you got greeter duty for the next half hour." She glanced at Callahan and said in a syrupy tone, "That enough time for you, honey, or are you a slow starter?"

"That'll do," said Callahan.

"Where you coming in from?"

"Reno."

"Casinos?"

"Sort of."

"Well, don't 'sort of' perform for me or you *will* get tossed out on that very cute ass. And I'll be the one doing the tossing."

"Just so long as we know where we stand," retorted Callahan.

Dawson said, "Don't worry, Archer, I'll have her back to you in half an hour, one way or another."

Before Shirley led him away Archer said anxiously to Callahan, "Hey, you okay with this?"

She smiled. "Not only am I okay with it, Archer, I'm really looking forward to it."

31

SHIRLEY GOT ARCHER A GIN AND TONIC and settled him in the back row of a large theater where the dancing girls were in high gear, parading to music played on a baby grand set off to one side of the stage. The pianist was a man in a black tux with a pompadour hairdo, a waxed and curly-tipped mustache, and hands whizzing over the keys like skates over ice. He watched the girls high-kicking it across the stage in unison and seemed to be changing the music to fit the dancing instead of the other way around. All the girls were tall and long limbed, which to Archer made them look a lot like Callahan. He wondered if maybe the competition here was stiffer than in Reno. And he also wondered how her audition was going.

The theme was a patriotic one, as the skimpy outfits were embedded with red, white, and blue sparkles and the top hats were of the Uncle Sam vintage. The legs were encased in fishnets, the shoes were silver and sparkled like diamonds, and every man in the front row was getting an enhanced view with each kick of the long legs and the accompanying lift of the dancers' skirts. All included in the price of admission.

Twenty-eight minutes went by. Archer checked his timepiece and began to grow a bit anxious, as there was no sign of Callahan. *Had* she gotten thrown out?

And then around ten or so the curtains parted, and Archer stiffened and sat up straight as Callahan walked out onto the stage at the same time the sea of chorus girls scampered off. She was dressed in the outfit Archer had first seen her in at the Dancing Birds Café minus the six-foot feather. Every eye in the house was on her, including Archer's.

She walked over to the pianist, said something to him, quickly skimmed through his music, and tapped her finger against a piece.

Then she backed up to the piano, gripped the sides with both hands, and nimbly launched herself on top of it, sitting on her bottom. She crossed her legs and gave a nod to the pianist, and he started tickling the ivories with enthusiasm, perhaps as intrigued as the rest of them with this recent development.

When Callahan began to sing Archer felt chills run up and down his arms. The song was one he knew well.

"That Old Black Magic."

Archer had heard Glenn Miller and his band play that song when he was in London in 1944, after Archer had killed enough Germans to make any human sick of war. At the end of that year, Miller would die in a plane crash in the English Channel, but that night the man could do no wrong. The song had sent chills up him that night, too, but not like Callahan's rendition was doing to him.

In midsong she slunk off the piano and marched across the stage in full command of both it and the audience. As she reached the end of the song, she tipped her head back, showcasing that long, elegantly curved neck, and held the final note for a remarkable period. She then let it die elegantly in her throat, like a thunderstorm dwindling to a gentle rain shower. There was silence for what seemed the longest moment and then the cheers rained down. The crowd lurched as one to its feet and thunderous applause filled the room. Hats and flowers and cash were tossed on the stage along with probably a few business cards and maybe a stray engagement ring or two. Callahan picked up one long-stemmed rose, cuddled it to her bosom, and blew kisses at the audience as she walked offstage looking like she owned the place. And right then, Archer knew, she did.

He felt the tug on his arm. It was Shirley.

"This way," she whispered.

Shirley led him backstage, where Callahan was sipping a glass of champagne and Dawson was staring at her like she was a bundle of cash with Dawson's name on it. She looked at Archer as he walked up.

"Okay, she says you're her agent. How much is she going to cost me?"

Archer shot Callahan a glance as she finished her drink and set it down next to the long-stemmed rose. She hiked her plucked eyebrows and said, "How about it, Archer? What am I worth to a joint like this?"

He didn't hesitate. "Two hundred and fifty a week. And she gets Monday and Tuesday off. After six months we look at your books and see what bump in pay she deserves for bringing in new business."

"You're nuts," barked Dawson. "That's what some Hollywood actors make."

"Did you see the audience out there?" said Archer. "Because I did. You'll need to get a bigger room or squeeze in more seats if you bring her on full-time. And if the pie gets larger it's good for everybody."

Callahan looked impressed by this but said nothing.

Dawson glared at Archer, grabbed the bottle of champagne that was chilling in a bucket of ice, and swilled right from it. She pointed at Callahan. "I'll need you to start this Friday. Get here around five. We have big crowds on Fridays and then through the weekend, of course. And it'll still give us time to get some posters and billboards up. You're a real pro, so we don't need to prep that much. Hell, you could do what you did tonight and it'll bring the house down again. You can do a quick rehearsal with the full band. And we can select a rack of songs for you to move through. We might want to throw in some dance moves, too, nothing too complicated, but I saw how natural you were onstage, so you'll make it look easy. Then you can do your big debut."

"And what will the billboards say?" asked Archer.

"I don't think they need to say much. They'll just have her picture. I had Barry, our staff photographer, take some stills of Liberty. We'll blow them up and use them on the billboards."

"How about something like, 'If you liked Liberty Bonds, you're going to love *this* Liberty," suggested Archer.

"I like that, Archer, it's catchy," said Dawson, who then turned to Callahan. "So how about it?"

"I don't have a car to get here."

"That's not a problem, because all of our performers live here. We'll have a nice room for you."

"I can go for that," said Callahan.

Archer said, "But nicer than what I saw in Ruby Fraser's place. And not in the nosebleed seats."

"Okay, okay."

"And her own bathroom," added Archer.

"*I* don't even have that."

Archer said nothing.

"Okay, okay," said Dawson again. She glared at Callahan. "If only you weren't so damn talented, I'd throw the pair of you out."

Archer looked at Callahan. "Well? Your call, boss."

"Get the contract printed up and we're good to go," said Callahan.

Dawson put out a hand for Callahan to shake, which she did. "With the dough we'll be paying you, this is a full-time gig. Starting Saturday you come in at four sharp every day—" she glanced at Archer—"except Mondays and Tuesdays. You'll start with rehearsal, then eat your meal and do your acts, which will also include some freelancing and playing to the crowd, pictures and handshakes and the like. You'll do four to five official sets a night. But you work until we say stop, which is usually two-ish. Understood?"

"Sure."

Dawson gazed admiringly at her. "I have to admit, I thought you were going to fall flat on your face with your audition." She looked at Archer. "She sang 'Boogie Woogie Bugle Boy' for me. I think Patty Andrews would've been jealous."

"It's a crowd pleaser, Archer, and that's the business I'm in," said Callahan.

Her face was flushed with her triumph, and Archer had to admit it was a good look on the woman.

"Well, well, what's all the fuss here? Good tidings, I hope."

The tall man had appeared in the doorway.

Archer saw that Dawson's smile faded and her confident look eroded. She took a step back and stared at the floor.

"Hello, Mr. Armstrong, I didn't know you'd be here tonight."

Sawyer Armstrong stood an impressive six feet five. He was lanky and loose-jointed, with long white hair and a beard of the same color that dipped slightly off his lean face. His nose ran a long, crooked line down to nearly his top lip. He wore a brown slouch leather hat, dark denim pants, a white vest with a blue collared shirt under that, and a brown corduroy jacket with green elbow patches. His skin was weathered and tanned, and the man's features seemed carved with the most precise of instruments wielded by talented hands. The eyes were flints of blue surrounded by a sea of shimmering white. He sort of looked like Walt Whitman, thought Archer, that is, if Whitman had been a throat slitter instead of a poet.

Armstrong put out a hand to Archer. "I'm Sawyer Armstrong. I believe you've talked to my son-in-law, Mr. Archer."

Archer shook hands while casting a look behind Armstrong, where two bulky figures lurked in pinstripes with bulges at their chests where large weapons presumably perched.

"Nice to meet you, Mr. Armstrong, I've heard a lot about you."

"I'm sure you have, Archer. You saw my daughter as well, I heard."

"Your hearing is real good, then," said Callahan, drawing Armstrong's attention to her.

"And you are?"

"Liberty Callahan. I'm Archer's *best* friend. We came to town together. Miss Dawson just hired me to work here."

"Did she now?" said Armstrong.

Dawson glanced up, her face full of trepidation as Archer watched this exchange warily. He had never seen a person change so much as the woman had, and there must be good reason for it.

In a timid voice she said, "I did, Mr. Armstrong. She's quite good. I think she'll really bring in the crowds."

Armstrong studied Callahan for a moment before turning to Archer. "And how is Willie Dash doing?"

"He's fine."

Armstrong put out a thin, long-fingered hand and gripped Archer by the arm. "Let's have a chat, Archer. I have a private room here."

"You want some company, Archer?" said Callahan quickly and looking uneasily at him.

Armstrong answered. "I'm sorry, Liberty. Maybe another time."

Archer said, "I'll meet you back at the bar. We'll toast your new career."

Callahan gave him a half smile that sank off her face as quickly as a cement block dropped over the gunwale of a boat. "Sure, okay." She glanced behind Armstrong as the two men stepped forward. Both were as tall as Armstrong but far bulkier, and their faces held nothing approaching human. "I'll come looking for you if you're not there soon," she added.

Armstrong said, "Let's go, Archer."

The two sides of beef immediately stepped forward and marshaled Archer out.

Armstrong eyed the two women. "Mabel, we'll talk later."

"Yes sir."

He glanced at Callahan, who stared resolutely back at him. Then, without a word, he followed the others out.

32

THE ROOM WAS SMALL, DARK, AND LOCATED in the bowels of the place where, Archer presumed, only the rats typically lurked. He was feeling like a trapped one right now.

The single bulb illumination overhead gave him no comfort.

One of the men, on a sign from Armstrong, searched him, found the .38, pulled it out, and placed it on a table out of Archer's reach, before the other man pushed Archer into a chair.

Armstrong sat down in the only other chair in the room, which faced Archer. He glanced at the gun. "Going around armed already? Do you feel that necessary? Are we that dangerous in Bay Town?"

Archer glanced at the men. "And what do they have under their jackets? Lollipops?"

Armstrong lifted out paper and tobacco from a pouch taken from his jacket pocket, dexterously rolled a small cigarette, and lighted it with a match struck against the table.

"The best tobacco in Mississippi," he said in a soothing tone as he sucked in a throat full and then let it ease out into the small space. "Have it shipped in monthly. You should try it."

"Is there something you wanted to talk to me about?" said Archer. "Or am I supposed to just watch you smoke?"

This statement earned him a staggering blow on the side of the head from one of Armstrong's men that knocked him from his seat. The other man lifted him up and slammed Archer back into the chair.

Armstrong made a clucking sound. "Tony is overzealous sometimes in his loyalty to me, Archer, though I can hardly fault him. You understand loyalty, do you not?"

"When it's explained to me," said Archer, rubbing at his face. A searing pain went from his head to his toes, and the ringing in his ears made it impossible for him to hear the accelerated beats of his own heart.

"Well, I can provide that explanation, then," said Armstrong, scooching forward a bit on his chair. "First of all, loyalty starts at home. I have a daughter whom I cherish and a son-in-law whom I respect."

"Loyalty, okay, that's good to know. Thanks. Are we done here?"

The second blow caught Archer on the other side of the head, and he slumped out of his chair, groaning. When Tony went to pick him up, Archer caught him in the gut with a pinpoint uppercut, doubling the man over and causing him to stagger back and retch up whatever was in his stomach. It came out as a pink slop that hit the floor. The other man grabbed Archer around the neck, lifted him off the floor, and slammed him into the chair. Tony recovered and gave Archer punches in the neck and oblique while the other man held him in place.

"Enough," barked Armstrong, and the breathless men released Archer and stepped back. "Archer, if you wish to be beaten to death, then by all means carry on as you are. But I see no future in it for you."

Archer fought back the urge to vomit, as the pains continued to radiate from his head and now to his gut and back. With an effort he managed to sit up straight. He reached into his pocket and took a few moments to pull out a handkerchief, which he used to dab at his mouth. He bent down and picked up his hat from the floor and put it on. "So where do I come into all this?"

"You are investigating the allegations against Douglas?"

"On *his* behalf. Which makes me wonder what I'm doing here getting my ass kicked by these two gorillas."

"What will make me happy, Archer, is that you do not *ever* question my daughter again. You should not have questioned her in the first place. She is not party to anything that her husband may be involved in. Do you understand that?"

"Okay. Yeah."

"And this Ruby Fraser woman?"

"What about her?"

"Is she having an affair with Douglas?"

"He says not. And she says the same."

"And what do you say?"

"I don't know. But if I tell you my opinion, am I going to get slugged again? If so, I'd just prefer to lie."

Tony started to swing a fist at Archer, but he ducked out of the way, pivoted on the balls of his feet, came out of the chair, and struck the man flush on the chin with a thunderous blow. Tony staggered back and slammed into the wall. His eyes rolled back into his head and he slid down the wall, unconscious. His legs splayed out and his pants were edged up enough to reveal the tops of pale, hairy ankles.

The other man pulled a black, square-muzzled .45 automatic from his shoulder holster and took aim at Archer's right eye.

Armstrong said, "Put that away, Hank, and give Tony a nip from your flask to revive him unless you want to carry him out of here."

While Hank did this, Armstrong eyed Archer. "You pack a pretty big wallop. Good to know."

Archer held up the set of aluminum knuckles he had pulled from his pocket under the guise of getting his handkerchief. "Yeah, pretty big."

"But getting back to the issue. Your opinion?"

"I haven't looked into it enough to have an opinion. We only started the investigation today. But if you want a half-assed opinion, I'd say that there's some truth to it."

"But that truth does not have to come out?"

"We were hired by your son-in-law. I would imagine he gets our report and no one else. So I don't see that as a problem for him and his campaign for mayor."

"I don't know about that. But I do know this, Archer. Bay Town is a deceitful place with secrets. You'll find that out soon enough." He paused. "If you make it that long."

"I survived the war. I think I can get through this."

Armstrong shook his head. "Wars are straightforward. It's you against the men in the other uniform. There is no nuance, there is no need to think about what you need to do. Here, it is quite a different scenario. It's a chess match with no room for error."

"Yeah, when you say it that way, I can see how that might be. Thanks."

"What do you intend to do now?"

"Continue the investigation."

"And what course will it take?"

"I got a list of people to talk to from Wilson Sheen."

"May I see the list?"

"And if I refuse?"

"I can assure you that all of our myriad interests are aligned here, Archer." He glanced at Tony, who had come around with two pulls on the flask Hank had poured down his throat.

"But I *can't* guarantee that Tony over there will not be so upset at being sucker-punched by you with a pair of aluminum knuckles that he won't resort to drastic actions. I could be wrong, but I wouldn't bet *your* life on it. Would you?"

Archer took out the list and handed it across.

Armstrong put on a pair of delicate rimless glasses and read down the names. "Interesting." He handed the paper back and removed the specs. "Now let me be clear, Archer. We are at a crossroads here. Bay Town has unlimited potential, but so do lots of other places. If we do not seize the moment others will. And what will we be left with? Not much."

"What do you want me to do, Mr. Armstrong? I imagine you brought me down here to provide some instruction."

"Follow your instincts, Archer. Do your job. Finish your investigation."

"And if it comes back against your son-in-law?"

"I care enough about this town that it takes precedence over family."

"After all your talk of loyalty?"

"The ultimate loyalty is to put the interests of many above your own. And that includes family. If you take away any lesson from this painful episode, let it be that."

"The guy may be cheating on your beloved daughter. How do you respect that?"

"I have no reason to answer that, and I won't." He sat back, took off his hat, revealing unruly thick, white hair, and ran his hand through it. "I know you have a client already, but I will pay you as well, to follow the trail to the truth, wherever it might lie." He put his hat on, took out his wallet, and lifted from it a wad of cash. "How much?"

"You can take that up with Willie. But I'm not sure we can have two clients for the same case."

Armstrong put his wallet away but held out a fifty-dollar bill. "I *will* take it up with Willie. But take this in payment for your assorted injuries. I apologize if you are in real pain."

Archer made no move to take the money. "I'll wait to hear from Willie." He glanced at Tony. "And that guy doesn't hit hard enough to be worth fifty bucks."

This comment earned a murderous look from Tony.

Armstrong stuck the bill in his pocket. "I like you, Archer. I'm not exactly sure why, but I do. But then my opinion is not set in stone." His face went dark, and he stood and walked out. Tony and Hank glared at Archer for a moment, as though they were contemplating killing him and wondering what to do with the body. Finally, they followed their boss out.

Archer picked up his gun and put it back in the clip holster. He stood up slowly and stretched out his torso, gritting his teeth with the cascading pain.

He gingerly readjusted his hat, as though the weight of the fedora was too much for his injured head to bear. He wondered if his skull was fractured and when he went to bed tonight whether he would wake up in the morning.

He slowly walked out of the room and headed back up to the light of the real world and away from the rats.

But, instead, maybe he was heading right toward them.

33

Jesus, Archer, did they do that to you?"

Callahan was looking at the purplish bruises on Archer's neck and face as he slowly drained a whiskey sour and ran his tongue over his teeth to make certain they were all still there. He came away unsure.

He set the glass down on the bar. "No, I just fell off the roof of this place and landed on somebody's fist. And then I did it three more times."

"But why did they work you over?"

"I'm not sure I have a good answer for that. I'm not sure he did, either."

"Armstrong, you mean?"

Archer nodded and waved to the waitress for a second round. She obliged and he sipped this one slowly.

"Does it hurt much?"

"Only when I blink." He rubbed his side where he could feel the swelling. Tony was good, he knew just where to hit to hurt a man. He called the waitress and asked for some ice wrapped in a cloth.

The waitress said, "You don't look so good, mister. Were you in an accident?"

"There was nothing accidental about it."

When she brought the ice in the cloth he took turns holding it against his face and his neck and his side.

"Is that helping?" asked Callahan.

"I'll let you know next week."

Callahan said, "I'm not sure I want to work for a man who beats up my friend."

"Thanks for elevating me to the status of a friend. What's the next level after that?"

"Archer, you know what I mean."

"Yeah, sure. We're pals, always have been, always will be."

"You want me to massage where it hurts?"

"Don't get carried away with all this friendship talk, Liberty. You might start getting ideas, and then I might start getting ideas, and we might end up killing each other over all those ideas."

She pulled her stool closer and said, "I can't believe I actually got the job."

He gave her an incredulous glance. "That's not how you were acting. You seemed really sure of yourself, like you were a shoo-in once Dawson saw your stuff."

"Yeah, well, that was just talk. I do that to boost myself up. Inside, I was a wreck."

"Good to know that about you. Maybe I do the same."

"So do you want to head on back to town?"

"Not yet. You forgot the other reason we came here."

"What was that?"

"To talk to Ruby Fraser." He looked at his timepiece. "We missed her show. She might be up in her room. I know where it is, come on."

He stood and then staggered a bit. She grabbed hold of him.

"You sure you're up for this?"

"No, but I'm going to do it anyway because according to Sawyer Armstrong, I might not get another chance."

"Hey, why isn't that jerk Willie Dash out here helping you? What a bum."

"He's not a bum. He's also not a well man." He laid the ice and cloth on the table. "Now come on."

They headed up the stairs and reached the top floor, which was empty at this hour.

"How come she has to live all the way up here?" asked Callahan.

"This is the hired-help section. According to Mabel Dawson, girls here work their way down."

"Hey, do you think they expect me to live up here, too?"

"No, you'll get a palace with your own bathroom at sea level, remember?"

"Oh, right. Hey, how come you know so much about negotiating contracts?"

"I knew what Ruby Fraser was making here. I doubled that amount and added fifty on top for good measure, and nicer lodgings."

"Well, aren't you a smart one, but then you are a college boy."

"I studied prelaw in college. Even worked for a lawyer during the summer. Got to see the law up close and personal."

"So you wanted to be a lawyer."

He lit up a Lucky and blew out smoke. "I *was* a lawyer, of sorts. Back in Poca City."

"What'd you do there?"

"Kept myself from being hanged."

"That's funny, Archer."

"It wasn't funny at the time."

Archer led the way down the hall to Fraser's door. He knocked but no one answered.

"She doesn't seem to be here," said Callahan, staring at the door. "Maybe she's off doing another show. Like Dawson said, they keep performing until around two-ish."

Archer knocked harder. "Ruby, it's Archer. We need to talk."

There was still no answer.

He said, "We can look for her downstairs and then ask around. Maybe she's doing another number, like you said. But I'd like to leave a note inside her room."

He tried the door. It was unlocked. He pushed it open and walked in.

Callahan nervously followed. "Archer, I'm not sure we should be doing this."

"It'll be fine." Archer turned on a table lamp and took out his notepad and pen, only he found that in the skirmish with Hank and Tony, the point had been broken off his pen. "Check in the kitchen for something to write with. I'll look in the bedroom."

Archer walked into the tiny bedroom and noted that the bed was made, but the room was messy with clothes and shoes everywhere. He found a pen in the nightstand next to the Gideon Bible and had turned to leave when Callahan filled the doorway like a tsunami coming right for him. Her face was drained of all color and she looked like she might be sick.

"What is it?" he asked sharply.

She stepped aside and pointed to her left with one hand while holding her stomach with the other. "In there," she said, her voice brimming with dread.

Archer raced past her and into the kitchen.

The room was illuminated by a single overhead bulb. But Archer could see enough.

Ruby Fraser was all dressed up, probably for her big number tonight. She was sitting in a chair that was pushed back against the wall. Her head was slightly tilted back, her long legs splayed out in front of her, and the woman's wide eyes were full upon Archer. Still, she could not see him.

Ruby Fraser could no longer see anything.

He gingerly stepped forward and bent down so he could ascertain more closely what had killed her. It wasn't difficult. Her throat had been cut so brutally that he could glimpse white bone through the fresh opening. The cut disappeared around both sides of her neck and ran along the back to nearly her spine. Another six inches and she would have lost her head entirely.

The woman had not been killed here. There was no blood on the floor, table or walls, though the front of her dress was coated with it, transforming white to crimson.

He felt her wrist. It was ice cold. He checked his watch. It was ten to twelve. If she had done her show at ten, and it had taken a half hour or so, how could she be killed, moved, and cold as ice barely an hour or so later? He lifted her arm. It moved freely. He replaced it exactly where it was.

"Don't do that, Archer. Don't touch her, it's…not right."

He turned to see Callahan staring dully at the dead woman from the doorway.

"She was really pretty," said Callahan in a hushed voice. "And really young."

"Yeah, she was," said Archer, taking a few steps back.

"Poor kid. Who could have done this?"

"What I want to know is how could somebody move a dead body in here and nobody see it. The lack of blood shows she was killed somewhere else."

Callahan still looked like she might be sick. "What do we do now? Call the cops?"

"There's a phone booth right off the front entrance. I'll make the call from there."

"Will you tell the police who you are?"

"My morals say yes, my survival instinct says no."

"I always go with survival."

"Let's blow this joint before somebody sees us."

As they turned to leave, Archer looked back at Fraser and said quietly, "I'm sorry, Ruby. Nobody deserves to go out like that."

Before they left, Archer took out a handkerchief and rubbed at all the places they had touched, including the doorknobs.

"What are you doing?" asked Callahan.

"Getting rid of our fingerprints."

"What for?"

"Because in the state of California they can send you to the gas chamber, that's what for."

34

Archer stepped into the phone booth, dropped in a coin, covered the receiver with his handkerchief, and dialed in the number for the police he'd found in the phone book dangling from a chain on the booth's inner wall. When the voice came on the line, Archer told the person about the body at Midnight Moods, giving the room location. He hung up, put his handkerchief away, and stepped out, pale and aching from his earlier beating.

Callahan was standing next to the booth and watching him carefully. "Well?"

"A radio patrol car should be here shortly."

"And where will we be? Long gone from here, I hope."

"Give me a minute. I want to check something."

"What?"

"Something that's bugging me timing wise."

They found Mabel Dawson in her office. She looked up from her desk where she was writing something on a piece of paper.

"I don't have the contract ready yet, Archer. I'm talking to the lawyer tomorrow, so just hold your horses. And we don't advance money on any contract, if that's what you're thinking."

"No, it wasn't that. I wanted to speak with Ruby Fraser. Do you know where she might be? I've been looking around but no one's seen her."

She put her pen down and frowned. "Now I'm really starting to get worried. She didn't turn up for her show tonight."

"She didn't?"

"You know she didn't."

He shot Callahan a glance. "How would I know that?" said Archer.

Dawson rubbed her forehead. "Oh, I'm sorry, I guess you wouldn't know. Well, it was because Liberty took Ruby's slot. That's why I had her go out onstage tonight. I mean, why'd you think I'd do something like that?"

"Wait a minute, you mean to tell me that Liberty sang *in place* of Ruby?"

"Yes. It was the only thing I could think of. I didn't have anybody else worth anything to stand in for her. Ruby has good pipes, but nothing like Liberty, so I told Liberty to go out onstage to Michael, he's the pianist, and find a song she knew. And that's what she did."

"I thought you were just putting me on the spot to test me," said Callahan.

"Well, maybe there was a little bit of that, but the main thing was I needed a singer to cover for Ruby."

"Did anyone check her room?" asked Archer slowly as he inwardly cringed at the mention of Fraser's "pipes."

"Yeah. I did before I made the decision to use Liberty."

"What time?"

"I got a message from the stage manager right after Liberty finished her audition that Ruby hadn't turned up for her warmup. So I went looking for her, starting with her room. The door was locked but I have a key. I thought maybe she was sick or had overslept or something. I went in. But there was no one there."

Archer glanced at Callahan once more. "And no one had seen her?"

"No. I thought she might have gone off somewhere with someone and left me in the lurch."

"Why would you think that?" asked Archer in a sharp tone.

Dawson looked at him warily. "No reason, Archer."

"Come on, Mabel, we're all friends here."

"Ruby liked men."

"Any men in particular?"

"Rich men," said Dawson.

"Okay, I guess that narrows it down. Any rich man in particular?"

"You're the gumshoe, I'll let you figure that out." She sat back, a look of clarity spreading over her features. "So that's why you were out earlier talking to her. It was about some man she might be seeing."

"It might have been. So what's the deal with Sawyer Armstrong?"

She eyed his damaged face and then ran her gaze over his stiffened posture. "Maybe I should be asking you the same thing."

"I understand he built this place."

"Before the war started."

"Is Armstrong married?"

"What do you care?"

"I'm just trying to get some information. That's what private detectives do."

"His wife, Eleanor, died in a plane crash a couple years ago."

"Do you know Beth Kemper or her husband?"

She laughed. "I don't move in those sorts of exalted circles."

"I understand that Douglas Kemper comes here to play cards. And maybe for other things?"

"Maybe *you* understand that. I don't."

"Meaning?"

"Meaning I'm not getting involved. If you have any other questions, ask somebody else."

"Okay. Well, if Ruby turns up, let her know that I want to talk to her."

Dawson looked at Callahan. "Don't be late on Friday, Liberty. We need to sign your deal and get things sorted out."

They left, got into the Delahaye, and were driving out when the first patrol car came flying up the road and passed them heading to the entrance. As they made their way down the road, two more prowlers sailed past them, their lights flinging away the gloomy darkness and their sirens cutting through the sounds of the breakers off in the distance.

"What now, Archer?" said Callahan.

"Now we go back to the boardinghouse."

"You want to go get a drink?"

"No, I've had enough."

"Okay, I guess I can understand that. I just feel bad leaving her there like that."

He gripped her shoulder. "Get that out of your mind. And don't slip up if anybody asks you, Liberty. We didn't go up there and we didn't see anything. You got that square?"

"Sure, Archer, sure."

"Because if the police start asking questions and you mess up, we're both in trouble. Big trouble."

They rode the rest of the way back in silence.

35

A DISTRAUGHT CALLAHAN HAD GONE to her room, and Archer to his. He got undressed and climbed into bed, but he couldn't sleep. He felt that if he closed his eyes, they wouldn't reopen. And his whole body ached even more.

It was nearly two in the morning now, but he rose, padded down to the bath, and splashed cold water on his face and neck. He went back to his room, slipped on the same clothes, and laced up his shoes. He opened the window and looked out. Even from the other side of Sawyer Avenue, he could hear the beat of the ocean, smell its pungent scent, and feel the mist from the marine fog that chilled him to the bone and made his injuries more painful still.

He pulled his PI license from his jacket pocket and looked at it.

Though it looked official and important, it represented nothing to him, really, because he'd done nothing to earn it. This could have been handed out to any Tom, Dick, or Harry.

Or Aloysius.

He was a shamus solely under the auspices of Willie Dash. Anyone could be under the *auspices*. It was like hitching a ride in someone's car and then claiming you owned it.

He pulled his pocket flask, and, despite telling Callahan he'd had his fill, he took several swallows of rye whiskey, which flamed his already inflamed body. It felt good, as though it was fire of his own making, and not a by-product of another's man angry attack.

He closed the window and went downstairs as quietly as he could. He had no desire to run into Callahan or anyone else. But that desire was to be defeated.

In the front room Madame Genevieve sat in an upholstered chair wearing a thick woolen robe and frayed white slippers. She was nursing what looked like a hot toddy in a clear glass mug with a handle. Her hair was mostly hidden under an old-fashioned cloth sleeping bonnet. Her ankles protruded from the robe and were bony and the color of the dead.

She looked up at him. "You cannot sleep, Mr. Archer?"

He leaned against the stair post and shook his head. "Might just be the new place."

"Your 'friend' does not appear to have that difficulty. I passed her door earlier and heard the snores. Soft but still audible."

"Well, she had a big night. We both did." Archer sat down in a chair across from her. "So what are you doing up? Can't sleep either?"

"I like this time of night. There is no one around and it is quiet. I can think. But I can also open the window and I can hear the water speaking to me. I can smell it. I can let it embrace me like a shroud."

"How many of those drinks have you had?" Archer said with a grin.

"It is not alcohol that speaks, Mr. Archer."

"What then?"

"Perhaps it is the wisdom of an old woman who has seen much. Perhaps too much." She cradled her drink. "What are you really doing in Bay Town?"

"Got a job. I'm a private eye. Working for Willie Dash. You know him?"

"I've seen the billboards. And do you like being a private investigator?"

He shrugged. "Haven't been doing it long enough to really

know. But it has its good points and bad points." He rubbed his neck. "I saw the bad points a few hours ago." He looked down at his shoes. "Look, you know anything about Sawyer Armstrong? Or Beth and Douglas Kemper?"

"Everyone in Bay Town knows of them."

"But you don't *know* them?"

"I don't know them, not really." She said these words as though they were distasteful lingering in her mouth for even a moment.

"You trying to tell me something? If so, I'd prefer if you just say it."

"I will not say anything of the sort. I live here. I have a business here that I need to operate in order to survive."

"We have the right to speak our minds in this country."

She glanced dourly at him. "Free speech is not really free if it costs you all that you have."

"Care to elaborate?"

She shook her head and held the glass against her withered cheek.

"Douglas Kemper is running for mayor," said Archer.

"I know."

"Thinking of voting for him, or for the dentist he's running against, Alfred Drake?"

"I haven't thought much about it, quite frankly. I liked our last mayor."

Archer perked up. "And who was that?"

"Benjamin Smalls. He was honest. He did right by the people."

"Why isn't he running again, then?"

"He died while in office, just a month ago. The upcoming election is a *special* election. The winner will finish out Smalls's term, which is three more years."

Archer squinted at her. "How'd he die?"

"They say he drowned in his bathtub."

"They *say*? You don't know for sure?"

"I don't know for sure, because the police don't know for sure.

No one apparently knows for sure. They only thing they know for sure is that Benjamin Smalls is dead."

"People *do* drown in their bathtubs."

"Yes, I suppose they do."

"I guess maybe he was old, or drunk."

She rose, went over to a bureau, opened the drawer, and took out a framed photo. "This is Benjamin Smalls. He was thirty-five and a teetotaler."

Archer looked at the photo that was signed to her and studied Smalls. He was tall, with slicked-back dark hair parted on the side. He had a dimple under his chin that must have been annoying to shave. He also had nice, comely features and wore a white linen suit with a Panama hat held in one hand. This was actually the second time he had seen a picture of the man.

"That photo was taken last year, when he won reelection."

"Maybe he died of a seizure, then, or a heart attack."

"The police could find no evidence of that."

Archer pulled out a Lucky and lit up, catching the ash in his hand. "You seem to think there was more to it."

"You're a private eye, maybe you should turn your 'eye' to that."

"I think I have enough on my plate."

She shrugged. "Why do you want to know about Armstrong and the Kempers?"

"Something to do with my investigation."

"Then I would be careful if I were you. Very careful."

"I'm starting to figure that out." He didn't think she could see the bruises on his face and neck in the dim light, but maybe she had better vision than he was giving her credit for. "I might go for a stroll. Is it safe out there at night?"

"Is anywhere safe at night, Mr. Archer?"

He tipped his hat and left her there with her toddy and her moody introspection.

Outside, he headed toward Sawyer Avenue, lighting another

cigarette on the way and feeling for the gun in the belt holster. Its presence lifted his spirits considerably. And if he ran into Tony or Hank again, he planned to shoot first and ask not a single question later.

There was no one out and about that he could see. All shops were closed at this hour, even the ones that, when open, catered solely to the baser pleasures of its patrons. A sliver of moon crept out from behind the clouds and cast a delicate glow over Bay Town.

A prowler slowly pulled up to him; he tipped his hat to the officer who stared suspiciously at him from the passenger seat. Archer tried to remain calm, but his aching body was stiffening all over with anxiety, and for an obvious reason.

Could this be about Ruby Fraser? Could they be here to arrest me?

"Everything okay, bub?" asked the cop, giving Archer a once-over.

"Yes sir, officer. Just got into town and couldn't sleep. Thought I'd walk around and get the lay of the land."

The cop at the wheel leaned forward so as to be in Archer's line of vision.

"That wouldn't include casing any joints, would it?" But he smiled to show he was kidding.

"Only the best liquor joints. But that can wait until the sun comes up," he said, grinning back, but his heart beat even harder.

They drove off and he picked up his pace.

He wondered how many cops were up at Midnight Moods right now. Maybe every one of them besides those two yokels.

Crossing Sawyer Avenue, he turned away from the fancy areas of furs and teas and Bentleys and headed to the working-class wharf. He wanted to hear the breakers better and smell the salt air with more vigor. He had no idea why, he just did. Maybe it would help him not to think of dead Ruby.

He reached the wharf after a brisk walk of fifteen minutes, during which he saw not another soul, or another car, prowler or not. Bay Town was clearly bedded down for the night.

He walked along the pier and finally settled on a bench built into the wooden wall there and which looked directly out to sea. The territory of Hawaii was out there, he knew, thousands of miles away. And beyond that, and more thousands of ocean miles, was Japan, which was still no doubt licking its war wounds after having two atom bombs dropped on it four years ago. Archer was just glad he hadn't had to fight his way to mainland Japan. He'd had enough of war to last him forever. Any man who had seen and done what he had would feel the same way. And if they didn't there was something wrong with them that nothing could fix except copious amounts of booze. He figured if Prohibition were still in place after the war, America would be no more. They would have rolled up the carpet and headed for Europe, where a man could get a decent shot of booze and a kind word from a woman at any time of the day or night.

The breakwater built out parallel to the land was made of enormous boulders which, like an iceberg, was just the tip of the rock out there. He sat staring at the jetty and the moored boats bobbing slightly, and worked through two more cigarettes and half his flask while he listened to the waves leisurely hitting the rocks and let the salt air carve his insides smooth.

The moon cast finger shadows over the water. The Pacific was basically flat and calm, the air not moving much, no storm clouds overhead to cause trouble. He might just sit here until sunrise and surprise the longshoremen and fishermen on their way to work. He closed his eyes and let his thoughts wander.

A few minutes later he opened them, and his thoughts focused on one thing. It was constant and perfectly replicated, meaning it was mechanical. As he continued to listen and watch, the motorboat came into view. There was a spotlight deployed on its bow, and the light gashed over the water as it tried to discern solids from fluids. As it came more fully into view and passed the breakwater, and started navigating through the minefield of moored boats, he could see that it was about twenty-five feet long and there were a number of people on board. It veered southward as it approached the pier and ran parallel to it for about two hundred yards, until it was well away from the port operations.

A minute before this, Archer had taken to his heels and was jogging along in that direction. He reached a spot where he took up position behind a waist-high wall and eyed the boat as it docked at a pier.

Two men got off and secured the boat's lines to the dock cleats. Then the bow light was extinguished and more people got off. Archer continued to watch as they walked toward the lot adjacent to where Archer was hidden. He sank lower, turned his head, and saw two vehicles parked there.

As the men drew closer to the cars, another automobile came down the wharf road, turned, and pulled into the parking lot. Due to the thrust and reach of its headlights, the group from the boat was fully revealed to him.

The tall figure of Sawyer Armstrong was prominent among them, as were his two goons, Tony and Hank.

And there were three other men that Archer didn't recognize.

The car pulled to a stop but kept on its headlights. Stepping out of the car was another person that Archer did know.

Beth Kemper hurried over to her father, and they held a quick and apparently heated conversation, at least by their body language, because Archer could hear none of it. The brief meeting ended with Armstrong and his group climbing into the two cars and driving off, leaving Kemper alone.

Archer saw the dot of flame emerge as the woman lit a cigarette and leaned against her car, which he now recognized as the little Triumph Roadster convertible he'd seen back at the Kemper estate. The woman stared out at the ocean and smoked her cigarette while Archer continued to watch and contemplated what to do. Part of him wanted to approach her, see what was going on. But his professional instincts—such that he had—told him that would be the wrong move, for any number of reasons. If he did that and she told her father that Archer had seen them come in on the boat from God knew where in the middle of the night, Archer figured he would get another visit from Tony and Hank, and it would be his last visit with anyone ever. His final resting place might be the very same ocean Beth Kemper was staring at, with cement shoes encasing his feet as he sank to the bottom to realize his new destiny as plankton.

She dropped her finished cigarette and scrunched it flat with the heel of her shoe, then got into her car and drove slowly off. Archer swiftly moved after the convertible. He knew full well there was no way he could really follow her on foot if she sped up and vanished from sight. Fortunately, she didn't go far. As Archer trotted along behind, she drove only three blocks before she parked the car at the curb and got out. Two motorcycles, one with a sidecar, were pulled up on the pavement in front.

Archer eyed the twenty-four-hour sign of the restaurant as she walked in.

He waited for a few minutes and followed.

36

Aʀᴄʜᴇʀ sᴛᴏᴏᴅ ɪɴ ᴛʜᴇ ᴅᴏᴏʀᴡᴀʏ of the hole-in-the-wall diner. Its yellow, pebbled floors were sticky linoleum, its booths shiny red vinyl, its tabletops slapdash laminate of no memorable design, and its walls painted a sea-foam green with the overhead whirly fans moving at the pace of a man with nowhere to go. There was a jukebox, but it was as dark and silent as the night.

There were three other customers in the place besides Beth Kemper. All three were around nineteen or twenty, and all were clustered around her booth, apparently giving the lady trouble, while a flustered waitress in her forties hovered nearby, looking uncertain as to what to do.

Archer heard one of the young men, tall and pudgy with a crew cut and muscled arms and shoulders showing under his T-shirt, say, "Hey, baby, we got some gin back at our place. You need to join us. Good times, sugar doll, good times."

His skinny, acned friend laughed and parroted, "Good times, sugar doll."

"Sure like to see your gams without anything on 'em," said Crew Cut. "Bet they're a knockout, like you."

The third man was lean and lanky, had dark, greased hair, and wore denim jeans stiff as a two-by-four, scuffed black motorcycle boots, and a brown leather bomber jacket; the fanned-out top half of a switchblade stuck out of his rear pants pocket like a cobra's head.

Kemper, for her part, was smoking another cigarette and looking extremely bored. She seemed to perk up when she saw Archer coming.

"Mrs. Kemper?" said Archer, walking over.

All of the men turned to eye him, and there wasn't a friendly look in the bunch, which was no surprise, thought Archer. What guy liked his crude lovemaking interrupted?

Crew Cut said, "Hey, Bud, we're having a talk with the lady here, so take a powder."

Archer drew closer. "That's funny. I have a scheduled meeting with the 'lady.'"

"Scram," said Switchblade, transferring an unlit cigarette from between his lips to behind his right ear, as though that movement constituted a plain threat.

Archer moved closer while Kemper continued to eye him with interest. "Don't make this difficult, boys," he said.

Crew Cut seemed to take this reference personally because he shoved Acne aside and said, "Who you calling a boy, mac?"

Archer looked around and shrugged. "We seem to be the only males here, so I'll leave it to you to figure out."

Kemper snorted at that one, which only made Crew Cut angrier. "You know him?" he demanded, wheeling around on Kemper.

She smiled benignly and waved her cigarette smoke away from her. "Not as much as I'd like to."

Confused by this, Crew Cut turned and shot Switchblade a glance along with a jerk of the head in Archer's direction that could not have been clearer.

Archer sighed. If he had a sawbuck for every time he'd seen that same look communicated in that same clumsy fashion.

Switchblade went for his knife, but before he could open the blade, Archer laid him out with a punch so hard, it knocked him into the next booth. He lay there, his nose bloody, a tooth wobbly, and his mind crushed into unconsciousness.

Crew Cut screamed profanities and drew a fist back. Archer swept aside the front of his jacket where the .38 sat prominently. Crew Cut froze.

Archer said, "You want to see my credentials now, or wait until after you get booked for harassing this lady and trying to have your buddy knife me?"

Acne said fearfully, "Y-you're…a cop, mister?"

Archer didn't even bother to look at him. He kept his gaze on Crew Cut with his fist still cocked. "In the meantime, unless you want your parents to have to spend their hard-earned money bailing you 'boys' out, grab your friend, throw some cold water on his face, get on your tricycles out there…and beat it. Now!"

Crew Cut and Acne grabbed their knocked-out chum and slid him out the door. About thirty seconds later Archer heard the bikes fire up. He went to the door and watched them ride off. Switchblade was slumped in the sidecar, as both bikes disappeared into the night with their owners' egos tucked between their legs.

The waitress said, "Gee, thanks, mister. They've been nothing but trouble all night."

"No problem. Can I get a cup of joe? Rumbling punks is thirsty work."

"Coming right up. And it's on the house."

She went off to get the coffee while Archer walked back over to the booth shaking out his achy hand.

"Mrs. Kemper," he said again.

She looked up at him, her expression one of intrigue.

"Mr. Archer, why don't you join me for our *scheduled* meeting?"

He slid into the booth, took off his hat, and set it next to him.

"That was impressive. And I so like to see a man enjoy his work."

He ran his eye over her. She was dressed far more casually than last time. Flared white pants with black buttons on the side, a checkered cotton shirt in blue and gold, a kerchief at her neck, and a fitted dark blue jacket over both. And a pair of gold hoops graced her delicately lovely ears.

"Surprised to see you here."

"As I am seeing you." She tapped ash into the ashtray. "I hope you haven't been following me," she said with enough behind it to put Archer on his guard.

"Following you?" he said with feigned incredulity that he hoped was genuine enough to carry away her suspicions. "That's your car outside. I recognized it from my visit to your house. If I'd been following you, you would have either seen my headlights, since there are no other cars out there, or heard my car. Did you hear a car behind you?"

"No, I didn't."

"I walked here from my place over on Porter. Asked my landlady for a place to eat. I woke up in the middle of the night all hungry. Turns out she's a night owl. She recommended here."

"Porter Street. Why didn't you drive?"

"Because I wanted to walk and smoke. And it's not that far. Your trip here was a lot farther. Must be tough navigating those switchbacks in the dark and the fog."

He pulled the ashtray closer, lit up, and tapped ash into it as his coffee arrived. It was hot and good.

"What, no notepad to write down my answers?" she said mockingly as the waitress departed.

"I'm off duty."

"I didn't come from my home," said Kemper.

"Really, where then?"

"That's no concern of yours."

"You're right, it's not."

"I spoke to my father. Have you heard the news?"

He exhaled smoke and shook his head. "What news?"

"There was a murder."

Archer furrowed his brow and said sharply, "A murder? Where?"

"At Midnight Moods."

"Hell, I was there last night, meaning about five hours ago. Went there with a friend who was auditioning for a job. Who got killed?"

"Ruby Fraser."

Archer let his jaw go slack and he laid his smoke on the lip of the ashtray before clasping his hands on the table and assuming what he hoped was a judicious look. "*The* Ruby Fraser?"

"Yes, the same one you were asking me about yesterday."

"How did she die?"

"My father didn't say."

"When was she killed?"

She spread her hands and shook her head.

"Who killed her?" he persisted.

"Apparently, no one knows."

"Where exactly was she found?" Archer was asking all the questions he would have asked of someone else if he hadn't known what had happened.

"I think in her room."

"How come your father knows all those details?"

She gazed at his injuries. "Come on, Mr. Archer, don't play me for a dope. You ran into my father there. And your *face* ran into the fists of two of his thugs."

Archer rubbed his bruises. "And did he tell you why that happened?"

"He told you to stop bothering me."

"Let's hope he doesn't walk in the door here, then. I might not get out alive."

"Don't make jokes like that."

"Why? Does your old man have a habit of knocking people off?"

"I'm not going to dignify that with an answer."

"I was surprised to learn he owned Midnight Moods."

She gave him a hard look. "He owns most of the town, so stop being surprised."

"Your husband is giving him a run for his money, though. A winery, the fancy-schmancy Mayport Hotel, a country club on the water. He runs a very efficient office. I met Wilma Darling. She could have been a ship's captain two hundred years ago. There never would have been even a hint of a mutiny with her at the helm. I don't know why he needs Sheen around with that gal on the job."

"You know, I've wondered that myself." She took a sip of her coffee and took out a fresh cigarette. Archer pulled out a match, struck it against the side of the table, and leaned over to light her smoke. She lightly cupped his hand while he did so.

They moved apart, their gazes averted after the intimacy of the subtle embrace. Archer dropped the spent match into the ashtray and waited.

"Where is Mr. Dash, by the way?"

"I hope asleep in bed. Why does your husband even want to be mayor?"

"Did you ask him?"

"I'm asking you."

"Afraid I can't help you there. I haven't asked him, either."

"Could it be your father's doing?"

"In what way?"

"Get your husband into the mayor's office. Help out his business interests."

"I'm not sure my father needs help in that regard."

"Did you know Benjamin Smalls?" Archer asked abruptly.

"Why do you ask?" she said warily.

"I saw his picture on the table in your library. It was signed, 'To Beth, All my best wishes, Ben.' It was right next to Jimmy Stewart's mug."

"I knew Ben, yes."

"He died about a month ago?"

"That's right. He drowned in his tub."

"So everyone keeps saying."

"What does that mean?"

"It means that's what everyone keeps saying."

"You don't believe it?"

"Well, I wasn't there to see it for myself."

"You don't accept things as facts unless you see them? You've got a long road ahead of you."

"How'd you know him?"

"Ben's father, Andrew, was partners with my father. He's dead now."

"I thought the Armstrong family had plenty of dough to do what they wanted."

"Andrew was a state senator and thus was very well connected in Sacramento."

"But he's dead?"

"He killed himself."

"How?" asked a startled Archer.

"They found him hanging in his barn."

She dipped her head and wouldn't look at him. She drew down thoughtfully on her cigarette. "With Ruby Fraser dead, things get complicated for you, don't they?"

Archer said, "I think they get complicated for a lot of people, you included."

"Me? What makes you say that?"

"Your hubby was maybe having an affair with her. And maybe you knew about it. That's what they call a prime motive. Have the cops been by to see you?"

"*Maybe* I have an alibi, or didn't I tell you?"

"How can you have an alibi when no one knows when she was killed?"

"Apparently, the police have a time *window*. I was at a dinner party from five in the evening until after midnight. In fact, I left for it right after you and your colleague finished interrogating me."

"Not right after, because you changed clothes. You had on a dress before, not pants."

"I went to the party in my dress. You don't wear an outfit like this to a dinner party. I changed into these clothes afterward."

"Did your father tell you about the time window?"

"I don't remember who did."

"And if your father did know, *how* would he know?"

"He has a direct line to the chief of police. They're old friends."

"And what's his name?"

"Carl Pickett."

"If the dinner party ended at midnight, what did you do between leaving there and coming here?"

"I went to a place with the thought of going to bed and then decided I wanted to get out. I like the coffee here."

"What place did you go to with the thought of going to bed?"

"It's here in town. I've owned it since before I was married. It's my little hidey-hole."

"Over ninety-nine percent of all dirty laundry gets lost in them."

She puffed on her cigarette. "What a wonderfully lurid imagination you have."

"When you were deciding to go to bed were you alone?"

"Don't get cute, it's not a good look for you."

"Yeah, I've heard that line before."

She stubbed out her smoke in the ashtray. "It really was quite masterful how you handled those men. Three against one."

"I probably could have huffed and puffed and blew them all into the Pacific from here." He tapped out his smoke, too. "Does your husband have an alibi for tonight?"

"I don't know. I haven't seen him."

"Does he have a hidey-hole in town, too?"

"I wouldn't know."

He cocked his head as he peered at her. "Why do you put up with it? They have divorce in California, I take it."

"It's not as easy as you might imagine."

"If you can prove he two-timed you, Mrs. Kemper, you can get a divorce."

"Maybe I like my life how it is. He goes his way and I go mine. How would divorce change that?"

"If you're okay with it, who am I to judge?"

"But you will anyway."

"Nah, I'm too busy. Besides, he must have some feelings for you."

"What makes you say that?" she said quickly. Her features tightened, and the look on her face was, at least to Archer's mind, caught between hopeful and hopeless.

"I saw a bottle of his wine. The BK. Stands for 'Beth Kemper,' right?"

Her features relaxed and all the light went out of her eyes. "Wrong, it stands for '*Best* Kemper.'"

He studied her closely before saying, "Sorry. My mistake."

"Yes, it is." She rose and looked down at him. "Do you need a lift back to where you're staying on dear old Porter Street?"

"Your Triumph's not very big, Mrs. Kemper. Things might get pretty tight in there."

"Make it Beth. And don't you know? Wonderful things come in small packages."

37

"Have you always lived in Bay Town?" asked Archer as Beth Kemper started the Triumph and pulled out from the curb. He had helped her put the top down because it was such a fine night.

The wind whipped Kemper's hair, and a few errant strands landed across Archer's face. *Lilac*, he thought as he leaned away from its clutches.

"Yes. My father was born here. His family's been here for generations."

"Willie Dash mentioned something about the cattle business from a long time ago."

"My grandfather, Atticus, raised and sold cattle, as did his father before him and so on and so on. Then he started investing in real estate, among other things. My father took over the family business when Atticus died. This was a long time ago. My grandfather died before I was even born. That's when my father and Andrew Smalls started working together. My mother, Eleanor, was born and raised in Seattle, but her family moved here when she was a teenager. She and my father met here and got married."

"I understand she died in a plane crash. Was it a passenger airliner?"

In a somber tone, Kemper said, "No, it was her plane. She was a licensed pilot."

"Female pilot? That's pretty nifty."

Kemper smiled sadly. "I used to go up with her all the time. My father was quite a bit older than she was. She had me when she was twenty-one. I couldn't imagine having a baby of my own at that age. She volunteered to fly during World War II, but they said she was too old. She was really upset about that. She used to be a barnstormer and trick pilot in the 1920s. She was really amazing."

"So what happened?"

"We don't know. It was a terrible accident. She was flying in her plane, a Stearman 75. It was a military trainer plane, but after the war they were sold to civilians and my mother bought one. She named it...she named it Elizabeth, after me, her only child."

"She must have loved you very much," observed Archer quietly.

She shot him a glance as though to check whether he was being sincere or not. "No more than I did her. Anyway, it was a two-seater single prop biplane. She could make it do anything she wanted. I was supposed to go up with her that day. It was beautifully clear, but Douglas had arranged a luncheon with some important clients and insisted that I be there. So, my mother went up...all alone."

She slowed the Triumph and put a trembling hand to her face. "It's been two years. You'd think I would have gotten past this."

"It's okay," said Archer. "I don't think you ever get past it." He pulled out his flask and handed it to her. "Rye whiskey always works for me."

She took a sip and let it go down very slow. She handed back the flask. "Thank you. That *does* do the trick."

The smell of the ocean hit them as they rounded a curve and the Pacific came into view. The breakers were rolling in hard and grinding the sand into even smaller particles.

"Did you learn how to fly?" he asked.

"No, I don't like to fly, really. In fact, I only flew with her."

"What about your husband? You said he was a pilot."

"After the war, he said he never wanted to get in another

airplane. He was shot down, landed in the Pacific, and floated in a raft for two weeks before being rescued."

"I had some 'plane' trouble in the war, too."

"But with my mother in the cockpit I was never worried or anxious. She would do barrel rolls and loop-the-loops and dives, and I would be screaming and laughing at the same time. It was the most exhilarating…the most…" She stopped and looked at Archer, her cheeks flushed. "I don't usually go on and on like that with someone I barely know."

"Yeah, I saw that personality trait the first time we met. But this is the second time, so there's that."

She smiled. "Are you going to make me change my opinion of you, Archer?"

"Oh, let's hope it doesn't come to that."

She laughed.

"But not being a pilot, there was nothing you could have done to save your mother that day, if that's what's hanging around your neck. You both would have died."

Her laugh died in her throat and her face flamed. She snapped, "You don't know that. You have no way of knowing that. You couldn't—"

He interjected. "I spent three years in Europe playing the what-if game. If I had only heard the sound a second later, or aimed a little less sharply, or turned left instead of right, I'd be dead instead of the other guy. It can eat you up, if you let it. So don't let it eat you up. From what you've said about your mother, she wouldn't have wanted that for you."

She slowed the car again and looked at him. And this time it seemed to Archer that Beth Kemper was actually seeing him for the very first time. "I…I didn't expect such nuance from you, Archer."

"I almost never expect it from myself. Sometimes it just pops out all by its lonesome."

She smiled and dabbed at her eye with her knuckle. She glanced to her left, toward the ocean. "She crashed about two miles off the coast. They found the wreckage the next day. People saw the plane just go into a dive. She never parachuted out. I guess she didn't have time. She wasn't flying that high."

"I'm really sorry, Beth."

"The news reached me when we got home from the luncheon. I...I couldn't believe it, not at first. They never did find her body. The water is very deep out there. And undercurrents are very fast." She hit the gas and they sped up. "And from that moment on my marriage seemed more a burden than a blessing."

"I doubt your husband wanted anything to happen to your mother."

"They got along all right, actually. More than Douglas and my father do."

"But your husband must owe a lot to your father. I mean, it must have helped his business prospects to have Sawyer Armstrong as his father-in-law."

"I believe Douglas thinks he's paid back any debt in spades. And maybe he has."

"How long have you two been married?"

"Nearly eight years. I met Douglas while I was in college. It *seemed* like a perfect match. We married after I graduated."

"Any kids running around?"

"No, Douglas...No. We don't plan to have a family."

"You're still young if you change your mind."

"That won't be happening."

She said nothing else, and Archer could think of nothing else to say, so they rode the rest of the way with only the Triumph's engine noise in their ears. When they reached Porter Street and the boardinghouse, Archer climbed out and tipped his hat.

"Thanks for the ride."

"I don't make it to this side of Sawyer Ave much. It's nice."

"You don't have to say that to make me feel better. I don't have a horse in that race."

"What will you do now?"

"Sleep. Then I'll hook up with Willie Dash and see where we go from there. He might not know about Ruby Fraser."

"This blackmail scheme. Was she involved in it?"

"She said not, but who knows?"

"But with her dead, does that mean the blackmail plan will fall apart?"

"You would think so, but honestly, my gut tells me no."

"You follow your gut?"

"It usually points me in the right direction. And I haven't found anything better, yet."

"Well, maybe I should follow my gut more. Good night, Archer."

"Good night, Beth."

She pulled off and he watched the little Triumph spurt along, and her long hair trailing out with the car's wake, until it turned at an intersection and she disappeared. Maybe back safely on the other side of Sawyer Avenue to her hidey-hole, where she would go to bed alone or with someone else. Or maybe the lady was going to go all the way back up the mountain and lose herself in her gated estate built by Daddy with the letter *A* all over the place to remind her—and, maybe more important, her hubby—that it wasn't really theirs.

Archer went to his room and wrote everything down he could remember about their conversation. Then he quickly undressed and got into bed in his skivvies and with his socks still on. He slept like a dead man for more than eight hours and awoke with bright afternoon sunlight dipping its toe into his room.

Shit.

He jumped out of bed, put on his robe, and headed to the communal bath at the end of the hall with his soap, scrubber, and shave kit. The water was lukewarm, and by the smell of it he wasn't sure it wasn't being piped in directly from the ocean. He dried off, combed his wet hair, and shaved in the humidity of the tiny room, where he had to keep rubbing the fog off the round mirror. Finished, he put his robe back on, and opened the door to find Callahan standing there in a sheer black number and white fluffy slippers and holding a shower cap and a scrub brush, along with a small leather toiletry kit.

"Wow, you're up bright and early, Archer," she said sarcastically.

"Look who's talking."

She rubbed his jaw with her hand. "You're all nice and clean and shaved."

"And a little salty, yeah."

"Where were you last night?"

"In bed."

She lightly slapped that shaved jaw. "Don't lie to me. You went out."

"How do you know that?"

"I got eyes and ears. And I saw you come back with the little dish in the convertible in the middle of the night like Cinderella getting dumped from the pumpkin."

"That little dish is Beth Kemper, the wife of my client."

"So why are you out with her in the middle of the night and not your client?"

"It's a long story."

"You couldn't sleep?"

"Not after what happened, no. But I understood you were sleeping like a baby."

"I was, until I wasn't. Are you *sleeping* with her, Archer?"

"I don't sleep with married women, even unhappily married ones."

"Says you, chump. And as a reminder, I'm not married and I'm happy as a clam."

She used her hip to bump him out of the doorway and she closed the door in his face.

He walked back to his room and dressed meticulously, down to his pocket square. He put his PI license in his jacket pocket, clipped the .38 to his belt, and drove out to the same diner near the wharf where they served breakfast all day. He ordered coffee and two over-easy eggs with crispy bacon, toast, and orange juice, which he knew they made in California in abundance.

He laid out the map of Bay Town on the table and started going over it. But this time with a different focus. He was looking at the water instead of the land.

He didn't know how far out Armstrong had gone in the boat, but common sense told him it couldn't have been too far. They sure weren't going to Hawaii in a boat that size.

His breakfast came and he ate and drank while he studied the map.

"What are you doing, Mr. Archer?"

He turned to see Madame Genevieve standing next to him clutching a sack about the size of his old Army duffel.

"Just learning more about the town. What are you doing here?"

She held up the sack. "I was at the dock buying fish for dinner tonight from a vendor and saw you through the window." She sat down across from him. "You know, for two dollars more per day you get breakfast and supper at my place. I make a better breakfast than they do here. And I get my fish fresh for dinner, as I just told you."

He lit a cigarette and nodded. "Thanks, I'll sure keep that in mind." He glanced at the map and then back at her. "Hey, how well do you know this area?"

"What do you want to know?"

He stabbed the Pacific with his finger. "What's off the coast here that a person could get to relatively fast by boat? I know about the northern and southern Channel Islands. Anacapa is the closest to the coast but it's still about twelve miles out and over an hour by boat. And it's about an hour-and-a-half boat ride to Santa

Cruz. The others are a lot farther out, up to seventy miles or so. Anything closer than that?"

Madame Genevieve studied the map for a few moments. "I do remember hearing about an island that was built about three miles out, so you could get there in about fifteen or twenty minutes in a fast boat depending on the sea conditions."

He looked at her strangely as his smoke dangled from his mouth. "Wait a sec, you said an island that was *built*?"

"During the war the military took over the Channel Islands, but they needed more capacity for some sort of special work. There was a very shallow spot about three miles directly out from here, where the land was just at the surface. The military built upon that base of earth to make a new island there."

"Who owns that piece of rock now?"

"I suppose the military still does. Why all the interest?"

"Just curious."

"I suppose all good private eyes are."

"We can assume that, yeah."

"Where did you go last night?"

"Just out for a walk. Found this place and had some coffee."

"And now you go to work as a detective?"

"That's right. A very tardy detective." He folded up his map and put it in his pocket. "See you later."

He put down money for his meal, tipped his hat, and left.

She watched him every step of the way.

38

Hᴇʏ, sʜᴀᴍᴜs, ʜᴏᴡ's ɪᴛ ɢᴏɪɴɢ?" said Earl as Archer stepped into the elevator car.

"It's going faster than I thought."

"Got you a juicy murder to work on?" said the little man as he closed the gate and hit the button for the fourth floor. He had on his uniform with the shirt untucked, and Archer spied a half-empty bottle of Southern Comfort tucked behind his fold-up seat.

"Why do you say that?"

Earl cackled. "Afternoon edition of the *Gazette*. Gal killed at Midnight Moods. You working on that?"

"It's confidential."

"Yeah, I thought so, all right. Now, don't you go get sliced and diced, Archer. Lotta that going around, it seems."

"I'll do my best."

The car clanked to a stop and he got off. He looked back to see Earl leaning out of the car and watching him like Archer was about to combust and the man didn't want to miss the spectacle.

Connie Morrison looked up from her desk as Archer walked into the office of Willie Dash, Very Private Investigations.

"Hey, sorry I'm late, Connie, I—"

She interrupted. "Willie is in his office. He wants to see you. Right now."

Her tone was a bit severe and her tight hair bun pulled her eyes back to such a degree that Archer wasn't sure if she was glaring at him or merely reacting to the pressure on her hair.

"Everything okay?" said Archer.

"Just go see him, Archer."

Archer hooked his hat on the wall peg, buttoned his suit jacket, and rapped on Dash's door.

"Come," said the voice.

He opened the door and walked in.

Dash was behind his desk, his jacket off and his sleeves rolled up to his elbows. His black toupee lay next to him, its wisps of hair sticking up like the man's finger had met a light socket while he was wearing it.

He took off his steel-rimmed spectacles and eyed Archer.

"Grab a seat, Archer, and let me finish this letter for Connie to get out."

Archer sat and waited patiently while Dash's ballpoint skated in cursive across the paper. Done, Dash rose, left the room with the paper, and came back a minute later without it. He was in his socks. Archer looked around the room for the bottle of Beam but didn't see it. The wall bed was nestled all snug up in the wall. He looked at Dash's eyes and saw not a trace of drunken red.

Dash sat down and eyed Archer right back.

"No, I did not sleep here, and no, I have not been hitting the bottle. And, yes, I know my toupee looks like a Sherman tank ran over it. Fact is, it blew off and landed in a ditch where a squirrel decided it was his new best friend."

"Keen eye, Willie. Sherlock Holmes has nothing on you."

Dash adjusted his plastic suspenders, smoothed down his shirt, and glanced at his watch. "You have a funny idea of a workday."

"I know, I'm sorry. But I was out really late doing some sleuthing." He paused and then let loose with his changeup pitch. "Ruby Fraser is dead."

"Yeah, I heard."

Archer looked deflated. "Okay."

"And you and your friend were at Midnight Moods last night?"

"How'd you hear about that?"

"I hear lots of things, Archer. What were you doing there?"

"My friend was auditioning for a job, which she got. And I went there to talk to Ruby again. I planned to have a second go at her. And when I got back here yesterday, Connie had my ticket ready and said I was to basically have at it, that you trusted me. Was she selling me a line or what?"

"Connie doesn't sell lines. So just drop the hurt-feelings crap, compose yourself, and tell me what you did after we parted ways yesterday."

Archer went through the whole gambit, from A to Z. Going to see Sheen and getting the list of names from him. Driving to Midnight Moods with Callahan. And then Archer got around to telling Dash about finding Fraser.

"So you walked in and there she was, dead?"

"And then I phoned the cops from the lobby, without identifying myself."

"You might have put you, me, and this agency in jeopardy, Archer."

"So you would have volunteered your name to the cops?"

"No, I'm not saying that. But did anyone see you and the lady go in or out? Because if they did, you two might be looking down the barrel of a murder charge, or at the very least intent to obstruct a police investigation."

"I don't see how I obstructed anything. But for me, they would've found Fraser a lot later than they did."

Dash stroked his chin. "What you say makes perfect sense, only some coppers have never quite grasped that concept. So you found Fraser dead, but no sign of anyone having been in her place."

"Right."

"Okay, you called the cops. Then what?"

"I went back to the boardinghouse where I'm staying."

"And then?"

"I went to sleep."

"I thought you said you had a late night. Hell, when I was your age, late to me was the next morning. But you got up and came here in the *afternoon*? So that was what, about thirteen hours' worth of shut-eye?"

Dash stopped talking and eyeballed him in a way that was making Archer wish he'd driven through Bay Town and kept going right into the ocean.

"Before you say anything, Archer, keep in mind that if you lie to me, and I'll know if you are, you're fired."

"I couldn't sleep. I went for a walk and ended up at a diner, where I saw Mrs. Kemper."

"What time was this?"

"Around three in the morning."

"What was Beth Kemper doing at a diner at three a.m.?"

"Having a cup of coffee and a cigarette. She said she has a place to stay in town, had it before she was married. So I don't think she went back up the mountain last night."

"How did you get home? Walk?"

"She gave me a lift. Let me check my notes." He pulled out his pad and consulted the pages, while Dash watched him with grudging approval.

"She said her old man told her about Ruby. I told her she might be a suspect, since Fraser might have been sleeping with her husband and they might assume she knew about it. But she said she had an alibi."

"What was it?" asked Dash sharply.

"She was at dinner with friends from five to midnight. She wouldn't tell me who with. She doesn't know where her husband was during that time. When I went over to his office to get the list, I don't think he was there."

"You found Ruby's body when exactly?"

"Ten minutes to twelve. I looked at my watch. One more thing—Ruby died from someone almost cutting her head off. But there was no blood around the body."

"Meaning she was killed elsewhere. Did you check out her rooms?"

"There was nothing anywhere. So she was killed somewhere else and her body carried to her room. Tell me how the hell does somebody not see that."

Dash took this all in and then focused on Archer's facial injuries. "Who beat you up?"

"Right. Forgot about that. Armstrong's boys did the pummeling. He was at Midnight Moods. He wanted to hire us to find out the truth behind the blackmail. I told him I'd have to take that up with you and that we already had a client paying us for pretty much the same thing. He didn't like it that we went to talk to his daughter. He made me show him the list of suspects I got from Wilson Sheen. And maybe I said some things they didn't like, and fists started flying and we got into it."

"For starters, Archer, Douglas Kemper did not hire us to find the truth. I'm not sure what he did hire us to do, but I'm certain it wasn't that."

"Okay, but I also told Beth that her husband would be a suspect. She didn't know if he had an alibi or not."

"Oh, so it's *Beth* now?"

"We had a cup of coffee last night. I saved her from a trio of punks. She was grateful."

"I bet she was. Only you don't want that kind of gratitude. And how does anyone know they have an alibi if no one knows when the woman was killed?"

"Beth said the police do. Her old man told her so."

"Sawyer Armstrong told her when? You found the body at 11:50. You called the cops. They came while you hightailed it.

You said Beth was at a dinner until midnight. Then she left, went somewhere, and then ended up in the diner at three a.m. So when did Armstrong tell her? And when and how did *he* find out?"

Despite the risk, Archer could not bring himself to tell Dash about seeing Kemper and her father together down near the wharf, when Sawyer Armstrong might very well have told his daughter about Ruby Fraser. "I don't know. Maybe he phoned her. And she said he's friends with Carl Pickett, the chief of police."

Dash sat back and mulled over this. "That could be. Carl Pickett is as big a brown-noser as they come. But why would he give Armstrong the heads-up about Ruby?"

"He might if he knew there was a connection between Ruby and Douglas Kemper."

Dash put out a hand. "Let me see the list Wilson Sheen gave you."

Archer handed it across, and Dash ran his eye down the page.

"I don't see much here, Archer. Looks to me more like a keep-us-busy list."

"So they want to keep us busy so we won't look where we're really supposed to look? This is a funny town."

"And getting funnier by the minute. Let's take a walk."

39

THE SUN WAS SHINING, and the breakers could be clearly heard. What looked to be a golden eagle soared above them with dizzying grace and power, while a black and white osprey spread its wings in another part of the sky and abruptly changed its vector to the oceanside as the bird no doubt went in search of lunch.

Dash had glued on his toupee before topping it with his hat. They walked for quite a few blocks in silence. One of Dash's shoes became untied as they crossed Sawyer Avenue and turned down De la Guerra Street. Dash stopped and bent down to lace it back up. Cars passed them and ladies window-shopping graced them with smiles, even as a beggar rumbled through in his near rags, hat in hand, to see what he could get from the women.

What he got were stern looks, tosses of hatted, refined heads, and sharp waves away. He headed toward Archer with not a hopeful look. Archer handed him a half dollar and the gent ambled on with a smile.

"Booze, you know," said Dash.

"Let's be optimistic. Maybe some soup. Surprised to see him on the rich side of town."

"He's doing what we're doing: following the money. You read up on this place before you came here, Archer?"

"Not really."

"A good shamus needs to know the lay of the land, the people who matter here. And I don't mean that everybody doesn't matter, but the way the world works there are two kinds of people: those with money and/or power, and those with neither one. And those with money and power have one thing in common: They can never get enough of either one."

"Okay."

"The Chumash people were here before any white folks. They had villages all over. This was hundreds and hundreds of years ago, you understand. Then the Spaniards came along in the 1700s to settle the area and to also fortify it. They tried to convert the Chumash to worship God; not sure how well that worked out. But what the Spaniards brought was smallpox and that came real close to wiping out the Chumash. So I guess if you can't convert 'em, you can kill 'em.

"After that the Mexicans came along and knocked out the Spanish, and their flag flew over this town but not for very long. That's why you have the street names you do here. Like the one we're on, De la Guerra, and then there's Carrillo, Torres, Alonso, Hernandez, Navarro, Gonzalez, the list goes on and on."

"But not the most important one, namely, Sawyer," said Archer.

"Right. Here's how that came about. The Mexican governors gave out land grants to prominent folks around here, like the Armstrongs. They did it to make them loyal and to cultivate allies. That's when the 'rancho period' started here. And those ranchos were used for cattle raising. And then they'd ship the cattle out for slaughter and the meat went all over."

"Beth said her grandfather, Atticus, was in that business. And she also said he got out and went into real estate. And you mentioned that the Armstrongs got out of the cattle business before it all went to hell. What happened?"

"A drought is what happened, Archer, like nobody'd ever seen before. And cows drink a lot of water. Now, Bay Town and Santa Barbara and other places in the region fell to the Americans when

John C. Frémont came calling with a bunch of armed soldiers. A peace treaty was signed, and this was no longer Mexican dirt. It was a dangerous place back in the Gold Rush days. Every sort of criminal type headed this way before the gold petered out. Then the Armstrong Wharf was built in the early 1900s, and that made Bay Town both a commercial and tourist town. Then the railroad came along and connected us to San Fran to the north and the City of Angels to the south. Now all things are in place for the town to really take off."

"Armstrong Wharf, huh?"

"Atticus Armstrong built it and Sawyer made a lot of improvements to it, bringing in new cranes and warehouse space. Everybody in town knows who they owe for that."

"How'd they make their money after the cattle business died?"

"Let's just say the Armstrong family knew how to relieve men of their dollars, whether it be by gambling, women, whiskey, or the long barrel of a gun. Then they discovered oil and gas out there in the bay. You can see the derricks pumping and you got the drilling operations down near the pier."

"Do the Armstrongs own that, too?"

"They have their fingers in every pie, Archer."

Archer looked out toward the water and thought back to the night before with Sawyer Armstrong in that boat. "So the point of the history lesson?"

"If you know the history of a place, you're not doomed to repeat the mistakes of others who came before you, Archer."

"And what mistakes are those?"

"Thinking you can hobnob with the likes of *Beth* Kemper and get away unscathed. You can't. And you won't. And I didn't get you that damn PI license just to see you end up in the ocean where the water's over your head." He looked at Archer's injuries. "It won't be bruises next time, it'll be something more permanent."

Archer kept his gaze on that very same water. "What's this I hear about some island out there the military built and now owns?"

"Who told you about that?"

"I forget. But what's the deal?"

"It's a chunk of rock with no more purpose in life."

"Okay. *Mrs. Kemper* told me about her mother's plane crash."

Dash's manner grew subdued. "Yeah, Eleanor Armstrong was a fine woman. Tragic accident."

"Her body was never recovered?"

"The wreckage was, but no, she wasn't. There are sharks out there, Archer. And other sea critters that just look at a body as a meal."

"And what caused the crash?"

"Some folks said they heard the engine cut off and the plane went into a dive. She never had a chance."

"I guess Sawyer Armstrong was real cut up about that."

"I'm not sure that man has the emotions of a regular person, Archer. But for now, we have a case to work."

"Well, if the list Sheen gave us is crap, what do we do?"

"We focus on Ruby Fraser. Which means we need to go have a chat with the police."

"Your buddy, Carl Pickett?"

"I never said we were buddies, Archer, did I?"

40

THE BAY TOWN POLICE STATION WAS LOCATED in a large one-story, cream-colored stucco building with thick, curved orange terra-cotta roof tiles to keep out the rain and enough wrought iron railing to keep the blast furnaces in Pittsburgh in business.

Archer noted the four prowlers slant-parked out front and the string of uniformed cops in their dark blue uniforms, chest straps, big, holstered revolvers, black boots, and crisp short-brimmed caps who lurked near the entrance. Two motorcycle officers were astride their Harley-Davidsons and passing the time with two young, pretty women in dark skirts, tight blouses, and high heels.

Dash led him inside to the front desk, where a burly man about six-four with shoulders as wide as a doorway and sergeant stripes down his sleeve sat in front of the large duty book in which he was carefully marking entries in pen.

"Steve Prichard," said Dash. "Long time, no see."

Prichard looked up, and his expression told Archer that the cop would have preferred the *no see* part going on indefinitely.

"What do you want, Dash?"

Dash smiled. "Is Carl in?"

"No."

Dash's smile broadened. "No really, or just not for me?"

"There's been a murder, or maybe you hadn't heard," growled Prichard, taking a look at Archer and coming away unimpressed. "Fresh meat, Willie? This one looks underfed."

"He's okay. And that murder is why we're here," said Dash.

Prichard perked up at this. "Is that so? What's your interest?"

"I'd rather talk to Carl about that. Professional courtesy, you understand."

"He's up at Midnight Moods looking into it. That's where the dame was killed."

"All right. Guess we'll take a ride over there." He hooked a thumb at Archer. "And this *is* my new associate, Archer."

"Who cares?" Prichard said, turning back to the pages of the duty book.

Archer looked over the man's shoulder and saw two photos on the wall. One was of President Harry Truman. And for the other he had to read the name on a brass plate at the bottom.

Governor Earl Warren.

As they walked out of the police station, Archer commented, "Boy, Willie, you got them wrapped around your little finger in that place."

"Let's go get that car of yours and take a run over to Midnight Moods."

"Is Pickett any friendlier to you than Prichard was?"

"Oh, me and Steve Prichard are good buddies. Play cards once a week over hooch and cigars, and spin tales about women we took to bed, none of which are true."

"Then I wouldn't want to see how he acts around somebody he *doesn't* like."

"I'm joshing you, Archer. He's my friend like Hitler was Roosevelt's. Same with Pickett."

"Okay."

"And unlike Armstrong's cronies, Big Steve hits where it doesn't show. He got more confessions that way than any cop on the force. And if you were colored or Mexican, you usually didn't live long enough to sign that confession."

"And they let him get away with that?"

"Get away with it? It's in the playbook, Archer. Big Steve just does it better than anyone else. Hell, son, didn't they teach you anything in prison?"

On the drive over to Midnight Moods, Dash patted the door of the Delahaye. "Now this is a fine machine, Archer. Puts a spring in my step just riding in it."

"Glad I could do that for you. What do you hope to accomplish at Midnight Moods?"

"I want to get in to see Ruby's room. Then I want to talk to folks who might have seen something last night. We need to narrow the time window down, to see who might be suspects and who might not."

"I guess they'll do an autopsy on her body."

"Yes, they will. I know the county coroner, Mortimer Wallace. He's a good man."

"Is he a doctor?"

"No, but he owns a funeral home and he's got experience doing the cutting. From what you told me it doesn't sound like the cause of death will be a tough one here."

"But can he tell us *when* she died?"

"Within reasonable parameters, Archer. It won't be to the minute. But we spoke with Ruby earlier that day. Other people will have seen her after we did. We can narrow it down that way if Mortimer can't be real specific. It's the only way we check alibis. Now, how long do you reckon she was dead when you saw her?"

"She was cold."

"How about her arms? Starting to get stiff yet?"

"No. They were soft as putty."

"So no rigor mortis then." He eyed Archer. "Body starts to get all stiff after death. But it takes a while for it to happen. Then you can't bend an arm or leg without breaking bones."

"Well, I can tell you she wasn't in rigor mortis then. Nowhere close."

Dash snapped his fingers. "Wait a minute, when was her act last night?"

"Oh, I forgot to tell you. She didn't show up for it, so my friend did the singing instead."

"What time was she supposed to be on again?"

"Ten. The thing is, Mabel Dawson said they went to look for Ruby but she wasn't in her room. This was probably around nine thirty or so."

"Okay. So she was somewhere else getting murdered."

"Seems like it."

"Who's your friend again?"

"Liberty Callahan. She drove with me from Reno. She's a singer and a dancer. Wants to be an actress in Hollywood."

"Her and every other dame. Think she's got a shot?"

"If anyone does, yeah."

When they reached Midnight Moods, two prowlers and a Chrysler as big as a tank were parked together next to the front entrance.

"That green Chrysler Town and Country belongs to Pickett," said Dash as they passed by it. "Small dick, big car. I've found that to be far more accurate than the weather forecast."

"Does he usually go out to all the murders?"

"Damn, Archer, how many homicides do you think we have around here?"

"I don't know. I was in a little town in the middle of nowhere and we had three in a matter of a few days."

"You weren't responsible for any of them, were you?"

"Only one, but it was self-defense."

Dash stopped and eyed him. "Well, well, am I going to have to reconsider my opinion of you, Archer?"

"Depends on whether that opinion will get better or worse if you do."

"You keep surprising me, Archer, you surely do."

"Is that good?"

"I'll let you know."

They ducked inside to see a lawman.

41

Lordy, lordy, look what just rolled in off the trash pile. I thought you was dead and buried, Willie boy."

The speaker was big, a slab of sloppy meat with thick legs and a square head stuck on either end. A cap of sweaty iron-gray hair hung limply on a scalp mottled with sunspots that spilled down to his forehead like tiny, irregular copper pennies. His brown suit had walked out of the 1930s in decent shape, but the decade tacked on to that journey had rendered it as limp and irrelevant as a politician's promise.

"Well, hello, Carl," said Dash, removing his hat. "Funny seeing you here."

Carl Pickett tugged a toothpick out of the gap between his front teeth and scrunched his nose back like a dog does before he takes a bite out of your leg.

"That's *Chief* Pickett to you."

"Okay, *Chief* Pickett, how goes it?"

Pickett glanced over at two men dressed more slickly than he was, but their youthful countenances together didn't relay a significant thought between them. They stood there, their hats tipped back on low foreheads and their elbows on the front desk, behind which Mabel Dawson stood. The woman looked like if a gun were handy they would all be heading to see the coroner for a final checkup.

Pickett said, "Boys, this is the mighty Willie Dash. You might 'a seen his billboards all over town. His hair wasn't that dark ten years ago. He must 'a stumbled on the fountain 'a youth, right, Willie?"

Pickett stuck the toothpick back in the slot and waited.

Willie looked at Dawson. "I'm truly sorry for your loss, Mabel. What a tragedy."

She sniffled and looked down at some papers lying in front of her. "Thank you."

Dash turned to Pickett. "So we came to get up to speed on the Fraser murder, poke around, ask our questions. I'm sure you have no problem with that."

Pickett rolled the toothpick out of the gap to the right side of his mouth and then to the left and all the time he was staring at Dash like the man could not have said what he just had.

"What you can do is turn around and march your fat ass right outta here, Dash. And take your little boy with you. This ain't amateur hour."

"Do I take that as a no to my request?"

"You can take it anyways you want, so long as you shove it sideways up where the sun don't shine."

The twin gumshoes thought this was mightily funny and yo-deled over it long enough to where Pickett finally had to shoot them a glance to silence the forced merriment.

Dash took his time edging up to Pickett, like a snake drawing mesmerizingly close to its prey. "A very important man in town has engaged me and my associate to look into this matter, *Chief* Pickett. But not to worry if you got a problem with that. Hey, Mabel, let me borrow your phone, hon, I got a call to make."

The toothpick froze right under Pickett's left incisor as he took a moment to process this new development.

"Bullshit," he said.

"Right, Mabel, just pass it to me, thanks."

She handed the phone across and Dash picked up the receiver and dialed a string of numbers from memory with Pickett watching. Finally, on the fifth number dialed, the police chief stuck his finger in a digit hole to prevent the dial from rotating back to where it had started, effectively stopping the call.

Dash looked up at him and smiled. "So you know Sawyer Armstrong's number by heart, too. How fascinating."

"What do you want?"

"I have already relayed my request."

"What's your interest in this?"

"My interest is my client's."

"Sawyer Armstrong really is your client?"

"You know I can't divulge that."

"You already did, asshole."

"Maybe, maybe not."

Pickett eyed Archer. "Who the hell are you?"

"Archer."

"Is that your name or occupation, dipshit?"

"Both, depending on the need."

Pickett leaned back against the counter and assumed a friendlier expression. "Yeah, go on ahead, Willie. I remember when you used to know what you were doing. Before the bottle kicked in. Worst thing you ever did was marry Connie. She cut your balls right off."

Dash put the phone receiver back in its cradle. "We're divorced."

"Yeah, right. You see her every day, I'm told."

"Well, thanks for keeping such a watchful eye on me, Chief. It's much appreciated."

"Uh-huh. Run along, you damn gumshoe, before I change my mind."

"I suppose you got uniforms up there?"

"And a suit, too. Just tell 'em I said it was okay. You can still spook people, Willie, and good for you. And if it gets real queer, just throw that rug you're wearing at 'em. They might think it's a skunk and run for it."

"And the body is still there? It's been quite a few hours."

"Mortimer was out of town. Didn't get here till a bit ago. So hold your noses, gents. The lady don't smell too good."

Dash eyed Dawson, who let out a sob at this insensitive remark. He gestured for her to follow them.

The three headed down the hallway. Dawson looked distraught and was blowing her nose into a hanky. She wore a long, dark blue silk robe that fit her like a bulky potato sack with no potatoes in it.

"I still can't believe it," said Dawson. "I mean, she was so young." She shot Dash a sudden look. "But you were here talking to her yesterday. Something's up. And she was killed for it, right?" she added in an accusatory tone.

"Well, you came out of your grieving at full stride," noted Archer.

She glared at him. "I don't take crap from anybody, especially men."

"Now, just calm down, Mabel," said Dash soothingly. "And tell us what you know as we head on up there."

"I can't see that body. I can't see it again. The cops made me identify her. Oh my God, I've never—"

"You won't have to. So tell me about last night, okay?"

"Like I told Archer here, Ruby didn't show up to do her act. I had his friend Liberty Callahan sing in her stead. We had looked everywhere for the girl. I mean everywhere, and then—"

"Yeah, so just slow down right there," said Dash. "Because this is important. When did you last see Ruby yesterday?"

"Cops asked me that. It was around eight o'clock. She came to get dinner. We have a separate room for the staff to eat their meals."

"Did you talk to her then?"

"No. I was just finishing up my meal with somebody."

"Pretty late for dinner," noted Archer.

"This place gets rocking later. We're usually not even a quarter full until nine. It is called *Midnight* Moods, after all."

"What time do you close?" asked Archer.

"We don't officially, but most people are gone by three a.m."

"Jeez, don't people sleep around here?" said Archer.

Dash interjected, "Did she seem upset? Was she alone?"

"No and yes."

They headed up the stairs.

"When did you know something was wrong?"

"When the cops showed up after midnight. They came tearing in here saying they got a phone call about a dead woman, Ruby Fraser."

Dash didn't look at Archer when she said this, and Archer kept his eyes on a spot on the ceiling.

"Then what?"

"They asked me where the body was. Hell, I didn't know anything about a body. So I took them up to her room. That's when they found her, and then made me take a look." She shuddered. "I know there are evil people in this world and maybe I've run into more than my share of them. But what they did to that poor girl...that takes the cake."

"Funny way to say it, but I get your meaning," said Dash. "Then what?"

"Then all hell broke loose. People running around, cops everywhere. And then, like the chief said, the coroner showed up a bit ago to tell us what we already knew about poor Ruby."

"I understand Sawyer Armstrong was here last night with two of his boys."

Dawson shot a glance at Archer and his injuries. "He might've been, yeah."

"He was," said Archer.

"Okay, he was."

"Why was he here other than to paint Archer's face purple and yellow?" Dash asked.

"He owns the place. He can come and go when he damn well likes."

"You ever see him with Ruby?"

"No, never," she said quickly.

"So you saw Ruby at eight. Have any idea where she went after that?" asked Dash.

"No. She was supposed to be on at ten. She normally comes backstage about a half hour or so early to warm up. But she didn't show, and the stage manager came and told me. I went up to her room thinking she might have overslept or something, but she wasn't there."

"So at twenty or quarter to ten, she was not in her room?"

"That's right," replied Dawson.

"Then you and the cops found her a little after midnight. So in four hours or so she went from breathing to dead. And in two hours or so she went from wherever she was killed to her room?"

"That's right," Dawson said again.

"You talk to anyone who might have seen her?"

She shook her head. "After I saw her...like that, I went to my room and killed half a bottle of bourbon. It felt like I was drinking water."

"I thought you said you didn't touch the stuff," said Archer.

"I was talking about *rum*, Archer. Bourbon and gin are just fine, thank you very much."

"And what sorts of questions did Pickett ask?" said Dash.

"Same as you."

"Funny, he has junior detectives to do that for him. Why is he here, then?"

"How the hell am I supposed to know?"

"Thought you knew everything that went on here."

She shot Archer and his injuries a glance. "Not everything."

They reached the room where a young uniformed cop stood guard.

Dash took out his license. "Chief Pickett sent us up here to have a look."

The cop looked startled but stepped back. "Okay."

Dash turned to Dawson. "Take a load off, Mabel, you look like you could use it."

She sat in a chair just inside the door while Archer headed into the kitchen to see a dead woman all over again.

42

I T WAS TOUGHER THE SECOND TIME AROUND, concluded Archer. He had seen violent death in the war, and while in prison. After a while, you didn't exactly get used to it, but it took you a shorter time to get over it. Until the next time came.

But this was different. This was a kitchen with a small refrigerator, a cooktop, a rug on the floor, and a cuckoo clock on the wall that he hadn't noticed before.

And a nearly decapitated young woman sitting in a chair. And now the body had started to decompose and smell and turn a color that no one would want to look at for long when it was stuck on a human being. And the smell was as bad as one would expect. Thankfully, someone had opened the window.

"Hello, Ern," Dash said to the small man in his late thirties standing in front of Fraser with his fingers tucked into his vest. The man's suit was blue serge, the tie partially undone, the hair, grizzled and unkempt, sticking out from under his brown fedora. But the green eyes were intense and searching.

Ern looked over, poked a cigarette into his mouth, and lit it.

With a grin he said, "Willie, how'd you get past the chief? Don't tell me he had a stroke when he saw your puss."

"Archer, this here is Ernie Prettyman, the best homicide detective north of San Luis Obispo. Ernie, this is Archer."

Prettyman came over to them and they all shook hands.

Prettyman said, "That's a mixed compliment on any day. What are you doing here?"

"We were talking to this poor woman yesterday in connection with a case."

"Who's the client?"

"Someone prominent and with some problems."

"No more than that you can tell me?"

"I could, and then I'd lose my ticket, and what would be the point of that?"

"Still," said Prettyman. "Whatever you can dish out."

"It was a confidential client matter," said Dash, "that we're following up. But if we find something that will help lead to her killer, I'll make the call to you."

"I guess that's the best I can do, then."

"Of course, Pickett would just send in Big Steve and club it out of me."

Prettyman frowned. "We don't do that anymore, Willie. At least on my watch."

"You're not always on watch, Ern. But to answer your question, Pickett told me to come up here and look around."

"Must be growing soft in his old age."

Dash said, "I knew just how to ask. What can you tell us?"

"As you can see, somebody nearly cut her head off. No blood here. She was killed somewhere else. How the hell she got in here, who knows?"

Dash looked skeptical. "Nobody saw anything? Place is pretty big, with lots of people coming and going." He glanced at the window. "And I doubt someone carried her in through the window over their shoulder."

"Right, but there's this. She was last seen around eight having dinner. Body was discovered after midnight. But whoever called it in did so at about nine or ten minutes before twelve. So the window is narrowed. Only at that time of night all the girls are out of their rooms and doing their things downstairs. And this is the top floor and Mabel Dawson told me there are only six gals up here, and those gals were all working last night from six o'clock on. They hand out the smokes and the whiskey and help run the card club and let the guys grab their asses as they go by for tips later. Fraser was the only song-and-dance *performer* up here. So her being alone on this floor before her act started wasn't unusual."

"I understand they have 'friends' visiting the gals here in the afternoon," said Dash. "When we came by yesterday the parking lot had quite a few cars. Even saw some prowlers in the mix." He gave Prettyman a look.

The man eyed him in understanding. "Que será, será."

"Murder weapon?"

"No. But whatever was used was as sharp as my wife's insults."

"How long did Mortimer think she'd been dead when he examined her?"

"He thinks she was killed between ten and midnight."

"Understand he didn't get here until this afternoon, though."

"That's right. He was out of town, and we don't like to move the body until he makes the call. But he was pretty sure of the timing based on the body's condition. And he did a pretty thorough exam."

"Not a job for the squeamish," noted Archer.

Prettyman nodded and said, "When'd you start working with Willie?"

"Yesterday."

"Nothing like hitting the ground running."

"Witnesses?" asked Dash.

"I've spoken to nearly all the staff. No one saw a body being moved into this room, I can tell you that. And I can't find anyone who saw Fraser after she left dinner. She could have come back up here or gone out. But if she went out, you'd think one of the valet boys would have seen her, and none did. And she didn't have a car, so somebody would have had to pick her up."

"How about out the back?" said Archer.

"That's certainly possible," conceded Prettyman. "But why go out the back?"

"If she was meeting someone she didn't want anyone to know about?" said Dash. "And just so you know, Sawyer Armstrong was here last night. With two of his 'associates.'"

"They weren't here when the first cops showed up, at least no one reported that they were."

"Funny thing about reports," said Dash. "They sometimes leave out more than they put in. Anything strike you looking around?"

"Yeah, she was a slob. And the fridge was empty. And the cooktop doesn't look like it's ever been used."

"Mind if we look around?"

"Go ahead, Willie. I need to go check in with Pickett."

"And why is he here when you're here?"

"Ask him, only I advise you don't."

"Advice I'll take."

After Prettyman left, Dash pushed his hat back and squatted down in front of Fraser. "She's in rigor mortis now," he said as he tried to bend one of her arms. "That dovetails with Mortimer's calculation." He gazed more closely at the wound. "Damn, that is a helluva way to kill someone. One stab to the heart would have done it. Why do it like that?"

"And how do you cut someone's throat like that and no one hears her scream?"

"Take a look at her right arm, Archer. In the crook of the elbow."

Archer drew closer and saw the small bump of red with a pinprick in the middle. "Someone shot her up with something to knock her out." He glanced sharply at Dash. "But you said she was a drug user. She could have done that herself."

Dash shook his head. "I see her as a pill popper. Needle folks have tracks long as my arm. That's the only one on her. Somebody else did it. Depending on what it was, Mortimer may find it when he checks her stomach."

"You think Prettyman saw the red bump?"

"I would be surprised if he didn't, considering I trained him."

Archer's jaw eased down in surprise. "He was a shamus before a cop?"

"Three years. I brought him on a couple years after I got here. He left and joined the police force when I had to take a leave of absence. That's why he's so nice to me."

"Why did you take a leave of absence?"

"None of your business." Dash walked around the space, taking in both small and large details.

"Got a question," said Archer.

"Shoot."

"How come I don't see any fingerprint powder anywhere?"

"That's right, you mentioned Irving Shaw told you about fingerprints."

"There's none on the doorknobs coming in or out. None in here, even though you'd think the killer might have touched the table, the chair, or something else. Prettyman seemed like a stickler for procedure but he didn't mention it."

"Ern's a good man who wants to keep his job."

"Is that supposed to be an answer?"

"I'll leave it up to you to muddle. Anything else you need to tell me?"

"Yeah, last night Dawson told me that Ruby liked men. Rich men. She thought she might have gone off with one of them."

"Well, why don't we go ask her about it?"

43

Dawson was not in the front room when they walked back in there. They headed down the stairs. Fortunately, Pickett was no longer in the reception area as they made their way to Dawson's office. She was seated at her desk, a bottle of gin sitting in front of her. She was staring at it like it was the second coming of Jesus. She looked up when they appeared.

"Dammit, can't you leave me in peace?" she moaned.

Dash sat in the chair across from her. "So Ruby liked rich men, huh?"

Dawson poured out three fingers of the gin and slowly spun the cap back while glaring at Archer. She poured in a smidgen of tonic, drank down a finger, tongued her lips, and said, "What young woman doesn't?"

"Don't play that game with me, Mabel. I'm trying to find a killer."

"What do I know about anything?"

"I think a lot more than you let on."

She let out a sigh so long it seemed to Archer like her dying breath. She lit up a Camel and blew smoke all over Dash, who just sat there and absorbed it, like a sponge.

"You private dicks are all alike, nag, nag, nag. Mark my words, in another life you're coming back as some poor schmuck's mother-in-law."

"That's a good description, actually. So, rich men?"

She tapped ash and polished off a second finger, holding the glass to her forehead after, as though she might get the final liquid dollop inside her via absorption.

"Tell me who your client is."

Dash didn't hesitate. "You already know."

"How?"

"We came here yesterday and pretty much told Ruby who it was. And there is no way you didn't get that out of the girl, because as soon as we left, you had a little talk with her, didn't you? I mean, you said that was your *job*: the girls?"

She took another puff of her smoke and eyed the man warily. "I know what you're thinking and maybe what you want me to say, but I never saw Douglas Kemper with Ruby, not once. She wasn't in his class. She was a kid from Kansas or Missouri or one of those places with more cows than people."

"So she did tell you we were asking about Kemper?"

"She...I mean...yeah, she did."

"Thanks for clearing that up. And she told us she was from Illinois, but they got cows there, too, so go ahead. What else?"

"She was pretty, she had a decent voice, and she was okay playing the dumb broad in the comedy skits. And that was it. She was not the second coming of Carole Lombard, trust me. She didn't have the brains or ambition for moving high up the social ladder."

"We heard different, at least about her and Kemper."

"Then you heard wrong, as far as I'm concerned."

"What if his wife thinks he might have been cheating with Ruby?" said Dash.

"Then maybe she knows something I don't. But if she can't keep her man happy it's her problem not mine."

"Can you think of anyone who might want to hurt Ruby?" asked Archer.

"We get all kinds in here, drunks, powder puffs, big men, small men, weak men, and mostly men who think way too much of themselves. But as far as I know, we don't have gents who like chopping a girl's head off, and I hope we never do."

"Well, you have at least one," pointed out Archer, drawing a glare from Dawson.

"*Was* Ruby seeing anybody, rich or not?" asked Dash.

"Truth is she didn't have nobody special. Working here doesn't really allow for that, does it? Part of the job is making *all* the men feel special. Hard to do that if you're gaga over somebody. Takes away your, um, generous spirit."

"I thought she was a performer on the stage, not a bedspring squeaker," replied Dash.

"And maybe she was making *one* guy feel special and then she stopped and he didn't like it," opined Archer.

"Well, I have no clue as to who that might be. Now, if you'll excuse me, I have some serious drinking to do."

Outside in the sunshine Dash looked around and said, "I remember when this was just an empty field."

"I guess it's good business for Sawyer Armstrong."

"He's always been able to sniff out the dollars."

"You said you've known him a long time."

"Sometimes I think too long. With him, one minute it's honey, the next a shotgun."

Archer rubbed his injured face. "It was pretty easy for me to figure that out last night."

"That was just him sniffing around the shrubs seeing if someone dropped something of value, Archer. Don't read too much into it."

"He really didn't like that we questioned his daughter."

"I'm sure he didn't, especially seeing as how she thinks her hubby is guilty as charged."

"And that might derail Kemper's mayoral run, you mean?"

"Well, I could see Armstrong thinking that way, sure."

"With Ruby dead, you think the newspapers will get wind of this?"

"I think whoever killed Ruby certainly hopes so."

"Again, to queer Kemper's shot at the mayor's office?"

"Maybe."

"You don't sound sure."

"We been working this case for one day. I'm not sure of a damn thing, except that Mabel Dawson knows more than she's letting on. Let's take a walk around back."

The rear grounds were made up of upper and lower terraces, paved courtyards, open spaces and private ones rimmed with hedges, along with tables, chairs, chaises, freestanding umbrellas to shield the sun's rays, and a large fountain on the top terrace that bled water down into a series of cast stone pods to form a gentle waterfall that somehow ended in a firepit before the water was recirculated to the top. At this hour of the day there were few patrons back here, but some of the staff were wiping off the furniture and others were restocking a large bar set on wheels that sat under a large circus-tent-sized pavilion.

Dash said, "At least two main doors that I can see leading out to the top terrace, but I'm sure there are more. Service entrances in particular are not always visible, and they like it that way. Tradesman's entrance is on the left side."

They walked over to a thin, reedy man with short white hair and a mottled complexion. He wore dark pants and a white collared shirt, and he was wiping down the furniture.

Dash flashed his license and said, "Besides the main doors up there, how else could someone who works here get out without being noticed?"

The man pointed to a paved path to the right of the upper terrace that curved past a row of green hedges.

"Up there is where we come and go. Boss don't like the hired help taking the main doors 'cept for the hostesses and the waiters and waitresses. Us riffraff got to hide if we can manage it. We ain't good enough to be seen apparently by the 'patrons' here." He plucked a cigarette from behind his ear and lit up before he grinned a gap-toothed grin. He smelled of smoke and garlic and sweat. "You're here about that gal, Ruby. Got her throat slit, somebody said."

"Did you know her?"

The man shook his head and puffed on his cigarette. "Look at me. Gal like that wouldn't give a guy like me the time of day."

"So you knew who she was?"

"Sure. Seen her around."

"And did the fact that she wouldn't give you the time of day make you mad?" said Dash.

The man's grin faded and his skin turned a soupy gray. "Hey, fella, I had nothing to do with what happened to her. I don't even work evenings. I was home with the missus."

"Name?"

"Tom, Tom Boswell."

"Address?"

"Fourteen Ocean Way."

"You on the water?" asked Archer as he wrote this down and then ran his eye over the man's plain clothes.

Dash said, "The street names in Bay Town are funny, Archer, and not in the way you might think. Ocean Way is close to the ocean the way the earth is close to the sun."

"That's a fact," said Boswell. "And the town dump is at the end of a road called Tuxedo Boulevard."

"You know anybody who might have had a beef with Ruby?" asked Dash.

Boswell shook his head. "No. I don't know nobody that knows her. I work out here for the most part, not inside."

"So you wouldn't know if she had any enemies or boyfriends?"

"No sir."

"Ever see anybody talking to her?"

"No sir."

A boy in a cap and buttons ran up to them waving a piece of paper. "Mr. Dash?"

Dash nodded. "That's me, kid."

The boy handed him a note. "This is for you." Then he turned and hustled away.

Dash opened the note and read it. "Well, Archer, we've been summoned by the king."

"The king? I thought we were a democracy, not a monarchy."

"In a few years you'll change your mind. You just need more seasoning."

As they walked off Archer said, "So is it Sawyer Armstrong?"

"Who else? Now, if his goons come after you again, *don't* lose your temper. This meeting might turn out to be very informative for purposes of our investigation."

"And how exactly am I supposed to handle it if they *do* come after me?"

"Hell, I know Tony and Hank. You're younger and in a lot better shape than they are, Archer. Just outrun the sons of bitches."

44

THE DRIVE UP WOULD HAVE GIVEN LIBERTY CALLAHAN a heart attack, thought Archer, as he piloted the Delahaye around the twists and turns and switchbacks and rising elevations, all while following Dash's directions. They were running on a road parallel to the one the Kemper estate was on, but Sawyer Armstrong had built his home on even higher ground.

When the land finally plateaued and they went around a curve, Archer glimpsed a house. "Is that it?"

"That's Armstrong's place, all right."

"After seeing the home he built for his daughter, I thought his residence would look like the Taj Mahal."

"Nope. It's a farm. He grows olives here. Don't know if he makes much money off it, not that he needs to, but apparently the man has a passion for it."

The home was about half the size of his daughter's, which made it very large indeed, and was constructed of red cedar siding and stone. The yard in front was a sculpted landscape of flower beds, large native trees and bushes, and a pea gravel path up to the front porch, which had a hundred-foot-long tin metal overhang and comfortable chairs, upholstered and wicker, spread along its length. Striped awnings hung over most of the windows on the western side of the house, and Archer could see how they might come in handy when the sun started to set. It would be quite hot and powerful at this elevation and angle.

As impressive as the casual house was in size, Archer could see about a dozen large outbuildings behind it, all constructed of red cedar with either shake shingles or tin metal roofs. Farm machinery was neatly parked across this stretch of land. There were horses in corrals and cows in other pens. He watched as men carried various tools, or else drove pieces of equipment designed to help grow or harvest things in the dirt. Stretching out behind all of this was a sea of what Archer surmised were the olive trees. The land seemed to go on and on right up to the foothills of the Santa Ynez Mountains. He could see lots of people with straw baskets and ladders swarming over the olive orchards.

"Are they harvesting the olives?" he asked.

"Yep," replied Dash. "It's tough work. You pick them by hand. Armstrong probably has about a hundred pickers here now, those folks you see out there. Mostly migrants from Mexico. He doesn't pay them much, but it's a lot more than they can make back home. They live in some of those bunkhouses you see around here. Feeds them, too, before he sends them on their way back across the border."

"Olives grow well around here, I take it."

"Yes. But it can be tricky. They need a lot of deep, infrequent watering."

"But you can't use salt water?"

"No. Armstrong told me one time the saline burns out the tree roots, and compounds coming from it can be toxic to the leaves."

Archer gazed out at the sea of green, healthy olive trees. "Where does he get his fresh water, then?"

"California has a complicated relationship with water, Archer. Orange growers need a ton of it, the cities need millions of gallons of drinking water every day, and farmers need it for their crops and livestock. There are pipelines and trenches and aquifers and a series of dams and reservoirs collecting water coming off the winter snow packs in the Sierras and the Cascades, and the Rockies, too. And folks fight over it. Some divert it, others outright steal it from their neighbor or duke it out in court. With regard to Armstrong, he's never divulged his source to me."

They drove up to the house and got out.

"What do you think he wants to see us about?" said Archer.

"I would imagine his son-in-law and his daughter."

"And Ruby Fraser?"

"Maybe. We'll find out soon enough."

A woman answered the door. She was of Mexican heritage, matronly and reserved, and casually attired in denim jeans with the cuffs rolled up and a colorful flannel shirt with a matching bandana. She told them she was Mr. Armstrong's housekeeper. And to follow her. And they did. The floors were polished wood and the walls were plaster. It was far cooler inside than out. Archer figured the walls were thick to make that the case. The interior decorations here were far less formal than at the Kempers' place.

They were led all the way through the house and out onto the back porch, which was just as sweeping as the front. At a round table set off to one side sat Sawyer Armstrong. He had on reflective sunglasses, though the sun was not in his eyes, and the man had just clipped off the end of a fat cigar before lighting and then puffing on it. He wore faded jeans, a white shirt, and a dark green corduroy vest. A straw hat with an olive green band sat on the table. His thick, unruly hair fell nearly to his shoulders. Scuffed boots rode on his long feet. His legs were stretched out. Three glasses and a pitcher of what looked to be sangria were set on the table.

And to Archer's surprise, Beth Kemper was also seated at the table, next to her father.

He waved them over.

They sat and took off their hats, and the housekeeper went on her way.

Armstrong poured three glasses and handed them out. "Nothing like a little Spanish honey in the afternoon," he said, taking off his sunglasses and slipping them into a vest pocket.

Archer looked at Kemper. "But not for you?"

She wouldn't meet his eye. "Sangria gives me migraines. My father insists that I learn to love it, but so far it just hasn't worked."

"Love the migraines or the sangria?" asked Archer.

Armstrong interjected, "I think we can move on from the chitchat."

"Sounds good to me," said Dash as he took out a pack of cigarettes and lit one. He took a puff and said, "You rang, Armstrong. We're here. But before we get going." He pointed to Archer. "Your boys didn't have to put the hurt on my associate here. That didn't show class."

Archer glanced at Kemper, but she displayed no reaction.

To him, the woman was like a flower in full bloom that had wilted to nothing because someone had thrown something toxic on it.

Armstrong nodded. "Yes, Willie, I agree with that. And I've had a talk with them both."

"Good, good. Now, Archer also told me that you want to hire us. Is that why we're here?"

"In part, yes," said Armstrong after taking a sip of sangria. "But it's more than that, too. There was a girl killed up at my place, Midnight Moods."

"Pickett himself is on the case, which I take to mean that you called him personally. Otherwise, he'd rather be back in his office banging that honey of a secretary." Dash glanced at Kemper. "Sorry, Mrs. Kemper, that just slipped out."

She smiled, briefly, then lowered her gaze.

"You don't have a high opinion of Carl, do you?" said Armstrong.

"I like competence and honesty, and you can throw integrity in there, too, if you want. Carl fails on all three counts in my book. And I'm sure he feels the same way about me, only he'd be wrong and I'd be right. I'm not telling you anything I haven't told him."

"I see," said Armstrong in a noncommittal tone.

"Now, we are looking into Ruby Fraser's death," added Dash. "We'd already talked to her because the case we're handling for your son-in-law involved her."

"You mean that they were 'seeing' each other? As I told Archer, it's something that my daughter here can ably handle. Though I doubt Beth much cares what Douglas does with his time."

Archer once more looked at Kemper. She finally lifted her gaze to his and said, "I believe I made my position on that very clear to these gentlemen."

Her father patted her on the arm. "And it's your right to do so, of course, Beth. If you remember, I told you to strongly consider not marrying the man, but you inherited your mother's stubbornness and you went ahead and did it anyway. And now look at where you are."

Archer watched as the pink rose in the woman's cheeks, and not in a good way. She looked angry but said nothing.

Dash said, "Regardless, someone was clearly trying to blackmail Kemper into dropping out of the race and using Fraser to do it. Now she's dead."

Armstrong sat up a little straighter and finished his glass of sangria. "I hope you're not implying that Douglas had anything to do with this girl's murder. I can't say that I like the man all that much, particularly after the way he's treated my daughter. But murder? That's preposterous."

Archer shot Kemper another glance. There was no expression on the woman's features. Archer could not reconcile the vivacious, quick-witted woman in the diner with this dull apparition.

"I'm not implying anything," said Dash. "I'm just saying that he had an obvious motive to get rid of her. And he didn't have to do the deed himself. There are guys who would do it for him for the right price." He glanced at Kemper. "Again, I'm sorry. I had no idea you'd be here, but these are things we have to discuss. If you want to leave, this might be a good time."

Archer saw the indecision on the woman's face until Armstrong put a big hand on her shoulder. "Beth is strong. She can deal with this, Willie. Isn't that right, my dear?"

Kemper glanced at Archer before saying, "I'm fine, Mr. Dash, please carry on."

"All right, ma'am, if you're sure."

Armstrong said, "I don't agree with that theory at all, Willie. Because now that she's dead, people will assume that Douglas *did* have something to do with it. And while adultery is not a good look for a politician, murder is far worse. So don't you see that this is an attempt to push the election to Alfred Drake?"

"So you really think Drake had her murdered?" said Dash, each word draped in more sarcasm than its predecessor.

"No, but politicians have backers. And Drake has his."

"And who are Drake's backers?"

Armstrong sat forward, looking pointedly animated now. "You should nose around about money men from Vegas, and mob types from New York who want to set up shop in Bay Town, Santa Barbara, Frisco, LA, and San Diego. There *is* a narcotics trade, Willie, that is very lucrative for the mob, and a lot of it comes over the border and over the water. These folks are invading this country, and nothing is stopping them so far."

"Yeah, did you happen to mention that to Carl Pickett? Because he doesn't even have a single police boat on the water. Maybe he likes the stuff coming in. Maybe he gets something from it. Maybe that's how he can buy big-ass Chryslers and toothpicks by the bushel on a policeman's salary."

Armstrong sat back, looking surprised. "Are you accusing the chief of police of taking bribes?"

"Not at all. I think he slipped and fell on the street and a bunch of money ended up in his pocket. But if you tell him I said so, I'll deny it."

Armstrong waved this comment away. "I don't care about Pickett at the moment. I care about this election, and I don't want to see my son-in-law's chances go down the tubes because someone is trying to frame him."

"The son-in-law you don't much care for?" said Archer.

Armstrong leveled his gaze at him. "I don't have to like the man to like his politics. Douglas will be a good mayor, and, more to the point, he is the man we need at the moment. And I consider Alfred Drake to be certainly a socialist and perhaps a communist. He would be a disaster for this town."

"You mentioned to Archer here that you wanted us to find the truth, no matter where it went. It didn't sound like you had a dog in the hunt, Armstrong, but now it sounds like you do. So which is it? I'd like to know before deciding on your offer of engagement."

Armstrong smiled and looked at his daughter. "I forgot how good Willie is at chess, Beth. I think he might have captured one of my pawns and one of my knights, and he's now bearing down on my queen."

"Is there an answer in there somewhere?" noted Dash.

"Look for the truth, Willie. And I do have a dog in the hunt, yes. But I'm confident of where the trail will lead you. How's that for an answer?"

"I guess it'll have to do, because I doubt another one will be coming along." Dash took a sip of the sangria and wrinkled his nose.

"You don't care for it?" asked Armstrong.

"I'm not much of a punch man. You introduce sweetness into

alcohol, you've pretty much lost me. Liquor should burn, make a man feel alive. Otherwise, you're just drinking something so you can piss it away an hour later. So, you had a look at the list we got from Kemper. Anyone on it look promising?"

"I'm not a detective."

"Just your gut, then."

"I think the list is pretty much worthless."

"Interesting." Dash rose and put on his hat. Archer did likewise. "So when did you and your boys leave Midnight Moods last night?"

"Right after our little encounter with Archer. You can check with the valet if you don't believe me."

"Okay, I will. You remember which one it was?"

"A man in a valet's uniform looking for tips and drunk women leaving alone."

"Thanks, that pretty much describes all of them. But it's a start."

"That's quite a place you built for the Kempers," noted Archer while looking directly at Beth Kemper.

"I built it for my *daughter*," said Armstrong. He put a protective arm around Kemper. "Douglas just came along for the ride."

"But you're backing your son-in-law for the mayor's race," said Dash.

"One does not have to love one's allies, Willie. One just has to use them."

45

W HEN THEY FINALLY ARRIVED BACK at the office the sun was dipping into the horizon and turning the dark ocean water salmon and gold in the process.

Archer said, "Didn't that seem weird to you back there? Beth Kemper didn't act anything like herself."

"Her old man takes up the whole universe when he's in the room."

They got out of the car and Dash said, "I've got some things to do, Archer. See you in the morning. Bright and early this time. But here's what I want you to do." He leaned back through the open window. "Tonight, head back over to Midnight Moods and see and hear what you can. Go over the room again and see what occurs to you. Talk to folks. I find it hard to believe that no one saw anything last night."

"Will do, Willie. Is Connie gone, do you think? I was going to head up to the office for a minute."

Dash checked his watch, dipped his hand into his pocket, and came up with a key ring with three keys attached. He took one off and tossed it to Archer. "Just don't lose it."

Archer watched as Dash walked off down the street, to where he didn't know. He went into the building to find the elevator car empty. Earl must have gotten off work, too, he thought.

He took the stairs up and unlocked the door to Willie Dash, Very Private Investigations.

Connie was indeed gone. He closed the door and entered his office and looked around. Small, spare, dowdy even, musty.

And my office.

He smiled and spent the next hour cleaning the place up and putting things just so. He almost felt like he was back in prison where small tasks like this—straightening something, cleaning something—allowed him to get through the day and the next day and the next. Finished, he looked out the small window and watched as two men walked down the alley four stories below smoking cigarettes and sharing a bottle.

Archer drove back to the boardinghouse and knocked on Callahan's door.

"Yeah?" she called out.

"It's me, Archer."

He heard footsteps approach. When she opened the door, he found himself a little disappointed that she had so many clothes on.

"What?" she said, her hand on her hip and attitude dripping from her features.

"You want to grab some dinner?"

"No. I'm not hungry. Did you find out who killed that girl?"

"We're working on it, Liberty. But I did have one favor to ask."

"Then you better come in. It would be humiliating for you if I turned you down in public."

She sat on the bed and he leaned against the wall. He could see that she had a number of outfits out on the bed and others hanging on various wall pegs.

"You going through your wardrobe?"

"Yeah. What Dawson had for me just didn't work. Luckily I brought a few things that will."

"More than a few. You excited about it?"

"It's not Hollywood, but it'll do. For now. What's the favor?"

"I was wondering when you start work there if you could keep your eyes and ears open at Midnight Moods and report back to me."

"You mean, act as a spy for you?"

"Well, that's one way of putting it."

"Seems to me like it's the only way, Archer."

"It might help us find out who killed that woman."

Callahan's hard features collapsed when he said that, and she looked down and started fussing with one of her nails. "Whoever did it, didn't have to kill her like that. They didn't have to...do that to her."

Archer sat on the bed next to her. "If you go all soft on me, I'll think somebody kidnapped the real Liberty and left you behind."

"What girls like me do, Archer, what girls like Ruby Fraser did, is hard. We have to navigate a thousand different things at once, most of them shitty and almost all of them having to do with men. All at the same time we're pursuing our dreams, or at least what we think we'd like to do with our lives. And unlike men, we can do a hundred things right and one thing wrong and our dream is over. That kind of gets to you, makes you...light on your feet, unwilling to..."

"To trust anybody. Including men like me."

She touched his face. "Does it still hurt?"

"Not when you rub it like that. Feels good, actually."

"I'll be your spy, Archer. And I need you to drive me over there on Friday to sign my contract."

"Okay, but you need to be careful. Something's not right at Midnight Moods."

"Something's not right with the whole world."

He left her there to continue her wardrobe choices, and ate a quick dinner at a place across the street. Steak, peppers, and onions washed down with a beer, and bread hard enough to hammer nails with.

Archer walked around the streets for a bit, enjoying the falling temperatures and light ocean breeze, and watched the marine fog build in the hollows leading up to the palaces resting above them. As he walked he thought about Beth Kemper, visualizing the woman in his mind. The first word that came to him as he did this was *fragile*. That surprised him because she didn't appear to be fragile. But he wondered what Beth Kemper's breaking point was. He thought at some point he might get to see it.

Having some time before he headed to Midnight Moods, he walked back to the boardinghouse and retrieved the Delahaye. He drove down to the wharf and saw that the boat Armstrong and the others had been on the other night was still tied up to the dock.

He sought out and found the harbormaster's office. The gray-bearded old man sitting in there had on a thick turtleneck sweater along with a sailor's pea jacket and a captain's hat. He looked like an advertisement for a seaman's life, at least from Herman Melville's time. He plucked his briarwood pipe from between tobacco-stained teeth and looked up at Archer from the perch in his quarters, which were not much bigger than a phone booth. Hanging on the wall behind him was a nautical chart of the harbor, complete with depth markings, the exact outline of the coast and seabed, along with navigational aids and hazards. Next to it was a picture of a pinup model who looked a lot like Callahan and was showing about as much leg.

Archer pointed out the window at the boat. "That's a nice-looking craft. Does someone own it, or can it be rented?"

The man said, "That there is Sawyer Armstrong's vessel."

"Sawyer Armstrong?" said Archer, feigning ignorance.

"Why, he's the richest man around here. Has a big place up in the mountains. Grows olives. But he owns most of Bay Town."

"Oh, right, I think I've heard of him. But I've only just moved here." Archer lit up a Lucky Strike and looked out at the boat. "Where do people go on boats around here? Are there islands and such?"

"Sure. The Channel Islands."

"Channel Islands? Can you get out there fast?"

"Depends on what you mean by fast, young man, and depends on which island. There're eight of them in what they call an *archipelago*. Goes from San Miguel to the north to San Clemente on the southern side. Santa Cruz and Anacapa are the closest to us, but you're still talking over an hour or more to get to them."

"Are the islands inhabited?"

"Just Santa Catalina, really. The others are either empty or just have a few folks. Used to be Indians lived on the Channel Islands. Chumash on the northern islands and the Tongva tribe to the south. But the Spaniards came and moved them out way back when. Now, on Catalina some rich feller built a town out there, like a tourist destination, so to speak. Avalon, it's called. Then he went broke and some other fellers tried their hand and kept building. Then they had a fire and money problems and had to sell out to other investors. Then that chewing gum feller, Wrigley, came along and bought most everything up. Spent millions out there, so's I heard. Catalina Casino is real popular."

Archer blew out a mouthful of smoke. "Casino? I thought casinos were outlawed in California."

The man chuckled. "Ain't no gambling there. 'Casino' is I-talian for 'gathering place,' at least some feller told me that. Anyway, Wrigley owned the Chicago Cubs. Team used to go there for spring training. Long time ago, I went over there once to watch 'em. Lotta fun. Then Mr. Chewing Gum died and his son took over and kept building it up. Then the military came in and took everything over during the war. They still do tests and stuff out there on some of 'em."

"How far is it?"

"Catalina's part of the Southern Channel Islands chain. Takes you about an hour or so by boat from way down in Long Beach to get there. Whole lot longer from here. Have to make it a full day trip."

"I hear there's another island out there, a lot closer to us here. Sort of a man-made place the military put together."

The seaman eyed him suspiciously and tapped the smoking end of his pipe against his desktop. "You hear a lot for someone who just got to town."

"I like to keep my ears open. Is it true?"

"Military folks did lots of things during the war. We don't know them all, expect we never will. Hush-hush, right?"

Archer eyed the man's seafaring garb. "So you've never been out there? Thought you'd have been all over these waters."

"No reason to go that way."

"Can I get out there, just to see if it's there?"

"Why would you want to do that?"

"I like trying new things."

The man shrugged. "You know how to pilot a boat?"

"I do, yeah. Army taught me."

"Funny thing for the Army to teach."

"You'd be surprised how much water you encounter in the Army."

"It's a straight shot west of here, pretty much from where I'm sitting. Two hundred and seventy-one degrees on your compass. Three miles. About fifteen to twenty minutes with the typical sea conditions we have here. Don't normally hit heavy water until farther out."

"Since you know the compass setting so exactly, then there *is* an island out there?" said Archer.

"Never said there wasn't, young feller."

"But you've never been there?"

The man bit down on his pipe and said nothing.

"So the military still owns it? Will I get in trouble if I go out there?"

"Maybe. But it might not be the military you have the trouble with."

"Who then?"

"Can't really say, young man, 'cause I don't know. And I don't *want* to know."

Archer kept his gaze on the fellow, but the man's mouth had closed up like a fish that had swallowed a hook.

He eyed the darkening skies. "Can I get a boat out early in the morning? Around first light?"

"Sure. Feller down near the port operations rents 'em out. You go that way there you'll see his sign. He's honest, or as close to it as you're going to get. He opens at six. Five dollars is the fee for the day. Eight hours or eight minutes, it's all the same. And that includes fuel."

"Thanks."

"Uh-huh."

Archer walked away and then glanced back to see the man now standing and staring after him.

You might have just made a big mistake.

But there might be a way around that.

Archer picked up his pace.

46

The man renting boats was just about to close when Archer reached him. At first, he didn't want to provide Archer a boat so late in the day, but when Archer waved a sawbuck in front of his face and said he was only going about three miles out, the man took the bill and said, "Okay, mister, just dock it nice and tight in the same slip when you come back, 'cause I ain't hanging around."

Archer filled out the necessary paperwork, and the man led him to the boat with a set of keys and a navigation map of the area. Along the way he grilled Archer on his seamanship and came away satisfied.

"Even three miles out weather can turn fast, so stay alert. And use your running lights. Shipping lanes out there. It's marked on the map. You don't want to get swamped by a tanker."

"Right, thanks."

"And what's so special about three miles out anyway?" said the man. "Nothing but water. Anacapa's a lot farther than that."

"Just checking out a tip I got on a fishing spot."

The man eyed him with skepticism. "Yeah, right. You ain't no smuggler, are you?"

Archer tapped his pockets. "Well, if I am, whatever I'm smuggling is really small."

The varnish was so freshly applied and smelled so strongly that Archer felt like *he'd* been lacquered as soon as he stepped foot on board the trim nineteen-foot Chris-Craft Barrelback with an American flag flapping from a post set on the stern. He stowed his hat, powered up the motor, flicked the switch for the running lights, and steered the boat due west. As he sped up the wind increased and the ocean followed this nudge, with the result that foot-high seas confronted him about a half mile out.

Archer pushed the throttle forward a bit more, and the heavy wooden boat handled the chop with ease. He kept his eye on his compass and then took a minute to look over the laminated map the fellow had provided, using a flashlight that had been clipped to a holder set on the dashboard. The island he was heading to was not marked on this map.

After confirming his route he put the map away and kept his eye on the compass, holding his heading steady at 271 degrees. He was cruising along at twenty-four knots and figured he would be at the island in less than ten more minutes. He let his gaze run from left to right and then behind him, just in case. The seas became heavier at around the two-and-a-half-mile mark, and he throttled down a bit to compensate, working the bow at a forty-five-degree angle into the oncoming waves to cleave their power in half. The moon was up and visibility was good. Everything was going his way so far. He knocked on the wooden dash for luck.

He had learned to pilot powerboats in these very same waters during his training back in 1942. The Army had worked with the Navy, and amphibious landings were going to be in his future, Archer learned. Thus, he had been given the skill set necessary for this, never realizing it would come in handy so many years later, and in American waters. He had been in far worse seas than he was currently in, but, like the boat rental man had cautioned, things could change quickly if the weather turned.

He slowed the boat as he approached a dark mass rising up out of the Pacific. He swung the light mounted on the side of the boat, much like a prowler's beam, so that it strafed the contours of the island he was heading toward. He turned north and navigated down the island's length, doing a rough calculation of its size and dimensions. Once he had returned to his starting point, he throttled down even more and pointed his bow at an enormous dock that his searchlight had revealed previously. There was another, smaller dock, about a half mile down on that side. He snagged two fenders and placed them on hooks on the gunwale on the port side to cushion the boat from the current pushing it against the wooden dock.

He glided in at an angle, then cut the wheel hard toward the dock, killed the motor, and jumped out as the stern swung landward. He quickly tied up the boat, grabbed his hat and the flashlight, and walked off the dock and onto the island.

He looked around, aiming the beam here and there. He was also wondering why, if the military still owned this piece of land, no one was here to challenge him for trespassing.

He walked in a westerly direction, shining his light over the dirt. The land was reasonably flat but then elevated to about forty or so feet as he drew closer to the middle of the island, which made sense to protect against flooding. There had clearly been structures here, large ones, if their remaining foundations were any indication. Like an archaeologist he could roughly determine what had been here by what had been left behind. He saw discarded cables, stacks of used lumber, chunks of concrete, and an empty crate that had RADAR stenciled on the side. There were old tires, the remains of a Jeep buried in the mud, empty boxes that had been filled with C rations, a sailor's white cap, an empty ammo chain for a machine gun, and a fifty-gallon oil drum that was labeled PROPERTY OF THE UNITED STATES NAVY. A little ways away he saw the rusted undercarriage of a Mark VI railway gun mounted on a rotating platform. He had seen these guns while training on the Channel Islands. They could move around in a circle and take on both enemy aircraft and ships.

Under the illumination of his light he spotted something inter-esting. He walked over and knelt next to a hole in the ground with a stake driven in next to it. Some number and letter markings were on the wooden stake, but he didn't know what they meant. This very same thing was also at several other places, all on the elevated portion of the island.

Then he saw another post in the ground with a name on it.

LANCET SURVEYORS AND ARCHITECTURAL GROUP, BAY TOWN.

There wasn't a phone number or any other information on the post, but he wrote down the name in his notepad.

Archer performed a run-fast walk until he reached the water on the other side of the island. He had measured his strides and gauged the island as being about three miles in width. He had earlier calculated it was about twice that in length. Three miles by six miles, or eighteen square miles in total. Not a lot of land, but certainly big enough to do something with, as the Navy apparently had. And it was an engineering marvel that they had created an island from basically a shallow spot in the ocean. And to his knowledgeable eye, the large dock located here could have handled the biggest destroyers the Navy had.

Farther out there was a long, shadowy form. It took Archer a few moments to figure it out.

A breakwater.

That would make sense when you were docking ships out this far from the mainland.

He looked up at the sky as the blinking lights of a plane buzzed overhead. Its angle of ascent showed that it had probably just taken off from the coast. It continued in a westerly direction, maybe on its way to Hawaii, he thought. To his practiced ear, it was a four-engine aircraft, and it would need all that horsepower to make it that far.

He trudged back to the boat, feeling disappointed. He hadn't really accomplished much of anything, and it had cost him ten bucks. Archer picked up his pace as a flash of lightning appeared far out over the ocean to the west. A storm was rolling in.

He jumped into the boat, fired up the engine, untied his lines, and pulled away from the dock. He pointed his bow east and throttled up. He could feel the wind at his back, and then the barometric pressure dropped with a rush. This was nature's warning sign of foul weather coming.

He pushed the throttle down further, and the Chris-Craft's powerful engine thrust the boat through the increasingly heavy seas. Archer listened to the cracks of thunder as the storm chased him all the way back to the California mainland. He slid the boat into its slip, tied it up, left the key under the seat as the man had instructed him, and hustled back to the Delahaye. He got the top on and the windows rolled up a few seconds before the rain began to fall in buckets. He sat in the car with the engine off and stared out to sea. Three miles out was an island. And he was pretty sure that that was where Sawyer Armstrong and those other men had gone. Now the question was why.

47

MIDNIGHT MOODS WAS STARTING TO HIT ITS STRIDE as Archer valeted his car at the front entrance. Apparently, a brutal murder of one of its employees wasn't going to interfere with business. People still wanted to drink, dance, gamble, and watch pretty young girls lift their legs and sing their hearts out.

The rain had already passed through, but it was still drizzling and about fifteen degrees cooler than before the storm had hit. He spotted the valet captain in his hat, buttons, and military-style uniform at the key desk. Archer walked over and held up his PI license.

The captain took a long look at the photostat copy. The gent was in his fifties, with thinning gray hair, a handlebar mustache, and a nervous tic at his right eye, which made Archer nervous just watching it. His lips and nails were stained yellow from his smokes. He was every inch of five-six, and that frame carried about thirty more pounds than it ideally should have.

"Okay, what do you want?" he asked.

"You know Sawyer Armstrong?"

"No, never heard of the guy," the man said, sarcasm dripping like the fake medals on his chest. "Oh wait a sec, ain't he the man who owns this place?"

"You can play me for a sap and this dance will just take longer than you want it to."

"The cops were already here, shamus. I talked to them but I don't have to do the same to you. So scram."

"We're working with Chief Pickett on this case, so you might want to rethink that position, chum, unless you want a trip downtown that might leave you black and blue, if you get my meaning."

The patronizing smile slowly faded from the captain's features. "Okay, don't get all tough, what do you want to know?"

Archer put his license away and said, "You have any idea what time Armstrong left last night? He was with two of his 'associates.' They were basically gorillas in neckties but not as good-looking."

"Yeah, I know them all right. Hank and Tony. Not a pair you want to get on the wrong side of, mister."

"I got that lesson yesterday right here and real good. So you saw them?"

"Yeah. I ordered Mr. Armstrong's car up myself. It's a Cadillac about as long as my house. He got into the back, Hank drove, and Tony sat in the passenger seat. Tony looked like he'd slipped and hit his face against something hard."

"Yeah, he did. So what time was this?"

"Oh, I'd say eleven, give or take."

"Give or take how many minutes?"

"Hey, what do I look like to you, buddy, a Timex? It was around eleven. They got into the car and drove off."

"Did you know the murdered girl, Ruby Fraser?"

"Just to see her around."

"You ever see her with a guy?"

"That's sort of the point of Midnight Moods, ain't it?"

"She was a singer, not one of the cigarette-and-brandy gals or the afternoon boppers."

His lip curled back in a sneer. "Well, excuse me, I didn't mean to speak ill of the dead. I'm sure she was a saint."

"So did you ever see her with a guy?"

"Maybe."

"Douglas Kemper, you know him?"

"Sure, he's here right now playing cards."

"You ever see him with Ruby?"

"Nope. Where is this going, fella?"

"Apparently nowhere. Thanks for nothing, Pops."

Archer walked over the drawbridge, checked his hat, and ordered a vodka martini that went down nice after his island hunting expedition off the coast.

He was directed to the card club room by a cigarette girl who did her best to palm off a pack of Camels on him.

"I only smoke Lucky Strikes," he said.

She looked him up and down and said in a husky voice, "You don't look like you need that much *luck*, handsome."

"Damn, I finally run into a gal who gets me and I have to go." He flipped her a quarter and took a pack of Luckys from her tray.

A boy in buttons opened the door to the card club room and Archer ducked inside. It was a large space about forty feet square, with tables set up nearly chairback to chairback. It was only men in here; Archer didn't know if that was a rule or not. The gentlemen wore expensive suits or high-dollar tuxes. They were smoking cigars, sipping what looked to be snifters of cognac, and looking amusingly content at their privileged status in life. Sitting on a tall stool in the middle of each table was a fellow with a colorful vest, sleeve garters, and a green visor who stood guard over the chute from which the playing cards were dealt.

It didn't take Archer long to spot Kemper. He was lounging in a chair behind five cards and a pile of chips with four other men who looked like clones of his, but without the indifference that oozed from Kemper. None of the men were Sheen.

He crossed the room, taking a last sip of his drink, and stopped next to Kemper, who put down a full house, kings over tens, and scooped up the chips in the pot to the chagrin of the rest of the elite herd.

Kemper looked up at him and set his Havana in an ashtray. "Archer, right?" He looked around. "Where's Willie?"

"He called it a day, but I'm more of a night owl." He knelt down and said in a low voice, "I'd like to ask you a few questions and give you an update, if you're interested."

Kemper glanced at the other players and smiled. "Okay, boys, I feel sorry for you, so I'm taking my toys and going home. You can duke it out for the few dollars you have left. And you can thank me later."

He glanced at the dealer and pointed to his chips. The man nodded. "Yes sir, Mr. Kemper. I'll take care of it."

"Scrape off fifty for your trouble, Harry."

"Thank you, sir."

Kemper rose and Archer followed him out of the room and over to one of the bars lining the grand hall that bisected the first floor. Archer refreshed his martini and Kemper opted for a stinger.

"Let's take a walk," said Kemper. "I don't really care for crowds while I'm answering questions and getting updated."

He led Archer out to the rear terrace and over to a covered area that had been sheltered from the earlier rain. They sat at a wrought iron table with orange-and-white-striped upholstered chairs set around it. The babbling waterfall Archer had seen earlier continued its walk down the terrace, ending in the spitting fire pit. The effect was nifty, thought Archer, if you were into all show and no substance.

"Give me the update first, Archer," commanded Kemper.

Archer took a swallow of his martini before answering, just because he felt like it.

He went through what had happened thus far, including the interviews done, steps taken, and information discovered. It was all perfunctory and necessary, and yet Archer just wanted to get beyond it and on to something meaningful.

Kemper listened to all of this and then took about a minute to clip and light up another Havana, puffing thoughtfully to get it primed. He sat back, took a sip of his stinger, and said, "Wilson filled me in on some of this. Now, I don't like it that you talked to Beth. I told you I didn't want her learning about this garbage."

"She was going to learn it whether you wanted her to or not. Better she heard it from us and not some rag."

Kemper looked him over but gave no opinion on this. He said, "Now, about this Fraser girl."

"What about her?"

"Any thoughts on who might have killed her?"

"Not yet. Have the cops talked to you?"

"Me? Why would they talk to me?"

Archer had had enough. He put his drink down and took his time lighting a cigarette from his new pack of Luckys. He waved out the match and put it in the ashtray.

"Look, I might have just started working with Willie, but I haven't fallen off a turnip truck since I was five. And to my knowledge, no one's removed my brain. So why don't we just jump over the horseshit and get straight on to one essential fact. Namely, that you had a strong motive to kill the lady, and that means the cops, even the bullshit ones in this town, will want to talk to you at some point."

"You haven't been in town long enough to know if the cops are bullshit."

"I'm a fast learner, and it wasn't that hard, actually."

"But they don't know about the blackmail attempt on me."

"There is no guarantee that will remain the case. And the fact that you hired us to look into it? You think us snooping around will go unnoticed? So why don't you drop your alibi on me and see if it passes muster."

"I don't like your attitude, Archer. As a general rule, people do not talk to me in that manner."

"Well, as a general rule, most guys I talk to aren't accused of having an affair with a woman who ended up murdered."

"I told you that I *wasn't* having an affair."

"And you're sticking to that?"

"Yes!"

"Do you know what your wife thinks?"

He sipped his stinger before responding. "I know, *generally*."

"Well, *specifically*, I don't think she believes your side of the story. Now, she probably hopes you haven't cheated on her, but that's all it is, a hope. So if the cops come to question her and she spills what she really thinks, the cops will be headed your way and that brings us back to: Do you have an alibi?"

"Why would they go to her?"

"I'll assume you're not really playing me for a dope and you actually want an answer, so here goes and listen closely. Your wife also has a motive to kill Ruby, and it's one of the oldest ones in the book: She thought you were sleeping with the woman. But she apparently has an alibi. She was at a dinner with friends from five to midnight."

His face clouded. "I see. When was the girl killed?"

"Say around ten."

Kemper's eyes eased to slits. He finished the stinger faster than he should have and looked around for the cocktail waitress to place an order for an encore.

She rushed over, bent low to flash some cleavage, batted her baby blues, and said in response to his order, "Coming right up, Mr. Kemper."

She swept away, apparently giddy with the prospect of serving the man cognac laced with crème de menthe.

Archer, who had watched this interaction closely, eyed the man and said, "All the gals come on to you like that?"

Kemper waved his Havana around like it was a wand that would make Archer and all of the man's problems just vanish. "I'm young, I'm wealthy, I'm well connected."

"And you're easy on the eyes," interjected Archer flatly. "Just in case you were too modest to say that."

"You have a quicker tongue than I initially gave you credit for,

Archer. I'm also married to the loveliest, richest woman in town. So naturally, some gals out there see me as a challenge. Can they get me to violate my marriage vows?"

"So, *can* they?"

"I'm a man, Archer. I'm not saying I'm any better than I am in that regard."

"Okay, now hopefully for the last time, do you have an alibi for the time Fraser was murdered?"

"I was with Wilson Sheen. We had dinner at the office and then we had a meeting there to go over campaign issues. I didn't leave there until well after eleven."

"Anybody else vouch for that?"

"No, but isn't he enough?"

"You better hope he is. And after that?"

"What does that matter? You said she died around ten."

"Just to satisfy my own curiosity."

"I went home."

"Anyone see you there? The Chinaman butler? Adam Stover, the chauffeur?"

"No."

"How about your wife?"

"You said she was at a dinner."

"How about later, when you went to bed?"

"We maintain separate bedrooms."

"Why is that?"

"None of your damn business."

"Okay, so you didn't see her at all? Or her car?"

"No. She might have stayed in town, for all I know."

"Where might that be?"

"She keeps an apartment in the Occidental Building. It's on Sawyer." He smirked. "Of course. She just can't get away from Daddy, can she? It's near the intersection with Carrillo Avenue. She had it before we were married."

Archer tapped out his smoke. "So not much of a marriage, then?"

"We've had a good run."

"I guess you missed the 'till death do us part' section of the negotiation."

"Don't give up your day job, Archer. You're not a satisfactory Abbott or Costello."

"Come on, Mr. Kemper, the line wasn't that bad. So you ever thought about kids? Sometimes that can make a difference."

"Thank you for the marriage advice, Archer. In the future keep it to your goddamn self."

The waitress brought Kemper's drink and placed it in front of him—as though she were presenting him with the crown jewels, thought Archer. "I hope you like it, Mr. Kemper. And if there's *anything* you need from me, all you have to do is say it and it's done. And I mean anything."

Yes you do, thought Archer. He half expected the woman to strip right there.

Kemper thanked her with a glance and she went on her way, smiling broadly.

Archer rose. "Well, I'll leave you to your drink and the fawning cocktail waitresses."

"I didn't kill that woman, Archer. I really didn't."

"Glad to hear it."

"Are you?"

"You're the client. It's not my job to put you in prison."

"Really? You strike me as more idealistic than that."

"Maybe once. Now, not so much."

Archer walked back inside, his work still not done. But then something happened to make him change course. Or, more specifically, *she* happened.

Bay Town was apparently a place where your intentions changed faster than the second hand on a clock.

CHAPTER

48

WILMA DARLING CAME OUT of the powder room and strode down the hall.

Archer ducked down another hall and then peered back around to follow her trek from powdering her nose. She pulled her gloves back on and drove her heels into the rug like American bayonets into Nazis as she marched to somewhere with a purpose that intrigued Archer. She was dressed all in crimson, and it was tight in all the places that counted. She had done something with her hair to make it even more luxurious, and it danced across her shoulders with every stride. The woman's makeup was immaculate. And from her resolute expression, Archer figured she was on the hunt for something.

The target presented itself when Wilson Sheen came walking down the hall in the opposite direction. He was dressed in a white dinner jacket, black bow tie, and dark pants. To Archer he looked like a headwaiter in a ritzy hotel. The short jacket didn't ride well on his wide, overweight frame, but Darling didn't seem to mind. She rushed forward and planted her lips over his, wrapping her long arms around his wide waist, while his hands patted her long, elegant back like a mom attempting to burp an infant.

When she pulled back, Sheen's face was coated with her attack, his face as crimson as her dress. He dabbed at the marks with his handkerchief, looking sheepish though pleased, as a few fellows passed by and gave him the universal male signs of success when hunting down the big game of females: the stupid schoolboy grins, the thumbs-up, and the tongues wagging like dogs in need of water…or something.

Arm in arm they ascended the stairs—Midnight Moods apparently did not have an elevator—and Archer followed at a discreet distance. They ventured all the way to the top floor and trekked in the direction of Fraser's old room. Archer kept pace with them, careful to keep his face pointed down and ready at a moment's notice to turn around if need be, though there were a few couples up here who looked to be heading toward the same Nirvana that Sheen and Darling were.

To his surprise, they entered the room right next to Fraser's, and Darling closed the door behind them. As Archer hustled to the spot, he heard the door being locked.

He glanced at Fraser's old room and decided it was worth a shot. The door was fortunately unlocked, and he entered, shutting the door quickly behind him. The body was thankfully gone. Archer found a water glass from the kitchen cabinet and made a beeline to the bedroom, which he figured would back up against the bedroom in the adjacent room. He placed the glass against the wall and his ear against the bottom of the glass.

He heard mumbles and heavy breathing and snatches of conversation that he couldn't understand. Something hard tapped against something else. Then laughter. Then moans. Then what sounded like two people disrobing as quickly as they could. Then a radio came on and he could hear loud music. Then he heard the sounds of bedsprings being bounced and then the movement settled into a rhythmic beat that, while he could appreciate it, helped him not one iota in his investigation.

He glanced around, wondering what to do, when he saw the small door in the ceiling with a short pull cord hovering right at the top. He grabbed a chair, stood on it, gripped the cord, and jerked, pulling down the hinged door. There were no dropdown stairs, but he got a handhold on either side of the opening, did a pull-up, and hoisted himself through. There was flooring up here over the ceiling joists and a chain with a light bulb at one end. He pulled it and the light came on, turning darkness reasonably bright.

He crawled quietly in the direction of the other apartment until he figured he was over it. Along the way he found some things that might actually be bona fide clues. But they would keep for now.

He found an identical door in the ceiling of the next apartment. With the loud music hopefully covering any sound he made, Archer decided to chance it and very slowly pushed down on the hatch.

He got it open about three or four inches, which gave him a sight line into the room.

Darling was on the bed, on her hands and knees. She was wearing nothing except her garter belt and the sheer nylons.

Sheen was completely naked, and Archer could see that the man looked just as fat unclothed, maybe more so. His skin was pasty; his chest, shoulders, and back were as hairy as a caveman's without an ounce of visible muscle. He was standing behind Darling and had a tight grip on her firm buttocks.

Archer felt embarrassed watching them, and he looked away. Part of him wanted to close the hatch, go back to Fraser's old room and run like hell. But then he asked himself: What would Willie Dash do? And it wasn't like he was watching out of purely prurient interest, he told himself. He was investigating. And what he was seeing didn't make a lot of sense. And that made him suspicious.

He looked back in time to see Sheen's efforts slow and he began to pant harder. Darling rose up enough for Archer to see her face. And now he was even more intrigued, and puzzled.

Her expression was a delicate mixture of boredom and disgust. The lady was clearly not there because she was in love with Sheen or found him attractive. Now the question was: Why *was* the lady there?

Archer once more averted his gaze, but he kept the hatch open so he could hear.

When Sheen again appeared to be fatiguing, she commenced pushing back hard against him and moaning louder, telling him he was bigger, harder, stronger, more virile than any man alive. It was like a coxswain calling out encouragement to the rowers to get them to accelerate their strokes. Sheen, thus puffed up, obliged her, but he was so unsteady on his feet he bumped into the nightstand and knocked both a half-filled glass and a Bible onto the floor.

In short order, the flabby man, thus inspired, finished his business and slumped over her, his massive weight forcing the woman down flat on the bed. Her expression was now one of irritation coupled with relief. Archer watched as she wriggled out from under him. Then she turned, smiled, and patted his cheek.

"Oh my God, Wilson. I'm gonna be walking funny for a week." He rubbed her cheek, smiled, and then promptly fell asleep.

She quickly rose, dressed fast, and headed for the door without even bothering to cover him with a sheet. Her glance back at the sleeping man was full of disgust.

Archer closed the ceiling door and retraced his steps to Fraser's door.

He looked out in time to see Darling's backside as she headed down the hall. Her stockings' seams were all off-center, but everything else seemed to be in place.

Archer fell in behind the woman and trailed her back to the first floor. She went to the check girl to get her hat, a little pillbox number the color of her dress with a little black veil tacked up. While she was doing that Archer spotted the cocktail waitress who had served him and Kemper earlier and asked her a couple of questions. She answered them, and he passed her a buck in thanks. She stuck it down her blouse, eyed him, and said, "Well, I get off at one if *you're* interested."

"Thanks, but I got other plans."

"Jeez, I can't buy a man tonight."

She flounced off, and Archer hustled over to claim *his* hat while Darling was adjusting hers.

"Well, funny meeting you here," he said to Darling.

She quickly turned. "Mr. Archer?"

"I thought this place was built mainly for the guys."

Her gaze inadvertently ventured upward, all the way, Archer thought, to the room where Sheen was now peacefully sleeping off probably the best sex of his life.

She blushed beautifully and looked back at him. "I was meeting a friend. And I come here for a drink now and then."

"Oh, well, then I'll leave you to it."

"No. I mean, I've met my friend and we're all...done now."

"Well, then how about that drink we talked about?"

"What? Oh, um, all right. What the hell."

"That's what I like to hear from a gal: 'What the hell.'"

He was rewarded with a crimsoning of her cheeks.

They got their drinks, he a beer and she a gin and tonic. He led her out to the rear terrace, and they occupied the same chairs he and Kemper had used earlier.

"So, was your friend one of the gals in the office?" he said.

"Um, yes, Sally. We had a drink."

"You like working for Mr. Kemper?"

"It's a job. I like the conditions."

"I guess you spend more time with Wilson Sheen, though."

She glanced sharply at him, searching his features for some telltale sign that his words meant something more. But Archer had prepared himself and gave nothing away.

"I mean, that's why he has Sheen, right? To handle stuff for him."

"Yes, that's right. I do deal with Mr. Sheen more."

She pulled out a pack of Pall Malls and he lit one for her. Her hand trembled. She took a puff and said, "Why were you meeting with him?"

"Something to do with Kemper's campaign. We're helping him out."

She said derisively, "If he can't beat a damn dentist, he doesn't deserve the job."

"Right. So you come here often?"

"Once or maybe twice a week. For a drink, like I said."

"You ever run across a gal named Ruby Fraser?"

"Was she the one who was killed here? I read about it in the paper."

"She was. So, did you know her?"

She tapped her ash into the ashtray a little too hard. It was like a toddler banging his toy against the wall right before she went truly berserk.

"No, no I didn't."

"I spoke with Kemper earlier. He was here. We sat at this very table."

Her eyes opened wider with interest. "Really? What did you talk about?"

"Just business. He said Wilson Sheen was here, too. Have you seen him? I think I spotted him a while ago. I wanted to talk to him as well."

"Mr. Sheen? No, no, I haven't seen him. If he was here, he might have left. I find he...tires easily."

Archer observed she had to struggle to keep the smile off her face. Finally she looked away from him and drank her gin and tonic nearly to the bottom of the glass.

"Oh, that's too bad. So how's business?"

"We're very busy. Mr. Kemper has his fingers in lots of pies."

"Do you know his wife?"

"I've seen her."

"She's quite beautiful."

"You know, Archer, the gal you're with is the one you should be complimenting."

He grinned. "Sorry. You don't need me to tell you that you're quite the looker."

"That's better. And I *do* need you to tell me."

"Okay, you're quite the looker. You stood out from the other gals in the office like a flamingo in the desert."

"First time I've been compared to a flamingo, but I'll take it. Even though those gals are younger than me, Archer?"

"Even though."

She looked over his shoulder and her gaze caught on something.

When Archer turned to look, all he saw was a waitress setting down a shrimp cocktail in front of an old man with a gal half his age on his lap.

"You know them?" asked Archer.

"He's a client of Mr. Kemper. Owns some property Kemper is trying to develop. His wife wouldn't like what he's doing right now."

"I guess not."

"So why do you want to talk to Sheen?"

"Part of the investigation. After this drink, I'm going to try to find him. He must be around here somewhere. I'll roust him."

She ran her eye up and down him to such an invasive degree that Archer felt his own cheeks start to burn.

"Why don't we blow this joint, Archer? My place is only twenty minutes from here."

"But what about Sheen?"

"Come by the office tomorrow. You can talk to him then. He's there every day, and this time I won't make you wait."

"So what are we going to do at your place?"

She gave him a look that raised one distinct possibility. "If I can't think of something and you can't think of something, then something is very wrong, mister."

"I've got a car."

"Good, because I don't."

"Do you mind if I ask you a few questions along the way?"

"Not so long as we get to where we're really going at the end."

49

"THIS IS YOUR CAR? REALLY?" she said as the valet brought it up.

Archer flipped the kid a quarter and held the door for her. "Yeah it is."

"Shouldn't I be getting in the other side?"

"The Brits do it differently from us," he replied.

"So this is a British car?"

"No, it's actually French, but it's a long story and not that exciting."

"Come on, where'd you get this ride?"

"Won it in a poker game back in Reno."

"Wow, you must be really *good*," she said. "Maybe I'll find out."

He smiled at her. "You know, you have a whole other persona at work."

"At work, everyone has to be someone they're not. I'm no exception. And I'm a gal who likes to have fun in her off-hours. All work and no play makes poor Wilma very dull indeed."

"Okay."

"So what questions do you have?"

"You ever see Kemper when you're at Midnight Moods? I understand that he's a regular."

"I see him sometimes. He plays cards. They only let men in there."

"Yeah, I saw that. How come?"

"They don't want to lose to women, that's how come."

"You ever see him with Ruby Fraser?"

"How should I know? I don't know what she looks like."

Archer described the woman for her.

"Well, that sounds like half the women who work there," she noted.

"Yeah, I guess it does."

"Why are you interested in her and Mr. Kemper?"

"Part of the business I'm doing with him."

"You think he was messing around with her? He's a married man."

"He ever mess with you?"

She shook her head. "To tell you the truth, Archer, I think he's in love with his wife."

"You're the first one to say that, and that includes him *and* his wife."

"Some of the gals at work have given it their best shot with the man, and came away with zip for their troubles."

"What about Sheen?"

"What about him?"

"You or the other girls ever make a run at him?"

"Maybe some of the other gals, but I don't like to bake, Archer."

"What does that mean?" he said with a puzzled expression.

"I don't enjoy sticking my fingers in dough." She let out a throaty laugh that was so spontaneous and unexpected that Archer couldn't help but join her.

"Hey," she said. "You look like a man who carries a pocket flask, and I need a drink."

He pulled it out and handed it across. She took a long sip and screwed the top back on before handing it back to him.

She directed him to her place, a one-story bungalow on the fringes of Bay Town in a quiet tree-lined neighborhood of like abodes. Like much of Bay Town, it smacked of Spanish influence, with stucco walls, wrought iron railings that were starting to rust from the salt air and stain the stucco, and a peaked terra-cotta tile roof. The front door was dark oak with black, strappy metal adornments.

She slid the key in and Archer followed her inside.

"Nice place," he said, looking around at the comfortable and plush furnishings, the colorful Oriental rug, the full mahogany bar set against one wall, with crystal glasses set on top and neat rows of bottles, along with a cocktail shaker and jigger set that looked well used.

She put her hat and purse on the coffee table and spun around to look at him, her fingers playing over the belt around her waist.

"I'm going to freshen up, help yourself to a drink. I've got cigarettes in that bowl over there."

"Thanks. What can I have ready for you?"

"Oh, we'll think of something when I get back."

She departed the room and a minute later he heard the shower start.

Part of Archer wanted to just walk out the door. He was investigating a case that had to do with the man Darling was working for. He had observed her having sex with that man's associate for reasons Archer did not yet know. Professionally, he told himself, it was better that he just walk away now.

But he didn't. Because he wanted to find out why she'd slept with the man. At least Archer told himself that was the only reason.

He poured himself a bourbon neat, lit up a cigarette, and walked around the room. He eyed Darling's purse and took a few moments to examine the contents. He was really getting into this shamus thing. There was a money clip with twenty bucks' worth of mad money, the pack of Pall Malls, a small pewter hip flask about half full, a lighter with a *D* engraved on it, and several ivory boxes that were empty. And a nickel-plated .22 Derringer with oak grips. It was loaded with four bullets and hadn't been recently fired, if Archer's sense of smell was any indicator.

He heard the shower stop and he put the items back in the purse and placed it exactly where it had been before. He moved over to the window, where there was a single streetlamp burning brightly but trying and failing to break through the marine fog rolling in. This place reminded Archer of London. Some days you could barely see a foot in front of you.

He was still standing there looking out when she came back into the room.

Darling had on a robe that was even more transparent than Archer's thoughts at the moment. Barefoot, she approached, a lioness to the lion, and it was not up for debate which would prevail.

"You freshen up better than anyone I know," he began.

She took his drink from him and set it down. She pulled his cigarette from his lips and took a long drag on it before bending down and tapping it out in the ashtray.

"You don't like to beat around the bush, I take it," he said.

"Life's short, so I don't have time to waste."

"You're young."

"We're all young, Archer, right up to the minute we're just a picture on the wall for someone to remember."

She put her arms around him and pressed both her body and her lips against his.

"As soon as I saw you at the office, Archer, I started having thoughts about you." She pulled away for a moment, looking at him. "You seem like you'd be good to a woman."

"I try to be good to everyone."

"You gonna kiss me back, or do I have to place an order for delivery?"

"You know, I am investigating a case."

"Investigate *me*, as much as you want."

"We probably shouldn't be doing this."

She kissed him so hard he tasted both the gin and the Lucky. It was an earthy combo. She took his hand and led him out of the room and into her bedroom, and there didn't seem to be a thing Archer could do about it.

Darling let the robe fall to the floor. Though he had seen her naked with Sheen, the woman's figure still left him breathless, particularly this close up. And there went any possibility of his walking out on her. What had Kemper said?

I'm a man, Archer. I'm not saying I'm any better than I am in that regard.

God help me, thought Archer.

She helped him undress and they slid into bed together.

After that it was a frantic twenty minutes of copulation that Archer wasn't even sure he could understand, much less rationalize. He wasn't one to jump into bed with a woman he barely knew, although this wasn't the first time he had done it. But Darling took control from the very start and never relinquished it. He was no babe when it came to sex, but the lady was clearly a few levels above him in that department. Archer felt like he'd been hit by a Mack truck, in the best possible sense, even as her nails gouged his back and slid all the way down to his butt.

Later, they lay together on top of the sheet, soaked in each other's sweat.

Her lungs heaving and her body still twitching she stroked his chest and panted, "Good God, Archer. How long since you've been with a woman anyway, mister?"

"Too long, apparently. And just for the record, you threw in a few moves that were new to me."

"See, that's what you get for going to bed with a 'mature' woman."

"Yeah. A mature wildcat, more like."

She sat up and played with his chest hairs while giving him a heavy-lidded once-over. "If I let you stay the night, you think you might be up for a repeat performance before breakfast? They say exercise helps the appetite. And I make a killer cup of joe."

"I like coffee. A lot."

She smacked him playfully on the cheek and then French kissed him. She pulled her lips away and breathed in his ear, "Mine's good to the very last drop, sweetie."

They slept heavily, and when they woke early the following morning Darling slid on top of him and they went for round two. After that they slept for another hour, and she made him a cup of coffee and two fried eggs with toast.

He showered, and when he got out he found her pressing his clothes while stark naked. He dressed and was giving her a kiss, his hand around her bare waist and thinking about maybe going back to bed for extra innings, when her phone rang.

And everything in the world changed.

50

ARCHER AND DASH WERE IN THE DELAHAYE on the way to Midnight Moods. He had called Dash from Darling's bungalow and filled him in on the call Darling had gotten earlier that morning. Then he had driven over to the office.

Dash said, "Who found the body?"

"Douglas Kemper told Wilma Darling that a maid found Wilson Sheen dead in a room at Midnight Moods."

"Which room?"

"If I had to guess, it would be the one next to Fraser's."

"If you had to guess?"

"Let me fill you in."

Archer told Dash everything about the night before, including meeting with Kemper and learning about Beth's apartment in town, and seeing Sheen and Darling together in bed.

"And in the crawlspace in the ceiling I found some bloodstains."

"So that's how they moved her body," said Dash thoughtfully. "From that room, through the attic access, and into Fraser's room. How the hell did the coppers not see that possibility? How did *I* not see it? I must be getting blind in my old age."

"Well, I didn't see it either the first time around. And who would think to move a dead body through the attic?"

"Well, the room where Fraser was killed probably has another body in it. Did Kemper say how Sheen was killed?"

"No."

"And you were with Wilma Darling when Kemper called?"

"Yes."

"Did she say how he sounded?"

"'Frantic' was the word she used. You think Pickett will be out for this one, too?"

"Carl can't find his teeth before nine o'clock."

They arrived at Midnight Moods to find prowlers everywhere along with the coroner's wagon. Ernie Prettyman was standing outside of the room where Sheen had been found.

"How'd you hear so fast, Willie?" asked a surprised Prettyman. "I've only been here an hour myself."

"Friend of a friend," replied Dash. "Can we see the body?"

Prettyman led them into the room where Wilson Sheen lay on his stomach with a sheet partially covering him.

"How'd he die?" asked Dash.

Prettyman lifted the sheet, revealing a wide, bloody wound in the middle of the back. "Knife to the heart. Quick, silent, and efficient."

"Was he here alone?" asked Dash.

"It was clear that he had been with…someone."

"A woman, you mean?"

"Yes."

Dash said, "Archer found the way that they shifted Fraser's body from here to there."

Archer led the way next door to Fraser's room and showed Prettyman the ceiling access door.

"It runs over to the next room where Sheen was killed. I found bloodstains up there that might be Fraser's. Her room is the last on the corridor, so that's the only room that's next to hers."

Prettyman looked at the door and then at Dash and then at Archer. "You found this last night?"

"Yes."

"What time?"

"Around ten."

"Coroner thinks Sheen bought it around eleven." Prettyman glanced at Dash and then eyed Archer. "So it's interesting that you were here around that time, right next door. And more than that, in the space over where the murder took place."

Dash said, "Okay, Ern, you got every right to ask questions and put the screws to Archer because he was here around the time in question. But he's got no motive to kill Sheen. We were working for his boss."

"Motives are funny things, Willie. They can turn on a dime if you look at things at a different angle." He paused. "I'm sure you remember telling me that."

"I do. And you're right. But Archer won't be leaving town. I give you my word on that. So he'll be around to answer any other questions you might have. But just to add my two cents, the guy who killed Sheen is not in this room right now."

Ern nodded slowly. "Okay, but I have to do my job."

"Yes you do." Dash glanced at Archer before saying, "Has this room been assigned to anyone here either now or in recent history?"

"Mabel Dawson said the last occupant was a vaudeville performer named Guy Parnell. But he left about a week ago. No one's been in there since." Prettyman glanced at Archer. "So you didn't see or hear anyone while you were poking around up there?"

"Ern, come on, what do you think?" said Dash, drawing a look from Archer, who was careful to avoid Prettyman's eye. "Now, we need to find the connection between Fraser and Sheen."

"If there is one," said Prettyman.

"We've both been doing this a long time. Two stiffs coming from the same room? There's a connection, all right."

"Any chance of your telling me who your client is now?"

"About the same odds as yesterday. Look, me and Archer have

to get going. Things are rolling fast now, and I don't like playing catch-up."

"Okay, but remember, Archer doesn't leave town."

Dash and Archer made their way quickly down the steps and outside.

"What was the deal back there?" said Archer. "You pretty much lied to the police."

"This line of work requires balance, Archer. And if you look at what I said, you'll find that I threaded that needle as well as it could be. Ern is a good guy but he's by the book, meaning whatever we tell him goes straight to Carl Pickett's ear. And right now, I don't want Carl knowing what we know."

"Right."

"One thing Wilma Darling said does surprise me," noted Dash.

"Just one? Then you're a better man than me."

"She said she really thought Kemper loved his wife."

Archer looked intrigued. "Yeah. And I believed her when she said it. And talking to the guy, well…"

"Well what?"

Archer said, "Some guys are genuine lotharios. And some guys want others to think they are. I believe Kemper falls into the latter group. He just tries too hard but then never seals the deal. I talked to the cocktail waitress who served us last night. It was pretty clear to me that he could've had her for the price of a Coke. She told me Kemper didn't even ask her what time she got off when she came back to pick up his empty drink."

"And I wonder when he actually left. And what he was doing between the time he left you and then left this place."

"What motive would he have to kill his second lieutenant and campaign manager?" asked Archer.

"I'm not looking purely for motives right now. I'm looking for connections. Nine times out of ten when you do that, the motives become apparent."

They climbed into the Delahaye and set off back to town.

"Drop me off at my garage. I'm getting my car back today. Then I want you to go and talk to Wilma Darling and see what you can get out of her, namely, who put her up to jumping Sheen's bones last night. Call the office when you have something."

"Okay. What will you be doing besides getting your car?"

Dash said, "Putting the pieces together. Gumshoeing sort of requires that."

AFTER DROPPING OFF DASH, Archer drove over to Kemper's office, but there was a sign on the door that read: "Due to unforeseen events, the office will be closed indefinitely."

Yeah, I guess a murder qualifies as unforeseen, to everyone except the person who killed him.

Archer ducked into a Rexall drugstore. He got a cup of coffee at the counter and smoked a cigarette while he mulled over things. Then he climbed back into the Delahaye and motored over to Darling's bungalow. There was a new two-door brown Ford coupe in the carport, something Archer had not noticed the night before, but it might not have been there last night.

He went up to the front door and knocked. It took a minute but he finally heard footsteps.

"Yes," said Darling in a tortured voice through the wood.

"It's Archer."

"Go away."

"I don't think you mean that."

"I damn well mean it."

"I need to talk to you, Wilma."

"Why?"

"Because Sheen's being murdered concerns you."

"I don't know—"

"I know you slept with him last night, Wilma. And I know he

was alive when you left him. But what I need to know is who put you up to it? Because whoever did might want to clean up loose ends. If you get my meaning."

The door slowly opened and she stood there in a thick white cotton bathrobe that went all the way to her bare feet. Her face was makeup free, her hair was a mess, and Archer thought she was more beautiful now than she had been last night.

"Come in," she said curtly.

He sat in a chair while she perched across from him. Archer saw an ashtray full of smoked cigarettes and a pitcher of something that was nearly empty.

"You okay?" he said. "You don't look so good."

"No, I'm not okay. And what the hell do you mean you knew Sheen and I—"

"I saw you go into the room together. And I listen well at keyholes."

"You son of a bitch. You rotten little sneak..." She grabbed the pitcher to throw it at him, but he was too quick for the woman and snatched it away from her.

He set it down out of her reach and said, "Calm down, Wilma. It's my job. Sheen is dead. We need to figure this out. You have a vested interest in doing so. I know you know that."

She pulled a tissue from her pocket and dabbed at her eyes. "What I know is that this is a godawful nightmare for me."

"It wasn't so good for Sheen, either."

She blew her nose into the hanky. "You want a drink?"

"No, I'm good. And it's a little early for me."

"Well, mix me a martini minus the olives and then think of a way out of this hell."

He fixed the drink, handed it to her, and sat back down. "Tell me about last night."

"What do you want to know?"

"Who told you to sleep with Sheen?"

"How do you know anyone did?"

"Come on, Wilma, I'm trying to help you. I know you didn't want to be with the guy. Someone put you up to it. Who?"

She looked at him in misery. "I don't know, Archer. I really don't know who it was." In her agitation she finished off the martini, rose, and padded around the room, lighting a Camel she plucked from the bowl.

"How can you not know?"

She pivoted to stare dead at him. "I'm not a whore, Archer."

"Wilma, no one's saying that you are, least of all me."

She sat down on the arm of the chair he was in. She took another puff of her Camel, tilted her head back, and drilled the ceiling with the smoke. "I...I got an unsigned note yesterday. It was in an envelope in my mailbox. It had a thousand bucks in it and a note that told me to sleep with Sheen last night at Midnight Moods. A thousand bucks, Archer! That's more than I make in a year working for Kemper."

"I think you're underpaid, then. But why do it at all? Why not just keep the money?"

"Because the note also said that if I took the money and didn't do it, well, that I would regret it."

"So it was a threat, then?"

"Look, I didn't want to do it, but I also didn't want any trouble. And I didn't know who to give the money back to. And if I left it out on the porch or in the mailbox, and somebody else swiped it, where would that leave me? With no money and somebody out there thinking I stiffed them." She got up and started pacing again. "So...so I did it. I phoned and arranged to meet Wilson at Midnight Moods."

"I saw you tackle him in the hall. I thought you were going to suffocate him with smooches."

She put a shaky hand over her face. "God, I can't believe I did it...It made me sick."

"I'm sure."

She stopped and looked at him. "What you must think of me."

"You did it for the money because you were caught between a rock and a hard place. A guy does it, he's smart like a fox because he's being paid to have fun. A woman does the same thing, and she's judged for it. I never really got that myself. I'm not judging you, Wilma. I don't have the right."

She perched next to him again. "Where do they make guys like you, Archer? I'd like to buy a dozen."

"Did the note tell you which room to go to last night?"

"Yes. They said it was empty, would be unlocked, and there'd be nobody to bother us."

"Do you know that right next door is where Ruby Fraser was found?"

"Oh my God!" She gripped his arm. "Look, Archer, I swear that he was alive when I left him. He was asleep, sawing logs. I swear."

"I know he was, Wilma."

She looked relieved but then gazed at him suspiciously. "You gathered all that from listening at the keyhole?"

"I trained under some of the best keyhole listeners in the business."

"So what do I do now?"

"I'd take you down to the police station where you could make a statement, only I don't trust Chief Pickett."

"Do you really think I'm in danger?"

"Yes. Whoever sent you the note used you to set up Sheen. But what I don't get is how did they know he'd fall asleep? He might have left the room with you."

Darling looked puzzled. "When we were going up to the room he was yawning."

Archer snapped his fingers. "Somebody slipped him a mickey. Did he say where he was before he met up with you?"

"Yeah, he was having a drink in the bar."

"Did he say who with?"

"No, he didn't. Maybe it was Kemper. You said he was there last night, too."

"Other people must have seen you and Sheen together. I'm surprised the cops haven't been to see you."

"They probably will be. And then what do I tell them? They'll never believe my story. They'll think I killed him. Shit." She looked as miserable as anyone Archer had ever seen.

"We'll figure this out, Wilma. Now, there aren't a lot of people who could come up with a thousand bucks, so that narrows the list of suspects."

She looked up. "But why get Wilson out of the way? What's the big deal?"

"He's Kemper's campaign manager. It might hurt his election chances."

"But if they really wanted to do that, why not just bump *Kemper* off? Then it's guaranteed he doesn't win."

"How long have you worked for Kemper?"

"Seven years. There aren't many office jobs for a gal around here that don't involve fetching dry cleaning and making coffee. I started out where the other gals are now and worked my way up. It might not sound like much to you, but it means a lot to me."

"So who doesn't want Kemper to be mayor?"

"Anybody pulling for Alfred Drake, I guess."

"Why is he running for mayor?"

She shrugged. "He was on the town council, so he has some experience."

"I've heard that Drake might have some serious money men behind him. Vegas types, even mobsters. You think that's possible?"

"Hell, Archer, in this world anything is possible."

Archer said, "Kemper closed the office. And it's Friday, so you have the weekend, too. Can you go to some place where you can be safe?"

She puffed nervously on her cigarette. "I used to drive down to Ventura and stay at a place on the water. I could go there."

"Then do it. Is that your brown coupe out there?"

"Yeah."

"Okay, why don't you pack and leave now? And give me the address just in case."

"Just in case what?"

"Just in case I have to come and rescue you."

"Archer, this is serious. Stop joking around."

"I'm being dead serious, Wilma. And that neat little Derringer you keep in your purse? Be sure to take it with you."

CHAPTER

52

Archer's next stop was the town library. He hadn't been to a library in a while, but whenever he had gone, it had been for a good reason. In the past, it was just about choosing a good book to read. Now, it was all about finding information that might help solve two murders.

He spoke with the woman at the front desk. She was elderly with a granny hump, and also knowledgeable and enthusiastic. She guided Archer to a shelf and helped him find what he needed. He sat down with the books that dealt with California law and started to read. He was there for seven hours. He made notes of everything and put the items back, thanked the librarian, and left. His next stop was the town hall, which he discovered was located on Sawyer Avenue, of course.

It was a three-story stone-and-stucco building with three faux bell towers, the ubiquitous red tile roof, and thick arched doorways. He made his way to the clerk's office, where a dour woman in her forties turned out to be very helpful once he showed her his PI license. She actually seemed excited to be assisting in a "very private investigation." She got him the records and ledger books that he asked for, though he had only a vague idea of what he was looking for.

Archer sat for another hour and went through each of the items methodically, tracking things down and having, in turn, to request other files. He made copious notes and thought about what he had found. When he was done he carried everything back up to her and thanked her for her help.

"Did you get your answers?"

"Along with more questions, yes."

"Well, isn't that always the case?"

Archer headed to the waterfront, but he didn't go back to the harbormaster's shack. He went to the rental boat man instead, who Archer had found out on his first visit there was named Reggie McKenzie. He asked Archer how his ride out had been.

"A little bumpy coming back in, but that boat was solid as a rock."

McKenzie smiled and pulled on the briarwood pipe clenched between his teeth. "Chris-Craft knows how to build a boat, that's for certain. Hell, I'd take that vessel pretty much anywhere without a worry in my head."

Archer gazed at the water. "About three miles out I nearly ran into a chunk of rock; it wasn't on the navigation map."

McKenzie shook his head, looking angry. "How many times have I said that to folks around here, eh?"

"What's the deal with it?"

"Navy thing. Not many know about it because not many go out there."

"I got pretty close but I didn't see anyone or anything on it."

"That's right. Navy moved out about, oh, six months ago. War's long over, what they were doing there is over, too, I imagine."

"I noted that there was a big dock on the island. Handle a destroyer easy."

"You're right about that." McKenzie took his pipe out and pointed the bowl out toward the sea. "There was a stretch of land that was right at the water line. Hazard to boats, I can tell you that. Had to be marked and all. Well, anyway, the Navy shipped in more dirt and rock and cement than you'd ever seen, mister.

Then they built on what was out there and raised it way above the water. Solid as the land we're standing on right now and high enough to where you don't have to worry about flooding 'less you get a typhoon or such out there. I sat here and watched the cargo ships heading out every day. But back then the military did some extraordinary things. Heard they built that there Pentagon in less than two years."

"But what was the point? I thought they took over all the Channel Islands."

"I'll tell you what I heard from some of the military folks coming through here." He settled back in his seat and pulled up his oilskin coat against the brisk breeze blowing in off the water as Archer leaned back against the doorjamb. "Now, back in forty-two, I think it was, a Jap sub come right up to shore around here and opened fire with its deck gun and torpedoes. Did quite a bit of damage. Found out later another sub did the same thing off the coast of Santa Barbara near the Ellwood Oil Fields. Hit some fuel tanks and other such things. Now, nobody was killed, thank God, but it scared the hell out of everybody." McKenzie took a moment to restuff and relight his pipe. "Anyway, it took so long for the Navy to get out there them Jap subs were long gone. See, Anacapa Island was the closest and it was still too durn far away. So the Navy got its marching orders. They searched for and found that bit of land just at the waterline barely three miles out and built what they called a 'rapid response' site on it. They had docks big enough for PT boats and even destroyers, like you said, and they also put radar out there and laid minefields for them subs, and had observation towers and God knows what else. They even had a runway there to land planes. And I saw them ship out a big gun, too."

Archer thought back to the remnants of the Mark VI railway gun and nodded. "Right. Then what happened?"

"Well, it operated all throughout the war. Kept the Japs off the coast here, I can tell you that. Would hear guns firing out there from time to time, see the sky all light up. Took a boat out once just to see and nearly got run over by a destroyer. Last time I did that. Then, like I said, about six months ago, it all went away. Ships went out there and pretty much dismantled the whole thing. I took my boat out and watched them do some of it. Pretty interesting."

"Who owns it now?"

"Now that's a fair question, young man." The man's eyes danced with a bit of excitement. "But I will tell you that some folks have been ferrying back and forth to that spot over the last few months."

"What folks?"

"Well, that I'm not sure about." McKenzie suddenly looked perplexed.

"What?" said Archer, who had noted the man's change of expression.

"Well, I hadn't given it much thought before, but your asking made me think."

"Think of what?"

"We had a mayor, a good one, name of Ben Smalls."

Archer tried to keep his features unreadable. "Right, I think I heard about him. Didn't he have an accident in his house?"

"He drowned in his bathtub, poor fellow. He was a good mayor. Nice, polite young man."

Keeping his voice calm, Archer said, "But what made you think of him?"

"See, he rented a boat from me about, oh, two months ago. No, I take that back. It was my wife's birthday, so it was six weeks ago. Anyway, he went out to that there island."

"How do you know that?"

"'Cause he asked me how to get there." McKenzie eyed Archer. "Hey, now, did you go out there the other night? Just asking, 'cause your fishing story sounded, well, fishy."

"Like I said, I almost ran into it. But as you know, it's not on the map you gave me."

The man's suspicious look faded. "Oh, that's right, sure."

"Did Smalls say anything to you when he got back here?"

"No, but he didn't look happy. I remember thinking, what's he all riled up about? Anyway, couple weeks later he's dead and buried. Makes you think, you know." He snapped his fingers. "We can all go just like that. Have to enjoy every day we got, yes sir."

"Right," said Archer. "Well, I hope you enjoy the rest of this day."

Archer got back to the boardinghouse just in time for Callahan to confront him on the stairs.

"Where the hell have you been? I'm going to be late."

"Late? For what?"

She tapped her high heel impatiently. "It's Friday, Archer. You were going to drive me to Midnight Moods so I can sign my contract. And then I've got to start rehearsals."

"Damn, that's right. Okay, I'm ready. You got your stuff?"

"I'll be down in five minutes, and then you better drive like you mean it."

* * *

"Wow, Archer, look at that!" said Callahan.

They were on the road to Midnight Moods and had come upon a billboard with her picture along with the caption, IF YOU LOVED LIBERTY BONDS, YOU'RE GOING TO LOVE HER. COME SEE LIBERTY CALLAHAN'S DEBUT AT MIDNIGHT MOODS, FRIDAY AT TEN SHARP.

"That must have gone up pretty recently. I was out there this morning and didn't see it."

She glanced at him. "And they used your idea."

"You're famous," said Archer. "Just don't forget me on the way up."

"Don't be silly…whoever you are," she said, slapping his arm, but her gaze was riveted on the billboard. Archer cut his speed so that she had longer to look at herself. He just had to grin watching the woman gazing at her image.

They parked in front of Midnight Moods, which was fairly empty at this time of the day. Later tonight it would be a different story, with large crowds coming to see the woman sitting next to him.

On the side of the building was Callahan splashed twenty feet high.

"That wasn't here this morning, either. They're really giving you the star treatment."

"Well, I'll show them that I'm worth it."

"So, you ready?" he said.

"I've been ready for a long time, Archer."

They met with Dawson in her office, where Callahan inked her deal. Callahan showed Dawson her outfits, and the pair settled on a slick, silver sleeveless number with fringe along the short hem.

"So does your agent there get his ten percent or what?" asked Dawson.

Callahan shot Archer a surprised glance. He held up his hands and said, "I was just being a friend. I don't want any commission."

"Okay. We can go into rehearsals now. Later, we got a gal to do your hair and makeup. The stage manager will do your sound check and make sure the acoustics are good. I don't know if you know, but we're charging five dollars admission into the theater for folks to see and hear you."

"How are sales?" asked Archer.

"We sold out," said Dawson. "Now I hope people show up."

"Why wouldn't they?" said Callahan.

Dawson glanced nervously at Archer and said, "We had some more trouble last night, but I think it'll be fine. Did you like the billboard we put up?" she added quickly, no doubt noting the puzzled look on Callahan's features. "And the one on the building?"

"Oh, yeah, they're terrific. I've never seen myself that big."

"Where's her room?" asked Archer.

"Follow me."

The room was on the second floor near the end of the hall.

"What do you think?" asked Dawson.

It was a four-room flat with a full kitchen, bedroom, bathroom, and a comfortable front room fully furnished.

"This looks swell," said Callahan looking around, her eyes dancing with delight.

"It should. It's the best we have." She eyed Archer. "Pass your test?"

"If Liberty's okay with it, then it's okay by me."

"Oh, hallelujah. Now let's go start rehearsal, young lady."

A few minutes later, Archer walked through the main bar area, only stopping when someone tugged on his sleeve and said, "Sit."

He looked down and saw Willie Dash perched in an armchair and cradling a cup of coffee in one hand.

Archer sat across from him. "What are you doing here? I thought you went to get your car, and then were going to do some piecing together."

"How long do you think it takes to pick up a car? And there is that thing in the detective business about coming back to the scene of the crime. And I *am* piecing things together right here in this chair. So what are *you* doing here?"

"I brought my friend, Liberty. She starts work here tonight."

"She the gal plastered all over?"

"She is."

Dash gave him a hiked eyebrow. "Well, lucky you."

"It's not like that between us."

"That's what they all say. Did you talk to Wilma Darling?"

Archer filled him in on their conversation.

"So she's off to Ventura," said Dash thoughtfully as he sipped his coffee.

"Is that a problem?"

"I don't know, Archer. I haven't quite got a handle on all this yet. Lot of moving parts."

Archer hadn't told Dash about going out to the island or his conversation with Reggie McKenzie, but he did want to run something by Dash.

"So, the only reason there's a mayor's election is because the former mayor died in the bathtub. Is it possible he was murdered?"

Dash eyed him severely. "Of course Ben Smalls was murdered, Archer."

Archer sat back, a little surprised by the other man's emphatic response. "But you didn't do anything about it. The police apparently never concluded one way or another."

"I'm not a cop, I'm a private dick, so what exactly *could* I do about it? But look at it this way—depending on who wins the election, certain things are going to happen in this town to benefit someone."

"So you think the murders are connected to the election?"

"They're both tied to Douglas Kemper, so I would say yes."

"What do you think about Armstrong's take on the mob and boys from Vegas?"

"Why would they want to come here? Like Armstrong said, they can get their hooks into Frisco and LA and Santa Barbara with the same amount of effort. And they're all bigger prizes than Bay Town."

"Like you said, you think Pickett is on the take. Low-hanging-fruit kind of thing, if they have him in their pocket."

Dash nodded slowly. "That's a good deduction, Archer. Very good. So Pickett might be at the center of this, clearing out the way for those boys to come here."

"So their preferred candidate is Drake, the dentist. Why?"

"Maybe we need to have a talk with old Drake."

"You know him?"

"Oh, yeah. Really smart guy, but he's a dishrag, Archer. With about as much curb appeal as a bag of trash. Kemper would win in a landslide, if he's allowed to keep running."

"If Kemper drops out, could someone else enter the race?"

"Deadline was last week. It's Kemper versus Drake, for better or worse." He looked at his watch. "Drake will probably be home by now. So let's go see the tooth fairy."

53

Alfred Drake's home was a large two-story dwelling made of red brick painted white. It had views of the ocean on an elevated plot of land that was lush and green and filled with palm trees, live oaks, and pretty much every native species in between.

"Damn, how much does it cost to get your teeth fixed in this town?" said Archer. He pulled the car to a stop in front of the columned verandah that spanned the entire length of the house, with a sea of emerald-green grass spreading out before it.

"For a while Drake was the only quality game in town and he made a tidy sum. Then he invested well and he's also done some real estate projects around here. He's a sharp guy, like I said. I found out his father was in real estate in New York and made a small fortune, which went to Drake. He built this place about five years ago."

Archer gave him a sidelong glance. "Why do I think you might have investigated Drake before?"

"Why, Archer, that's confidential." But Dash tacked on a grin. "Number of years ago some guy got really upset over a deal he did with Drake. He thought Drake had cheated him. Turned out my client was the one cheating and just hired me to hassle Drake into a quick settlement. But Drake stuck to his guns. I always respected him for that."

A black woman in a maid's uniform answered the door and told them that Drake was out by the pool. She took Dash's card and left them there while she checked to see, as she put it, "whether Mr. Drake is accepting visitors at this time."

After she left, Archer said, "I thought we were going to see a dentist, not the president."

"The man *can* put on airs," noted Dash. "In that regard, he's just like most politicians."

"Right. Are there any *honest* politicians?"

"Sure. They're mostly all honest in the first six months. It's only the time after that where they convince themselves they can do no wrong and everything that comes out of their mouths is the gospel, but all they really care about is getting reelected."

"Franklin Roosevelt was pretty good."

"He was already rich. Nobody could touch him."

Archer gave him a dubious look. "So you're saying only rich people are incorruptible?"

"Hell no, they're the most corrupt of all. But FDR was different. He was rich but he inherited it and then he got polio. That made him see the world in a different light, least I think it did. He got the plight of the workingmen and -women like nobody else since Teddy Roosevelt. Too bad we don't have more Roosevelts waiting in the wings."

The maid returned and without a word escorted them back to the rear terrace and left them there.

Alfred Drake was tall and skinny with a sunken chest. He had few hairs left on his head and had perhaps compensated for that by growing one of the biggest mustaches that Archer had ever seen outside of a carnival. He was dressed in a white terrycloth robe, and his pale, thin, bare legs protruded from underneath. Though the evening was cool, his droopy mustache and wet footprints on the pool surround showed the man had already taken a dip. He had sandals on his feet that revealed neatly trimmed toenails. He was holding a martini complete with a trio of olives on a toothpick and sitting at a table with an open white umbrella poking through a center hole. He was staring out toward the ocean and gave no indication he even knew they were there.

"Mr. Drake?" prompted Dash.

Without looking at them, Drake pointed to two empty seats at the table.

As they drew near Archer could see that the bottom of the pool had inlaid aquamarine tile in the shape of a large stallion in full gallop. The rear grounds were as immaculate as the front. In the distance Archer could see a muscular, bare-chested young man shoveling a hole with a large bush standing next to it, presumably waiting to be planted.

Whether Drake was really staring at the ocean or the young man, Archer couldn't tell for sure. He thought the odds were fifty-fifty.

After they sat and put their hats on the table, Drake said, "Well?" He still had not turned to look at them and didn't seem inclined to offer them a drink.

Archer took out his notepad and readied his pen.

"This is Archer, my new associate," said Dash.

"Am I supposed to applaud or do you want to get to the point?"

"Hope there's no hard feelings after that case I worked involving you."

"You were professional and honest, Willie" was Drake's surprising reply, at least to Archer, who was still sizing up the man's hostile attitude.

Drake continued, "It was your client who was neither of those things. I appreciated how you got him to back off when you realized the truth."

"Well, thanks for being understanding. Now, we wanted to talk to you about the upcoming election."

Drake turned his chair around to face them. "Why is it any of your concern?"

Before Dash could answer, a Persian cat ambled out from somewhere and jumped onto Drake's lap. He absently stroked the animal while he waited for an answer.

"Two people have been recently murdered."

"What does that have to do with me?" said Drake bluntly.

"Did you know them?"

"Why don't you tell me who they are and maybe I can answer the question."

"You don't know?" said Dash skeptically.

"Enlighten me."

"Ruby Fraser. She was a singer at Midnight Moods."

"I've never been there. It's not really my thing, if you get my meaning."

"So you don't know her?"

"I thought I just said that."

"The other victim was Wilson Sheen."

Drake flinched just a bit, causing the Persian to hiss. "I knew him. We weren't friends or anything, but I knew him through the usual social circles. And also from the election. He's running, or he was running, Kemper's campaign."

"Do you know of any reason why someone would want to kill him?" asked Dash.

"I just told you I didn't really know the man. I guess he had enemies, what man doesn't?"

"So how's the campaign going?" asked Dash.

"You've seen the ads in the paper, and heard the radio spots, I'm sure. And the billboards where Kemper looks off broodingly into the distance, or the future, or maybe he's gazing at some woman's ass, who knows? Anyway, they're everywhere. And he owns a hotel and a country club, and a winery and has a beautiful home and a beautiful wife. And look at me and look at Kemper. Physical appearance shouldn't matter, but it sure as hell does. Just ask any woman. He's got that vote wrapped up."

"Women might just vote on the issues, not someone's jawline," noted Archer.

"I used to think that," said Drake in a tight voice. "But not anymore."

"So why are you running for mayor?" asked Archer.

Drake ran his gaze over Archer, and Archer didn't like the expression on the man's face. He involuntarily glanced over at the bare-chested man as he hefted the bush into the freshly dug hole.

"Oh, so you want to hear my stump speech?"

"Sure, why not?" answered Dash.

Drake took a long—almost luxurious—sip of his martini before setting the glass down and munching on one of the olives he plucked from the drink.

"Bay Town is a place of the haves and have-nots. I'm one of the haves. Sure, I worked hard, but my parents gave me an excellent education and I inherited wealth from them. So when I moved here from the East Coast, I had a lot of advantages. However, with that said, opportunities should be equal and we don't have that here. Take Sawyer Armstrong as an example." Drake glanced at Dash, perhaps to see how this provocative statement was playing with him.

"Okay, how so?" asked Dash.

"His initial wealth came from old family money. Now, no one can say that the man is not ambitious and all that. But he had quite the boost because the Armstrongs have owned this town for nearly a century. They own the lion's share of the wealth and leave the crumbs for just about everyone else. I stand for better working conditions for the poor. More money for education and health care. We have kids dropping out of school and working adult jobs, and no one gives a damn. We treat the Mexicans coming across the border to pick our vegetables and fruit as less than human. That's wrong. That needs to change." He paused and looked thoughtfully at his pool. "But in the long run, people like the Armstrongs should thank me for the positions I take."

"Why is that?" asked Archer.

"Because the have-nots greatly outnumber the haves. But the have-nots will only put up with so much for so long. Then they start scaling the walls of the elites' estates, and the results will not be pretty. I include myself in that group. I'm not asking the Armstrongs of the world to give up their wealth. I'm asking that others have the full opportunity to earn their share by being fairly compensated for their work. Right now the system is rigged. It makes a laughingstock out of the American dream."

"You actually sound like FDR," noted Dash, glancing at Archer.

"Good, be sure to vote," said Drake.

"Did you know Ben Smalls?" asked Archer.

If Drake was surprised by this segue, he didn't show it. "Yes. He was a friend, a *good* friend. We got to know each other when we served on town council together. And then when Ben became mayor, we worked on projects together. The stump speech I just gave? A lot of it came from my discussions with Ben. He was of the same mindset. He is greatly missed."

"I understand his father was partners with Sawyer Armstrong," said Archer.

"Andrew Smalls was a good man."

"But he killed himself," noted Archer.

Drake's head dipped. "Yes. That...that was so out of character for Andrew."

"And do you think his son's death was just an accident?" asked Archer.

Drake picked up his drink again and took another sip. He set it down and pressed the sleeve of his robe against his moistened lips. "That's what the police say."

"Some folks think he might have been murdered," noted Dash.

"Well, you can't control what some people might think," replied Drake.

"Just like that, you dismiss your friend's death?" said Dash.

"What do you want me to do about it?" Drake shot back.

Archer said, "Well, maybe as mayor you can do something about it, because it doesn't seem like the police did much of an investigation."

A small smile escaped Drake's lips. It was the saddest smile Archer had ever seen.

Drake said, "Maybe I could, in an ideal world. When you find one, let me know."

"Nothing else you can tell us to help our investigation?" said Dash.

"Excuse me, but who exactly is your client in all of this?"

"That's confidential."

"Really? Bay Town is still manageable when it comes to gossip. And my gossip tells me that you're working for my opponent."

"And if I told you that finding the truth trumps that?"

"Then I think you'll be trying to sell me the Golden Gate Bridge next."

Dash grinned. "You know, just to be brutally honest, I told Archer here that you were pretty much a dishrag without a chance in hell of beating Kemper."

"I've been called worse."

"But now I see you in a different light. And it's a much better picture."

"Don't patronize me, Willie."

"If I was patronizing you, Alfred, you'd know it."

Drake took a moment to study Dash's earnest features. "All right. I wish you luck with your investigation, even if it *does* help Kemper beat me."

"Maybe it will, and maybe it won't," said Dash. "But you'll always be a damn good dentist."

Drake chortled. "Maybe I'm seeing you in a different light now, too, Willie. Who'd 'a thunk?"

Dash rose and so did Archer, who said, "So you really think you have no chance against Kemper?"

"*I* have no chance. We'll just have to see, won't we? Stranger things have happened."

They left him sitting there stroking his cat and staring out toward the ocean.

54

"He doesn't strike me as a man who has sold out to mobsters from Vegas," said Dash as they drove back to town.

"He actually seems like a good guy who cares about people."

"Like he cared about the young buck planting the bush?" said Dash.

"Thought you might have noticed that. Any rumors about him on that score?"

"None that stuck. And for a guy like Drake you'd need some hard proof, otherwise he'll sue your ass off."

"But you did refer to him as the tooth *fairy*. Or am I reading too much into that?"

Dash's features became deadly serious. "That sort of behavior is illegal, Archer, it comes under sodomy and sexual perversion. You can go to prison for a long time for that, and you have to register as a sex offender."

"Really?"

Dash looked uncomfortable. "Hell, some private eyes spend their careers drilling holes in walls and taking pictures of folks engaged in such…activities."

"Why?"

"Because they're hired by neighbors, disgruntled family members, or people who believe themselves to be the guardians of 'morality.' Folks went to prison and often died there or were sterilized to 'cure' them. My take is, if a guy's different, so what? Live and let live."

"Didn't figure you'd be sympathetic to that sort of thing, Willie."

Dash looked out the window. "Yeah, I guess I look like an old, fat son of a bitch with all the prejudices that come with it." He patted his chest. "But my ticker ain't just there to keep my blood pumping, Archer. Doesn't the good book say to love thy neighbor?"

"The one I read does."

"Yeah, well…" He lapsed into silence and ran his fingers along the car window.

"Did you ever do that sort of work, spying on people?"

Dash slowly nodded. "For about a year. And then I'd had enough."

"So what happened?"

"None of your business."

"Okay. But I hope I've proved over the short time we've worked together that you *can* trust me."

"I don't trust easily, Archer."

"And you think I do?"

"You got your flask?"

Archer handed it to him and Dash took a belt, screwed the cap on, and passed it back to Archer. He settled in his seat and started smoothing down his tie.

"One day a lady comes in and hires me to spy on her fifteen-year-old nephew. She told me she just knew he was engaged in *lewd* behavior. But when she told her sister her suspicions, the sister was having none of it. Said she needed proof, so the lady comes to me. Later, I realized the broad just hated her sister and wanted to use the kid to stick it to her. But she was paying me money I really needed, so I took my little bag of dirty tricks and went to work. I followed the kid to this abandoned building that had the rep of being a safe place for guys who were 'that way.' I snuck in, got the lay of the land, figured out where he was, and drilled a hole in the wall and took my little pictures of him and another kid. I handed them over to my client, who promptly passed them over to the boy's mom."

"What happened?"

"The mom and dad apparently went berserk on the kid."

"That must've been tough for the boy."

"I wish that were the end of the story, Archer. See, the client wanted more evidence."

"Why?"

"She told me her sister wasn't *sufficiently* alarmed by her son's 'perverted' qualities. Her word, not mine. She wanted me to go back and get even more dirt. I learned later she just wanted to rub her sister's nose in it."

"So what did you do?"

"I went back with my camera to my dirty little hole and...and when I looked through it there he was hanging from the light fixture. I rushed in, cut him down, and tried to revive him, but he was already dead, Archer. Only fifteen and he was dead."

"Jesus."

"Yeah, I talked to Jesus a lot after that one. After I drank enough whiskey to fill Drake's swimming pool. Took me a year to get back to work. Pretty much lost every damn thing I had. And you know what?"

"What?"

"I got off a lot easier than the kid did."

"I'm sorry, Willie."

"Don't feel sorry for me," Dash snapped. "I had it coming. He didn't."

Neither man said anything as they drove along. Dash was staring out the window and Archer kept his gaze on the road.

Finally, Archer said, "So that's why you took a leave of absence?"

Dash turned to look at him. "You ever been so ashamed of

yourself you can't even stand to look at your reflection in the mirror?"

Archer slowly shook his head. "No."

"Good. I hope you never get there."

They drove back to the office building. Then they took the elevator up and settled in Dash's office. The man poured out two fingers of Beam each, sat across from Archer, and said, "Okay, you brought up the trust issue, so let's talk that through."

Archer took a sip of the Beam and said warily, "Okay."

"When were you going to tell me that you've been asking questions about that island, Archer?"

Archer set his drink down and leaned back in his seat. "I *did* tell you about the island but you blew it off. So I thought I'd go it alone. For now."

"Okay, 'for now' is over."

"How'd you know? Were you following me?"

"If I were, you'd never know it. Reggie McKenzie is a buddy of mine. He's a sloppy drunk, but okay when he's off the booze. He told you all about that chunk of rock's history. You also went to the library and looked through a bunch of materials. Sharon Aster helped you there. Nice gal, but too highbrow for the likes of me. Then you went to the town hall and did the same. Linda, the town clerk, is also a friend of mine."

"You got lots of friends."

"It's not by happenstance. Most PIs cultivate them. At least the good ones do."

"How'd you find all that out so fast?"

"I just piggybacked on you, Archer."

"So you *were* following me."

"I never said I wasn't. Library, town hall, McKenzie, back to your boardinghouse to pick up your lady friend, and then up to Midnight Moods. I just had my cup of coffee and waited for you to show."

"You said you were going to pick up your car and do some thinking."

"I *did* pick up my car, which I used to follow you. And I did do some thinking. I was thinking about *you*."

Archer smiled appreciatively. "Mr. Shaw said you were the best, Willie. And he was right."

"I'm not busting your chops, Archer. Yes, you did mention the island, and yes, I did blow it off. And you did what I would have done—you followed up a hunch on your own. So let's compare notes."

Archer took out his notepad. "I found out in the real estate records at the town hall that the island was sold by the federal government six months ago to a company called Stearman Enterprises. Even though it was federal property, I guess Bay Town had to have a record of it because Stearman has its office here. The man listed on the paperwork for Stearman—"

"—was Douglas Kemper," interjected Dash.

"Right," said Archer. "How'd you know? I never mentioned it to the town clerk lady."

"Great minds, Archer. Now, at the library you researched certain laws and statutes."

Archer consulted his notepad again. "A state has all water rights up to three miles off its coast. That's important for fishing rights and the like. The feds control everything out to twelve miles."

"And anything beyond that is international waters," added Dash.

"But in 1947 the Supreme Court ruled that the federal government owns all the *seabeds* off the California coast, even within the three miles. It's just the water the state controls."

"The Supreme Court? How'd you think to check that?"

"When I was in college I wanted to be a lawyer. Things didn't pan out, but I studied some law and then worked with an attorney. I learned a lot."

"So this pertains to the island?"

"Right. When the Navy was done with it and pulled out, the federal government assumed its rights to the island. Along came Stearman and bought those rights. I think the law really was meant to deal with oil and gas rights. You have to drill into the seabed to get to those."

"That's right," agreed Dash. "But where does the mayor come into this?"

"That I couldn't find. I mean, if the state governor has no power over that island, why would a mayor?" Archer paused, recalling a snippet of conversation. "But your buddy Reggie McKenzie did tell me something interesting. He said that about two weeks before he died, Ben Smalls took a boat ride out to that island, and McKenzie said when he came back he did not look happy."

"Fascinating," said Dash, his mind clearly moving at high speed.

"Beth told me that his old man, Andrew, hanged himself in his barn."

"That's right, he did. I wondered how you knew that when you mentioned it to Drake."

"I also took a boat and went out to the island. It's bigger than you'd think. And you can reach it in about fifteen minutes. And there's something going on out there. I found survey stakes in the ground and a post with the name Lancet Surveyors and Architectural Group on it."

Dash rubbed his cheek. "So there's going to be a building put up."

"Right. And there's something else." Archer looked at the man nervously.

"Is this where you tell me what you haven't told me so far?"

"That night I saw Beth Kemper? I was down at the harbor. I saw a boat coming into shore close to three. It was Armstrong's boat, and he and Hank and Tony and some other folks were on it. I'm sure they'd been out to that island. That's what got me thinking about something like that in the first place. Beth Kemper pulled into the parking lot as they were heading to their cars. She and her old man had a heated argument. I followed her to the diner."

"And you didn't tell me this before because...?"

"I don't have a good answer."

"If you had pulled this from the get-go, Archer, you'd be looking for another job. But I know now you got the chops and the instincts. And I was clearly holding back from you, so there we go. I just got some of my own applesauce thrown in my face. Now, let's look at this again. Armstrong went to the island. Kemper's on the documents of the company that bought the property. Fifteen-minute ride out is pretty convenient for carrying folks back and forth who might just want to stay for a few hours and not overnight."

"But what sort of place would that be?"

"We'll wait until later, then go find out."

55

A GUMSHOE'S STOCK IN TRADE, ARCHER," Dash said quietly, as he pulled the small leather case from his pocket and opened it, revealing a neatly arranged set of small tools. They were at the back door of the offices of Lancet Surveyors and Architectural Group, two blocks off Sawyer Avenue. It was a two-story nondescript brick building. If this was the height of the firm's design powers, thought Archer, he might look elsewhere if he was ever in the market for inspired architectural work.

Dash inserted two different lock picks in the upper lock and worked away. After twenty seconds, Archer heard a click. Dash next inserted one of the tools in the lower lock and did the same. Then he put his kit away, turned the knob, and opened the door to the darkened building.

Inside Dash whispered to Archer, "There's an old cop that makes the rounds of these buildings at night. He's pretty much deaf and blind, but he carries a gun. He'll never hit anything on purpose but will by accident. So we can't turn on any lights."

Archer nodded. They felt along the walls until they reached a door. They went through it and eyed the space they were in. There was enough moonlight along with a streetlight's glare coming in through the broad windows to give them reasonable illumination. They searched the rooms on the lower level, found nothing, and took the stairs to the upper level. The door of every room up here was unlocked except for one.

That naturally garnered their interest, and out came Dash's lockpick kit once more. The door was soon defeated, and they walked into the windowless office.

Dash slipped a small flashlight from his pocket and turned it on. It was more than enough light to see what they needed to see.

On a large table in the center of the room was an architectural mockup of a series of enormous buildings without roofs.

"The Golden Rock," said Dash, reading off a sign on one of the buildings. Then he cast his gaze lower to look at some drawings that had been set next to the building mockup.

"What does that mean?" asked Archer.

"Well, for starters, the Rock is what they call Alcatraz, but it's sure as hell not golden and this sure as hell isn't a prison." Dash looked over the buildings more closely. "Damn, Archer, these are *casinos*." He pointed to the interiors of the buildings, where miniature pieces of furnishings and equipment were set. "See there, craps tables, roulette wheels, poker and blackjack tables. Over there is the cashier, in that corner the mother of all bars. Over there are slot machines."

"They're building gambling casinos on that island?" said Archer.

"Looks like it. And I've been to Vegas, and if this place is to scale it's way bigger than anything they got there. Now, you remember me telling you that they outlawed *gambling* boats off the coast?" said Dash.

"Yeah, which means this building makes no sense unless they're going to overturn the law."

"That would be incredibly difficult because gambling is actually outlawed in the California State *Constitution*. And I told you our now governor Warren led the drive against gambling boats when he was attorney general. The big lawsuit was about Santa Monica Bay. Point being, where did you measure from the shore out three miles? Did you start at Santa Monica itself, or the two farthest points out of the bay? See, the latter would put you in really heavy water, where folks aren't going to gamble and puke at the same time."

"When I was out there I saw there's a big breakwater west of the island, so I imagine it's pretty calm waters around the island for the most part."

"Another reason to buy and develop it."

"So it's serious money, then?"

"Serious enough. Before Warren pulled the plug, a guy named Tony Cornero, with his ship the *Rex*, was making two hundred grand a month in profits. Just one ship."

"But gambling is still illegal. Like you said, it's in the state constitution."

"Not so fast, Archer. In 1948 Truman signed the Knowland Bill. It outlawed gambling in all territorial waters as well as the transport of folks to those gambling *vessels*."

"Okay, but—" Archer caught himself. "Wait a minute. The law only applies to *ships*?"

"That's right. If you're on land off the coast that is not under the jurisdiction of California, there's apparently no applicable law against gambling and no law against ferrying folks out there *to* gamble."

"But hold on. If the governor was so against gambling on boats, why would he allow it on land?"

"The Navy *built* that island. And even if they hadn't, it's just over three miles out, and there's no dispute about the measurement from the shore here the way the coastline is configured in Bay Town. So California has no say in the matter. It's in federal waters."

"But Catalina Island and the other Channel Islands are even farther off the coast. Why hasn't anyone tried to get gambling on them?"

"Because even though the military is all over them they're officially part of California, so the governor has control over what happens there. There was some question about whether the treaty signed with Mexico way back that ceded northern Mexico to the U.S. included them, but a few years ago Mexico confirmed they have no rights to them. But even if they could be used for gambling they're a lot farther out, Archer, *and* in heavy water. You want to spend an hour or two or three in heavy seas to play blackjack or craps? And drink your fill and come back in heavy seas and stand at the gunwale and contemplate killing yourself because you're so seasick?"

"No, I wouldn't."

"Yeah, sometimes it really is the little things. That island is in the perfect location to be a gambling joint. A fast ferry ride out and back in relatively calm waters. That's why the ships were so popular. But this island setup is even better. The floor's not moving while you're rolling the dice."

"But they could outlaw anybody getting *ferried* out there."

"Guess who controls that in each locality, Archer?"

"The mayor?"

"Bingo. And the town council. Which explains what happened to Ben Smalls and why this election is so important to some folks. And Kemper's country club is right on the water and has a marina with a big dock. They could have the ferries leave from there."

"But if President Truman signed a bill about boats, what's to stop him signing a bill about an island?"

"If Kemper was a real smart guy, and I'm thinking he is, he's paid off some powerful folks in D.C. to make sure there's no Knowland Bill number two and that the state of California is not going to make this a priority. Hell, America is just now digging out of a war. They want some fun. Now, gambling is fun. Sure, most lose their shirts, but they're smiling while they get stripped naked. And if one ship can make two hundred thou a month, what do you guess a bunch of mammoth casinos out there could do? Folks will do a lot for that much dough."

"Well, the short time I was in Reno, I can vouch for that. Casinos are raking it in."

"You have to follow the money, Archer. It usually takes you where you need to go."

"Then Armstrong and Kemper are in this together?"

"Could be," said Dash.

"But then who's trying to blackmail Kemper into getting out of the race?"

"How about Drake?"

"But he seemed like a straight shooter with good motives."

"Drake is an idealist. He may believe if Kemper gets in there it's the same as having Armstrong in charge again. He knows he can't win the election on the up and up; there's too much money and other things aligned against him. So he finds or makes up dirt on Kemper and tries to win the race that way so he can get in there and do a lot of good."

"And the murders of Fraser and Sheen? You think Drake is involved in those?"

"Haven't figured those out yet. And Archer?"

"Yeah?"

"Remember this, son, if you remember nothing else. What I just laid out is a *theory*. Theories are not the truth. To find the truth a gumshoe's got to keep digging."

CHAPTER

56

ARCHER DROVE BACK TO MIDNIGHT MOODS and was in the audience when Callahan made her formal debut later that night. To say she was a success would have been like saying the Allied countries had fought to a draw with their Axis counterparts.

The theater was filled to standing room capacity and Archer noted, with some surprise, that the number of women in the audience roughly equaled the number of males in attendance.

The curtains had parted and out had marched Callahan in the outfit she and Dawson had selected. Her long, dramatic strides bore the confidence of someone at home in the spotlight. Indeed, her smile seemed to outshine the stage lights. When she reached the microphone, Callahan motioned at the piano man to prime his fingers. He started to play and his skill was obvious; yet when Callahan opened her mouth and the sounds poured from it, Archer didn't give the man tickling the black and white keys another thought.

One hour later the last note of her final song held in the air like cannon smoke after a twenty-one-gun salute. She took a bow, stood straight, and let the appreciation of hundreds of people rain down on her for holding them in luxurious captivity for the previous sixty minutes.

A man in his fifties seated next to Archer elbowed him and said, "Damn, son, is she a keeper or what?"

Archer smiled and nodded and concluded that Callahan was right where she was meant to be—in front of large crowds and sending them into a better existence than reality ever could.

As his gaze ran over the audience, Archer spotted him. He bent forward for a better look. Yes, it was definitely the man.

Douglas Kemper hadn't grieved long for his campaign manager. He was in the front row, cigarette and drink in hand, and seemed to be fixated on Callahan.

Archer went backstage after the show to see her.

She was in her small dressing room with LIBERTY freshly stenciled on the door. There were baskets of flowers littering the floor, while she sat in front of her mirrored vanity table and reapplied her stage makeup.

"Well?" she said, looking at him in the mirror.

"I think you did okay."

"Well, don't give yourself a heart attack slinging out praise, Archer."

"Do you want me to say you're a star? Okay, you're a star, Liberty. But you don't need me to tell you what all those people already did. And you had as many ladies as gents in the audience. I'd say that's something, all right."

"You got your flask?" she asked, giving him a pretty smile.

He handed it across and she took a sip. "So, that was just the first act. I've got three more sets and then some hand shaking and drinks with some of the big players here, and the local rag is going to interview me and even take my picture."

"You good with all that?"

"Hell, Archer, I was born for 'that.'"

"Yeah, I guess you were."

She lit up a Camel, blew smoke out, and swiveled around to look directly at him. "I heard someone else got killed here. That's what Dawson was referring to, right?"

"Wilson Sheen. He worked for Douglas Kemper."

"Kemper, huh? Someone told me he was in the audience tonight."

"He was. In the front row looking very appreciative of your *many* talents."

"Moneybags, right?"

"And married to a very lovely woman, so don't get your hopes up."

"So he has connections to Fraser and this Sheen guy. Is he a suspect in your book?"

"Everyone's a suspect in my book, Liberty."

"You wanted me to be your spy here. Should I start with Kemper?"

Archer hesitated. "You know, what I told you before probably wasn't a good idea. It could be dangerous."

"*I* can be dangerous, Archer, or have you already forgotten?"

"Yeah, well, you're dangerous when someone is threatening you. These guys don't wait around for that."

"You're worried about me, Archer. That's very touching."

"I *am* worried about you. Two people have bought it in this joint over a really short time."

"Well, just so you know, I worry about *you*, Archer. And *I've* done a little snooping already since I've been here."

"What do you mean?"

"I'm observant. I keep my eyes and ears open."

"And what did you find out?"

"Oh, so now you're okay with me spying?" said Callahan.

"Liberty!"

"Okay, okay. Anyway, I finished my dinner and took my cup of coffee and found a little room to just have some quiet time and get my nerves under control."

"And?" said Archer expectantly.

"And I heard some noise in the room next door. And your name came up."

Archer frowned. "Who was it?"

"It was those same two thugs that roughed you up before, Archer."

"Hank and Tony? But how do you know what they sounded like? You only *saw* them before. They didn't say anything."

"Easy. When they mentioned your name, I snuck out and peeked through the keyhole."

"Liberty, that was a big risk."

"My whole life has been a big risk. Anyway, I saw them."

"And what did they say about me?"

"Oh, that they were going to kill you."

Archer sat back and dead-eyed her. "Thanks for saving the best part for last."

"You can take care of yourself, Archer, I've seen that. And now that you're forewarned? Well, my money's on you over those two goons."

"They say *why* they want to kill me?"

"I heard them mention you were snooping around an *island*?"

Archer told her about the architectural mockups he and Dash had found and their connection to the island. And then his suspicions about the death of Benjamin Smalls.

"A casino, huh? Makes sense. And dying in your bathtub, Archer? Puhleez. That's mob stuff. They either machine-gun you or do the ankle grab in the tub and under you go."

"How come you know so much about that stuff?"

"You think the mob passed Reno by for some reason?"

Archer looked at her closely. "Is Max Shyner part of the mob?"

"I got out, Archer. Read into that what you want to. You got a gun?"

"I do."

"And you got your aluminum knuckles?"

He nodded. "And I'm wearing underwear, too," he said with a grin.

"Really? I'm not."

His features sagged and his cigarette drooped. "Not now, Liberty. For chrissakes."

She smiled demurely. "What's your next move?"

He rose and put his hat on. "And the room where you overheard them?"

"Go right down this hall, turn left, and then right again. Second door on the left."

He tipped his hat. "You got great gams and a great voice, but you've also got a great brain. Don't let anybody ever tell you otherwise."

"You got style, Archer, don't let anybody ever say you don't."

57

THE DOOR TO THE ROOM WAS STANDING OPEN and it was empty, Archer could see. Hank and Tony apparently had flown the coop. He walked out to the terrace, found a seat, ordered a gimlet and a rack of olives and—because he hadn't had his dinner yet—a roast beef sandwich with a side of potato salad. He drank and ate, and was lost in thought until he heard the voice.

"You don't look so good, honey."

He looked up to see it was the same waitress who had taken care of him and Kemper.

"Nah, I'm fine. Hey, you seen Kemper tonight?"

"I'm not that lucky."

"You ever seen any other skirt here reel him in?"

"Not a one. And there wasn't a lack of effort. Least it ain't just me, right?"

"Right. Hey, you know Hank and Tony, Sawyer Armstrong's bouncer boys?"

"Sure."

"They're here, right?"

"They were. Seen 'em leaving, oh, about an hour ago."

"You ever try your chances with them?"

She planted a hand on her hip. "Hey, fellow, I'm not that desperate. And I like my guys with a little class. I mean, I don't even think those goons can read. I got standards."

Archer slipped her a buck and added a wink to it. "Thanks. And keep aiming higher. Who knows, you might just end up running General Motors one day."

She tucked the dollar down her blouse. "What a comedian. You should try vaudeville."

As she walked off, Archer checked his watch. He decided it was time to drive up the mountain again. And maybe bag two for the price of one.

The Bentley was gone, but the Triumph and the Phantom Rolls were out front. The door opened and the same servant appeared. He looked at Archer like he'd never seen him before.

"Are Mr. and Mrs. Kemper in?"

"Who shall I say is asking, sir?"

"It's Archer. I was here before, with Willie Dash?"

"It is very late, Mr. Archer. I believe you should come back—"

"It's all right, Chen, I'll see Mr. Archer." Beth Kemper had appeared next to her butler. "Follow me, Archer. You look like you could use a drink."

And so, just like that, Archer followed her. He liked following her. He liked how she moved, like a panther slinking through the brush. It was inspiring, actually, simply how the lady walked. You couldn't teach it, he knew. You could either do it or you couldn't. And this lady could do it in spades. Just like Callahan.

She took him into one of the rooms he and Dash had passed on their previous visit. It was all marble and white and cold and, despite all that, interesting. He stared at a large figurine of a naked woman looking at something over Archer's right shoulder.

He pointed his hat at it. "Does it cost more *not* to have clothes on?"

She sat beautifully on the couch, her bright red skirt fanning out and covering her legs all the way to her calves. The blouse above it was a creamy white. She looked like some sort of exotic flower in full bloom.

"In life it usually does, Archer, so why not in art? *Would* you like a drink? I'm going to have one."

"You look very comfortable sitting there, so let me do the honors. Dry Manhattan do the trick?"

She smiled and waved her hand at the bar. He guessed they had a bar in every room, and wasn't that just the stuff of everyone's fantasies?

He poured and measured and jiggered his way through the concoctions. He presented the Dry Manhattan to her and took a seat facing the woman.

They raised the glasses to each other and took sips.

She said, "And what can I do for you so late at night?"

He dabbed a bit of vermouth off his lip. "I think your father might be mad at me, again."

"Why do you say that?"

"Well, you know Hank and Tony gave me the once-over when your father learned that we had come up here to question you."

"But I thought that was all forgotten and forgiven after we met at his house."

"But then I was a bad boy a second time and gave them more reason to give me the treatment again."

"And what exactly did you do now?"

"If I tell you, you'll tell your father, right?"

"Not if you don't want me to."

A smile eased across Archer's face. "Now that's a good line, Beth. Although Willie doesn't want me to call you Beth."

She set her drink down, took out her cigarette case, tapped a smoke on the top of the coffee table, and lit up. "Why is that?"

"Something about different classes of people. You're up here on the mountain and I'm down on Porter Street with the dirty rabble."

"I don't see it that way, Archer, I really don't."

"Anyway, your instincts were right the other night. I *did* follow you to that diner. Which meant I saw you and your father in the parking lot of the wharf. Which of course means I saw him come in on his boat from visiting that island that a company with your hubby's fingerprints all over recently bought from the feds."

Kemper sat back, tapped ash into an ashtray, and took a swallow of her Manhattan.

"You were a busy boy, then, although I have no idea what you're talking about. I thought you were going to tell me you burned down one of my father's olive trees."

"So the island was owned by the feds. And now it's not. It's owned by your husband, apparently."

"No, it's damn well not."

This didn't come from Beth Kemper. It came from her husband. They both turned to see him standing in the doorway, his hat in hand. His necktie was undone, his shirt was wrinkled, his hair was disheveled, and he didn't look like the sparkling golden boy at this precise moment in time.

Beth rose and said in a concerned voice, "Douglas, are you all right?" There was genuine concern in both her voice and expression.

"No, Beth, I'm not. I'm really not, honey." He paused and looked at her. "I...I just need some...help."

Douglas walked forward while Archer watched both of them closely.

Beth reached her arms out to him and Douglas did the same, and a moment later they were wound as tightly as wire on a coil. They stood like that for a full ten seconds before they stepped back from one another.

Wilma Darling was right—he does *love his wife.*

Douglas looked at Archer. "I have no interest in that island."

"Paperwork filed in the town hall says otherwise. You're listed as the chairman of the board."

"Anyone can list anyone else."

"Any idea who might have *listed* you?"

"No, no idea. What was the name of the company?"

"Stearman Enterprises."

The Kempers exchanged nervous glances.

"Yeah," said Archer. "That was the model of your mother's plane. The Stearman 75. Someone's being either ironic or downright cruel."

She looked at Douglas. "Do you know anything about this? I want the truth!"

"No. I swear. I'm involved with no company by that name. And I...wouldn't have named it that."

"The money behind Alfred Drake, maybe?" suggested Archer.

"Maybe," said Douglas doubtfully.

Archer shook his head. "Wrong. There is no money behind Drake other than his own. He's getting swamped by the bucks you and your father-in-law are throwing at this election. He knows he's going to lose." He glanced at Beth before saying to Douglas, "Would you say your vision of Bay Town coincides with what Ben Smalls had in store?"

"I would say so, yes. I know what it's like to be wealthy. But I also know what it's like to be poor."

"And Alfred Drake also admired him, or says he did."

"I believe they were friends, yes."

"And you were friends with Smalls, too, correct, Mrs. Kemper?"

Douglas said, "His father was partners with Sawyer. You two grew up together, and he was at that luncheon."

"When my mother died," said Beth, without looking at him. "But I met him other times, too. We *were* friends."

"Now that's interesting," said Archer. "Would you like to tell us what those other times consisted of?"

"No, I wouldn't," she said heatedly, which answered the question for Archer pretty well.

Douglas fast-walked over to the bar and poured himself a

bourbon on the rocks and swallowed half of it before he got back to his wife and looked at her in a way that surprised Archer. It wasn't angry or hurt or full of bluster. It was a look of resignation, of hopelessness. They sat hip to hip in the same chair, one of her hands resting on his thigh, Archer noted, in a protective manner.

Douglas said, "I wish I knew more to tell you, Archer. But things are not adding up."

"Sheen's dying, for one," noted Archer.

"I can't understand who would want to hurt Wilson."

"You want to hear my theory?"

They both settled their gazes on him.

"You actually told me yourself," said Archer.

Douglas frowned. "You're going to have to spell it out, Archer. My thoughts are not too clear right now."

"One question. Have the police been by to see you?"

Douglas wiped his brow. "No. But I think that situation is about to change, from what I've heard. But tell me why someone would want to kill Wilson."

"Your wife has an alibi for the time Ruby Fraser was killed. She was with friends for dinner. Now, that alibi needs to be verified, and it will be. But the thing is, as you told me, Wilson Sheen was *your only alibi* for the time Fraser was murdered. You had dinner with him and then a meeting during the time Fraser was killed. Which means you no longer have an alibi, because dead men can't give them."

Douglas swallowed the rest of his bourbon and collapsed back against the chair. "Right," he said. "I hadn't thought of that."

Beth looked worriedly at him and then said to Archer, "What can be done?"

"I'm not sure. But I do know that your husband is being set up as a patsy to take the fall."

"I never had anything to do with Ruby Fraser, I swear."

Archer glanced at Beth. She had told him she didn't know

whether her husband was sleeping with the lady. But now, in her countenance, he only saw belief in Douglas's words. She gripped his hand to show her support.

"Okay, I believe you," said Archer.

"You do?"

"I've seen and heard of other ladies throwing themselves at you. No go on their part. Why would that be?" He looked at Beth. "Because he loves you."

Beth looked at Douglas, and Archer saw a glimmer of tears there, from *both* of them.

"But you're not out of the woods," continued Archer. "Talk to me about the island."

"I don't know anything about—good Lord, what is that?"

A door could be heard banging open; there was a shout followed by mingled cries, and feet pounding fast toward where they were. Archer had risen, his hand moving to his .38. The Kempers stood, too, staring at the doorway, their arms around one another.

Archer quickly moved the hand away from the gun when he saw who was arriving at the party.

Chief Carl Pickett and four of his beefy coppers, looking all nice and shiny in their brass buttons, clipped hats, shoulder straps, big guns, and brash countenances.

Archer could see they were all excited, and he knew why. Rousting a poor slob was not a thrill; they probably did it every day. But slinging mud at the rich, carrying them out of their palaces, now that could get a man's blood going.

Pickett eyed all of them there, and a grin spread over his face as he extracted a small stogie from his pocket and took a moment to light up.

"Well, well," said Pickett as the three stood there staring at him.

"What do you want?" demanded Douglas. And it was clearly a demand.

Pickett strolled over to him. "Don't go all high and mighty on me, Kemper. You might be married to the boss's daughter, but that means shit to me."

"I'm my *own* boss."

"Whatever you say. But what *I've* come here to say is, you're under arrest."

"For what!"

"Do I really have to spell it out for you and upset the missus?"

"You're damn right you do," insisted Beth.

"Okay. You're being arrested for the murders of Ruby Fraser and Wilson Sheen."

"What would possibly be my motivation?"

"You were bedding Fraser, and Sheen found out and was blackmailing you for it," replied Pickett. "That comes out, you're not going to be the mayor of this town."

"That's absurd," cried out Beth. "He was not sleeping with that woman."

"Well, then, how did we find a pair of his cufflinks in her bedroom? Along with a shirt belonging to him that has blood on it, and that matches the blood type of the deceased woman? How did two witnesses swear on the Bible that they saw him in the company of Miss Fraser on the night she died? And that they had seen the two a week earlier in Mr. Kemper's Rolls-Royce Phantom?" Pickett sidled up to Kemper and said in a low voice. "If you want to screw around with other women, you really need to do it in a low-down Ford."

"And Sheen?" said Archer.

Pickett gave him a withering look. "What are you doing here, whatever your name is? Willie off in the bottle and sent the schoolboy to cover for him?"

"The name's Archer. And what evidence do you have that Kemper killed Sheen?"

Pickett got so close that Archer could smell the cheap gin on the man's breath. "Well, let me tell you, *Archer*, the autopsy on Sheen showed enough barbiturates in his stomach to make a horse go nighty-night. And Sheen and Kemper were seen having drinks at the club earlier that night. A perfect setup to slip the man a mickey and then come back later and kill him."

"You're crazy," said Kemper. "I was having dinner with Wilson when Fraser was killed."

"Sure, sure you were. Anybody else verify that?"

"No, we were at the office alone."

"And he's dead and can't verify that. Right," scoffed Pickett. "Of all the lame excuses." He looked at his men. "Take him away."

"I'll call my father," Beth said quickly, giving her husband a kiss on the cheek before he was handcuffed and led away.

Pickett said. "Not even Daddy will be able to get his little prince out of this jam, lady."

And Archer thought he might just be right about that.

58

Now it was just Beth and Archer.

"This is ridiculous," said Beth. "Douglas wouldn't harm a fly."

"They didn't arrest him for harming a fly," Archer pointed out.

"My father will know what to do."

She rushed from the room, leaving Archer alone. He mixed himself a whiskey and soda. He was drinking it in his chair when Beth returned about fifteen minutes later.

"My father will be here shortly. He's as distraught as I am."

"But what do you really think he can do?"

"He can...do something. You don't believe Douglas killed those people, do you?"

"No, but I can't prove it."

"He hired you. You have to help him."

"He hired us to find the truth. That's the road we're going down."

"The truth will be enough," said Beth firmly.

"Yeah," said Archer. "That and ten cents won't get you a cup of coffee. So talk to me about the island."

"I don't know anything about it."

"I need you to try. You were at the harbor that night when your father came back in on the boat. Why were you there?"

"I...thought he might be there."

Archer shook his head. "It was almost three in the morning.

You didn't take a ride down there on the *chance* that you might run into him."

She lit another cigarette and blew puffs of smoke to the ceiling. She finally looked at him. "I need a drink," she said.

"Dry Manhattan again?"

"Something stronger than that."

Archer rose and poured out three fingers of scotch, neat. "If that doesn't do it for you, go to the hospital and get some morphine." He sat back down and picked up his glass and watched the lady drink hers. "When your father gets here, will the two palookas be with him?"

"I don't know. Probably. They usually go where he goes."

"I have it on good authority that they've been ordered to do me in on account of I've been snooping around that island."

She glanced up sharply. "What good authority?"

"*Good* authority."

"You're saying that my father wants to have you killed because of your snooping around that island?"

"You need to try that line again, Beth, and add in *surprise* this time. It's like eating spaghetti without the meatballs."

"Oh, so now *I'm* in on the conspiracy against you?"

Archer swallowed the rest of his drink and shook his head. "Wanting a man dead doesn't have to constitute a conspiracy. You just need someone willing to do the deed and a weapon with which to do it. And there are lots of both around this town, I've found."

"Well, then you better scram before the death squad gets here."

"Since you won't spill on the island, let *me* do some spilling." He lit up a Lucky, bent the match, and flicked it into the empty fireplace. "Casinos on that island would be worth more money than even your old man has ever made, I'm thinking."

"You can't have casinos in California. You can only bet on horses and play in card clubs."

"Yeah, like the ones your hubby likes to frequent. He was at Midnight Moods tonight in the front row watching my friend Liberty Callahan light up the place. She's the only woman I know around here who might give you a run for your money in the loveliness business."

"My, my, Archer, you're so free with your compliments."

"My point is, why go out for filet mignon if you already have it at home?"

She looked down and said demurely, "Sometimes, the grass is greener. But casinos really are a no-go in this state. So why all the interest in that island?"

"That chunk of rock *isn't* part of California. It was owned by the feds and then sold to Stearman Enterprises. The surveyors have already started to work it."

"Which surveyors?"

"Lancet."

He watched her catch a breath and her face changed color.

"Yeah, I thought that might be the case. There's only one hitch in the giddy-up I haven't pegged yet."

"What's that?" she said dumbly.

Before Archer answered, they could hear footsteps. A few moments later Sawyer Armstrong appeared, hat in hand, and, thankfully, with no Hank and Tony behind him.

59

Armstrong's gaze flicked around the room before alighting and holding on his daughter.

He hurried across and wrapped his long arms around her. "Oh, honey, this must be very distressing for you."

Archer watched Beth Kemper. If he had used the flower metaphor before, now it was like acid had been thrown on the bloom. She wilted as though every molecule of water had been drained from her at the man's touch.

He tilted her chin up so she would look at him. He was dressed more formally tonight, a three-piece wool suit with a colorful cravat. His hat was a dark brown fedora with a crimson band. A pair of specs poked out from his breast pocket.

"We will make this right, Beth," he said.

Archer thought, *Well, there's a lot of wriggle room in that statement.*

He looked around and spotted Archer. Armstrong slowly let the woman go and faced him. "I was under the impression that you had been warned to stay away from Beth."

"It's all right, Dad," said Beth. "I said—"

He put up a hand, and she stopped and stepped back. "Archer? I'm waiting for an answer."

"I didn't hear a question. But maybe that's just me. By the way, where are Laurel and Hardy? Out beating up some old ladies for their church money?"

Those lines didn't even warrant the tiniest of smiles from Armstrong.

The man turned to Beth. "I'll talk to Carl. I'm sure this can be rectified."

"They have evidence, or so they say," commented Archer, one eye on Armstrong and his other on the doorway waiting for Hank and Tony to appear. "Pretty compelling stuff. Cufflinks, bloody shirt with guess-who's blood on it, eyewitness testimony, stomach contents from Sheen. I'm no lawyer, but even a bad DA could make hay out of that."

Armstrong said, "You and Willie never gave me an answer on my offer. I don't like to be kept waiting."

"I work for him. It's his call."

"Then tell him what I said. And just do it."

"By any means necessary?" asked Archer, with a glance at Beth, who looked at the floor and nothing else.

"I won't tell Willie or you how to do your job. I'd appreciate the same courtesy."

"Yeah. Well, I guess I'll be going then." He looked at Beth. "You going to be okay?"

"She'll be fine, Archer, now that *I'm* here," Armstrong answered for her.

The night sky was bursting with stars, the air chilly enough to make him feel alive, and yet with all that, part of Archer felt dead inside as he steered the Delahaye back down the mountain. The scent of eucalyptus was so strong he felt his eyes start to water. He glanced at his timepiece. He debated whether to go back to Midnight Moods, but then decided against it. He opted to return to the office, call Dash, wake him up if necessary, and get his advice.

He pulled to the curb in front of the office building and got out. The front door to the building was unlocked and Archer proceeded down the hall toward the stairs. He reached the elevator and stopped. The elevator's outer door was partially open because there was something blocking it. And that something was an arm, with a gnarled hand at the end of it.

Archer quickly pushed the door all the way open, revealing Earl lying there, his face pointed to the side.

"Earl, you okay? Earl?"

The man's eyes were closed, and it was dark enough that Archer couldn't see whether he was breathing or not. He might have had a heart attack or maybe a stroke.

He knelt down and felt around the man's neck. He didn't need to check for a pulse, because when he pulled his fingers back the clotted blood came with them. Archer pivoted on the balls of his feet for a better look at the little man. He tipped the chin back a bit and saw the slash across the neck.

This was Ruby Fraser all over again. The man was cold. He'd been dead awhile, but his limbs weren't stiff. Archer looked around the elevator car and saw what looked to be a pile of blankets in one corner along with a newspaper and the bottle of booze he had seen before. Archer sniffed the air. From out of the pile of blankets he pulled a raw onion, half eaten, and a knuckle of bread with some roast beef inserted in it. Along with a pair of underwear and a torn sock.

The guy was living here?

He backed out of the car and hurried toward the stairs. And stopped again.

A door off the hall was open. The doorjamb was shredded and the locking side of the door had a long crack in it.

Archer eyed the name stenciled on the door.

MYRON O'DONNELL, M.D.

Archer recalled the name because O'Donnell was the surgeon who'd recently removed Beth Kemper's appendix.

He eased the broken door open.

"Hello? Dr. O'Donnell, you okay? It's Archer from upstairs. I work for Willie Dash."

There was no response. The place had the feel of a tomb. Archer nipped out his gun and pointed it around. He worked his way through the front reception room, which had six wooden-back chairs all in a row, and a coffee table with magazines spread out on it. He spied an old *Look* magazine from 1948. And a *Life* magazine from August with a toothy Joe DiMaggio on the cover.

"Hello?" said Archer.

He reached another door and pushed it open. This must be where O'Donnell kept his drug dispensary. The glass cabinet was smashed open, and bottles and spilled pills littered the floor.

Archer left this room and headed on. The next room was O'Donnell's office. Archer could tell because the man's diplomas were on the wall. There was a desk with two chairs on the patient's side, and one office chair on the other.

And in the office chair was a dead man.

60

ARCHER RUSHED UP TO THE FOURTH FLOOR to make sure that Dash had not been a victim as well. When he unlocked the door and burst into Dash's office's a few moments later, he heard a voice call out, "One more step and you get a third eye, buster."

"It's me, Archer."

Dash turned on a light revealing him sitting on the side of the bed holding a lethal-looking .32 Colt. "What the hell are you doing here?"

And Archer told him what he was doing there. Dash hurriedly dressed and raced out without bothering to don his toupee.

They first went to look at Earl. "Shit," Dash said.

Then he followed Archer to the doctor's office.

Dash looked down at the body. "Shit twice," he muttered.

"Who is it? Dr. O'Donnell?"

Dash nodded, picked up the dead doctor's phone, and made a call.

"Ernie Prettyman on duty? Yeah, right. Tell him it's Willie Dash. Thanks."

A few moments passed and then Prettyman came on. Dash told him what had happened.

"Okay, Ern, we'll be here," said Dash in reply to whatever Prettyman had said.

Dash put down the phone and said, "Okay, you look like you have something to tell me."

"Pickett arrested Kemper for the murders of Fraser and Sheen." Archer told him about all the evidence Pickett said he had on Kemper. And the fact that Beth had called her father and that Armstrong had shown up a bit later.

"I'm sure Pickett paid top dollar for the eyewitness accounts," said Dash. "And the other stuff is easy to massage into evidence of anything you want it to."

"We can't fight the whole police force, Willie."

"Maybe not. Let's go analyze this sucker and see what they were really after."

In the dispensary Dash carefully looked over the tossed bottles and spilled pills. Then he stepped back and said, "Tell me what you see here, Archer. Take your time and think it over."

Archer bent down and picked up some of the bottles and scooped up some of the pills. He compared some pills with some bottles and even put some of the scattered pills back in the bottles. He looked up at Dash.

"This thing was staged, to make it look like a robbery with drugs as the loot."

Dash nodded. "You're right. But explain to me your reasoning."

Archer stood and held out two half-empty bottles and a handful of pills. "This is morphine. And these pills are amphetamines. Worth a small fortune on the street."

"That's right."

"But when you compare the pills they spilled with the space left inside the bottles, they pretty much tally. So they didn't take any narcotics with them."

"And they didn't have to smash the cabinet open. The key's in the lock. The idiots obviously didn't see it, or else they would have taken it with them."

"Did you know O'Donnell?"

Dash nodded. "He was a good guy. A good doctor."

"Why would anyone want to kill him?"

"That's principally why they call it a mystery, Archer."

"So do we wait here for Prettyman?"

"Now that I know Pickett has arrested Kemper, I'm pretty damn certain that Ern's not gonna show up here. Pickett will. And then I think I might actually fear for *our* safety."

"So what do we do?"

"You got your car out front?"

"Yeah."

On the way out, Dash stopped at Earl's body. He knelt down and closed the man's eyes.

"He was a crook, and he hated my guts, but anybody who thinks they had a harder life with fewer opportunities than Earl is seriously fooling themselves."

"You think he was in the wrong place at the wrong time?"

"Maybe. Let's hit the road before Carl Pickett hits us."

"Where are we going?"

"I think it's time to check in with our client."

61

"WHAT THE HELL ARE YOU DOING HERE?" snarled Steve Prichard, the front-desk sergeant. He apparently had the graveyard shift tonight and was not happy about it.

"We're here to see our client," said Dash calmly.

"Your *client*?"

"Douglas Kemper. I understand he was booked for a double homicide. I presume an alleged murderer would not be able to post bail."

"He's here, but you can't see him."

"How many years you got to your pension, Steve?"

"Five, why?" growled Prichard.

"Because you're never going to make it with that attitude."

A pulse beat in the blue vein at the cop's temple. "You threatening me?"

"No, just stating a fact. *Rogers versus California*, 1934. Cops denied a suspect seeing his attorneys *and* private investigators. All charges were dropped, a writ of habeus corpus was issued by the court, and the suspect walked free. And the cop who did the denying was busted down to riding in a prowler for a month. Then, for good measure, they canned his ass seven months before his full ride kicked in. You want to go down that road, Stevie boy, it's okay by me." He glanced at Archer. "Let's go wake up

Kemper's lawyer and get the lawsuit filed before this lug uses what little brain he has and comes to his senses."

"You ain't bullshitting me?" Prichard barked.

"Look it up, Steve. You can read, can't you?"

Prichard glanced at Archer and then grabbed a set of keys off a hook.

He pointed a big finger at Dash. "Just one night I hope to run into your fat ass all alone on a dark street."

"Why, Steve, you ain't one of them guys that like guys, are you?"

Prichard's face flushed, but before he could say anything Dash continued, "Our client? Before I really get mean."

Prichard led them back to the holding cells and over to the cage containing Kemper. He was seated on a metal bench, his back to the wall and his collar and necktie still undone. His very expensive suit jacket rested on the bench next to him. He had a shiner on one eye and some hardened blood on his lip.

As Prichard unlocked the door, Dash said, "Who roughed him up? You?"

"He tripped and hit that handsome puss of his on the wall," said Prichard with a grin.

"How is it that everybody who gets arrested in this town suddenly forgets how to walk?" Dash eyed Prichard and the ring of keys. "Call Ernie in here."

"Why?"

"Because I'm not letting you lock us in there and then forget you did."

"I don't know if he's here."

"He's here. And I know Pickett's not."

Prichard left and came back with Prettyman, who said, "Willie, I'm sorry—"

"I know. Now take the keys from Steve and sit down with us and maybe you'll learn something along with me and Archer." After Prichard left, they all sat across from Kemper.

"Which one did that?" asked Dash, pointing to his injuries.

"Does it matter?"

"Probably not. Heads-up for you, the elevator guy at my building named Earl had his throat cut and Doctor Myron O'Donnell has a third eye. I'm thinking O'Donnell was the target though they clumsily tried to make it look like a narcotics steal."

Kemper sat up straight, looking scared. "What the hell is going on?"

"That's what we're going to find out."

Archer interjected, "You told us that O'Donnell had performed a recent surgery on your wife for appendicitis?"

"That's right."

"And you said her mother and father had used O'Donnell as well?" added Dash.

"Yes. Eleanor caught her arm in a piece of machinery at the shop where she kept her plane. She lost a lot of blood, but O'Donnell fixed her right up, good as new. And Sawyer had to have an operation after a car accident years ago."

Dash said. "Now, whose idea was it for you to run for mayor?"

"It was *my* idea."

"Armstrong didn't put you up to it?"

"Look, I know everyone thinks I'm his lapdog, but the fact is, I don't need help from him. When I told him I was running, he raised no objection, but I'm funding the campaign myself. He hasn't put up one dime, nor would I take it if he offered."

"You led us to think that he was supporting you," said Archer.

"Did I? Well, maybe I did. But he's not."

"Why did you come to me to look into this blackmail scheme?"

"I asked my lawyer. He knew about you."

"And does your lawyer know your father-in-law?"

"Well, yes. Sawyer recommended the guy to me. But what does that have to do with anything?"

"Your wife called Armstrong tonight," explained Archer. "He showed right up."

"I bet he did," Kemper muttered.

"Whenever father and daughter are together she becomes a different person. And not in a good way."

Kemper seemed to appraise Archer in a new light. "You just described my marriage." He paused and ran a hand through his hair. "I love Beth. From the moment I saw her, I was nuts about the woman. I loved her mother, too. Eleanor was a dynamo and Beth took after her." He paused again. "That was when Sawyer wasn't around. When he was, Beth just clammed up, became a totally different person, like you said. She'd defer to him on all subjects. Took his side against me. It made me mad. It enraged me, in fact."

"And how did you manifest that rage, Mr. Kemper?" said Dash.

"I never touched a hair on her head and I never would. But...but I started going out on my own, pretended to play the field, acted like some sort of sap you'd see in the movies. Slept in separate rooms. I...I guess part of me thought it would make Beth jealous. The only thing it did was—"

"—it drew her to Benjamin Smalls," said Archer. "They were having an affair, weren't they? Ironic, since you were the one playing the ladies' man, but had remained faithful."

"I don't blame Beth for what she did. I feel like I drove her to it. And I know Sawyer was in the background feeding her all sorts of lies about me, trying to destroy our marriage. And he intimated to me that Beth was sleeping with our chauffeur, Adam Stover. I didn't want to believe it, but it made me suspicious."

"Yeah, we met handsome muscle boy. He's definitely not your wife's type. But you made Armstrong's job easy, you dope," pointed out Dash.

"But I never did anything with the woman who was killed. And I sure as hell would never have murdered Wilson." He paused and looked at Archer. "Why do you know about the island? What the hell would anyone do with it?"

"Well, I think your father-in-law is planning to build a huge casino complex on it," answered Dash.

Prettyman interjected, "You can't have a casino in California, Willie."

"That chunk of rock ain't part of California," retorted Dash before turning to Kemper. "Your country club that has the marina and big dock. Does Armstrong have an ownership interest in that?"

"Yes. It was my first big project. I needed his backing."

"What's the ownership split?"

"Fifty-fifty."

"Not to be blunt, but what happens to it if you get gassed in the chamber at San Quentin?" said Dash.

Kemper paled. "I...Beth gets everything that I own."

"Meaning, realistically, Armstrong will own it all."

"Yes, I suppose so. Beth just can't seem to say no to him."

Archer said, "The day Eleanor Armstrong died in that plane crash, Beth was supposed to go up with her, but instead she went to a luncheon that you had arranged. How did that come to pass?"

"It was Sawyer. *He* really arranged the luncheon and he insisted that Beth be there."

"I think Armstrong told Beth that it was your idea, not his."

Kemper slowly nodded. "It seemed like the light went out of our marriage after Eleanor's death."

Dash glanced at Prettyman. "Carl's going to come up with anything he can to lock me and Archer up. So we're going to have to lie low for a bit."

"Okay, Willie, but watch your back."

"Hell, Ern, you know I'm as familiar with my back as I am my front."

They walked out of the cell, where Dash buttonholed Prettyman out of Kemper's earshot. "Okay, here's the deal, Ern, you got any guys on the force who actually know Pickett's a bad cop or who aren't on the take themselves?"

"Yeah, sure. A few."

"Good. Call 'em in and have them help you play guardian angel. If Kemper bites it, all my plans go sideways."

Archer and Dash left.

"Where to now, Willie?" asked Archer.

"Midnight Moods."

"Why?"

"I have to ask Mabel Dawson about an old vaudeville performer named Guy Parnell."

"And that case you told Prichard about? *Rogers versus California?*"

"The technical term for that, Archer, is 'bullshit.' But it's all in how you sell the line."

CHAPTER

62

THEY FOUND DAWSON BACKSTAGE watching Callahan perform another set.

Dash glanced at the packed house, checked out Callahan doing a song-and-dance routine, and said, "And tell me again how you're not the luckiest sap on earth, Archer?"

"It's complicated."

"In my day, it wouldn't have been." Dash eyed Dawson. "Okay, Mabel, we need to talk."

"Not now. I'm busy."

"There have been two more murders."

"Here?" she snapped.

"No, but they're connected. Now, why did you kick Guy Parnell loose early?"

Dawson slowly turned to look at him as Callahan belted out Dinah Shore's "I'll Walk Alone."

Archer thought, *Well that song fits her to a T.*

Dawson said, "I...I guess he had a change of plan."

Dash shook his head. "It's what we in the business call a rhetorical question, Mabel, because I already know the answer. I dropped enough coins to talk to Parnell long distance. He's in Detroit with an extra five hundred bucks in his pocket on top of his full seasonal wages courtesy of *you.*"

She licked her suddenly dry lips. "I...I don't recall."

"Sure you do. Armstrong told you to do it, and so you did what you always do when Armstrong tells you to do something. Now the question is *why* he wanted you to do it."

"Is this another *rhetorical* question?" asked Dawson, looking ill now.

"Yeah, it is. They needed his room to kill Fraser and Sheen. They transported Fraser from that room to hers after she was dead using the connecting attic space between the two rooms. They left Sheen in Parnell's old room after the poor guy was murdered."

Dawson took a deliberate step back. "I don't know nothing about that."

Dash shook his head and smiled. "Come on, Mabel, you're up to your baby blues in this, honey. See, you told us Fraser liked rich men. Now, who's the richest of all in this town and a widower and available to boot?"

"You're nuts. Armstrong's almost old enough to be her grand-father."

"You'd be surprised at how millions in dough can make people seem a lot younger. So you arranged for poor Ruby to meet up with Armstrong in Parnell's old room, only it was Tweedle Dee and Tweedle Dum in there and not Armstrong. They pretended her throat was a steak, and then they deposited the lady in her own room through the crawlspace after cleaning up the blood. When you went looking for her, why do I think you skipped Parnell's old digs? If you had opened that door and seen them cutting up poor Ruby, they might have had to kill you, too."

"This is crazy talk, Willie," said Dawson.

"Then why are your eyebrows sweating? Armstrong already knows what I'm about to tell you and here it is: You are what we call in the business a loose end. He's had four people killed so far. What's one more, sweetie? You get my drift, or are you under the delusion that you're actually something special?"

Dawson plopped down in a chair that Archer had hastily drawn up for her while Callahan launched into Sinatra's "Five Minutes More."

Dash knelt down next to her and gently patted her hand. "Come on, Mabel, I got nothing against you. And I bet you didn't know what they were going to do to poor Ruby."

She shook her head and said in a hushed voice, "I didn't. I swear to God. I thought I was doing her a favor. You know, hooking her up with money. The poor kid. Why...why would they do that to her?"

"She was just a murder to pin on somebody else," said Dash. "Look, you got someplace safe out of town you can go to for a few days?"

"My sister's. In Long Beach."

"Okay, but first, we're going to my office. I'm going to have an affidavit typed up and you're going to sign it."

"What affidavit?" she said, her eyes bugging out at the man.

"Just saying what you already told us. I'll get my secretary to come in, type it up, and notarize it."

"But then I'll be—"

"What you'll be is *smart*. You'll get a deal. No jail time. And your story is memorialized for all to see if need be."

"You swear?"

"So long as you've been square with me on your involvement, yeah, I swear. I'll fix it with the DA. Now go pack a bag and we can drop you off at the bus station after we go by my office. Memory serves, there's a southbound bus that leaves in about two hours that stops in Long Beach. You give me your sister's phone number and I'll be in contact. Okay?"

She nodded dumbly.

Archer went with her while she packed a bag, then they drove to Dash's office. He had phoned Morrison from Midnight Moods and she was already there, waiting.

Archer looked at Morrison, all efficiency and professionally outfitted at this time of night, and wondered if she just waited by the phone all night for a call from Dash to say he needed her.

Dash and Dawson wrote out what she was willing to say, and Morrison typed it up in triplicate. Dawson signed three times and Morrison notarized all of them.

After that they drove Dawson to the Greyhound terminal.

She said, "Since I signed that paper, will you still need me?"

"We'll have to see how it plays out. If it goes to trial, I'll personally come and get you."

They watched her get on the bus ten minutes later.

Archer said, "So, we can bring it all down with her affidavit?"

"Not even close, Archer. He said, she said. And unfortunately Armstrong's words will carry far greater weight than a dame who runs a burlesque."

"So why'd you have her do it?"

"Every little bit helps, and it was a way to scare her into getting to a safe place."

"That was good of you, Willie."

"I don't have much good in me, Archer. But when it does come out, it feels pretty swell. Can I take another pull on your flask?"

Archer handed it to him. After Dash gave it back, Archer stared down at it as something occurred to him. An awful something. He said, "Look, I just had a thought and need to run it down. You going to be okay?"

"When Pickett and his clowns finish there, I'm going back to the doc's office."

"Why's that?"

"To figure out why somebody needed to kill Myron O'Donnell."

CHAPTER

63

ARCHER LOOKED ALL OVER MIDNIGHT MOODS until he found the old gent. He was the one Wilma Darling had pointed out to him the night they'd been having a drink on the terrace. He had the same lovely young lady sitting in his aged lap. Archer asked his questions and got his answers, which he grimly accepted as they proved his forming hunch correct. Then he drove straight to Wilma Darling's bungalow, where he confirmed that the Ford coupe was gone and the place was empty. Next, he pulled out his map and saw the general direction he needed to take. He figured forty minutes if he made the Delahaye get real excited.

He kept the pedal to the floor, and thirty-eight minutes later he pulled into Ventura. He stopped at an all-night dance club—where people seemed to be having a good time without getting murdered—and asked for directions to his final destination. The bouncer actually knew the address and told Archer how to get there.

"That's Wilma's place," said the man, a beefy gent with a bald head and hands the size of watermelons.

"*Her* place?"

"Yeah. Hey, you one of her customers?"

"Customers?" Archer said, puzzled. Then he quickly recovered and said, "Yeah, yeah, I am. Any idea where she is?"

The bouncer's friendly features fell away as it was clear he did not believe Archer. "Forget it, mac, just forget it. Now beat it, I got work to do."

He walked away, leaving Archer deeply disturbed.

The house was a one-story stucco with a red tile roof and enough plants, trees, and flowers to hide it from its neighbors. Its backyard was basically the ocean. A storm was drifting in, as Archer had found storms often did around here. It was like the Pacific wanted the coastal residents to be as wet as it was.

The Ford coupe wasn't in the carport. The porch light was on, and that was it for illumination at this time of night. He pulled the Delahaye farther down the road and out of sight of the house. He got out and flitted back up the quiet street. He chanced looking in the mailbox and pocketed a couple of pieces of mail he found in there, which told him a lot, although the bouncer had already done that. He next circled back around, jumped a fence of the house next door to hers, and traversed the backyard, where the smell of charcoal from a recent cookout competed with the eucalyptus trees for dominance of his nostrils. Although he could still smell his sweat and the stink of fear that went along with it.

Archer squatted down behind the fence separating Darling's place from her neighbor's.

He waited for a few minutes there, reconnoitering the land in front of him. Finally satisfied, he gripped the top of the wooden fence and easily propelled himself over, landing in the wiry grass of Darling's yard. He threaded his way up to the back door and tried the knob. It was locked. He didn't have Dash's lockpick kit, but he had a pocketknife. The blade was enough to push back the simple latch. The next moment he was inside and on the wrong side of the law, where Archer was getting to be more comfortable than was probably good for him.

He moved through to the kitchen, where he found a small refrigerator that held a glass jug of buttermilk, two eggs, a bunch of apples, and a wedge of cheese. The buttermilk smelled fresh.

In the living room he saw the monogrammed cigarette lighter on a table.

Okay, here we go.

Archer sat down in a chair facing the front door and waited. He checked his timepiece. It was almost four in the morning and he had never felt further from sleep. It was like every nerve in his body was doing the jitterbug.

Thirty minutes later the beams from a car's headlights cut across the front window. He sank down a bit deeper in his chair. He heard the car door open and close, and listened to the high heels poking into the sidewalk until their owner arrived at the front door. A key was inserted and the door opened, and there she was. In the illumination of the porch light he could see that she wore a narrow-brimmed, angled hat, a dark green dress that flared out from the hips, and a white, short-waisted jacket, long white dress gloves, and green pumps that lifted her impressive height ever more skyward. Her purse hung over her forearm. She looked like a knockout, thought Archer. And that cut both ways.

Archer eyed the purse and thought about the two things of importance that might be inside it, because he knew they weren't in here.

She closed the door behind her, flicked on a switch, and dark became light.

And Archer went from invisible to revealed.

She froze and then gasped, her hand flying to her chest, which was heaving.

That sight made Archer feel better.

"You scared the hell out of me. How did you get in here?"

"Back door was unlocked."

"No it wasn't. I distinctly remember locking it."

"You missed my meaning. *I* unlocked it."

Her fearful expression faded and was replaced with a look that under other circumstances might have intimidated Archer. But not tonight.

"Explain yourself."

"I need a drink. Couldn't find one in here. Got your flask?"

She opened her purse and looked inside it. "I've got rye. Is that okay?"

When she looked up, Darling was staring down the barrel of the .38.

She coolly eyed the gun. "If you don't want the rye, Archer, just say so."

"Yeah, I wish a funny line would cut it, Wilma. Have a seat and take it real slow. Anything fast or sudden from you would not be healthy. And hand your purse over."

"What, are you an armed robber now? It doesn't suit you, Archer. Admit it, you're a Goody Two-shoes."

She tossed the purse to him. He caught it in one hand and set it on the table next to his chair while he watched her perch on the settee across from him and cross her long legs at the ankles, her gloved hands in her lap as prim and proper as could be.

"You want to tell me what this is all about?"

"You never should have given me the address of this place, you know."

"Yeah, I'm starting to see that was a mistake."

"But it's a nice place, Wilma. Real nice. Cost a pretty penny, no doubt."

"It's not mine. I'm just renting it for a few days. And *you* told me to come here."

"Starting off with a lie? Not the way I want this to go."

"I'm not lying, Archer," she said smoothly.

He pulled the letters from his pocket and tossed them down on the table that sat between them.

"People don't have mail addressed to a place they're *renting* for a few days."

She looked at the letters with her name and this address on them. Archer could see the wheels spinning as she tried to think of a plausible counter to what he'd just said. But then her expression finally showed that she had come up empty.

"So what?" she said.

"Yeah, so what. And tack on to that the bouncer at the nightclub near here knows this as *your* place." He opened her purse and took out the flask. "And so what that on the drive to your place after Sheen got croaked you asked for a drink from *my* flask when you had this one in your purse. But then you couldn't drink from this one without getting very, very sleepy. Like Sheen when you slipped him the mickey. You lured him to the room on the pretense of showing him a good time. You let him ride you till he had his fill, and then he went beddy-bye courtesy of what was in your flask. You got dressed and left and someone else came in, maybe Hank and/or Tony, and they introduced a hole through Sheen's heart that he didn't have before."

"You're talking nonsense, Archer."

He cocked his head at her and waggled the. 38.

"You think I could sleep with you, knowing that somebody was killing Wilson? I'm not a monster, Archer."

"You got me out of Midnight Moods for one reason only. When we were sitting on that terrace you looked over my shoulder and your gaze froze on something. You told me it was the old guy with a taste for young gals. You said he and Kemper were doing a deal. I asked him about that tonight. He doesn't even know Kemper and he doesn't do deals. You lied to me, Wilma. I don't like that."

"Why would I lie?"

"Because who you really saw over my shoulder was whoever killed Sheen. They were giving you the high sign. And I told you I was going to go look for Sheen. You couldn't have that. So what did you do? You invited me to your place for a little fun between the sheets, and I forgot all about Wilson Sheen until you got the call the next morning. And since I was with you at all relevant times, you got yourself a prime alibi to boot. It was on the fly and neatly done. I'll give you that."

She took a cigarette from the bowl and lit it. "You're nuts."

"Am I? I'd explain it all like they do in the detective novels, but it would take too much time and you already know what I'm going to say."

"You're making me out to be some criminal."

"You made yourself out to be one by committing criminal acts. Funny how that works." He took out a pillbox from her purse and withdrew a pill from it. "I saw this pillbox in your purse before, but it was empty. And that same bouncer asked me if I was a customer of yours. A customer for what, I wonder?"

Darling just stared at him, lips pursed, legs still primly crossed at the ankles, the smoke in her hand.

"You sell drugs, Wilma." He looked at the pill. "Amphetamines."

"You know about amphetamines, Archer? I'm impressed."

"Army used to give them out like candy in the war. Made you not feel tired even though you hadn't slept for days. Made you not feel hungry so they didn't have to stop the fighting to feed you. Made you act like a lion when you felt like a mouse." He put the pill back and returned the box to the purse. "And you're also selling to the gals in your office. That's why they could work dawn to dusk and move like someone had stuck their fingers in a wall socket. Must pay well. You got the place in Bay Town, this place here. A new car. Nice clothes. Yeah, what a success you are."

"Everything I have I worked for."

"Oh, yeah, you did. And you said you went to Midnight Moods regularly. I'm betting you sold to the gals there, too. Like Ruby Fraser. You sold her pills. And I'm thinking you were the one who fingered her to be the patsy in all this. Put her at the center of this phony blackmail scheme with Kemper, and then they cut her throat out. And then you set up poor Wilson Sheen and removed any alibi Kemper has for Fraser's murder. You probably got that info from one of them while at the office and passed it along to the appropriate party."

"You weave a good tale, Archer. Good thing for me the cops only care about facts."

"Let me give you some then. They killed Dr. Myron O'Donnell tonight and made it look like a narcotics hit. In the process, they slit the throat of a harmless old man who spent his days going up and down in an elevator reading the *Gazette* and swigging his cheap rum after a really shitty life. I look down on folks who kill other folks, unless you happen to be in a war. So that makes you an accessory to two more murders, Wilma. Even if they don't send you to the gas chamber you're getting at least twenty-five to life." He checked her purse again. "Where's the Derringer?"

"A lady has to protect herself, Archer. You got a gun. Why shouldn't I have a gun?"

"Under any other circumstances, I would agree with you. But I'm fresh out of understanding right now. So where is it?"

"I dumped it. It was making me nervous."

He decided to let this pass, for now, and kept the gun pointed right at her, his finger on the trigger guard.

"So I get no points at all for screwing you? 'Cause I know you enjoyed it, lover boy. Guys can't fake it, only the gals can do that, only I admit I didn't have to with you."

"Yeah, and now that I know the truth about you, I'll be taking three showers a day to try to get the stink off."

"A girl has to do what a girl has to do to survive, Archer. But being a man, you would have no clue."

"I know lots of gals who get by just fine without selling drugs and helping people kill other people."

"I never wanted to be like 'lots of gals.'"

"And thank God lots of gals never want to be like *you*. I hope

the money you got paid was worth it. And I'm betting it was a lot
more than a grand."

She hiked her eyebrows. "So where does all this leave you
and me?"

"In a difficult spot."

"You have no proof of anything."

"That's *my* difficult spot. But I just wanted to let you know that
I know the truth."

"How decent of you, Archer. I was half serious when I asked
where I could get a dozen of you. Of course, you'd start to bore
me at some point. See, I don't like the shiny knights. I like the bad
boys who take what they want when they want."

"Yeah, I know all about them. And the bad *girls*, too, like you."

"What a choirboy you turned out to be."

"I tell you what. Give up Sawyer Armstrong and get a few years
shaved off your sentence. He framed his son-in-law for a double
murder that Kemper had no part in. Can't let a guy like that walk
the last mile to San Quentin."

"And why not?" She ground out her cigarette on the tabletop
and sat back.

"If you have to ask, any explanation I could give you would be
a waste of time."

"We seem to be wasting a lot of time tonight, Archer. But one
thing I wanted you to know."

"What's that?"

"I wasn't surprised to see you here. I was just faking. How'd
I do?"

"I'd rate you right up there with Bette Davis. But why weren't
you surprised?"

"I was at that dance club tonight. And the bouncer's my friend.
And he told me all about you."

She did move well, very well. The Derringer came out from a
pocket on her jacket and she got off two quick shots.

Both missed.

Archer's did not.

Darling lowered her gun and then looked down at her front. The dark green cloth was sprouting another color.

The crimson patch kept growing as she looked up at him, her facial muscles as tensed as a person surprised that she is suddenly dying can make them. A bit of blood emerged at the corner of her mouth as the internal hemorrhaging expanded upward.

She fell to her knees and glanced up at him. Her mouth moved but no words came out. Her head hit the table on the way down. It didn't matter. She didn't feel the impact. The dead felt nothing.

Archer looked behind him where the twin Derringer bullets had slammed into the back of his chair right on either side of him.

Part of him thought it would turn out this way. He'd only hoped *that* part of him would be wrong.

He rose and looked down at her. Fleeting images of their first meeting and their lovemaking raced through his thoughts. Part of him felt lucky, part felt depressed, and part of him, maybe the largest part, just felt sick to his stomach.

He left the way he had come, after wiping his prints off everything he had touched. If he could have dug the bullet out of her he would have. Now he had to be worried about getting fingered for her death.

He drove fast back to Bay Town because he knew there was more to be done.

CHAPTER

64

ARCHER RODE THE STORM ALL THE WAY BACK. It looked like the entire coast of southern California was getting the same treatment. On reaching the town limits he drove straight to his office building. There were no prowlers out front, nor did he see Pickett's big Chrysler. They must have come and gone, thought Archer.

Dawn was still over an hour away as the storm continued to rage overhead. He hadn't slept in nearly twenty-four hours, but he had never felt less tired in his life. Killing a person, particularly a beautiful woman with whom you'd previously slept, just did that to you, he supposed. It didn't make him feel good or bad. He didn't feel anything, really, and he couldn't really handle that so he stopped thinking about it.

He entered the office building through a back entrance and crept along the first-floor corridor until he neared the elevator. He got a sight line that showed Earl's body was no longer where it had been before. He moved forward and saw that the car was empty. He passed by it and drew closer to O'Donnell's office. He waited, crouching in the darkened hallway, listening and watching. Satisfied that an army of cops wasn't lurking to bash him in the head, he eased the office door open and peered inside.

Empty and dark.

He hurried through the reception area and thought to pull his gun, just in case. He had five shots left in the barrel. He hoped he didn't need any of them. He didn't like the exposed position he was in, but he had to find Dash, and fast.

He nearly jumped out of his shoes when he heard the voice.

"Archer, is that you?"

"Yeah, it's me."

Dash appeared in the doorway leading into the interior hall of the office space.

Archer put the gun away.

"Where did you go?" asked Dash.

In sixty seconds, Archer told him what had happened and why.

"Okay, Wilma Darling bit the dust. She was in on it. And she was selling drugs on top of it. What a piece of work. Nice catch on the flask. But you got some exposure there when they find the body."

"I know."

"We'll have to focus on that later."

"What did you find?"

"Come on. I'll show you."

He led Archer into another room that was filled with metal file cabinets.

Dash turned on the light and took a file off the table in there.

"What's that?"

"*My* medical file, Archer. O'Donnell wasn't just a friend, he was my doctor, too."

"Okay," said Archer, looking confused. "How does that help us?"

"Lots of good stuff in here. My age, height, weight. Medical history. Blood type. Blood pressure." He blanched. "Not a number I want to really dwell on. But before you go under the knife, they have to know this stuff."

"What'd you have done?"

"Ulcer surgery."

"Yeah, Connie mentioned that."

"O'Donnell cut out some of my gut, so most nights I eat Cream of Wheat and buttermilk."

"Should you be drinking, then?"

"Hell, Archer, I can only get the goddamn Cream of Wheat down if I *do* drink."

"So did you find anything helpful?"

"It's what I *didn't* find that was helpful."

"Come again?"

"What I didn't find were the medical files for Sawyer and Eleanor Armstrong, and Beth Kemper. They're missing."

"What? Why?"

"Because I'm sure they provided the same sort of information as mine does. So I sat here going over my file to see what sort of information someone wouldn't want someone else to know. And then I had to take it a step further and see what sort of information someone wouldn't want someone to know, when they put all *three* of those files together. See, it's important to note that they didn't take one or two of the files. They took all three and they took them for a reason. You see that, right?"

"Yeah, when you lay it out like that, it makes sense. So what did you conclude?"

"I think they took all three because the files had their individual blood types. Sawyer's, Eleanor's, and Beth's. You know about blood types?"

"Sure. They have to know that when they need to give transfusions. Otherwise, it can kill you if they get the blood types mixed up."

"That's right. But blood types are important for something besides making transfusions safe."

"Like what?"

"They can prove whether someone *isn't* the parent of a child."

Archer stiffened but remained quiet and looked at Dash expectantly.

"There was the Charlie Chaplin case back in the early forties. It happened right here in California. Chaplin slept around and one woman said she had a child by him. They did a blood test on the kid and Chaplin and the woman to see if he could be the father. Turns out he wasn't the dad, though the jury held him liable for other reasons. But the point is if the kid has AB blood and the mother has A blood, the father has to have B or AB blood. If not, he's out. Now, it can't say for sure you're the parent if you have one of the right blood types, you see, but it can rule you *out* for certain depending on the blood types of the interested parties. Nice thing about science. It is what it is."

"Who exactly are we talking about here, Willie?" Archer said this although he was pretty sure he knew the answer.

"All three of them—Beth, Eleanor, and Sawyer—were treated by O'Donnell. All three involved surgery, potential blood loss. So all three would have had to have their blood types checked in case they needed a transfusion. Now, Eleanor's and Sawyer's operations were a long time ago."

"But Beth's was recent," interjected Archer.

"Right, the last piece of the puzzle. I think it occurred to Armstrong how he was exposed on that and he decided to nip it in the bud, even if O'Donnell hadn't made the connection. But he couldn't take a chance, which is why the doc had to die and the records had to be taken."

"So you're saying...?"

"I'm saying that Armstrong is not Beth's biological father."

"That means Eleanor had an affair?"

"Yes."

"Any idea who it was?"

Dash took out his pipe and chewed on the end without lighting it. "I know that Beth Kemper just turned thirty-one. It was in the papers. Well, thirty-one years ago I wasn't in this town. But somebody else was."

"Who?"

"Andrew Smalls."

Archer looked startled. "Armstrong's partner who killed himself."

"Well, maybe he did and maybe he didn't."

"Are you saying he was having an affair with Eleanor?"

"More than that, Archer. I think he's Beth's father."

"But…but that would make her and Benjamin Smalls—"

"—half siblings, yeah."

Archer scratched his head. "Then this is all about what?"

"Revenge. Cruelty. And maybe something else that's sicker than both those put together. The point is, anyone gets close to Beth Kemper gets taken away, somehow, some way. Andrew Smalls, Benjamin Smalls."

"And her husband," said Archer.

"And her mother," added Dash.

"Her mother. But she died in—"

"Yeah, a plane crash. A *Stearman* plane crash, which is the name of the company that bought that island out there. And everyone in town knows Beth was supposed to go up with her mother that day, but she went to a luncheon with her husband instead. And Kemper told us it was Armstrong who made that happen."

"But why kill Eleanor? Because she cheated on him? He sure as hell waited a long time, unless he just found out two years ago."

"I think it's more complicated than that, Archer. Beth loved her mother far more than she loved Armstrong. And maybe he just couldn't take that anymore. And then, in his warped mind, Eleanor had to pay the ultimate price for cheating on him. But everything was just fine until Beth had her surgery. Now O'Donnell had *all* of their blood types. And I think it was then that he could see for himself that Armstrong *couldn't* be the father. I can envision Armstrong sitting up there surrounded by his olive trees brooding about it. And once he figured the man had that leverage over him, the doc was as good as dead."

"Why would Armstrong think O'Donnell would even put the three together? And why would Armstrong believe that O'Donnell would use it against him?"

"A good question, and here's my answer. A man like Armstrong believes that everybody else thinks like him. Meaning if Armstrong had that information on someone he would sure as hell use it against them. So he just assumed that O'Donnell would put the screws to him. He sees the world and everyone in it through his own warped perspective. All of his actions are dictated by what is best for him, nobody else."

"Okay, let's say that's all true. How does that tie into this blackmail plot against Douglas Kemper? Armstrong's backing him for mayor."

"Is he, Archer? Who really told us that? Douglas Kemper never did, quite the opposite, in fact. And Armstrong hedged his bets talking about it. But look at it this way: If Armstrong wants his son-in-law out of his daughter's life, here's what he could do: He sends a blackmail letter to Kemper saying they know he's sleeping around with Fraser. Then Kemper hires us to look into it because Armstrong's lawyer recommended me to him. Fraser denied the affair, since it was all a load of baloney, but that still gives Kemper every motive to kill her. Then, she *is* killed."

"And the only guy who can give Kemper an alibi for Fraser's murder is Sheen."

"So he dies too, and they frame Kemper for that. Then they got the medical records and the doc is dead and that loose end goes away. And Kemper goes to the gas chamber, and Armstrong is left to pick up the pieces with a woman who is *not* his daughter."

"Do you think..." began Archer, his face growing pale as a number of sickening thoughts invaded his mind.

Dash looked at him knowingly. "I don't know, Archer. But I do know that Armstrong is one dangerous man."

"And what about Benjamin Smalls?"

"Smalls found out Armstrong was planning to build a casino and had a confrontation with him about it. The law may allow gambling out on that rock, but as mayor, Smalls could have made Armstrong's life miserable and put his scheme in real jeopardy."

"But we have no proof of any of this."

Dash stroked his chin. "And Pickett is so far up Armstrong's ass you can't even see the man's wingtips."

"So what do we do?" asked Archer.

"We go see the dentist."

65

THE SUN WAS BREAKING THROUGH the remnants of the passing storm. Both men stared out the windscreen of the Delahaye as they drove to Alfred Drake's home.

"What's your angle on him?"

"He has a backer, all right. But it's not the Vegas mob. It's Sawyer Armstrong."

Archer jerked the wheel of the car. "Armstrong?"

"We've been played for dopes, Archer. Like everybody else in this business."

"You're going to have to explain that to me."

"Drake is a grown-up version of the kid I saw hanging in that room. Armstrong knows it, and I'm betting he has hard proof and he's blackmailing Drake with it. He'll have to approve whatever the man wants in connection with that casino. And remember what Drake said when we were leaving his house? You asked him if he really believed he had no chance against Kemper? And he said something like '*I* have no chance. But we'll have to see.'"

Archer added, "And then he said, 'Stranger things have happened.'"

"Right. But the point is, Drake was being literal. *He* doesn't have a chance against *Kemper.*"

"But if Kemper isn't running against him?"

"Then he's going to win."

"But Drake doesn't strike me as a guy to just meekly take it on the chin, Willie. Like you pointed out before, the guy fights back."

Dash suddenly got a disturbed look on his face. "You're right, Archer, so step on it!"

They roared up to the front of the residence, and Dash had his door open before Archer even stopped the car. He ran up and pounded on the front door. It took a while but the same woman as before answered. She was cinching her robe around her waist, and her hair was disheveled from sleep.

"Do you know what time it is?" she began angrily.

"We need to see Drake now," said Dash. "It's an emergency."

"He's asleep. And so was I."

"Then we'll wake him up." He pushed past her. "Which way?"

"You can't just—"

He grabbed her arm. "Which way, lady? This is life and death."

The woman quickly led them down a long hall to a set of double doors situated at the end of the corridor.

Dash tried the door but it was locked.

"Drake, it's Willie Dash. Alfred, open up." He pounded the wood again. There was no reply from within.

"Do you have a key to open it?" he asked the woman. She shook her head.

"Archer!" Dash motioned to the door.

Archer took a few steps and exploded forward, his shoulder smashing into the wood. It buckled but did not give. Archer retreated and then charged forward once more; this time the door flew open, and he was in the room. Dash and the woman followed him.

She screamed, and Archer just stared.

Drake was in a chair. The gun he'd used to kill himself was still in his right hand, his index finger wedged in the trigger guard. He was dressed in a dark blue silk robe with white pajamas underneath. There was a single hole in his right temple. It was blackened and burned in the center and crimsoned with blood on the rim. It looked angry and foul and wrong.

Dash walked over, felt his wrist, and leaned in close to check the wound. Finally, he felt the gun muzzle. He glanced up at Archer. "Doesn't seem like he's been dead long." He looked at the woman, who had finally stopped screaming and was swaying like a pine tree in a windstorm.

"When did you see him last?" he asked.

"I...I..."

He guided her to a chair as far away from Drake as possible and pointed away from the man's corpse. "Just take a deep breath and collect yourself. I know this must be a shock. Archer, your flask?"

Archer drew it from his pocket and passed it over. Dash unscrewed the cap and encouraged the woman to take a sip, which she did. She handed it back and looked up at him.

"What's your name, hon?" asked Dash.

"Ruthie."

"Okay Ruthie, just take your time and tell us what you can about last night."

She took another replenishing breath and began. "Mr. Drake had an early dinner and then sat up reading in the library. Around nine or so I saw him go to his room. That's the last time I saw him."

"He seem okay?"

"He seemed...normal. He's never one for small talk, but he...he didn't seem like a man ready to shoot himself, either."

"Did you hear any noises? Like a gunshot?"

She shook her head. "Me and the cook sleep at the other end of the house. This is Mr. Drake's private wing. I didn't hear anything. Not until you knocked on the door."

"Okay. Did he have any visitors last night? Phone calls? Get any messages delivered?"

"No, nothing like that. It…it was a typical evening." She glanced at Drake's body and shuddered.

Dash eyed the phone on the nightstand. He picked it up and dialed.

"Yeah, I want to talk to Ernie Prettyman, tell him it's Willie Dash." He paused and then stiffened. "When? Shit. Okay."

He slammed down the phone and looked at Archer. "Ern's in the hospital unconscious. Some goons jumped him and the two guys guarding Kemper."

"And Kemper?"

"Looks like they took him. Son of a bitch!"

He picked up the phone again and stared at it like he'd never seen one before. Turning to Ruthie he said, "But you wouldn't know if *Drake* called someone, would you?"

"No sir. I would have no way of knowing that."

"Willie!" exclaimed Archer.

Archer was kneeling and looking down at the carpet near a set of French doors opening to the outside.

Dash hurried over to him.

"It was raining up until about an hour ago," said Archer.

Dash examined the wet footprints on the carpet. "Those weren't made by Drake; they're too short."

Archer opened one of the French doors. "Not locked."

Dash walked over to the woman. "Ruthie, that young fellow we saw planting a bush when we were here before? Who is he?"

"You mean, Bobby?"

"Yeah, Bobby."

"He's the gardener. Takes care of everything outside."

"He live here?"

Ruthie nodded. "In a room over the garage."

"Thanks."

66

THEY HEARD THE SOBS AS THEY APPROACHED the garage. They cut through the still morning air like a machete through bamboo. The garage was a three-bay setup with a full floor above, where, presumably, Bobby lived.

The exterior door was locked, but Archer managed to push up one of the garage doors and they went inside, passing a Buick and a trim little green Hunter convertible with the canvas top down on their way to the set of interior stairs. The sobs were now even louder, and in them Archer thought he could hear an anguish associated with only the deepest of personal losses.

They reached a doorway at the top of the stairs. The cries continued, with the person inside seemingly oblivious to their presence.

Dash whispered, "Pull your heater, Archer, just in case."

The gun came out. Archer stepped in front of Dash, put his hand on the doorknob, and slowly rotated it. The next moment he eased the door open and peered into the room.

The space was small, with bead-boarded, whitewashed walls and plenty of windows to let the emerging dawn peek through; one of the windows was open. That was no doubt how they could hear the crying all the way outside. On the wall were framed publicity stills of Cary Grant, Montgomery Clift, and other male actors. A two-drawer dresser painted a pale blue, some built-in cabinetry, a banjo leaning in one corner, and a mahogany four-poster bed were the only things to be seen—other than the young man lying in the bed and sobbing his heart out.

Archer and Dash stepped into the room and Archer closed the door behind him hard enough to make the man sit up and stare in fear and confusion at them.

"Who...who are you?"

Dash came forward. "You're Bobby, right?"

"Yes sir." He sat up and pulled the covers up over his bare chest.

Seeing him up close, Archer figured he was no more than twenty years old, with fine, delicate facial features and large blue eyes.

"I'm Willie Dash and this here is Archer. We're private eyes. You know about your...employer, I take it?"

Bobby wiped his eyes and nodded. "He shot himself. Did...did you see him, too?"

"Yeah. Hey, Bobby, let me see your hands for a sec."

Bobby held out his hands, and Dash wiped them with his pocket handkerchief. He looked at the cloth and then sniffed it.

"Well, you didn't fire that gun."

"I would never hurt anyone, especially Mr. Drake."

"Okay, calm down and tell us all about it."

Bobby glanced at Archer, who put his gun away, leaned against the wall, and said, "Must've been pretty upsetting to see him like that."

Bobby nodded and wiped his face on the sheet, looking anxious. "Yeah, it was."

"You went to see Drake sometime really early this morning, right?" asked Dash.

"I, uh..."

"Look, Bobby, I don't give a damn what you had going on with Drake. I just want to hear any information you might have so we can find out why Drake did what he did."

"You're in no trouble, Bobby," Archer added. "And what you tell us goes no further."

Bobby glanced at Dash, who nodded. "That's right, son."

Bobby grew calmer and sat up against the headboard. "I usually go to...see Mr. Drake around three in the morning, unless he tells me not to the night before."

"Why at that hour?"

"Well, the ladies are sure to be asleep by then and..."

"Okay. So you went there around three?"

Bobby nodded. "His bedroom door, see, I can walk right in off the rear verandah. Don't have to go into the house."

"We saw your footprints," noted Dash. "And saw that the door was unlocked."

"Well, I opened the door and walked in, like usual...and there he was." Bobby's eyes filled with fresh tears. "It was like he was staring at me, but he was...he was all dead and everything."

"Did you touch the body?" asked Dash.

"No sir," he said quickly. "I...I just turned and ran back here. And I been here crying the whole time. I mean, Mr. Drake was real good to me. I...I can't believe he's gone."

Dash glanced at Archer. "Now, Bobby, this is real important, okay?" He paused and drew closer to the bed. "When did the men come out here? You saw them, right?"

Bobby looked at him in surprise. "H-how'd you know about that, mister?"

"I didn't, at least not for sure, until now. Tell me about it."

"About twenty minutes after I got back here, I heard a car pull up real quiet like. I looked out the window. They had stopped right near the garage. Two men got out and went over to Mr. Drake's bedroom door. They opened it, but didn't go inside. But I saw a light flashing around."

Archer said, "That's why we only saw one set of footprints—Bobby's."

Bobby said, "Then they closed the door and got in their car and drove off."

"Two big lugs with stupid faces?" said Dash.

"Yeah, that's right. I saw 'em clear enough in the light next to the garage door."

"Hank and Tony," said Archer. "They were here."

Dash edged over to him and spoke in a low voice, "That's why they took Kemper, Archer. With Drake dead, Kemper is the mayor. Armstrong can't have that."

"So Drake must have called Armstrong and told him what he was going to do? That's why you mentioned back there about him maybe calling somebody?"

"And the two goons came here to make sure Drake wasn't bluffing. See, that was the ace in the hole Drake always had. Armstrong just figured he'd never play it, because it meant Drake would end up six feet under. But old Drake had his principles and he was apparently sticking to them. He wasn't going to be Armstrong's rubber stamp, no sir. Gotta admire the guy for that. I would like to think he died with that thought in mind and a smile on his lips."

He turned back to Bobby. "Drake ever talk to you about the campaign for mayor or Sawyer Armstrong?"

"No sir. We never talked about stuff like that."

"Okay, you got somewhere you can go, or people you can stay with?"

Bobby shook his head. "I...ran away from home a few years ago when..." He looked at them anxiously.

"Yeah, I understand. Okay, Ruthie knows that Drake is dead. She knows we came over to speak with you. For now, you just play dumb, okay? You don't know anything. You got that, Bobby?"

"S-sure, okay. Hey, mister, with Mr. Drake dead, will I...will I have to leave here? I don't have no other place to go."

Dash looked uncomfortable. "I could lie to you, son, and say you can stay here for as long as you want. But fact is, Bobby, I have no idea. But for right now, you can stay, okay?"

"O-okay, thanks." He looked past them and out the window

toward the house. "He was a really nice man. He treated me okay, he really did." He wiped his face on the sheet again, but it came away looking as tear-streaked as before.

"Unfortunately, all good things must come to an end sometime," noted Dash. "And for some people in this town, all I see are bad times coming."

67

ARCHER AND DASH PULLED AWAY IN THE DELAHAYE as the dawn
kept creeping up on them.

Archer said, "Where would they have taken Kemper? And what's
Armstrong's game? How is he going to get out of this one?"

"From his point of view, he's home free. He just has to get
rid of Kemper, and his star keeps shining bright. No one will
ever point their finger at him. Kemper was his beloved son-in-law.
Armstrong was supporting his campaign. He loved and respected
the man. He shows up after he gets arrested and tells you to do all
you can to save the man. He'll cry some crocodile tears when and
if they find his body, and that'll be it."

"But if we find out that he was the one who snatched Kemper?"

"He'll be nowhere near that, Archer, with an unshakable alibi.
And he won't have used Hank and Tony. Some boys from out of
town were no doubt paid to do the job and keep their mouths
shut later."

"So what do we do, then?"

"We *find* Kemper."

"He could be anywhere, though."

Dash looked at him and smiled. "I think we need to go to the
hospital."

"But Ernie Prettyman is unconscious. He can't tell us anything."

"This has nothing to do with Ern. I just want to prove to myself that Armstrong isn't as smart as he thinks he is."

* * *

Bay Town General Hospital was a large, whitewashed building, four stories tall, with lots of windows, a flat face, and no interesting architectural elements. It looked about as appealing to enter as a morgue. At least to Archer.

"Look here, Archer, while I'm in here checking things out, I want you to go to the Occidental Building and see if Beth Kemper is there. You said she has an apartment there. It's only one block over in that direction." He pointed to his right.

"Beth? Why would she be there?"

"For some reason I don't think she wants to be anyplace right now that has an *A* on the gates."

"You think she knows her husband's been taken?"

"Doubtful. So I want you to tell her. And then I want you to persuade her to throw in her lot with us. She needs to tell us where Armstrong might have taken her hubby."

"You think she'll tell us?"

"Depends on how persuasive you are."

Archer dropped Dash off, and Dash told Archer he would meet him at the Occidental as soon as he could.

Then Archer parked the Delahaye at the curb and got out. He stared up at the façade of the Occidental Building. It was constructed of white and brown slabs of stone with emerald-green slashes thrown in, probably to make the architect happy. A long burgundy awning was emblazoned with the name of the place in case the two-foot-high chrome letters on the side of the building weren't clear enough. There was a doorman out front wearing a black top hat, and a long coat the same color as the awning with brass buttons and a vest the color of a British redcoat. Long, white gloves covered his hands. A cab whistle dangled on a chain around his neck. To Archer, the man looked as embarrassed as he probably felt wearing that get-up.

He walked over to the man and said, "Hey, pal, checking to see if Beth Kemper is at her place here."

The gent looked him up and down in a disinterested way. "Who wants to know?"

Archer produced his PI license, which had about as much effect as if he'd stuck out his tongue and tried to pull the guy's pants down in a fit of mild mischief.

"You'll have to do a lot better than that," said the man. And he looked like he meant it.

"Then *Lincoln* wants to know."

The man looked dubiously at the single bill Archer held out.

"And his twin brother," Archer added, producing a second five-spot.

"Lady *is* in, and it's Apartment 411, *pal*," said the man, sliding the two Lincolns into one of his numerous pockets.

Archer cleared the set of double doors and took the stairs up to the fourth floor.

He hurried down to 411, knocked on the wood, and did it twice more before there was a response.

"Who the hell is it?" called out Beth Kemper.

"Archer. We need to talk. It's about your husband."

He could hear feet running toward the door and it was thrown open a moment later.

There stood Kemper in a nightgown and bare feet, her hair disrupted by sleep. "Yes?" she said breathlessly. "What about Douglas?"

Archer took off his hat and said, "Can I come in?"

"Yes, yes, of course."

He stepped through and she closed the door behind her.

"Have you proven that Douglas didn't kill those people?"

Archer sat in a chair and waited until she did the same. "No, we haven't. Not yet. But there have been developments, lots of them."

"What developments?"

"For starters, Alfred Drake shot himself this morning at his home. He's dead."

Her hand flew to her bosom. "Oh my God. Why would Alfred do that?"

"Let's just say he played his winning card. He didn't want to be your old man's lackey as mayor."

"That's ridiculous. My father wasn't backing Drake."

"You're right about that; he was *blackmailing* him."

"Blackmail? I don't understand, Archer."

"You don't have to, but it's true. Drake was a key to the casinos that were going to go up on that hunk of rock out there your father bought. Your husband would never agree to do his dirty work, so he couldn't be allowed to be mayor. Your father was the one who sent the blackmail note to your hubby. He was the one who had Fraser and Sheen killed. And now he, with the help of Chief Pickett, is framing Douglas for the twin murders and hoping he spends his last few minutes on earth breathing in cyanide in the gas chamber at San Quentin."

"You...you must be mad," she said breathlessly. "Even if what you say about the election is true, my father wouldn't have to try to frame Douglas for murder and see him executed."

"He already *executed* Benjamin Smalls. So what's one more?"

She stood, her fury evident in the reddened cheeks, the slash of her mouth, and the trembling arm that was pointing to the door. "You just get up and march the hell out of here. I never want to see your lying face again, do you hear me?"

"Well, you're going to have to endure it for just a while longer. By the way, do you know your blood type?"

This comment might very well have been the only thing that Archer could have said to stop the lady in her tracks. "What?"

"Your blood type. Everyone has one. Mine's AB."

"I'm...I'm a B," she said slowly.

"Okay, do you know your mother's blood type?"

"No, I don't."

"How about your father's?"

"No," she snapped, obviously growing irritated at these queries.

"How about Sawyer Armstrong's?"

She started to say something, but as she got the point of his question the look on her face made Archer tense.

"What exactly do you mean by...*that*?" she said in a low and threatening voice.

"I think you know exactly what I mean."

"How dare you? You are a lying, filthy—"

"They killed Myron O'Donnell last night. And the only things missing from his office were the medical records for you, your mother, and Sawyer. See, the doc had all three of them. He'd had your mother's and Sawyer's for a while. But then you just had your appendix operation. And Sawyer realized that what O'Donnell could have seen from that was that one plus one does not equal...you."

Archer barely caught her before Kemper hit the floor in a dead faint. He picked her up and carried her into the bedroom. He laid her down on the bed, propped up against the pillows, found some smelling salts in her medicine cabinet, and also poured out a snifter of brandy from the small bar set up on a stainless steel rolling table in the front room.

The salts did their duty, and she jerked and sat up, gasping. He gently but firmly pushed her back against the pillows and held up the snifter.

"Drink this," he said. "It won't make you feel any better, but it won't make you feel any worse, either."

She took the drink without a word and finished it in one impressive swallow. "You...if you're lying to me, Archer—"

"I don't have anywhere near that sort of imagination, Beth. They shot O'Donnell, made it look like a narcotics job, and slit the poor elevator guy's throat, just like they did Fraser."

Kemper dropped the empty glass on the bed, slowly sat up and put her face in her hands, and started moaning.

Archer gripped her shoulder. "I didn't mean to drop this on you like an A-bomb, but you needed to know."

Through her hands she said, "You mentioned that you had news of Douglas?"

"You might need some more brandy."

She shuddered and lowered her hands. She looked up at him hopelessly. "Please... please don't tell me that he's..."

"He's not dead. But the jury's still out on whether he will be. That's why we need your help."

She shuddered again and said in a whisper, "I have whiskey out there."

"I have whiskey in *here*," he replied, pulling out his pocket flask and handing it to her.

She took a swallow, handed it back to him, and said, "Now, tell me what's happened to Douglas."

"They took him from his jail cell. They knocked out the guys that Willie had set up to guard him."

"Why? Why take Douglas?"

"With Drake out of the picture, he's the mayor by default. Sawyer can't have that."

"And you really have proof that he's not my father?"

"We're trying to get it. And even though you fainted back there, something tells me that you're not as surprised by that as you should be."

She wouldn't look at him but she didn't have to. The eyes welling with tears and the tremble of her delicate mouth were enough.

"He... he didn't always act like a *father*... around me."

"Yeah, he also found it difficult allowing anyone to grow close to you. Benjamin Smalls, your husband." Archer paused for a moment and then decided to launch it. "Your mother."

She didn't move even the tiniest of her muscles. She just sat there staring at nothing like nothing was the most fascinating thing ever.

"We talked to your husband in jail before he got snatched. He said the idea for the luncheon that day was Sawyer's. He insisted you be there. So your mother went solo, right into the Pacific. That's what happened, right, Beth? Douglas said the light went out of your marriage then. He thought you blamed him. But did you?"

She looked up at him with such a sorrowful expression that Archer's mouth started to tremble.

"I...I questioned my fa—I questioned Sawyer on...what happened to my mother."

"You questioned him on whether he sabotaged your mother's plane?"

"It took all the nerve I had. And...and he answered my question with a question. He..." She broke down at this point and seemed to be struggling to keep from collapsing.

Archer just held the woman for a long minute in silence, except for her sobs. When they finally subsided, Archer handed her back the flask and said, "Just finish it, Beth. The whiskey and your story. You can do this."

She drank the whiskey but held on to the flask, gripping the metal hide like it was her last attachment to life. Her words came in a rush, like they had been bottled up inside of her for two centuries instead of a mere two years. "He said he wondered whether people would think it odd that I didn't go up with my mother that day. That I *should* have been with her, but let something as unimportant as a luncheon prevent me from being with her, when she might have most needed me. Because a second pair of hands, even untrained ones, and another mind to troubleshoot the situation might have made all the difference." She stopped and stifled a sob as she leaned her head against Archer's chest.

"In other words, he guilted you."

She glanced up at him. "He did worse than that, Archer. He made me *doubt* myself."

"What possible motivation would you have to kill your mother?"

"Oh, he supplied that, too." She ran her fingers down the flask as though it held all the answers she needed, only in Braille. "He again wondered whether others would think I wanted her out of the way so I could be the reigning queen of the Armstrong family. He even suggested that some might think with Eleanor gone, he was the only one standing in the way of my inheriting a vast fortune. He joked that he would have to watch himself around me."

"I think you needed to watch yourself around him."

"So he's really not my father?"

"No, he's not."

They both looked up to see Dash standing in the doorway holding a piece of paper.

"Now we just need to find Armstrong. Because when we find him, we find your husband. Do you know where he might take Douglas if he intended that the man would never come back alive?"

Beth Kemper nodded. "I do, Willie. He would have taken Douglas to the Cliffs, his little retreat high up in the mountains."

"Can you tell us how to get there?"

"Yes, I can."

CHAPTER

68

It cost me two sawbucks and a promise to the records clerk that I'd provide him with lascivious details about some of my cases," said Dash.

Dash and Archer were in the Delahaye starting their climb up into the mountains. Daylight had brought increasing clouds, and a huge storm system was coming in off the water like an armada ready to do some serious business. The mists and fogs were already making their ascent treacherous.

They had stopped at the office, where Dash had picked up something that he said would probably be necessary. When Archer saw it, he couldn't disagree with the man's logic.

"Why would the clerk want to know those sorts of details?" asked Archer.

"He's really a Hollywood screenwriter masquerading as a records clerk, at least in his own mind." Changing gears, Dash said, "So, the Cliffs. Armstrong's little retreat high up in the mountains. A man might just go up there and have an accident."

"But if he kills Kemper, surely the jig is up for him."

"Why? Particularly if the body is never found? Armstrong's already laid the groundwork for Drake's campaign being backed by Vegas mobsters. Then Drake offs himself and the mobsters are getting concerned because their guy is out of the race and Kemper is the only game in town for the mayor's slot. They get to him in jail and ask for his loyalty. He refuses. So what do they do? They take him and kill him, and the mob guys disappear and are never seen again. Where does Armstrong come into the equation in a court of law? He'll have a dozen alibis that he and his goons were nowhere near the jail because they weren't. And what evidence do we have that he had Fraser killed except for an affidavit by a lady who's so scared of Armstrong that if she does come back and testify, she'll probably claim *we* killed everybody, instead of Armstrong being behind it?"

"So that's why we're heading up to the Cliffs? To rescue Kemper?"

"Yes, but Archer, pull off the road, I don't want you getting us into an accident when I tell you what I have to."

Archer stopped on the shoulder and stared at the man. "What are you talking about?"

"I made two phone calls from the hospital. One to Connie. She's fine. The other call I made was to Midnight Moods."

"Why'd you call there?"

"The thing is, Archer, we have to assume that Armstrong knows all that we know, okay? So knowing what we know, what does the guy do?"

"Well, if he thinks we're coming after him, he might want to get some leverage over us."

"That's exactly right. Now, Connie is the only person in this town I really care about. But like I told you, she's safe." He stopped and stared expectantly at Archer, who, to his credit, had seized on where Dash was going halfway through his last sentence.

"They have Liberty. You called Midnight Moods and she's gone."

"I'm sorry, Archer."

Archer drove the car back on the road. "No, Willie, you're wrong there. *They're* going to be the ones who are sorry."

The rain started to fall a quarter of the way up. Halfway up they could barely see out of the windscreen. The fog was so thick, fledgling day had been turned into night.

Archer was gripping the wheel so hard his forearms were growing weary. All he could think about was Liberty and what they might be doing to her right now. Especially Hank and Tony.

He suddenly realized something. "Wait a minute, what'd you find at the hospital?"

"Exactly what I hoped to find. Now don't ask me anymore. Just concentrate on your driving," he added as a curve shot up.

Archer had to brake and cut the wheel hard to navigate it. The edge of the Delahaye came perilously close to a thousand-foot drop.

"You scared?" he asked. "I don't mean by the ride up. But when we get there."

"Well, I'm not stupid, Archer, so of course I'm scared. How about you?"

"Yeah, but it's neck and neck with anger in me."

"Channel both to your advantage. Armstrong won't be alone and there's hostages, so it's complicated."

Archer fought the storm two thousand feet higher. The farther up they went, the worse it got. Finally Dash said, "Slow it down, Archer. From what Beth told us, the place is right at the end of that road."

"Okay."

He turned down the road, and then stopped the car.

"Cut the lights."

Archer did so. They didn't bother to try to see what was up ahead. Even God was probably having a hard time doing that this morning.

"She gave us the layout of the place," said Dash. "We need to hit it from front and rear. Which one do you want?"

"I've always been partial to the back door."

"Smart man. Me too. So seniority here dictates that you go in through the front." Dash took a moment to remove from the floorboard what he had brought. "You ready, soldier?" he asked.

"I thought 'liberty' was worth dying for in the war. And my opinion hasn't changed."

They moved off silently into the darkened mist.

69

ARCHER MOVED JUST LIKE HE HAD AS A SCOUT in the Eighth
Army, first in Italy and then in Hitler's Rhineland. That is, he
moved like a ghost. And next to him Willie Dash did the same.
They had grilled Beth on landmarks around the Cliffs, and Archer
and Dash came upon one of them. It was one of the largest oaks
Archer had ever seen, but either lightning had struck it years
before or a forest fire had come through at some point. It still
clung to the dirt, a blackened husk of electrified wood that was
apparently too stubborn to fall down.

They passed that and they had three hundred yards to go before
they got to the log cabin that was Armstrong's sanctum sanctorum,
according to Beth, a place he came to think and brood and plot the
doom of others, Archer figured.

At that point he and Dash parted company. Before he disappeared into the mist, Dash said, "Good luck, Archer, but it won't
really come down to luck, will it?"

"No, it won't."

A few moments later Archer slowed his pace and looked to his
left and right. No one guarding these premises would think that
anyone coming by stealth would stick to the road. They would be
watching the paths and trails that meandered through here like a
chipmunk on a stroll looking for its next meal. So stick to the road
Archer did.

After another one hundred feet he looked to his right and squatted low.

The man was neither Tony nor Hank, but he was about the same size. Armstrong apparently liked his henchmen in one size only—extra large.

Archer took a widened route and came up on the man's rear flank as he sat there on a rickety chair behind a rock that was, apparently, his cover. He was smoking. That was his first mistake. He was nipping something from a bottle. That was his second mistake. His third and final mistake was having his .44 holstered.

He never sensed anyone until Archer introduced himself by parking the muzzle of his .38 against the fellow's skull.

"The lady you took, she okay?" said Archer in a voice that brooked nothing but a straight answer. About two pounds of trigger pull and the mistake-prone guard was a dead man.

"Yeah, she's okay," the man hoarsely answered.

"You lying to me, I'll be back. And what I'll do to you you'll never forget right till the moment you close your eyes for the last time, you understand me? Nod or say yes because I need confirmation."

The man nodded.

The sharp blow from the butt of the .38 put a depression in the fellow's head and he slumped forward, hit the rock, and slid off the side into the dirt. The fog was so thick Archer could barely see the gent a foot below him.

He took off the man's suspenders and used them to hog-tie his wrists and ankles together.

One down, who the hell knew how many to go. But Archer would get to every last one of them to bring Liberty back safe and sound.

Archer kept going, and the log cabin came into view around a bend strewn with fallen rocks. Two big sedans were parked out front, looking as out of place there as a horse at a dog show. And one of them was Pickett's Town and Country. Lights were on inside, and Archer could see a power line snaking from a tall pole to the side of the cabin.

There was no guard out front, and Archer realized the tactic Armstrong was employing.

He's pulled back, built his interior line, and he's daring us to cross it.

The next step Archer took, he stumbled over a small fallen branch, cracking it in half. The sound shot through the misty air like cannon fire.

The voice calling out to him sounded confident and unsurprised, and also confirmed Archer's theory.

Armstrong said, "Willie, is that you? Please come in and have a drink. I know it's still the morning, but this evening is guaranteed to none of us, unfortunately."

Archer made no move to do as the man asked.

"Archer, if you're out there, too, I want you to know that your lady friend is a feisty one. I don't think I've seen a woman get hit harder and not even one little moan. I have to respect that. Now come in here and let's discuss this rationally."

The next sound Archer heard was Liberty screaming.

This was followed by someone roaring with laughter. "Okay, that one got her, yes sir. I knew there had to be some point of vulnerability. I mean, she is flesh and blood, and what flesh and blood she is."

Archer watched as the front door to the cabin slowly opened, but no one appeared.

"Now, the next sound you hear from this young lady will be her death rattle," Armstrong called out.

"Archer, don't!" cried out Callahan.

The next sound was a dull thud like something hard hitting a watermelon.

"All right, all right," called out Archer. "I'm coming in. Lay off her."

"Without your weapon. And take your jacket and belt off."

Archer did so because he had no choice. He decided against trying to wedge the .38 in the rear of his waistband, because without the belt his pants were bound to sag, which was why Armstrong had demanded that he shed his jacket *and* belt.

He walked slowly toward the open door and passed through. He immediately felt cold metal against his neck. He knew without looking that it was a man with a gun.

He surveyed the area in front of him as the door was closed behind him.

Sawyer Armstrong was sitting in a rocking chair, a thin, dark cigar stuck in his mouth. His straw hat was on his head and his faded blue shirt was neatly tucked into dark brown corduroys. Next to him was Hank. Next to Hank was Tony, who looked like he wanted to claw Archer's eyes out of their sockets, and that was just for starters.

Douglas Kemper sat on the floor with stout rope bound around his arms and legs.

Next to him was Liberty, dressed in the robe they probably let her put on before they insisted at gunpoint that she leave her nice suite of rooms at Midnight Moods on her very first night there.

He looked at her and she looked back at him. The blackened right eye matched the one on her left. She was holding her left arm funny and though there was not a single tear in her eyes, Archer could see the pain the woman was in. He nodded at her, trying to convey a sense of calm in his look. He didn't know if she received it as such, but it really didn't matter. Not much mattered right now.

Next to them was Carl Pickett, looking more nervous than Archer would have given the corrupt cop credit for. And on the right of Pickett was Steve Prichard in plainclothes and looking even more menacing than normal, which was saying something.

"Now, Archer, where is Willie?" asked Armstrong.

"Probably having his breakfast back in town."

Armstrong shook his head. "There is no possible way he sent you up here alone. It was Beth who told you about this place, wasn't it?"

"With Drake dead, you seem to have lost your horse in the race," said Archer, ignoring the man's questions.

"That's the wonderful thing about horse racing, Archer—you can always find another ride."

"We told Beth, you know."

"You told Beth what?"

"Why you had O'Donnell killed." He looked at Hank and then Tony. "And did you have to kill Earl?"

"You mean, the colored boy?" said Hank. "Hell, that don't count."

Archer turned back to Armstrong. "Beth knows you're not her father."

"What?" gasped Kemper.

"Now just hold on there, Archer," said Armstrong with a smile. "You're getting way ahead of yourself. Where is your proof of that?"

"O'Donnell had it. That's why you took it."

"You're not her father?" snapped Kemper. "Then who is?"

"Carl," said Armstrong sharply. "I can't hear myself think. Take care of it."

Pickett looked at Prichard, who clocked Kemper so hard he hit his head against the wall and slumped over onto Callahan's lap. She put her hands protectively around Kemper even as blood from his nose and mouth leached onto her robe.

"Leave him alone," she cried out.

"Now, Archer," said Armstrong in a scolding tone. "You really can't go around spouting lies. When I see Beth I will tell her the truth."

"No, you won't. Because the truth is, Andrew Smalls was her father."

From Armstrong's expression, Archer could tell that Dash's theory on this point was correct.

Archer continued, "And while we're at it, you killed Andrew Smalls. You sabotaged Eleanor's plane, and you dunked Benjamin Smalls in his own tub."

"My goodness, Archer, is there anyone I didn't kill?"

"Yeah. Me."

"Well, it's early in the day yet."

Prichard guffawed at that one, but no one joined him, and he quickly grew quiet.

"Well, here I am, Armstrong," said Archer.

"Yes, here you are. I would prefer that Willie was standing next to you. There aren't many in town that give me pause, but he's surely one of them. So where is he?"

"I don't know what to tell you."

From his pocket Armstrong produced a squat, black automatic pistol and pointed it at Callahan's head. "Now, I don't want to do this, Archer. She is a lovely young lady—not in Beth's class, you understand, but not someone in whose pretty head you want to place a very large hole. So, this will be the last time I will ask: Where is Willie?"

For over five years Archer had not heard the sound that exploded around all of them in the next moment. For the three years preceding that, he had heard it pretty much all the time.

The windows shattered and the wooden walls were hit with such force that pine shrapnel went flying off in all directions. An antler chandelier was blown loose from its tethers overhead and fell to the floor with an ear-splitting crash. Those standing dove for the floor. Those already on the floor looked to burrow into the planks.

When they all looked up after the shooting stopped, Willie

Dash was standing at the open back door holding his still-smoking tommy gun.

"Here I am, Sawyer." He brandished the weapon. "I took this from Ma Barker's cold, dead hands. Forgot the kick the sucker has. But it's an attention getter."

Archer was already on his feet. He picked up the gun that his captor had dropped on his way to the floor. He pointed it at the guy and motioned with the muzzle for him to join the others.

Pickett, Prichard, Hank, and Tony slowly rose to their feet, looking stunned, perhaps, that they were still alive.

Only Armstrong hadn't moved. He had remained sitting in his rocking chair. And he still held his gun. And he looked not intimidated at all.

Dash slowly came forward, his tommy gun leveled at Armstrong. "While it would give me great pleasure to empty the slugs remaining in this gun's drum into your face, Armstrong, we need to jaw a bit before I seriously consider doing that."

"I'm all attention, Willie," said Armstrong, still not lowering the gun.

"First things first, put down the gun."

"I will, if you and Archer will."

"Was the casino really worth all this?" asked Dash.

Armstrong looked animated by the question. "I calculate it would be worth at least fifty million dollars a year. And even to me, that's a lot of money."

"How much money do you need?" barked Archer.

"Well, to tell the truth, it's not really the money. It's the excitement. And I'm a man who's easily bored."

Archer said, "And I guess your excitement level went up when Benjamin Smalls took a boat out there, found out what you were planning, and was going to find a way to stop it."

"But then, most conveniently, he died."

"You mean, you murdered him."

"A murder charge requires proof. You have none."

Dash took a bulky envelope from his pocket and tossed it to Archer. "But, Sawyer, you messed up. Hospitals are a business, you know. They have to document everything, and everybody has to get their copies. One copy for the patient, one for the doc. And one for the *hospital*."

Armstrong said nothing to this, but Archer could see the man run his tongue over his lips to moisten them.

Dash said, "Read it out, Archer. First line on each page."

Archer jammed his gun into his waistband, opened the envelope, and took out the papers. He looked down at them. "Eleanor Armstrong, Blood Type A." He flipped to the next page. "Sawyer Armstrong, Blood Type also A." Archer glanced up. "Beth told me her blood type is B."

"It is," said Dash, "which means Armstrong can't be her father. Two As can't produce a B, at least when it comes to blood types."

"You bastard. I knew something was off with you."

This came from Kemper, who had regained consciousness and was sitting there listening, with Callahan's arm still draped protectively around him.

"Very off," said Dash. "In his weird, creepy mind he had to kill off anyone who grew close to Beth. Why is that, Sawyer? You want her for yourself?"

"Well, for starters, unfaithful wives don't deserve a lot of respect in my book," he replied calmly. Too calmly, thought Archer.

"Married to you, I don't wonder why she got the wandering eye, particularly when it seems all you wanted to do was dominate the daughter that really wasn't yours, not love the woman who really was your wife," countered Dash.

"So, I have a gun and you have a gun. How do you see this ending, Willie?"

"My gun has a lot more bullets."

"All I need is one." In an instant he pointed the gun directly at Archer. "When you shoot me, I shoot Archer. Care to sacrifice your new boy, Willie? Like a good racehorse, you can always find another."

For the first time Dash looked uncertain of the outcome, at least it looked that way to Archer, who was staring at him.

"No reason to do that, Sawyer. It's a fair-and-square game, just admit it. You don't need to go down in a blaze of glory like Dillinger, because it's not a blaze of glory, it's just dead."

"Don't begrudge me taking one of your pawns," said Armstrong. "As my final act."

The bullet was fired, and everyone just stood there. Except for Callahan and Kemper, who stared openmouthed from their seats on the floor.

Armstrong seemed to be the last person in the room to comprehend that *he* was the one who had been shot. He finally looked down curiously at the gaping hole in his chest. He looked up and saw Beth Kemper standing in the doorway, the smoking gun she held still pointed resolutely at him, like an accusatory finger demanding justice.

Beth Kemper looked prepared to take a second shot. However, Sawyer Armstrong slid dead to the floor, so it didn't seem necessary to kill the man twice.

Kemper calmly set the gun down on a table, walked over to her husband, knelt beside him, and hugged him as tightly as she could.

Callahan moved her arm away and looked at Archer. He was not looking back. He was watching Dash, whose gaze was squarely on the dead man.

When he finally looked up to see Archer staring at him, he shrugged and said, "Now *that* takes the cake."

70

SEVERAL DAYS LATER, AROUND LUNCHTIME, Archer drove to the office and rode the elevator up, pushing the necessary buttons as Earl no longer could. He said hello to Connie Morrison, who smiled sweetly at him and told Archer that Dash wanted to see him.

Archer pecked on the man's door and was told by a gruff voice to enter.

Dash was on the davenport, his shoes off, his feet up, and his jacket off. He had a tumbler of scotch in one hand and a cigar in the other. "Take a seat."

Archer sat.

"First things first. I got five names for your license application. You'll be happy to know that both Carl Pickett and Steve Prichard signed the list, their last official acts before they retired from the force."

"Retired, huh? How come?"

"I strongly suggested it and they finally agreed."

"So who's going to be the new chief?"

"I've told Ern to make a run for it. He's young, smart, talented, honest as the day is long. Which means he doesn't have a chance in hell of getting the job."

"Okay."

"I'm writing a letter to the Board of Prison Directors. Connie will include that with the application she's typing up now for your signature. It basically says you're a helluva gumshoe, are of outstanding moral character, and helped solve a big case and saved a bunch of lives, blah, blah, blah. You'll get the license."

"But you said they might do their own investigation into me, my background. Hell, I killed a lady down in Ventura, even though it was in self-defense."

"Yeah, I made discreet inquiries into that, Archer, through some PIs I know down there. The lady's body *was* found, the cops did their investigation, and they concluded that it indeed looked like self-defense. She had fired two rounds into the chair, I assume, you were sitting in. She missed, you didn't."

"They're really going to leave it like that?"

"You deduced that the lady was selling drugs. Well, the cops down there were already looking her way on that as well. So the consensus in Ventura is she got what was coming to her. End of story."

"Damn, I didn't expect that."

"Second thing, the Kempers added another nine grand to the retainer already paid, for a total of ten thou in appreciation of a job well done and a cancer named Sawyer Armstrong no longer being in their lives. So my money problems are over, for now, at least."

"That's great. So, what is my salary and when do I start getting paid? Connie didn't know, and you never said."

"Third thing, all the folks who were at the Cliffs are keeping their traps shut. Pickett and Prichard, Hank and Tony, and the other two goons know they're looking at murder and kidnapping and assault charges and a long stint in the big house if they say one word. So we're good there. Now, in an ideal world, they'd all be going to the slammer or the gas chamber, but proof is hard to come by, and I doubt Hank and Tony can make a living without Armstrong around. They'll melt into the dirt, like a water lily in the Sahara. And Pickett and Prichard are leaving town. And good riddance."

"Okay."

"Fourth thing, Beth inherited everything that Armstrong had. So she's even richer than she was. And Douglas is going to be the new mayor, so that hunk of rock out there will stay a hunk of rock. And it looks like with Armstrong out of the way, those two are going to make it. True love wins out, right?"

"Right. And fifth?"

"There is no fifth, except what's in that bottle of scotch over there. Okay, I'm done, Archer. Go off and play today."

Archer rose and headed to the door.

Dash said, "Hey Archer?"

"Yeah?"

"You got the makings of a decent gumshoe. Just keep at it, okay?"

Archer nodded. "That wasn't really Ma Barker's tommy gun, was it?"

"Who the hell knows? But when you pick up a weapon like that, you got to do it with style."

Archer signed his application and Morrison said she would be mailing it out that day. And then she did something that surprised Archer. From behind a vase of flowers she lifted up a long-stemmed glass with some liquid in it.

"What's that?" asked Archer.

"Champagne, of course. Lots to celebrate. You want a glass?"

"Thanks, but I'm saving myself for something a little more amber in color." He crossed the reception area and went into his office. He sat down at his desk and noted the single sunflower that presumably Morrison had put in the vase. It was already drooping from lack of sun. Archer moved it to the windowsill, and it seemed to perk right up.

There was a knock on his door.

"Yeah?"

It opened and there stood Dash.

"Forgot something, Archer." He took out his wallet, peeled off eight C-notes and ten Jacksons, and handed them to Archer. "Your weekly wages. Just don't expect that kind of dough every time, capiche?"

"Thanks, Willie," said Archer.

"Now how about using some of it to buy me lunch?"

"I know a place down by the water."

"I know you know a place down by the water, only my gams aren't nearly as fetching as Beth Kemper's, so don't get your hopes up, son. Hey, I wonder if they serve Cream of Wheat?"

The two men walked out into the clearest sky Archer had seen since he'd been in Bay Town.

71

Early the following afternoon Archer drove to Midnight Moods. Mabel Dawson was back from Long Beach, and she nodded to him as he walked in.

"Long time no see, Archer."

"Yeah, I can't seem to stay away from this place."

"This *place* is under new management," she added. "Beth Kemper came by this morning. Told me no reason to change a ship's course midvoyage, though she did say the girls can't have 'visitors' at lunchtime."

"They were probably bad for the digestion, anyway."

"You're here to see Liberty, I suppose?"

"I am."

"Well, considering it's only just after one, you'll probably find her in bed."

He headed up to Callahan's room and knocked on the door.

"Yeah, who is it?"

"It's Archer. You decent?"

"Same answer as last time, Archer."

The door opened and there she stood in a sheer black silk number, her hair tousled and her face puffy from sleep. And she looked more beautiful than ever, Archer thought. If Beth Kemper was all cool class, Liberty Callahan was the white-hot flame of the working-class gal used to the rough and tumble of the world. And it wasn't a close competition which one intrigued Archer more.

"Miss me?" he asked.

"Yeah, you're all I've been thinking about, buster."

She stepped back so he could pass through.

He looked around and saw the few personal touches she had made to the place.

"How're your eyes?" he asked, noticing they were still a bit swollen but the black and yellow was fading back to pale white.

"Nothing makeup can't take care of. Nobody notices when I'm doing my act. And my arm's all better where they twisted it."

"Still packing the house?"

"What can I say? I'm a star."

"Beth Kemper owns this place now."

"Yeah, I heard. Good to see a woman taking charge."

"So you still happy here?"

"Well, I signed a contract for a year, as you know. After that, I'll probably be taking a bus to Hollywood. That's where I need to be. I'm not getting a star turn in Bay Town, at least the one I want."

She sat in a chair and crossed her legs and that got Archer's attention, and he sat, too, and tried not to think about her leaving in a year, or about how little she was wearing.

She looked at his gloomy expression. "Why, you going to *miss* me?" she said.

"Yeah, I will, actually."

"Don't make me get all weepy," replied Callahan in a mocking tone, but her expression showed that his words had touched her.

He twirled his hat between his fingers. "Look, I came here to apologize for getting you involved in all this."

"No need. Almost getting killed makes a girl feel more alive than a dozen roses, a plate of oysters on the half shell, or soaking in a tub full of Chanel Number Five."

She lit a cigarette and Archer mimicked her.

They blew smoke and stared across at each other, maybe both looking for some sign of something in the other.

"Decent of you to see it that way."

She crossed her legs again and she said, "That's me, Archer, *decent* to my core, as you can see for yourself."

"So what are we really doing here?" said Archer.

"Beats me. I'm just making it up as I go along. And, in case you forgot, *you* knocked on *my* door."

"Yeah, I did," he said and then fell into an awkward silence. This was clearly not going how he intended.

"You want a drink?" she asked in a helpful tone.

"Sure, why not? Seems like everybody's drinking these days."

She rose and went to a small cabinet. She got down on her knees, opened one of the doors, and pulled out two glasses and a bottle of bourbon. He could see that the bottoms of her feet were pale and smooth, and that, of all things, made something go haywire in part of his brain.

"You know, technically to be called 'bourbon,' it has to be made in Kentucky," said Archer quickly, loosening his tie to allow more air to come in.

She poured out three fingers each and said, "There goes the college boy again."

They sat and drank and stared at each other.

"Anything you want to tell me?" asked Archer.

"Should there be something?"

"I don't know, that's why I'm asking."

"I don't like running in circles. I get dizzy easily."

Archer was going to say something right back, but he took a page from his old friend Irving Shaw's book and slowed down. He looked at Callahan and she looked right back at him. She just wanted to get out of Reno, just like Archer. She wanted to chase a dream to the West Coast.

Just like me.

She saved both our lives up in those mountains.

At first, it had shocked him, that a woman could do that. But if he'd had the gun and not Callahan?

I would have shot all three and felt like a hero.

She tries to be confident and in control, but it's sometimes just a show, because, inside, she's scared to death.

Just like me. We're actually a lot alike.

"Archer, you still breathing in there, or should I call a doctor?"

He came out of his musings. "I'm here." He took a nervous sip of his drink. "I know we both said some things we probably regret. At least I do."

"It happens, Archer. But I think we both made up for it, right?"

"Yeah, I guess we did."

"I mean, we've been through a lot. More than most married couples have, right?"

"I didn't come here to propose."

She laughed a deep, throaty laugh that, for some reason, made Archer feel wonderful about himself. "I'm not ready to settle down, Archer, not by a long shot. But if I ever did, well, I could do a lot worse than taking a ring from you."

He held up his glass to her and added a warm smile.

She stretched her leg out and touched his shoe with her bare foot and kept it there. "So that thing that happened in the mountains? Are we good on that?"

"They killed Bobby H. They were going to kill us. They deserved what they got. Hell, we let the little guy off easy."

"You didn't think that back then," she pointed out.

"And maybe I was wrong."

She took a sip of her drink and studied what she had left. "No, you weren't, Archer. If I'd shot that little weasel in cold blood?" She shook her head. "I'm not sure what it would have done to me, but none of it would be good. So, I have to thank you for doing what you did."

"Okay."

"I see their faces in my sleep," she said quietly. "I see how they died."

"Yeah. I suppose you do."

She shot him an anxious look. "Does it ever go away?"

"Not completely, no. But you see the faces less and less as time goes on and not nearly as clearly."

"That's good to know."

"But if you ever see them so much that you can't handle it, give me a call. I'll be right over."

"You're a good man, Aloysius Archer."

"Surprised you remembered my given name."

"I plan to keep on surprising you. They say it's good for a relationship."

He grinned, and took another swallow of his drink. "Oh, so we have a relationship now?"

"I think so."

"I actually know so. And I'm lucky for it."

"Hell, we're just gushing over each other. I'm starting to feel giddy."

"I'm feeling something too, only it's not that."

This was the first and only time he had ever seen Liberty Callahan blush. It was a lovely look on the woman.

"You want to take me to lunch?" she said, a bit breathlessly.

"No, but I will take you to dinner."

"So what do we do in the meantime?"

Archer put his glass down, took off his jacket, undid his tie completely, and started unbuttoning his shirt.

"If you have to ask, lady, then I'm really doing something wrong."

She stood and slid her soft hand along his hard jaw.

"Oh, you're not wrong, Archer. You just need to work on your timing, is all. But I got at least a year to help you with that."

She took him by the hand, led him into her bedroom, and closed the door.

ACKNOWLEDGMENTS

To Michelle, back to the forties with Archer. Right now, it beats the present day. And I wouldn't want to spend it with anyone else.

To Michael Pietsch, Ben Sevier, Elizabeth Kulhanek, Jonathan Valuckas, Matthew Ballast, Beth de Guzman, Anthony Goff, Rena Kornbluh, Karen Kosztolnyik, Brian McLendon, Albert Tang, Andy Dodds, Ivy Cheng, Joseph Benincase, Andrew Duncan, Morgan Swift, Bob Castillo, Kristen Lemire, Briana Loewen, Mark Steven Long, Thomas Louie, Rachael Kelly, Kirsiah McNamara, Nita Basu, Lisa Cahn, Megan Fitzpatrick, Michele McGonigle, John Colucci, Alison Lazarus, Barry Broadhead, Martha Bucci, Rick Cobban, Ali Cutrone, Raylan Davis, Tracy Dowd, Melanie Freedman, Jean Griffin, Elizabeth Blue Guess, Linda Jamison, John Leary, John Lefler, Rachel Hairston, Suzanne Marx, Derek Meehan, Christopher Murphy, Donna Nopper, Rob Philpott, Barbara Slavin, Karen Torres, Rich Tullis, Mary Urban, Tracy Williams, Julie Hernandez, Laura Shepherd, Jeff Shay, Carla Stockalper, Ky'ron Fitzgerald, and everyone at Grand Central Publishing, for running on all cylinders for me.

To Aaron and Arleen Priest, Lucy Childs, Lisa Erbach Vance, Frances Jalet-Miller, and Kristen Pini, for making my life much easier.

To Mitch Hoffman, for doing what you do so well.

To Anthony Forbes Watson, Jeremy Trevathan, Alex Saunders, Sara Lloyd, Claire Evans, Sarah Arratoon, Laura Sherlock, Stuart Dwyer, Jonathan Atkins, Christine Jones, Leanne Williams, Stacey Hamilton, Charlotte Williams, Rebecca Kellaway, and Neil Lang at Pan Macmillan, for continuing to knock it out of the park.

To Praveen Naidoo and the stellar team at Pan Macmillan in Australia, for doing such an amazing job for me.

To Caspian Dennis and Sandy Violette, for being such great advocates for me.

And to Kristen White and Michelle Butler, for being the absolute best.

In a town full of secrets who can you trust?

Have you read the first Aloysius Archer novel?

One Good Deed

Freedom never tasted so sweet

Poca City 1949. Fresh from serving time for
a crime he didn't commit, Aloysius Archer is ready
to put the past behind him and start again.

Who can you trust?

Accepting a job as a debt collector for the local tycoon
he gets embroiled in a long-running feud between
the town's most dangerous residents. When one of them
is found dead, Archer is the number one suspect.

Framed for murder

A bloody game is being played in this town.
Should Archer run or fight for the truth?

Read it now!

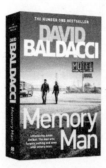
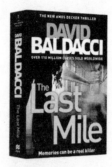
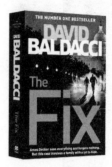
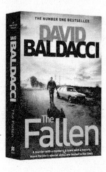
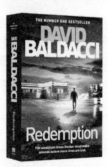
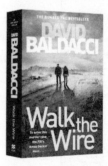